His Desire Sealed Her Fate

"Accept me," a harsh, husky voic

Like quicksilver, excitement er breath rushed from her lungs. ng so, she would deny herself. She closed her eyes her loosened. Finally, she would know how it felt.

In answer, she undulated beneath his hardness as it pressed for entry.

He put his lips to her ear. "Say the words: I accept you."

She gasped at the raw passion of his words, the tone possessive and commanding.

"Say it!" he hissed. His body coiled above hers, like a serpent ready to strike.

"I-I accept you," she breathed.

Praise for the novels of Karin Tabke

"A blast of hot air; a fun female fantasy; an erotica novel with a good plot." —*Fresh Fiction*

"Tabke masterfully creates sexual tension." —*Romantic Times*

"I enjoyed this book not just for its eroticism, but for the powerful storytelling." —*Romance Junkies*

demanded above her.
thrummed through her veins. Heat
she would not deny him. In de
every part of

BLOOD LAW

KARIN TABKE

HEAT
NEW YORK

THE BERKLEY PUBLISHING GROUP
Published by the Penguin Group
Penguin Group (USA) Inc.
375 Hudson Street, New York, New York 10014, USA
Penguin Group (Canada), 90 Eglinton Avenue East, Suite 700, Toronto, Ontario M4P 2Y3, Canada
(a division of Pearson Penguin Canada Inc.)
Penguin Books Ltd., 80 Strand, London WC2R 0RL, England
Penguin Group Ireland, 25 St. Stephen's Green, Dublin 2, Ireland (a division of Penguin Books Ltd.)
Penguin Group (Australia), 250 Camberwell Road, Camberwell, Victoria 3124, Australia
(a division of Pearson Australia Group Pty. Ltd.)
Penguin Books India Pvt. Ltd., 11 Community Centre, Panchsheel Park, New Delhi—110 017, India
Penguin Group (NZ), 67 Apollo Drive, Rosedale, Auckland 0632, New Zealand
(a division of Pearson New Zealand Ltd.)
Penguin Books (South Africa) (Pty.) Ltd., 24 Sturdee Avenue, Rosebank, Johannesburg 2196,
South Africa

Penguin Books Ltd., Registered Offices: 80 Strand, London WC2R 0RL, England

This book is an original publication of The Berkley Publishing Group.

Cover photograph by Claudio Marinesco.
Cover design by Rita Frangie.
Text design by Laura K. Corless.

PRINTING HISTORY
Heat trade paperback edition / May 2011

Library of Congress Cataloging-in-Publication Data

Tabke, Karin.
Blood law : a blood moon rising novel / Karin Tabke.—Heat trade paperback ed.
p. cm.
ISBN 978-0-425-24092-2 (trade pbk.)
I. Title.
PS3620.A255B56 2011
813'.6—dc22

2010049800

PRINTED IN THE UNITED STATES OF AMERICA

10 9 8 7 6 5 4 3 2 1

To Sylvia for lighting the fire,

and to Bonnie, a true heroine

BLOOD LAW

The Truth

In medieval Europe, wolves were feared and looked upon as the scourge of the earth. Many people lost their lives to wolf attacks. In 1281 Edward I, Longshanks, king of England, commissioned the great hunter, Peter Corbet, to eliminate the wolves in England. Peter, who would come to be known as Peter the Wolf, accepted the charter with bloodthirsty gusto, and soon hundreds upon thousands of wolves were slain. The devastation of wolves did not end with their demise in England and Scotland. As the centuries passed and the wolves fled into other parts of Europe, the hunt continued.

The Lore

In Peter's time, there was a deformed wolf, Fenrir, an outcast born of an alpha and his mate.

All of the alphas, even Fenrir's own sire, were so disgusted by Fenrir's deformities that they banished him from all the packs. Furious that his own kind would shun him, Fenrir struck a deal with Gilda, the Druid witch of the Marches. She would grant the outcast wolf alpha strength and immortality in return for the slaying of twin wolves and the delivery of their souls every one hundred years.

Fortified and hungry for vengeance, Fenrir offered his services to Peter Corbet.

With Fenrir's help, Peter hunted the packs and slew them. Only the strongest survived. Most fled north into Scotland, then into Norway and Russia. In Russia the great pack, Vulkasin, was born. Another pack fled south into France and across the Great Pyrenees where they settled and coexisted with the fierce Basque people. There, the formidable Mondragon pack multiplied and thrived.

Before Peter Corbet's death, King Edward rewarded the great hunter for his fearlessness with a gold ring fashioned in the image of a howling wolf. Set as the eye, a rare, bloodred ruby. Peter dubbed the ring the Eye of Fenrir. And it was passed down to the eldest Corbet son.

The wolf hunts did not end with Peter's death. With Fenrir's guidance, Peter's progeny picked up where their sire left off, as did their descendants through the ages, who would come to be known as Slayers.

The centuries passed, the hunted wolves moved into the vast Siberian wasteland and then across the great Bering Sea and into the New World. There the mystic Inuit people who had great respect for the wolves befriended them. But the Slayers, led by the vengeful Fenrir, followed.

On a fateful night, one that coincided with the sun reflecting on the full lunar eclipse and turning it bloodred, the Slayers, led by Fenrir, attacked the great wolf packs—both the Mondragon in Europe and the Vulkasin in the New World. Both packs fought valiantly. But Fenrir's vengeance was too potent.

Seeing that the great packs were on the verge of extinction, Singarti, the great spirit guide of the Inuit, called to the gods for intervention. Lightning struck the master Slayer known as the jager, killing him. Singarti took the Eye of Fenrir from his hand and turned it on its namesake, forcing Fenrir's spirit into the ring. Singarti cast a sealing spell, trapping Fenrir within, then buried the ring deep into the frozen tundra of the North.

Singarti knew for the wolves to survive into the next millennia they must be able to shift into human form. And so she raised her arms to the great gods once more and asked that they have mercy on the wolves. The gods were benevolent that day. The surviving wolves shifted into human form and were called Lycan, only to take their natural wolf form for twenty-four hours during each full moon or when provoked by great rage. Singarti further protected the Lycan with the gift of her daughter, Sasha, to the great Vulkasin alpha, Arnou. With an infusion of Inuit blood, the Lycan thrived.

This infuriated Fenrir. Through the confines of the ring, he called upon the dark gods and demanded they favor him with a chance to raise his Slayers against the Lycan. And the gods scoffed but promised him this: when he found one who was equal to him in power but pure of heart, the gods would release him from the ring and grant him the chance to defeat the Lycan on the next rising of the Blood Moon.

The Slayers continued to hunt wolves and Lycan alike. The wolves continued to grow fewer in numbers, but the Lycan thrived. With no help from the banished Fenrir, the Slayers turned to black magic to aid them in their efforts to annihilate all things Lycan.

Ten generations passed. The Eye of Fenrir lay buried deep in the snowy tundra of the North. With the second coming of the Blood Moon looming, the two great packs, Mondragon and Vulkasin, united. Tamaska, pack Vulkasin's alpha female, conceived and bore twin males, Rafael and Lucien: one dark, the other light. The births set off a year of countless other births, strengthening the bloodline and guaranteeing yet another generation of Lycans.

Though buried deep in the northern ice, Fenrir's senses were so great that he was aware of the twins' birth. Furious and more desperate than ever to be freed, he used all of his dark magic and called out to the jager, *Thomas Corbet.*

Thomas heard the call and unearthed the Eye of Fenrir. Knowing the power the ring possessed and what would happen if Fenrir was freed, Thomas kept the rising of the ring to himself. But Thomas exploited the ring's power. The Lycans who had thrived were systematically hunted and slain at an alarming rate.

Tragedy struck on the Vulkasin twins' tenth birthday. Their parents were slain by Thomas, his two brothers, and his marauders. Vulkasin's powerful medicine woman, Layla, was kidnapped by Thomas Corbet. Though it is forbidden for a Slayer to lie with a Lycan, Thomas could not control the overwhelming desire he experienced when he was in the presence of the soulful Lycan. Shamelessly, he took Layla; she bore him a child, a girl she named Falon . . .

Fourteen years ago . . .

FOR LONG MINUTES, Rafael stood silent outside the two-story cinder-block walls that shielded pack Vulkasin from the world. Thick rolls of concertina wire topped the five-brick-thick concrete, and behind that, the hot currents of high-voltage electric wire hummed. Although it was spring, a chill still lingered from a rough winter, and gray smoke wafted in great arching swirls from the chimneys inside the compound. Soon, the pack would rise, only to find that something had changed.

After being gone almost a year, Rafael Vulkasin was home.

But his homecoming was not one to celebrate. It did not signify the completion of Rafael's spirit journey in the North, but rather the confrontation he'd been long hoping to avoid.

Alpha against alpha.

Brother against brother.

Even as he clenched his jaw, resolute in what was to come, Rafael set one of his two duffel bags down on the ground, pressed a code into a keypad that opened with a soft click, revealing another keypad, then pressed his right hand to the biometric pad. Slowly the heavy metal gates clicked open. Grabbing his bag, Rafael slid inside as the gates clanged shut behind him.

Gravel crunched beneath his booted feet as he strode deeper

into the compound and paused to take in the two-story log cabin–style building. He hated this place as much as he loved it. His chest tightened as memories stirred in his heart. Memories of his mother's warmth and comfort, of his father's strength and power, and of his brother's unconditional love and loyalty. Memories of feeling secure—of knowing as long as his parents were alive, he, his brother, and the rest of the pack would be safe.

But they weren't alive—not anymore—and the pack had nearly died right along with them.

Rage snapped, hot and vengeful, in Rafael's belly. The beast within him snarled, gnawing at his gut, demanding release.

Retribution.

It was what he and Lucien lived for. It was why they had jointly challenged their cousin, Tallus, almost three years ago, for alpha rights. And while it was often the cause of tension between them when they disagreed about how to proceed, their goal had always been the same: hunt down *Jager* Thomas Corbet and his two brothers, Balor and Edward, and destroy them. To avenge the helplessness and despair he and Lucien had felt when they'd been forced to hide while the three Corbet brothers skinned their mother alive as their father and the rest of the pack helplessly watched.

Now Lucien was endangering the success of that goal.

According to Talia's—his pack's healer and spirit guide—dream visit, Lucien had brought someone into the compound walls that threatened their revenge as well as their pack's strength—a human. A human his brother intended to claim as his mate.

As Rafael's lip curled with distaste, Anton, Rafael and Lucien's second-in-command, greeted him with a somber expression. The same somber expression that never changed. Though he was only a year younger, Anton's face bore the stress lines of one who had witnessed unspeakable horror. As Rafael and Lucien had watched as their parents were eviscerated, so, too, did Anton witness the mutilation of his mother. Their bond went far deeper than their heritage. Their suffering had solidified their friendship for life.

"It's been a long time," Anton said, extending his arm but casting his eyes down in a show of submissiveness. Rafael grasped Anton's arm at the elbow then quickly released it.

"Too long by some accounts," Rafael clipped, staring hard at Anton. "How fares the pack?"

Anton's glance shifted momentarily up then sideways before he nodded and met Rafael's gaze. "There is unrest. Talk of mutiny. Some say your brother would sacrifice us for his own pleasure. I don't agree, but Lucien . . ." Anton shook his head. "The human has a strong hold on him."

"Where is my brother and his—flavor of the week?"

Anton hesitated, then jerked his head toward the south wing of the compound. "He calls her *elegida*."

Rafael scowled. Usually his brother's conquests didn't last long enough for a name exchange, but for him to go further and call her his chosen one? His scowl deepened. What hold did this woman have on his brother? "What do you think of her?"

Anton shrugged. "She makes your brother happy, but . . ."

"But?" Rafael questioned.

"But there is something not right with that one. Even for a human."

For a moment, Rafael was tempted to share what he'd learned on his spirit journey—that an enemy was closing in on the pack, one with the power to destroy it completely. He didn't think such a thing could be accomplished by a mere human female, especially one that his brother thought was his chosen one, but still . . . As he often did, Rafael chose to be cautious. Until he talked to his brother, he wouldn't reveal too much. Rafael dropped his duffels to the plank wood floor. "Have the females prepare my quarters, and rouse the pack in an hour. By then, the human will be gone."

Rafael turned and moved toward the south wing, halting in his tracks when Anton's voice followed him.

"Lucien will not cast her out, Rafe. He loves her. He believes she is his chosen one."

Not turning around, Rafael said more to himself than to Anton, "Lucien has no choice. I am taking control of the pack." It had to be. If Lucien would jeopardize the welfare of the pack for an unworthy life mate, he did not deserve to lead it.

Without another word, Rafael strode into the large, sprawling building he had left on his eighteenth birthday. It was as he remembered it: dark, depressing, but home. Lucien's dominant scent pricked at his nostrils, but other scents mingled with Lucien's. The scent of a human female. The scent of sex. And something darker . . .

Urgency pushed Rafael faster. He could only hope his brother had not yet marked her; had he, there was only one thing that could separate her from Lucien: death.

That she was merely a weaker species, one unworthy of sharing its blood with the powerful Lycans and thus weakening the pack as a whole aside, something dark and terrible grabbed hold of Rafael.

As resolved as Rafael was to remove the human from the pack, he didn't want to kill her to do it. Not only would he lose his own brother in the process, but there would be the Blood Law to answer to. An eye for an eye.

"Damn you, Lucien!" Rafael growled. He took off toward the heady scent of sex.

HE KICKED OPEN his brother's door and stopped short at the shrill scream of a woman.

Rafael's eyes narrowed in on the sight of his brother vigorously fucking the female from behind.

For a moment, her beauty, so spectacular, mesmerized him to stillness.

Thick auburn hair, deep-set blue eyes, high cheekbones, and lips so succulent he instantly imagined his dick shoved between them topped her voluptuous curves. His hands twitched at his sides. Her best asset, however, were her ripe tits. She slyly watched him watch her then wriggled her ass under his scurrilous glare, her tits bouncing in response.

Rafael's blood quickened as the sudden urge to take her struck him. If it were under any other circumstances, he'd take a dip in that pond himself. But these weren't other circumstances. Intuitively, he knew there was something terribly wrong here.

Jerking himself forcibly from the unease that has settled upon him, Rafael shouted, "Lucien. Stop!"

Unbelievably, even as the female met his gaze, as if he were in a sexual trance, his brother paid him no mind—didn't even acknowledge his presence. Instead, he continued to pump into the woman, eyes closed, his fingers digging into the flesh of her hips, his own thrusting with manic power as low groans of pleasure escaped his throat.

Rafael stepped deeper into the room for a closer look at the girl's neck for signs of his brother's mark. It was smooth and unblemished. He was not too late.

In the next instant, his brother brought himself and the girl to a raucous climax without attempting to mark her. Their heavy pants filled the small space as their bodies slowed.

Without breaking her stare, the female brushed damp hair from her brow and licked her full lips. She smiled deviously and straightened, arching her back and wrapping her arms around Lucien's neck so that her breasts thrust tauntingly in Rafael's face. Rafael swallowed hard. Her mysterious, musky scent called to him as it must have to his brother. His gaze dropped to her flat belly, her flared hips, then lower to the fiery red curls at the juncture of her thighs. They were tight and glistened with moisture. She spread her thighs wider, giving Rafael an unfettered view of her pink, swollen lips cradling his brother's dick. More of her potent scent released, snaring his rapt attention. He felt her pull, like sweet-smelling angel vines slowly winding around his chest, intoxicating, tightening, lethal . . . he resisted. She was all things carnal, and for a brief span of a second, Rafael understood his brother's infatuation. Heavy lids dipped over passion-dark eyes. "Lucien, my love, we have company," she purred.

Breathing heavily, Lucien opened languorous eyes and locked gazes with Rafael. Although his eyes appeared dazed, almost drugged, there was no surprise in their golden depths. No welcome, no joy, only indifference.

"The fair-haired son returns," Lucien slurred. "Come back later. I'm busy." Lucien grabbed the woman's hips and thrust into her again. If Rafael didn't know better, he'd swear his brother was on drugs. Something he would never do.

The woman gasped, her eyes rolling back into her head, each time Lucien impaled her from behind.

"You've had your fun, Lucien. Release her," Rafael said softly to his brother. "Now."

Grasping her hips tighter to him, Lucien narrowed his eyes, defying Rafael's command. He thrust harder into the female—once, twice, three times. The woman's gasps turned into high-pitched, "Oh my God!" shrieks.

"You don't command me, Brother," Lucien gritted out between thrusts. "I have ruled this pack for a year in your absence, and I will continue to rule even if it's with you by my side. Now leave us. Find your own mate."

Quieting now even as her body shook with the power of Lucien's penetration, the woman sneered, "Do as your brother commands, Rafael, before I have you banished from the pack."

Lucien snarled loudly, grabbed a hank of the woman's hair, and wound it around his fist and pulled hard, causing her to scream. "Silence, woman!" His eyes glittered, seeming to clear momentarily from their lust-induced trance. "You may be my chosen one," he growled, yanking her hair for effect, "but Rafael is my brother. He is your alpha just as I am. Do not—"

"This human," Rafael snarled, pointing an accusing finger at her, "is *not* your chosen one. Such a thing is impossible. She is not our kind!"

Lucien's head whipped back, his glare menacing. He growled, showing straight white teeth. His eyes still on Rafael, Lucien nipped the female's shoulder. "You're wrong, Brother. She is mine. It has been foretold that my mate will be human, and so now it will be done." He thrust into her again, and the female cried out.

Rafael shook his head, unsettled by the belief in his brother's eyes. Lucien had always been impulsive and rash, ruled more by his emotions than by caution. If it had been up to him—if Rafael hadn't finally convinced him otherwise—Lucien would have risked the pack before it had regained its full strength to go after clan Corbet. Now, this female had made him forget almost everything but the need to mark her. That alone told Rafael something was wrong.

"Fuck her all you want, Lucien, but don't mark her. Not now," Rafael tried to reason. "Not with the coming of the Blood Moon."

"The rising is over a decade away."

"She will corrupt you before then."

Lucien didn't respond, and once more Rafael glanced at the

female as a snide smile tilted her full red lips. Her eyes darkened to onyx and lasered in on Rafael. The tendons on her neck stood out as she arched into Lucien. Her head held high, her black eyes unwaveringly locked onto his. Terrible realization sprouted to life in Rafael's belly.

She was not just an outsider to his pack.

She was the enemy.

She was Slayer.

And if Lucien marked her, his seed would bear fruit. It would mean not just the weakening of their pack; it would mean its utter destruction.

As if reading his thoughts and mocking them, the female rubbed her slick cunt against Lucien, making small mewling sounds. Her sinister scent clamped down around Rafael's head, tightening around his chest, making it impossible to draw a breath. His anger flashed red, and the beast within him snarled, clawing for release.

Striding toward them, Rafael grasped his brother's shoulder. "Dark magic oozes from her scent, Lucien! Can't you smell it? She is Slayer! Kill her now, or she will be the death of us all!"

Totally consumed by her, Lucien shrugged off his touch. Shaking his head, he looked down at the undulating body connected to his own. Adoration shone in his tawny eyes. He traced a finger along the curve of her back then looked up at Rafael. "You are wrong, Brother. Yes, I smell her magic, but it will only strengthen the pack. Our children will rule for the next millennia!"

Lucien shoved him, sending Rafael stumbling back against the wall. As Rafael righted himself, Lucien pumped wildly into the Slayer, sweat slickening his body as once more he and his consort shuddered through another impending climax. Lucien threw his head back and snarled, "She is mine!" Teeth bared, he lowered them to the pulsating jugular of the woman beneath him, to mark her as his life mate, his chosen one, forever forming a blood bond that could only be broken by death.

"You defy the Blood Law!" Rafael shouted, lunging upon them. And for doing so, Lucien would pay with his life!

Even if it were not written that no Lycan shall lie with a Slayer, Rafael would never allow his brother to blend the blood of a Lycan and Slayer. It was sacrilegious treason.

Just as his brother's teeth sank into the tender flesh of the girl, Rafael's beast roared furiously and sank his fangs into her chest. She screamed, a bone-chilling, agonizing sound of misery and furious defeat. Her body contorted and convulsed; blood spurted from her punctured heart in a high arch across their faces as her life force dwindled. Her screams turned to low gurgles before trailing off to silence.

"No!" Lucien roared, the sound of his voice filled with despair. Frantically he pressed his fingers into her gaping chest, trying to stem the streaming blood from her heart. "What have you done?" he demanded, his voice choked in harsh sobs. Her black eyes glassed over in hardness as her lifeblood ebbed from her body. "No," Lucien cried, this time barely audible. He pulled her limp body to his chest, clutching her tightly as if his strength could restore her life. Then slowly, hypnotically, he began to rock her, murmuring soft words of comfort against her cheek.

Rafael stood firm, resolved, knowing that despite his brother's terrible pain, he did what had to be done. He had saved his brother's life as well as the lives of his pack.

After several long minutes, Lucien abruptly stopped. Gently he laid her down on the bloody sheets. He smoothed her blood-soaked hair from her lifeless eyes then gently shut her lids. Her blood smeared across his body, slowly his brother rose on the bed, his eyes glowing red.

"Rafael!" Lucien raged. "You will pay with your life!"

"I saved yours, Brother! She was Slayer!"

Lucien shifted into a huge black wolf, his glossy pelt shining beneath the morning sunlight.

And so it had come down to the survival of the fittest.

PAIN TORE THROUGH Talia's heart. "*Rafael! Lucien!*" she screamed, jumping from her bed. An urgency so strong it nearly toppled her with its power propelled her from her rooms at the far end of the compound to Lucien's quarters. As she rushed into his room, she screamed, slid in a pool of warm blood, and landed spinning on her knees. The woman Lucien had meant to mark lay dead on his bed, steam rising from her eviscerated chest.

In the corner, amid the shambles of splintered furniture and broken glass, lay Rafael, his tawny fur matted with blood, his turquoise colored eyes glazed as death took him. Next to him lay the black furry body of Lucien, his golden eyes dulling as his lifeblood streamed from his chest.

"Noooooo!" she cried, "Noooooo!" On hands and knees, she scurried across the slippery hardwood to them. Kneeling between the brothers, Talia pressed a bloody hand to each of their hearts, stemming the blood flow. "Please," she whispered to the gods. "Please, spare them." The panic that had initially seized her evaporated as a deafening calmness settled within her. Slowly, reverently, she began to chant, summoning all of her power and calling upon the Great Spirit Mother, Singarti, the mother of all healers, the mother of all Talia's grandmothers, to preserve the Lycans she'd created three hundred years ago.

Energy crackled and snapped around her head in a myriad of metallic colors. Wide-eyed, she stared as they began to form into a vision of a noble woman dressed in white-fringed leather robes, with eagle feathers woven into her long, flowing black hair, two great wolves, one black, one golden, lying obediently at her feet.

Raising a slender hand, her ocean blue eyes glowing fiercely, Singarti whispered, "As you ask, so it will be done. The brothers will live, but only as one. Day and night. Light and dark. Mated and mateless. For all eternity, only one hour shall separate them. Until the Blood Law is avenged."

AND SO THE years passed . . .

Present day

THE HARD THRUM of the V-twin vibrated between his thighs, up to his hips, then along his spine. His corded muscles bunched in tension as he focused on the dark thread of highway ahead. He was wound tight, every sense on high alert, ready to uncoil, to strike at the slightest provocation.

The cool spring air tore through Lucien Mondragon's long black hair. He didn't wear a helmet; he didn't care about the law. Not man's law anyway. There was only one law he respected, and that was the Blood Law of revenge.

Throwing his head back, Lucien howled at the rising moon. It was dusk, and the Blood Moon called to him. It was time. The quickening had begun. In three months, the lunar eclipse would occur, and with it, he would stand as undisputed leader of the northern packs with more power than any alpha before him. More power than one leader had a right to posses, but the power he was due. And with it, he would destroy every living descendant of Peter Corbet, the original wolf Slayer. But he had another just as important slaying to do first.

Lucien opened the throttle wide, and the chopper lunged beneath his thighs, like an ardent lover arching into his deep thrusts. Only Lucien had no lover. No mate. No mistress.

Rafael Vulkasin had made sure Lucien would never have more than one-night stands with pack whores.

Snarling, Lucien pictured his nemesis's blood running in thick rivulets from his torn-out throat. The vision swam in macabre glory before him. He could almost taste the coppery thickness of Rafael's blood on his tongue.

It would be Lucien's pleasure to end that betraying bastard's life. And he would do it slowly. Lucien would savor each one of Rafael's gasps for air, each plea for his life, each pulse of his heart as his life-giving blood ebbed from him.

But first, Lucien would force Rafe to watch as he slowly, methodically, strangled Rafael's mate. She'd beg for her life, too. But she would die.

He grinned in the darkening light and snarled again.

An eye for an eye.

It was the way of the pack.

He would see it done.

One

FOR FALON CORBET, being special sucked. A lot.

Because in today's world, her rages, which were coming more frequently, and the dead people that seemed to follow her even into her dreams were not *en vogue*. There were other things, too, things she pretended weren't there. Things that got her into trouble.

It was why she was constantly between jobs, always broke and never spending more than a month anywhere. It was also why she lived in a closet-sized room on the fifth floor of a flophouse in the dregs of Sacramento.

And most of all, it was why she was hungry all of the time and why her most viable dinner option was yet another one of those nasty prepackaged sandwiches. The ones with soggy yellow bread and a limp pickle.

She hated them so much that the thought of choking another one down was enough to consider the pros and cons of living. For the third time that day, she contemplated ending it all. She felt as if her life held no purpose. Survival had become increasingly difficult. No one would miss her . . .

Yet.

There was that niggling thought in the very back of her mind that told her she was destined for more. That she had a very specific purpose for living. That if she took her life, many more would be lost. So she persevered.

And since beggars couldn't be choosers, Falon decided to make a dinner run to Del's market.

Quietly, she slipped into the hallway outside her room, pulling the door shut behind her.

Cringing when the rotting wooden floor creaked beneath her stealthy step, she glanced quickly behind her, afraid she'd see her slumlord, the ever watchful Mr. Sabo. If he caught sight of her, he would corner her then press her hard about her late rent. Then, even as she tried to put him off, he'd bluster inches from her face, his spittle spraying her cheeks and nose as he told her how, if he let her slide on her already past due rent, he'd have to let *everyone* slide, and he wasn't in the *goddamn* business of enabling losers to continue to be losers.

Did Sabo actually think she was happy with how her life had turned out? Of course, he never bothered to ask. Then again, it wasn't like she was Chatty Cathy either. But whenever Sabo compared her to a loser, something deep and terrible inside of Falon wanted to hurt him. Such feelings terrified her. She was not always prone to violence, but sometimes . . . she couldn't control it.

Holding her breath, Falon flattened her slender limbs against the murky hallway, down the five flights of stairs, and then inched her way into the dingy gray vestibule. She nearly collapsed in relief. The old codger was nowhere in sight. For someone who hadn't eaten since peanut butter toast and a banana more than twenty-four hours ago, she darted out the front door with Olympic sprinter speed.

She raised her face to the crisp evening breeze and inhaled. Spring had sprung in Sacramento, but there was more than the fragrant scent of blossoms in the air. The stench of decaying flesh, though barely perceptible, hung like a fog bank along the streets most nights.

Recently, her senses had honed. Unusually so. Just another anomaly that was Falon Corbet.

With each passing day, it seemed the stench around her grew heavier, more prominent. Tonight it combined with a dark energy that was so palpable Falon hesitated in her step and seriously considered returning to her room. The vitality of it felt like an electrical storm in her body, her veins live conduits. Her breath came hard, fast, and warm. She could feel it curl around her each time she exhaled. But as aware as she was of the dark forces that seemed to follow her no matter where she went, she was even more aware of the auras around her. Not the bright colorful ones of those who embraced life in happy accord. It was the dark, malevolent ones, like dirty dredge oil that slithered along corners or along the street gutters, careful to stay undetected, from who or what she wasn't sure.

Most days she didn't pay them much mind, like the cockroaches under the trash cans, they were just a part of the world as she knew it. Squeezing her eyes shut, Falon mentally pushed back, blocking the wild, chaotic swirls of emotion that pierced her brain. Normally, if she concentrated hard enough and long enough, she could push it all away. But some nights when she opened her eyes, she saw the haunted souls who walked the streets, like holocaust victims, their deep, dark, sunken eyes begging in silent agony for glorious release.

She couldn't help them. She didn't know how to, and even if she did, the darker, more powerful auras that swirled around them would prevent it. Intuitively, she knew that.

Hastily crossing the street, Falon glanced up at the waxing pink moon shrouded in dark, wispy clouds. She tried to make light of the sinister sight, thinking the only thing missing from the eerie vision was the lone howl of a wolf. Instead, shivers slithered across her back like giant cold worms, and she felt the hint of something else in the air. Something dark and powerful. Primal. Something that would irrevocably change the course of her life.

Something she wanted no part of.

Using every ounce of her concentration, Falon closed her mind to every flick and flare of energy around her. It cost her. More of her precious energy drained in her efforts to keep her mind closed to things that did not concern her.

She was not at her strongest, having eaten only enough to feed a bird more than a day ago.

Head lowered, Falon trudged down the sidewalk, crossed the oddly quiet street at the first corner, then stopped just outside the metal and glass door of Del's grocery. She raised a hand to push the door open, then hesitated. Guilt gripped her.

Unable to stand the tragedy of the souls who haunted the many soup kitchens in town, or endure the recrimination at the local churches, she'd become the lowest of the lows—a petty thief. Yet, if she got over that sad fact and went in, she'd eat again, and if she ate, she'd live another day. Hunger pains jabbed at her belly in a harsh, grinding staccato. They were becoming unbearable. Despite her aversion to them, when she pictured a soggy sandwich wrapped in cellophane, her mouth actually began to salivate.

"Jesus," she hissed, staring at her trembling hand. She'd eat a damn brick she was so hungry.

She almost regretted her blasphemy. Despite her guilt, she knew

God would want her to eat. Wouldn't he? Yes. After all, he'd guided her here before. Closing her eyes, like a repeating movie reel, she played her artful pilfering out in her head. She knew exactly how many steps it took to get from where she stood to the refrigerated food section in the back. Once there, she'd smoothly duck behind the towering paper towel display, out of sight of the big round mirrors mounted in the ceiling, and slip a sandwich down her bulky sweatshirt. And then, eyes cast to the floor, she'd walk past Mr. Delico, through the front door, without any fear she'd be stopped.

She opened her eyes, blinking away the hot sting of tears.

Yes, she'd stolen from Mr. D before. Tonight, though, something significant was going to be different. Tonight, she'd walk out of the store without leaving her usual quarter. Tonight, she didn't even have that. Which meant she'd have to pay with something more . . . special—in a currency only she knew existed. Maybe warn Mr. D when she sensed trouble heading his way. She'd done it before. The first time she told him he might want to close early, he hadn't listened. He'd been robbed and pistol-whipped three hours later. After that, he never questioned her. After that, he let her walk out with dinner, her cost, a quarter.

With a weary sigh, Falon pushed open the front door to Del's and stopped short. Pressure swirled about her, pushing against her in a tentative, probing way as if trying to get into her head. The hair on the back of her neck stood straight up. It didn't take a PhD to know something was different in Delico's grocery.

Son of a bitch.

She knew she should have stayed in her room!

Tentatively, Falon cast a slow glance around the small grocery, looking for the jovial face of the owner. He was nowhere in sight.

The pressure mushroomed, followed by an unexpected jab of pain in her belly. Falon grunted as if she'd been mule-kicked in the gut. Another hard punch racked her. Hot tears welled in her eyes. Grabbing her midsection, she slowly turned to face the counter.

The thin, blond man behind the register bore no resemblance to the chubby olive-skinned Italian shopkeeper. She stepped toward him, gasping when another hard jab of pain twisted her innards. This pain wasn't from hunger. This was different.

A warning.

Taking a shallow breath, Falon slowly faced the blond man and demanded, "Where is Mr. Delico?"

The guy merely swept his gaze over her from head to toe, then nodded with a slow, satisfied gesture that surprised her as much as his lopsided leer. He must have X-ray vision. Her depleted curves were hiding beneath a baggy black sweatshirt and two-sizes-too-large desert cammies and combat boots. Her black hair, a shield to her soul, hung like a sheet halfway across her face and down to her ass.

When he continued to leer, Falon turned and walked stiffly toward the back refrigerators. Subtly, she glanced up at the round mirrors mounted in the back corners of the store. Through a slit in the wave of her hair, she watched his dark eyes follow her. Then his eyes shifted to his left and his mouth moved slightly, as if he was talking to someone behind the counter.

She'd bet the rent she didn't have that the person he was speaking to wasn't Mr. D. So where was he? Trussed up like a holiday pig in the storeroom?

"Damn it," she muttered softly.

Slowly, she turned. As she did, she tossed the long waves of her hair off her face. She straightened to her full height of five foot eight and looked pointedly over the stacked aisles to the blond man behind the counter.

"Walk out of here now," she said softly, "and I promise not to hurt you."

The blond's thin lips turned up into a smile then widened, showing badly stained teeth. As he stepped to the side, another man rose from behind the counter. As he appeared, his deadly aura blasted her entire being with hot, searing pain. The force of it knocked her backward into the thick glass refrigerator doors.

"Shit!" she woofed as her back shattered the glass and the velocity of the hit pushed her into the unit.

She really hated being special.

Two

EMBEDDED IN THE broken glass of the refrigerator door, with the shelves inside holding her upright, just like in cartoons, Falon heard birdies chirping as they circled around her head. But unlike a cartoon character, Falon recovered quickly. Shoving the metal shelves and broken glass off her, she jumped to her feet and prepared to fight. She might not like facing unpleasantness, but she wasn't a shrinking violet either. Her heretical life sucked, but she wasn't going to give it up without a fight.

"Oh, holy hell!" she gulped, catching sight of the massive hulk that materialized before her.

The skinny dude had nothing on this guy. This dude looked like a Conan the Barbarian.

Thick brown hair hung straight around a sharp, angular face, a face embedded with the deep lines of experience and age-old hatred. Black, penetrating eyes locked onto her with such fervor she shivered. A thick leather strap crossed his worn leather jerkin that was open at the throat. Brown suede pants were tucked into doeskin moccasin-type knee-high boots. Huge gnarled hands clenched and unclenched at his sides. Despite the power exuding in waves from the man, if she wasn't so terrified, she'd laugh. He looked ridiculous in that getup.

Falon tilted her chin up defiantly. He could smash her with a flick of his wrist, but only if she gave him the chance.

"I might be half your size, mister," Falon challenged, "but I'm quick, and I know kung fu." She postured in what she hoped looked like a credible karate chop position. The scuzzy blond man behind the counter walked silently up behind his big friend and stopped. Not, she was sure, because he took her threats to heart but because something had fundamentally changed between them. Instead of a leer, his long face had turned solemn. Like she had passed some sort of sniff test, and she was now due his respect.

Conan scowled and quietly contemplated her. Every instinct told her to turn and run as fast and as far as she could, but she didn't.

Mr. D was trussed up somewhere, probably needing medical attention. She wasn't going to thank him for looking the other way when she ripped him off by turning yellow.

She took a threatening step forward and raised her karate-chop-ready hands higher. "Go now, and I won't call the cops."

"Cops cannot help you, Slayer," Conan said in a thick accent she could not place. He extended his ham-sized hand, his thick, callused fingers distended toward her. A large gold and ruby ring glittered on his third finger. The stone, depicting the eye of a howling wolf, glowed. "Your place is with your people."

Pain jabbed her temples. She blinked several times. She'd seen that ring before. A long time ago . . .

"Come with me, now," he softly commanded.

Stunned, Falon could not react. Her brain fogged. Her joints froze as if clogged with Play-Doh. Somewhere in the midst of her fear, however, she felt the bubbling of astonishment.

If this guy thought she was going to trot out of here with him and his blond sidekick, he was too stupid to live.

"*My* people?" she choked out. "*I* have no people. You have me mixed up with someone else."

He stepped toward her, and somehow, despite her terror, she was able to hold her stance. "I have not made a mistake, Falon Corbet. I have searched for you for nearly a decade. You are the one I seek."

Her jaw dropped. *No one* knew her real name. No one except her long-gone foster parents and the poor excuse of a caseworker who had turned his back on her when she needed help all those years ago. She'd been on her own since she was fourteen, and since then had always used an alias. Better to keep the cops at bay when she skipped town and her financial obligations and to keep her name out of the system that had turned on her.

Despite wanting to show this guy some game, Falon took several steps back. "Who are you?" she whispered. "How do you know my name?"

"I am Viktor Salene." He gave her a short, curt bow. "*Jager*, master Slayer of Lycans."

She narrowed her eyes. The guy was definitely smoking something. "What's a Lycan, and how do you know who I am?"

The man scowled, his eyes darkening until he looked demonic. "Lycans are an abomination of nature. The scourge of the earth! They are the creatures a great king charged our ancestors to destroy over seven hundred years ago. The creatures I have spent my life hunting."

Falon took another step back. The guy was crazy. She looked past him to Blondie, who was nodding reverently.

Right.

Okay.

She almost made a crack about Halloween being months away, but didn't. These guys were serious. Crazy, but serious. And that just made them all the more dangerous.

"I'll tell you what, boys. Tell me where Mr. D is. Let me make sure he's okay, then we'll take our conversation outside."

"If it is the shopkeeper you speak of, he cannot be helped," Conan the *jager* said.

As his words trailed off, Falon felt it. The bitter coldness of death followed by a profound sense of loss. And guilt. Mr. D was dead because he had befriended her. "*You killed him?*" she demanded incredulously, knowing, yet still not wanting to believe what she instinctively knew to be true. Falon cringed, squeezing her eyes shut. She also knew poor Mr. D did not die easily or quickly. Her eyes flashed open. Heat radiated from her face, and the rage erupted. This time she didn't fight it.

The barbarian nodded.

Her vision clouded then cleared as fury ripped through every part of her, pumping more adrenaline into her system. The kick of it gave her a sudden urge to retch, but she swallowed the bile back. "You bastard! He was a kind old man! You had no right to kill him!"

She grabbed a box cutter from where it lay on top of a partially unpacked box of produce and swung it wide. It caught Conan's face, slicing open his right cheek. He didn't flinch. The only clue to his fury was the narrowing of his shiny black eyes and the intense wave of pain that flashed over her. The bastard! He'd attacked her with—what? Some kind of invisible force? Whatever it was, it hit her like a wall, but one she held her own against. Her fury and despair over Mr. Delico's fate reigned supreme, causing something unbelievable to happen.

Conan's massive body jolted as if *he* had been slammed by a wall.

Instinctively, Falon knew she had done it, but she had no idea how. She didn't question it. She'd never know, so she'd just go with it. A snide smile twisted her lips.

His eyes narrowed to black slits. "Do not challenge me, Slayer!" he roared. "I am *jager*! I will cut you down where you stand for your insolence!"

Visions of poor, sweet Mr. D begging for his life as these two thugs ripped him to shreds nearly brought her to her knees in anguish. The anguish, however, made her stronger. It fueled the rage in her. It gave her the will to see if that small jolt of power had been real and if she could do it again. She leaned forward, as if pressing against a great wind, when in truth it was the force of Conan's will she battled. Concentrating, she pulled the furious energy swirling around her inward, until it was pulsing inside her chest like a fireball. In one Herculean surge, Falon flung her hands forward with her last ounce of strength, expelling the buildup. And it was enough to nudge Conan the *jager* aside.

She bolted for the front door.

Conan cursed, and his mad aura took the form of a steel blade that speared her from behind. Searing jabs of heat pierced her skin. This time, however, the pain was more than mental.

Her skin split open.

Blood erupted from the wound. She felt the warm rivulets drip down her back.

He followed with another sharp slice of heat, this time cutting through the black leather of her left boot and across her ankle. Falon howled in agony. Stumbling, she zigzagged awkwardly through the store. The front door was only a few feet away. If she could . . . just . . . get . . . to it—

Another searing shot of heat cut across the back of her ankle, severing her Achilles tendon. She screamed again and fell face-first, sprawling onto the hard linoleum floor. Blood, warm and slippery, pooled around her, preventing her from getting the traction she needed to crawl to the doors.

Hard footsteps thudded behind her. She focused, pushing the agony from her mind, and concentrated solely on escape.

Deep laughter infiltrated her focus. Large hands grabbed her by the hair and pulled her up. "You cannot outrun your destiny, Slayer."

Falon closed her eyes. With every cell in her tattered body, she channeled her rage and mentally forced a harsh shot of pain into her captor.

He yelped, his hands loosening. She watched his dark eyes widen, then narrow. His face morphed into something so disturbing she thought she'd lose control of her bodily functions. When he opened his mouth, long sharp teeth glinted under the fluorescent lights. "You will learn, Slayer, I am *jager*, and as such, I own you."

He lowered his face to her chest but kept his gaze on hers. "Now," he hissed, "we will become a part of the other. The next time you lash out to inflict injury on me, you will also inflict it on yourself!"

"No," she screamed, thrashing against him.

"Don't fight me—" he growled just as the front doors of the small grocery slammed open. A harsh, hot wind chaotically swirled inside, swooshing across Falon's face, lifting her hair in a spiraling torrent before sending items from the surrounding shelves flying across the aisles and crashing to the floor.

Conan's head jerked up, eyes narrowing as if catching sight of an enemy. "Take care of him, Barrak," he growled furiously to his flunky. Blondie stepped forward. Before he took another step, he screamed and went flying across the top of three aisles before crashing onto the floor.

"Still picking on little girls are you, Viktor?" a deep masculine voice sneered.

Falon tried to raise her head to see who was speaking, but Conan's gaze snapped back to hers at the same time he shoved her down. His eyes glinted with a preternatural shine, warning her off. Despite his superior strength, she felt a shift in his body and energy at the other's presence. Falon forced her head up to get a look at what caused the satanic bastard such anxiety.

For the brief span of several heartbeats, she could not breathe. She could not have uttered a single syllable had her life and the fate of the free world depended on it. Fierce gold flashes of energy snapped and popped around the blond, black-leather-clad man. He was, in very plain speak, magnificent. And lurking beneath his glory was a deadly supernatural energy. The commanding presence of the man standing at the threshold of the store could not be denied. Nor could the contempt twisting his lips. She swallowed hard and wondered which man was more of a threat.

"Vulkasin, you cur. How dare you show yourself!" Conan spit.

Vulkasin strode into the store, his chin raised, his nostrils flaring. "The stench of death follows you, Slayer. Do you never grow weary of the kill?"

Conan raised Falon up and held her out toward the intruder. "The quickening has begun, Lycan. Prepare yourself." Falon tore her gaze from the intruder, who had not even glanced at her, and turned to the lunatic who held her so tightly she could scarcely breathe. He turned rabid black eyes on her.

"No," she croaked, knowing he was going to bite her. She shoved at him, madly trying to gather her thoughts and blast him one last time. His grip tightened. He ripped the front of her sweatshirt open with his teeth, revealing her naked breasts. His eyes glinted hungrily. Not, she realized, with lust but with possession. As if he had won the lottery and he was mentally counting all the terrible ways he could spend the money.

"We are destined to be one," he breathed.

A dark shadow fell over them. Falon screamed, not sure if it was because of the bite Conan was about to take out of her or because she'd locked gazes with the one he called Vulkasin—the one that looked as if he'd just escaped the bowels of hell with every intention of bringing them right back with him.

Three

CONAN DROPPED FALON to the floor, then swept her behind him with a booted foot to her chest. She slid several feet on her own blood before slamming into a wall hard enough to force the air from her lungs.

Even as Falon gasped for breath, she was very aware of the two furies before her, and of her need to get the hell out of there. *Fast.*

But even as she tried to flee, her bloody hands offered no traction on the slippery floor. Her right foot throbbed with pain as she tried to backpedal away from the two whatever-the-hell-they-weres.

The sharp shaving sound of steel against steel echoed in the small grocery. Aside from her gasps for air, it was the only sound. As the two beasts circled one another to the left of her and away from the door, Falon rolled, trying to inch closer to escape. She turned over and looked up, paralyzed by awe.

The fantastic sight before her was breathtakingly terrifying. Vulkasin stood battle-ready with two gleaming broadswords, one in each fist, the fluorescent lights glittering off the sharp edges in a weird play of colors.

Conan held only one sword, but it was larger, with a hook at the end of it. He slashed it down on the dark one's right sword and yanked. Vulkasin yanked harder, pulling Conan toward him. Mere inches from Conan's nose, Vulkasin sneered. "Do you really think, Viktor, you can best me at swords?"

The barbarian spun around, shoving the hooked end of his sword down to the pommel of Vulkasin's. Vulkasin laughed and kicked Conan in the chest. "Is that all you have? And in front of the girl? How do expect to win her with such a pathetic show of strength?"

"You overrate yourself, Vulkasin. My powers are equal to yours, but my mind is not befuddled with your archaic sense of honor." Conan flew backward in the air, but even as he did, he twisted in a Matrix move, landing squarely on his feet. Fear turned Falon's blood to ice. She told herself to run, to flee while they were distracted, but her body disobeyed her. Stunned, she could not look away.

"You flaunt your arrogance, Viktor. How do you think I found you so easily?" Vulkasin leapt high over Conan, tiptoed across the ceiling, then—with arms extended wide—somersaulted in beautiful symmetry. Body and blades formed a perfect iron cross. As he came down, the *jager* leapt up in the air to meet him. The two furies clashed in a spellbinding kaleidoscope of furious blade sparks. Red, black, and orange rained down upon her, the heat prickling her skin. The sensation jolted her, ripping her body from its paralysis. Falon rolled over again, concentrating on her path toward the door.

They could kill each other for all she cared. She prayed for exactly that even as she continued to roll. As the furious clash of steel continued, Falon made it to the closed doors. She pushed with her hands and opened them just a crack. On her elbows, she dragged herself forward, ignoring the harsh scrape of her skin against concrete as she made it outside. It occurred to her that the sidewalk was eerily quiet even as she collapsed on the dirty concrete. In slow, thick flows, her strength drained from her body.

No food in more than a day, coupled with what was going on behind her and the continued blood loss had taken its toll. If she didn't find a trash can to crawl into soon, she'd die on the street.

At least in a trash can she'd have some privacy. The shattering of glass and the subsequent pelting of needle-sharp shards into her skin forced Falon to roll into a fetal position with her hands over her head. She prayed once more that the two demonic warriors would just go the hell away. Didn't happen. One of them—she didn't dare uncurl her body to see which one—slammed to the ground beside her with a hard thud. A harsh whoosh of air expelled from the body's lungs, and she heard the crunch of broken glass beneath the feet of the other. "Please, please, just leave me alone," she begged.

A large, powerful hand grabbed her, its thick uncompromising fingers wrapped around her biceps. Falon gasped, opened her eyes, and froze. Deep turquoise-colored eyes blazed down at her. Her skin chilled, then heated before he yanked her up as if she didn't weigh more than a small sack of potatoes.

"Get your damn hands off me!" she shrieked, kicking at Vulkasin.

Instead of obeying her, he shook his head as if she were naught but an annoying child begging for a piece of candy. He had sheathed one sword but held the other high in his right hand. With his left hand, he pulled her up to him and held her firmly against his chest. He turned easily and pointed his sword at Conan, who glared from where he lay broken and bloodied on the sidewalk. Malevolent heat radiated off his body. Falon cringed into the hardness of the man holding her. He laughed and pressed the tip of his sword into Conan's jugular. "I'd planned on killing you, Viktor. Do you think I'm here by accident? I've been tracking you for days." Vulkasin sighed as if bored. "Your death will be my pleasure." As he pushed the tip into Viktor's skin, a small fountain of blood sprayed onto the blade. "But I may spare you, for a few minutes."

Conan sneered and spit at Vulkasin's sword. Vulkasin jabbed the sword deeper into Conan's throat. More blood spurted. Falon cringed at the gory sight.

"Tell me where Balor has gone and why, and I will give you a ten-minute head start."

Conan's black eyes snapped in fury. "I do not know. I broke with my clan years ago, as you know."

Vulkasin tsked tsked and shook his head. His blade sliced deeper into Conan's throat. Blood squirted in short thick pumps from the artery. Falon was going to be sick.

"Back East! The clans converge for the rising!" Conan screamed, pushing as far back into the asphalt as he could.

"The rising you will never see," Vulkasin sneered, but retracted his blade. "You just bought yourself ten minutes."

With her still clutched to his chest, Vulkasin whipped around and strode toward a shiny, sleek motorcycle surrounded by more choppers. Behind the sleek cycles stood dark, hooded figures, all the more menacing for their silence. "*You* will not see the rising of the Blood Moon, Vulkasin!" Conan shouted.

Falon trembled with her desire to flee, but she didn't dare move a muscle. She was too afraid that if she struggled, the demon who held her so tightly against him that she could scarcely breathe would drop her and leave her for Conan. Unfortunately, she was just as terrified of where she would end up if this whatever-the-hell-he-was took her away. The thought had her suddenly finding her voice as well as her courage.

"Let go of me!" She kicked with her good leg against the iron-hard thigh of her captor. He readjusted her weight in his arm and turned toward Conan. Just as they turned, a blazing force of energy slashed across her waist up to the bottom swell of her breast. Falon screamed in anguish. The initial pain from the attack had been bad enough, but instantaneously the wound burned as if someone had poured a bottle of alcohol into it. She hissed and writhed, unable to find a way to deal with the ungodly burn. She was going to die.

"You push me too far, Slayer." The man holding her tightened his grip, and with a mighty hurl he let his blade fly. In the white-hot haze of her pain, Falon heard the sickening thunk of steel penetrating flesh and bone, the harsh scream of a man in agony, then the slow hiss of air as it escaped his lungs.

Unable not to, she turned. The steel blade had impaled Conan straight through the heart, passing through him and into the concrete as easily as if he were butter.

"He won't be pissing me off again," Vulkasin said in a deadly whisper.

Fear and unholy agony pushed Falon's heart into overdrive, the force of its beating jamming her throat. She couldn't swallow, couldn't speak, couldn't breathe. She prayed for sweet, blissful death.

Vulkasin turned a scorching grin on her. Then, thankfully, the world went dark.

RAFAEL SIGNALED FOR his men to mount up. Harleys revved around him. His sergeant at arms, Anton, inclined his head toward the crumpled body hanging in Rafe's arms.

"What do you want me to do with her?" Anton asked.

Rafael looked down at the ashen face. The girl—woman, he amended, as he felt the lush weight of her breasts against his arm—weighed much less than half his two hundred and forty pounds. Her height was a good hand and a half less than his own six foot three. Except for her breasts, she was nothing but a bag of skin and bones.

Her state of health didn't concern him, however. That she'd seen and heard too much, did.

He looked around and noted no other strange faces around him. Had his men not been circled around the corner grocery scaring those off who might have rubbernecked the fray, he would have had to do some serious cleanup. As it was, there was merely this sole slip of a woman to deal with.

For a moment, he studied her, remembering the fire and courage she'd shown as she'd fought the Slayer and tried to flee them both. A grudging admiration swept through him, and he hesitated. But only for a second. She could only bring trouble. He didn't need the attention, and he sure as hell didn't want it.

He turned, nodded, and made to hand her over to Anton. Her eyes flickered open, and deep murky pools of what he thought might be blue eyes beneath all of her suffering stopped him. Once again, he hesitated, but as Anton grabbed her arms, her ripped sweatshirt fell open, exposing full, creamy breasts. Blood shot to his cock. Rafe growled but released her to his sergeant at arms.

His desire sealed her fate. He wanted no woman clouding his resolve. No woman for his brother to use against him.

As he looked down at her, Anton licked his lips.

"Make her end painless," Rafe softly said.

Anton nodded, but his eyes sparked in undisguised lust.

"No, Anton. Leave her some dignity."

Anton scowled but again nodded. As he turned toward an adjacent alley, Rafael strode to Salene, pulled his sword from his chest, and deftly decapitated him. Seconds later he watched the Slayer turn to dust. He wiped the sword blade across his right thigh, cleaning any vestige of the Slayer from it. As he sheathed it with its twin behind his back, he caught the twinkle of something under the sputtering streetlight.

He reached down and picked up a chunky gold ring from the

gray dust that was once Viktor Salene. It warmed in his hand. Awe-struck by its simple beauty and the fact that it was of a howling wolf similar to the wolf emblazoned on the back of his black leather duster, Rafael held it up to the dim light.

The ruby eye blazed. A harsh wave of frigid air moved through Rafael as he realized what he held in his hand. The Eye of Fenrir. The savage wolf of doom. A traitor to his own kind. The talisman of the wolf Slayers. Enemy of the Lycan nation. Rafe's eyes narrowed. The ring, lore told, held the captured spirit of Fenrir. Fenrir had been lured into the ring by Singarti, the great spirit woman of the Inuit, during the great battle of the North more than three centuries ago. And there, buried deep in the frozen tundra, it was supposed to stay, keeping the spirit within frozen for all eternity. It possessed great power and if in the wrong hands could unleash Fenrir to his terrible physical form. However, if kept secured, the ring bearer had the potential to wield greater power. Rafael smiled. Was this a sign? His smile faded. Or a precursor to their doom?

How did Viktor get his hands on it? No word had leaked that it had been unearthed.

Did Balor, master of the Slayers, know of Viktor's possession of it? Rafe doubted it. The ring was too powerful, doubly so with the coming of the Blood Moon. Balor would never stand for anyone other than himself to possess it. Was that why Salene had gone off on his own?

Rafael folded his fingers around the ring. Heat lasered painfully into his hand. He clutched it tighter, unwilling to give in to the savagery of Fenrir. He was alpha, leader of the great Vulkasin pack. Only death by a Slayer could take his power. Many had died trying over the last three decades of his life, and many more would meet the same fate. Heat flared in his hand, as if to say he was a fool to think he could survive the coming of the final battle, a modern-day

Ragnarok. He smiled grimly and opened his hands. The ruby eye dimmed. He slid it onto the third finger of his right hand. "You have been delivered to me for a reason, Fenrir. But rest assured, you will not be the death of my pack."

He looked over his shoulder to see that Anton had faded into the black jaws of the alley. As more questions swirled in his mind, an uneasiness overcame Rafael. What did Viktor, a rogue wolf Slayer with an inflated ego, want with a homeless girl? He had been close to marking her, something the Slayers did only when the person being marked held value to the clan. Though Viktor was known as a mercenary rogue, one who did not limit his kills to Rafael's people, he had blood ties to the direct descendants of the original Slayers. If the girl held value to a Slayer, she would hold value to Rafael.

"Anton!" Rafael strode toward the alley just as his sergeant at arms emerged empty-handed. "The girl?"

Anton's dark brows crowded together, forming a thick mono-brow across his deep-set pale eyes. He jerked his thumb over his shoulder. "I took care of her as you commanded."

Rafael sprinted past his man in a blur. He did not need his keen sense of smell to locate her because his eyes immediately adjusted to the darkness. He found her lying in a crumpled heap next to an overflowing Dumpster, buried beneath several stacks of cardboard. He swooped upon the lifeless form.

Shoving the debris aside, Rafe grabbed her to him, grateful that Anton had not snapped her neck. His powers were not so great that he could fuse bone and nerves. Not yet anyway. Thankfully, Anton had only smothered her. Rafael sank to his knees and carefully pulled her into the cradle of his arms. Pushing her head back and her jet black hair from her ashen cheeks, he opened her cooling lips, pressed his own warm lips to hers, and gently blew.

Four

AS THEY HEADED out of the city, Rafael could not fight the feeling that the human draped across his gas tank was going to create an uproar with his pack. They were no more accepting of humans than he. While he did business with humans because he needed their money, Rafael was staunchly opposed to any human for any reason breaching his tightly controlled world. He went to them; they were not permitted to come to him.

He could barely stand the stench of humans. Prejudice, hate, and greed clung to them like stink on shit. Were it not for humans, his race would not be dying out, and they would still thrive in Europe.

There was little solace in the fact that if his kind were not able to take human form and walk among them as equals, Rafael would not have been born. And while that may be true, it was the human ancestors of the original wolf Slayers who were as hell-bent on eradicating his kind as the day Peter Corbet accepted the charter to eradicate wolves from the British Isles by his king, Edward I.

Since the violent split of the pack fourteen years ago, the necessity for humans to survive had increased tenfold. Rafael resented it. He resented his brother more for making it so. By refusing to see that Rafael had saved him from a death sentence for lying with a Slayer, Lucien insisted Rafael had intentionally slain his chosen one, then hammered home a deep wedge between what had been a healthy, thriving pack. Once, pack Vulkasin was the undisputed alpha pack among all the packs in the world, leader in commerce, military, and in government. But his brother ruined it all in one furious act of selfishness. And now, Rafe needed humans to support his pack.

Rafael sighed, weary of his brother's continued acts of vengeance. The time was at hand. Rafael knew what he had been in denial about for years. For the greater good of his pack and the Lycan nation at large, he must eliminate his brother. He cringed as he always did when the realization hit him. He loved his brother, Great Spirit Mother, help him, but he did. And there were times like now when he despised him. So much at stake, so much to lose, so much pain and suffering, for what? Lucien's refusal to see that he was duped by a woman? A Slayer?

Rafael set his jaw. He had no choice. And therein lay the rub. The Blood Law. Murder of an alpha was punishable by death. Then who would lead the nation against the Slayers?

But it had to be done. There would finally be peace the nation desperately needed, and once united, they would defeat the Slayers once and for all.

Rafael set thoughts of his brother aside and focused on getting home. His almost nightly hunts over the past three months had proven fruitful. His Slayer count had gone up exponentially. He smiled in the night wind. He would take the next week to regroup, strategize, and rearm. Then strike when Lycans were their most powerful, during the full moon.

Now, miles north of California's capital, high atop a mountain, two dozen blacked-out choppers rumbled into the pack compound. As the thick iron gates closed with swift precision behind them, Rafe sneered. His brother's scent, though faint, wafted through the air. It wasn't the first time his brother had skulked close when Rafael was hunting.

As he drove past several outbuildings then around to the clubhouse—the main compound building—Rafael glanced up at the shrouded moon. It was well past midnight. He didn't have much time if the girl was to survive.

He looked down at her in his arms. She had not stirred once on the long ride home; she didn't stir now but remained half draped across the gas tank and half sitting against his chest. With her added weight, maneuvering the bike had been a tricky feat, especially through the twisting Sierra road that led to the compound. But he was strong, and his strength didn't waver. He couldn't say the same for her. As he came to an abrupt stop, the girl's body slid from his grip, causing him to curse. He grabbed her by the arms and pulled her back across his blood-soaked leathers.

He stared down at her, resisting the urge to push her hair away from her face. The ruby eye on the ring glowed, its heat stinging his flesh just as it had done whenever he'd looked down at her on the ride home.

If only Talia, his pack's healer, was here. Not only would he know that the girl's life was in good hands, but Talia had a way of getting into human minds. There was much she could tell Rafe about the woman the Slayer had wanted enough to mark.

But Talia wasn't here. Instead, she was being held captive by his brother. Which meant Rafael would have to care for the woman, and that meant taking unnecessary risks.

Rafael cursed. "Damn you, Lucien!" And damn himself for

falling for Lucien's schemes. It was his fault Talia was locked away in the dragon's lair.

Recognizing how his thoughts had spiraled, Rafe mentally shook himself. He didn't have time for this, and neither did the woman. Grabbing her up to him, he toed the kickstand out from under the bike, cut the engine, and stood, bringing the injured woman with him.

"Anton," Rafael called over his shoulder. "Release the Berserkers."

"Are you mad?" Anton screeched.

Rafael sighed. In another place and time, he might have laughed his ass off at his sergeant at arms' squealing. Or, more likely, he'd have cut him down so low for questioning his authority that Anton would've been fodder for the omegas of the pack. But Anton was not his concern at the moment. Saving the girl in his arms was, and so was sealing the compound from all threats, especially that of the Slayers, who would know of Viktor's death by now and likely come charging in with a vengeance.

Rafael growled low. "Do as I said." He kicked open the front door to the clubhouse. His eyes instantly adjusted to the darkness, yet he didn't need a light to navigate the large room. Even if his night vision hadn't been so sharp, he could navigate the entire compound blindfolded.

"Alert the pack," he called to Anton, who had not moved since he'd dismounted his bike. "Stay within the compound walls until dusk tomorrow."

Anton called out to Nazz and JorDon, his right and left arms, informing them of Rafael's command. Incredulous voices drifted to Rafael.

It was rare that the Berserkers were released outside of the compound walls, and even then, it happened only when Rafe was there to supervise. There was nothing living or dead that could survive even a scratch from one of them. Their fangs were hollow and filled with such toxic venom that even a drop of it into a bloodstream would render the victim paralyzed. What the Berserker did after that was what nightmares were made of. Rafe was the only creature that could command a Berserker. As he was alpha, the mutant wolves had to obey him or die.

A jolt of fire sparked on his finger, and he looked down at the ruby eye of the ring. Fenrir could learn a trick or two from his Berserkers. They came to heel at his first whistle. They owed him their lives. They obeyed. So, one day, would Fenrir.

"Rafael?" Anton called from the doorway. "You must give them their command. Otherwise, they'll run loose through the woods and destroy every living thing!"

Rafael halted in midstep and readjusted the slippery body in his arms. He put his fingers to his lips and, in several short, earsplitting whistles, he called to the Berserkers. He was immediately rewarded with loud snarling barks from the other side of the compound.

"Open the gate to the outside. They will obey. I'm going to my rooms. Do not disturb me unless you have no recourse."

Anton nodded. Once the Berserkers were released to patrol the outside perimeter, Anton and the rest of the pack would see to the security of their own homes within the high concertina wired steel block walls. Since the day after his parents' deaths, the walls had held against several Slayer attacks as well as a few from the Vipers, a Slayer-backed gang of bikers, but Rafael knew he would have to reinforce every inch of the compound with the coming of the Blood Moon. The quickening had begun. But their survival rested on surviving the rising.

Over the last two decades, the Slayers had systematically reduced Lycan numbers to fewer than a thousand worldwide. Add to that the division of the Vulkasin pack, and there were fewer to protect the bloodline. He and his brother were the last alphas of the pack. Until he marked his chosen one—the alpha female who matched him in courage, heart, and strength—the line could not continue.

The irony twisted within him. Of course, once he found his destined mate, she would be offered up to Lucien as the payment for Rafael's deed. It was why he had refused to choose and mark his mate. How could he knowingly sacrifice her? He couldn't. Yet, if he did not, his line would die.

Rage at his brother intensified. Would that Lucien admit his woman was Slayer, there would be no sacrifice. But if Lucien did admit it, the Blood Law would demand his life as payment.

It was an impossible situation, one that would only be remedied by death.

Rafael kicked open the door that led to the more private rooms in the communal building. Then, after striding across a wide expanse of hardwood floor to a steep stairway and down a short hall, he kicked open the thick oak door into his own quarters. He moved through the main room and into his bedroom.

He grimaced when the subtle scent of lemony spice wafted around his nostrils. Lana. She was always leaving her scent on his bedpost in hopes of driving him mad with lust. She refused to accept that he took from her only what his body needed, never his heart.

Never his heart.

Rafe fought back a bitter laugh. As alpha, he had his pick of any female in his pack, even the paired ones. Not wanting to create harsh feelings among his pack males, Rafael stayed away from their females. He would rather be a lone wolf than share his mate, even with the alpha, so how could he expect his pack to? He made a point of taking only the unattached pack females to his bed. Their scents appealed to him for only a brief time before he set them aside. Yet they all vied for his affection, even knowing that in the end, it would mean their deaths to love him. He could not bring himself to mark a Lycan, only to see her sacrificed. His decision not to pull the trigger, so to speak, had become an increasing problem. For his pack to survive, he had to take and mark a mate.

So lately, he had taken to fucking human females. Unless marked, a human could not conceive with his seed, and he was immune from human disease. But the best part of sex with a human was that he never had to see her again. No longing looks, no whines for attention, no backbiting. He'd taken more and more to cruising the cities for human sex to quench his ever growing primal fire. But even so, lately, his moods had darkened. He spent most days running through the forests until he had no strength to run another step and his nights hunting Slayers. He had a hunger for something else. Something with meaning, something out there, something . . . taboo.

It was a double-edged sword he wielded. There was no debating the three-century-old covenant. Though many council meetings had convened to sidestep or find a loophole, the laws were written in Lycan blood after the great war of the North and could not be challenged.

He would take a mate, and Rafe could only hope she lived long enough to conceive, for once she conceived, so, too, would the females of the pack, and the line would survive another generation.

He growled, frustrated and angry. Resentment for what he could not change ate at him, but when he laid the girl down on the linens, he did so carefully.

Her long body molded into the thick down comforter. In seconds, the pale yellow cotton was blood-soaked. She groaned in pain. When she moved her right leg, the groan became an excruciating cry. His anger softened. Human or not, she was innocent, and he wished no pain on innocents.

He didn't understand her continued bleeding. The tourniquets had not worked. Why hadn't her blood clotted? Swiping his hand across his face, Rafael could think of only one way to ease her pain and stop the bleeding.

His skin warmed at the thought. His eyes narrowed and his fists clenched, white-knuckled.

He didn't want to heal her. Doing so would create a bond between them, one that Rafael wanted with no woman. But if he didn't do it, she would die without giving him the information he needed. What choice did he have?

Rafael jerked off his leather duster and tossed it to the floor, then sat down on the edge of the bed. He reached out to her, the heat of her fevered body causing him to recoil. Despite her grave state, a low buzz of energy radiated from her. He pressed his hands to her back, her skin burning him with the same intensity of the Eye of Fenrir.

He ripped her sweatshirt in half and hissed as he laid it to the sides of her pulpy back. Salene had done a number on her. Her flesh was peppered with gaping wounds, as if she'd been stabbed then burned. He rolled her gently to her left side and looked closer at the deep gash that ran from the middle of her rib cage up the bottom swell of her breast to her pink nipple.

Anger amplified. Viktor Salene was a fool. Rafael's hatred for all Slayers ran as deep and as passionate as his love for his pack. Soon, soon it would come to a bloody end. Only one race could survive the Blood Moon rising. The Lycan nation had triumphed three hundred years ago with the coming of the first Blood Moon; they would triumph with the second rising as well!

Rafael lived for the honor of finally slaying the master of all Slayers, Balor Corbet, along with his entire bloodline. After nearly eight hundred years of bloody battle, Rafael would end the cursed killing of Lycans.

He looked down at the woman's ashen face. His blood quickened as her body thrummed in his arms. She had a place in the rising; he knew it in his gut. He laid her back down. As easily as he had ripped the sweatshirt in half, he did the same to her baggy pants and pulled them from her. The leather boots took more effort, especially the one housing her swollen foot. Clumps of blood stuck to the inside of the leather. She cried out again, this time taking a swing at him.

"Shhh, I will not hurt you," he soothed.

He was answered with a low moan. She lay completely naked, facedown on his bed. The sharp bones of her spine stuck up along her pale skin. The long curve of it reminded him of a sea creature just surfaced. He swept her long hair from her back and knelt down beside her.

He closed his eyes and hesitated. Once more, he considered letting her die, but intuitively he knew her death would not be in the pack's best interest now. And—*if* he were honest with himself—he would grudgingly admit there was something about her that intrigued him on a very primal level.

He lowered his lips to the topmost wound, just at the base of her skull. Despite her injuries, her skin smelled fresh, sunny, and sensuous. Arousal flared. Blood warmed in his veins, and the beast within him stirred. He closed his eyes, wrestling with the power that grew within him even as her female essence called to him.

The beast growled. Valiantly Rafael wrestled it back to obedience.

Slowly, he pressed his lips to her mauled skin. His body swelled at the first taste of her. Her blood mingled with his saliva, the coppery taste ambrosia even as he licked the poison of the Slayer's black magic from her flesh.

She moaned beneath him. He licked her more deeply, a moan escaping from his own lips. Confused by his immediate and voracious response to her scent and the taste of her blood, Rafe grabbed fistfuls of linen to keep from touching more of her. As alpha, he had the power to heal. So he would heal her, but their bond would begin and end there.

The beast growled again, clawing at his gut, restless for more than a healing bond. With honed discipline, Rafael pushed it away. Not completely out of him but far enough that *he* had the control and not the other way around.

As he soothed each wound with his tongue, he traveled lower. When he pressed his lips to a deep slash just above what he knew would be a sexy ass with a little more meat on it, he hesitated. He squeezed his eyes shut and inhaled. Her female essence filled his nostrils. It wasn't the first he'd smelled of her. He'd been ignoring it, but now, so close to her thighs, he no longer could. He pressed his palm against her right cheek, marveling that for one so thin she still maintained curves.

Unable to get enough of her sultry female scent, he closed his eyes and inhaled more of her. It wrapped around his head like a vise, circled his neck, caressed his chest, then slid past his belly to his groin. His cock thickened beneath his leathers, returning the call. The beast snarled, insisting on release. Its fangs slashed at his guts, and it demanded to be heard.

Confused by its determination to be free when it had never been so insistent, Rafael moved away from the girl.

Take her! the beast howled. *Take her, mark her,* do not *let her go.*

"No," Rafe shouted. "*She is a* human. There can be no mixing of the blood!"

Do not deny it.

He tried, yet he could not deny that he had taken her blood into his own body to save her. And in doing so, recognized the call of her blood to his.

He shoved away from her and stalked across the room. Raking his fingers through his hair, Rafael denied it again. His equal, *his* chosen one would be Lycan, like himself. He would not, as his brother had been so willing to do, throw away the future of their race for a human!

"No!" he shouted at the form on his bed. "Never!"

The beast howled. Insistent. *Mark her.* Unrelenting. *Mark her now before it is too late.*

Rafael shook his head. "No! You cannot force me! *Not* with a human."

He turned to leave the room, to let her die. To let her be taken from him and his people. She was not what his pack needed. If he succumbed, she—because he chose her—would be the downfall of not only his bloodline but all of the packs who barely survived.

He reached for the doorknob. The ring on his finger glowed hot. He looked down at it and cursed again. He tried to wrest it from his finger, but it would not budge. It burned hotter, so hot he could barely stand the pain of it. He reached for the knife sheathed in his belt. He'd cut the damn thing from him.

The ruby flared white-hot. The pain was intolerable. Rafael raised his hands to the heavens.

"Leave me!" he called out to the forces beyond his control. "Leave me!"

The ring seared his skin. Refusing to allow him. The stench of burning flesh assailed his nostrils. "Damn you, Fenrir! Damn you to hell!"

He stalked back toward the bed. With each step of his approach, the burn lessened. Incredulously, he looked from the dimming ruby to the woman who lay naked on his bed. Unwanted realization dawned. Was Fenrir insisting he mark her as well?

The eye flared.

"I'll cut my finger off before I give you control over my destiny," he said to the ring. But the beast within him snarled in protest, just as the ring heated again.

The constant burn on his finger finally penetrated his resistance.

The Blood Law could not be denied. An eye for an eye. It was time to pay.

Looking at the woman sprawled naked on his bed, Rafael accepted what he must do. He accepted *only* because she *was* human. And as such, he would never succumb to loving her. But still, she would be his mate. For how long he did not know.

"Son of a bitch!"

She would be his, and he would lose her.

Maybe this was best. She was human. She would be his, but he would never be hers. And when she died, she would take the stain of her humanity with her, easing his conscience in some small way. And when Lucien came to claim her, he would be free.

For his pack, he would do it. He had waited too long.

Resolved now, Rafael sat on the edge of the bed, reached out a tentative hand, and pressed it against the wounds he had just tended. They were merely smooth pink blotches on her creamy skin now. That skin, however, burned hot, with the same intensity as the ring. He crawled onto all fours, hovered over her, and carefully rolled her over, exposing the ugly slash along her belly and breast.

With a will of their own, his lips dropped to her breast. He hesitated before he licked the pale pink nipple that immediately stiffened beneath his touch. She moaned again. Rafael growled, clutching the sheets in his fists, twisting the fabric. When her hips slowly undulated beneath him, he squeezed his eyes shut, not wanting to want her. But he could not escape what the fates and his body demanded. With each slow undulation of her hips as he licked, hot blood filled his veins.

FALON MOANED. PAIN mixed with an inexplicable pleasure slid sensuously across her skin, sinking into her muscles and bones, then deeper, to her womb. Moist heat trailed across her nipples then, painstakingly slowly, down her belly. Anticipation flared with a want so deep, so profound, she sobbed. Hot breath hovered just above her mons. The need for more took her over. Grabbing the sheets she lay upon, Falon twisted them tightly around her hands, afraid if she reached out, the sensations would evaporate. She craved this touch with every cell in her body. She had lived her entire life without it.

She wanted more. All of it.

Her thighs parted, her hips rose. Hot breath fanned the tender flesh there.

"God," she moaned. "Make it stop."

Possessive hands cupped her breasts.

"Ah," she gasped, melting into the erotic pressure. "More," she begged. The urgency in her blood demanded more. More pressure, more intensity. Penetration.

It was the most erotic dream she had ever had.

No longer did she feel the pain from that terrible attack. She shut out the horrible memories of Mr. D and the debacle that followed. It was a nightmare. But this . . . this was pure bliss . . .

Firm lips pressed between her thighs. Falon shuddered, the intense pleasure of the contact too much for her to bear. Releasing the sheets, she dug her fingers into the thick silken hair on the head between her thighs. An erotic rush coursed through her. She could feel the muscled jaw, open and moving as he . . .

"Oh, God," she moaned as a thick wet tongue swirled across her hardened clitoris. "Oh, God," she moaned again, her breath hard and forced. "Oh, God." She couldn't help herself. She dug her nails further into the thick hair, raking his scalp. A low masculine growl vibrated against her.

Lips gently suckled her labia as big hands fondled her breasts and fingertips plucked her nipples. Sensation shot through her nervous system, lighting her up. She arched her back, spreading herself wider, wanting all of the man who tortured her so.

She'd been alone so long. So cold. So hungry. This extraordinary feeling of being wanted felt too good to stop.

Magic hands and supple fingtertips caressed her skin, branding every inch of her. Falon writhed, barely able to control her body's voracious response to this master's touch. She held nothing back; every inhibition had fled at his first touch. It was a dream or she had been drugged. She didn't care which, she only cared that it never stopped.

Strong hands grasped the cradle of her hips, lifting her drenched pussy more firmly to molten lips. "Please," she begged. "Please."

He growled, attacking her with the ferocity of a starved man. Fear shimmered through her at his rough handling. But her body wept for more. He caught her clit in his teeth and tugged, laving her to soften the intensity. The air around her simmered; she gasped, unable to breathe. He sunk a long, thick finger into her virgin body. Her liquid muscles hugged him in welcome. Falon's eyes rolled back into her head as her body wracked with exquisite pleasure. Her lungs hurt in their desperation for air. Perspiration erupted along her flesh, slickening her eager hot body. Her hips bucked wildly, demanding more. He gave it to her.

He slid another finger into her wanton pussy, then in a slow, deliberate cadence, he fucked her as his lips clung possessively to her clit.

It was too much. Falon cried out in sensation overload, yet her fingers clutched and clawed at him, wanting him to go deeper.

He snarled. The tension in her body rose. Fingers dug into her ass. Her body thrashed. The fingers inside of her curled and tapped a sweet spot. Falon screamed. The tension snapped. Her body shattered. She didn't know if she would live or die. She didn't care.

"You are mine," a rough voice growled against her trembling thighs. "Mine."

"Yes," Falon gasped.

Cold air spiraled across her body.

"No," she gasped when she wanted to scream. Weep.

Her dream, her lovely, lovely dream, was ending.

The bed dipped on either side of her head as her dream lover planted his hands there. She was afraid to open her eyes, afraid if she did, her dream would be gone from her forever. Warm breath caressed her cheek. Warmer lips pressed to her neck. Her body liquified as the tension eased. He wasn't leaving her.

A long, lean, blistering body pressed against hers. Power washed off him in waves. Even if she wanted to run, he would never allow it. His possession was final. She knew it intuitively.

Falon held her breath for one long moment as she steeled herself. Anticipating . . . His cock pressed against her belly. She moaned as he dragged its heavy thickness downward, stopping between her thighs. He grabbed it with his hand and rubbed the wide head up and down along her drenched lips. She moaned, wanting all of him but suddenly afraid. She stiffened.

He growled and nudged against her slick opening. Unbelievably, despite how much she knew her body wanted it, she felt its instinctive resistance.

"Accept me," his harsh, husky voice demanded above her.

"Please," she begged. "Don't hurt me."

He growled, the sound not threatening but indignant.

His long fingers dug into her hair. His warm breath caressed her cheek. She dared to open her eyes. Her heart stopped. Deep ocean blue eyes glittered like molten jewels above her. Wide-eyed, she could not look away.

"Accept me," he said again roughly, nudging her.

Like quicksilver, excitement thrummed through her veins. Her breath rushed from her lungs as her heart restarted. She would not deny him. In doing so, she would deny herself. She closed her eyes as every part of her loosened. Finally, she would know how it felt to have a man inside her.

In answer, she undulated beneath his hardness as it pressed for entry.

He put his lips to her ear. "Say the words: I accept you."

She gasped at the raw passion of his words, the tone possessive and commanding.

"Say it!" he hissed. His body coiled above hers, like a serpent ready to strike.

"I-I accept you," she breathed.

He growled low, then in a quick move that startled her, he flipped her over onto her belly and pulled her up to all fours.

A long, muscular arm snaked around her belly as his knees widened the chasm of her thighs. His other hand tipped her hips upward. She was so sensitive; she shivered as cool air swept across her swollen pussy. Falon's need for him was so acute, she reached behind her and grabbed his heavy cock. She nearly let go, so shocked by the heat and the satiny feel of him. The throb of his heartbeat pulsed through him. Fascinated by his passion, she rubbed her thumb across the dewy head. He swelled in her hand, then he groaned, bucking against her palm.

Her grip tightened, his muscles stiffened. "You're so hard and warm," she whispered.

He responded by pressing a thick finger against her anus. Falon gasped, grasping his cock tighter in her hand. Her hips tipped upward, then back in a slow undulation. Her hand around his cock moved in the same slow cadence. She felt him fighting his need to let go with her with his determination to stay in control. She wanted control. But he was having none of it. He pulled his cock from her hand at the same moment he sank his finger slowly into her. "Ah . . ." she breathed, sucking in her belly, unable to process the sensation overload. Every nerve in her body fired up, burning, on the fringe of complete incineration.

Falon's knees and elbows shook. His strong hand slid along her back and around to her chest, where he splayed his fingers across her breasts, maintaining her balance for her. She would need it. When, in a slow in and out motion, his finger moved inside of her, Falon's body jelled.

Hewn thighs pressed against the back of hers as his big body hovered above her. His breath was as ragged as her own. The slick sounds of her juices as his finger moved rhythmically in and out turned her on. Wildly her hips pumped against his hand. She rose higher than a kite, warm and cold and hot all at once. Every sense flared more acute than ever.

He bent low over her and nipped at her shoulder blade. The action was, in many ways, more intimate than his finger inside her.

Desolation engulfed her when he withdrew. She cried out, but his large hand stayed her hips. He was not leaving her. Hard, thick heat pressed against her wetness. She pressed back into him, her need for his cock driving her mad. She felt drugged, out of control, and more wanton than she ever thought herself capable of being. He nuzzled the back of her neck, his breath warm, his lips warmer, his tongue searing. Teeth pressed against her jugular.

He nudged into her. She held her breath.

Wild sensations swirled in exciting disarray inside of her body—sensations she'd never dreamed existed. His teeth pressed more firmly against her skin just as he moved deeper inside her.

Her breath sloughed in and out before she sucked it in and held it again. Her entire body trembled violently with anticipation. He was just on the precipice of taking what she had never offered a man.

Then, it was taken.

His teeth pierced her skin as the cock inside her pierced her hymen. She opened her mouth to scream her pleasure and her pain, but no sound came forth. Her body was too racked by a catastrophic wave of pleasure. Falon's eyes flew open, then she squeezed them shut, overwhelmed by the sensations running rampant throughout her body. His hips thrust in an agonzily slow undulation. Finally, her voice. "Faster!" She couldn't stand the blistering tension in her womb. It needed to be consumed so that it could consume her. Wildly, he pushed in and out of her. In a primal, sweaty dance of give and take, they mated.

She came in a blistering orgasm, so deep and so powerful she screamed until her throat was raw. He bit her again, this time not releasing her until his body bucked and he howled with his own earth-shattering orgasm.

MILES AWAY FROM where Rafael found his pleasure, the golden eyes of a wolf snapped open. Unsure why he had been woken, the black wolf snarled, leaping from his bed in one swift, elegant movement, then catapulted through the open window to the roof. Raising his snout, he faced north to the shrouded moon that would soon be overtaken by the sun. He grinned a wolf grin at the thought, knowing exactly what kind of suffering the Blood Moon would bring.

Suddenly, the wolf inhaled the musky scent of mating. It taunted him, causing his blood to still. His heart stuttered and twisted with pain. He howled in both denial and anticipation.

Rafael had found his mate.

Even now, he was experiencing the kind of joy that Lucien never would again.

Once more, Lucien threw his head back and howled, a long lone howl.

Defiantly, he pushed his own grief aside. Revenge would soon be his.

This time when he howled, it was a horrific, fearful sound.

It carried north to the other compound. His brother would hear, and when he did, he would know Lucien knew.

He howled again, this time in joy.

An eye for an eye.

'Twas the way of the pack.

Blood Law.

Five

FALON TRIED TO open her eyes, but the pressure on her lids was too great, as if sandbags had been plopped on her face. Just the slightest movement, and her eyes burned, felt gravelly. So heavy, so . . . She yawned and stretched. Her right hand touched something big and warm . . . and . . . furry?

She jackknifed up and immediately knew three things. She was naked. She was in a strange bedroom. And from the scent in the air and the ache between her thighs, she'd been properly fucked. But by who?

Movement to her left caught her attention and she turned, instinctively moving slowly. "Holy sh—!"

Next to her, a big tawny-colored dog lay on its stomach, its muzzle resting on its paws. Even as her skin skittered with goose bumps—even as she thought, Dog? That's no dog . . . it's a freakin' wolf—it lifted its regal carry-on luggage–sized head so its deep turquoise-colored eyes were level with hers, gleaming with both an intelligence that defied the species and a masculine laconic ease.

She scooted slowly away from it, not liking the way its gaze followed the blanket as it slipped to her waist. She quickly yanked it up so she was covered. "Nice doggy," she whispered, feeling around for her clothing. The beast growled low, barely audible, deep in its chest. Falon froze and swallowed hard, trying to remember what happened and how she had gotten here, wherever *here* was.

She had been hungry. Had gone to Delico's . . .

She stiffened as the horrible images of the previous night flared in her memory banks.

Mr. D dead, that Conan guy and then the other one. The pain Conan inflicted. And those crazy mental lightning bolts! How the hell had she managed to pull that off? Were the planets cosmically aligned?

She pushed back in the bed as panic overcame her. That big blond dude in black leather with the double swords. He'd killed Conan, right there on the street. Then he'd picked her up; she'd been too terrified to run. Had she fainted? She must have. It was the last thing she remembered. Self-recrimination slapped her. Why hadn't she tried the mental lightning bolts on him? And run. Oh, wait, she couldn't run.

She flexed her right foot. No pain. What the hell? Conan had shredded her Achilles, and—she looked down at her chest. Reached her hand over her shoulder and touched her shoulder blades. She'd been torn to shreds. The pain of the wounds excruciating. Now, not even a tingle. Had it all been a dream? She shook her head, closed her eyes, and told herself it had to be a dream. A terrible, terrible dream. She opened her eyes, wishing to be back in her dingy one-room hovel.

But she wasn't. It had all happened and, somehow, she had survived it. Instead of a dream, her life had become a nightmare of biblical proportions, and now she was in bed with the big bad wolf. Only, who and where was his owner?

She glanced past the wolf to the windows. Sunlight streamed in, warming the large room that screamed testosterone. Everything in it was big and sturdy, including the bed she lay in. It was double the size of a normal king, supported at each corner by thickly carved oak totem pole posts. Handmade Indian rugs covered the rich hardwood floor, their crimson and black accents echoed in the heavy earth-toned drapes. Under different circumstances, she would have reclined back on the comfortable mattress and enjoyed the atmosphere. Instead, despite the warm decor and the sunshine blazing through the glass windowpanes, she shivered.

Delicately, she sniffed. Her sense of smell heightened. There was a particular scent in the air—the musky scent of sex and something else, something dark and male that immediately had her picturing the sword-wielding blond.

Falon shook her head, rubbing the heels of her hands into her eyes. Realization struck. "Oh, no!"

The blond dude.

This was *his* place! She inhaled sharply, the musky scent of their sex clogging her throat. She lowered her hands, her eyes narrowing when she spotted the spots of crimson on the rumpled sheets. She groaned. Proof positive. He'd—he'd had his way with her! And his way had probably been every which way she could imagine and then some.

Even her own thoughts made her cringe. At twenty-four, Falon certainly wasn't the world's oldest virgin. It would have been easy to blame that fact on her wandering lifestyle, since she was never in one place long enough to find a man she was attracted to and wanted to have sex with. But the truth was, it had been her choice. Call her old-fashioned, but she'd wanted love first, and she knew she'd never find love while she was running. But she had hoped that, one day, she *could* stop running and that maybe . . . well, maybe she could have a semblance of a normal life.

The only normal thing about her life and where it had landed her today was how *abnormal* it was and how complicated it had suddenly become.

Anger flared in her chest.

It wasn't the loss of her hymen that upset her but the fact that he'd taken it. She didn't have much in this life, but her body, her right to choose who and when she slept with someone—that was one thing she'd always had and fought hard to keep. That bastard! Now she didn't even have that to give.

A sound—close to a whimper—escaped her. Horrified, she watched the wolf's head tilt slightly, as if in concern. It made her boiling anger ignite. She flung back the sheets.

"Your owner is a prick!" she seethed at the wolf dog. Although she moved slightly, he countered, blocking her with his big baseball mitt–sized paw.

She felt no fear, only resolve. Between clenched teeth, she said, "If you don't move off the bed, I'm going to call the dogcatcher, and all hell is going to break loose!"

Interpreting her threatening tone correctly, the wolf barked at her, as if to dare her. She almost smiled. And that shocked her and disturbed her more at the moment than her lost virginity.

Falon shook her head. She had to get out of there before the wolf's owner returned. She didn't want a repeat performance of last night. Didn't want him to find her naked. Didn't want to see him naked—

She shivered, and her skin flushed. She knew what he looked like naked. How warm he was. How wide his shaft was as it cleaved into her flesh. To her horror, her nipples tightened.

The wolf whined, its tongue flicking out along her breast in a way that made her shiver, and not in a bad way. She crossed her arms over her breasts and shot it another glare. "Pervert," she hissed, unsure whether she was talking to the wolf or herself.

Out of here. *Now*, Falon.

She almost fainted with relief when she spied a pair of folded black jeans, a black shirt, a pair of doeskin UGG-type boots, and socks, all resting on a chair cushion as if they were waiting for her. Backing completely off the bed, she groaned when her knees wobbled and her head throbbed. She raised a shaky hand to her forehead, and her body immediately overwhelmed her with a barrage of intense sensations. She had to pee. She was cold and hot. And she was disoriented, that damn dog staring at her like it was human or something. Thank God it stayed on the bed.

She grabbed the clothes and boots to her chest, casting her gaze around the big bedroom until she spotted a door in the corner. *Please be the bathroom.* "Excuse me," she murmured to the dog as if he could give her permission to leave the room. She hurried past it and soundly shut the door behind her.

The bathroom was as big and masculine as the bedroom. Timber beams supported the rich inlaid black granite and wood-paneled walls. An oversized claw-foot tub took up one side of the room, and a tall granite and oak vanity with built-in drawers beneath took up a corner. A toilet and doublewide granite shower encompassed the wall opposite the tub. Her bare toes dug into a thick alpaca throw. One thing she could say for Blondie, he liked creature comforts, and he liked the high-end kind. Too bad for him, but she had no intention of becoming part of his collection.

Quickly, she used the facilities, turned the shower on high, and let it run. Not that she was going to be using it. She was fastidious, yes, but not insane. She dressed, opened the bathroom's single window, and climbed out onto the slant of a wood shingle roof. She squinted in the sunlight. From the position of the sun, she figured it was just before noon. She was at least two stories up, in some kind of compound, surrounded by high cinderblock walls topped with razor-sharp rolls of concertina wire. To keep intruders out or prisoners in?

Crouching low, she maneuvered across the roof, stopping each time a voice filtered up from below. Once she reached the edge of the long, log cabin–style structure, she could see the forest—and freedom—over the high-wired walls. If she dropped to the ground, she'd have to climb the wall and take the chance of being seen and caught. Her only chance was to go over the wire. And how the hell was she supposed to do that? Hop over it?

Yes! A voice inside of her matter-of-factly said.

Falon squeezed her eyes closed. Great, now she was hearing voices.

She looked back at the high fence. It was her only option. So be it.

Falon moved around to the back of the structure where the rooftop edge was closest to the fence. If she got a good running start, she could jump onto the fence, grab onto the wire, and climb the rest of the way over. She cringed, thinking of the pain grabbing the wire would bring. It didn't matter. She'd take her lumps if it meant her freedom; to Falon freedom was everything.

As she backed up to get a good head start, Falon ripped the long sleeves off her shirt. She wound each piece around her hands and tied them securely to buffer the razor wire. She heard voices. Close. Then a shout followed by a flurry of heavy feet moving in her direction.

She'd been spotted.

Taking a deep breath, Falon focused on the other side of the fence. Slowly, she exhaled and then took off. As she leapt high into the air, she felt an exquisite sense of euphoria as well as shock. Her body was lighter, her muscles stronger, her reflexes that of a cobra. Her feet barely touched the top coil of wire as she flew effortlessly over the wall. She landed in a patch of soft grass squarely on the other side of the wall. In disbelief, she glanced back and up at the high wall she had just cleared, then sprang like a tiger and took off for the hills.

How? How had she just jumped like a kangaroo over a two-story-high, concrete, wire-rimmed wall? How had she healed? Had the supernatural energy she'd detected in Vulkasin rubbed off on her? Had sex with him infused her with some of his power? It didn't take a genius to figure out that Vulkasin was as different as she was. Maybe he was like her? Maybe he was the one person who might be able to shed some light on what it all meant. As much as she wanted answers, she wasn't going to stick around and find out if he had them. He terrified her. Falon ran. Blood pumped in her veins with the velocity of ten engines as she raced to put as much distance as she could between herself, the blond, the wolf, and the shambles her life had become. She pushed everything that had happened to her in the last twenty-four hours out of her head. Ostriches had nothing on her—running was how she'd survived all these years. It was how she would continue to survive.

Hair prickled along her neck and arms. Her skin suddenly felt cold.

She was being followed.

Falon kept her frantic pace but dared to look over her shoulder. Her heart nearly stopped.

A pack of beasts—enormous, long-fanged, black, slobbering beasts—were hot on her heels. Miraculously, she dug deeper and her speed increased. This time she didn't question it, she just went with it. A thick copse of trees was dead ahead. If she could just get to them before . . . She tripped.

She rolled over and hurried to her feet only to fall to her knees. Pain shot from her left ankle straight up her calf to her thigh. She leapt up again only to fall face-first to the loamy ground. Fresh pain radiated in hot pulses to her groin.

Her leg was broken, but she didn't have the luxury to cry about it. Crawling toward the nearest tree, she hoisted herself up and reached for the lowest branch.

She heard their panting first. Then hot, wet breath licked at her back. She turned, back flush against the trunk. The beasts surrounded her, their red eyes ablaze, their fangs exposed, their tongues lolling out of their long mouths.

"Nice, doggies," Falon softly said, once again reaching for the branch above her head. "Nice doggies."

The largest of them, looking like it weighed a good three hundred pounds, lowered his head and flattened his ears. Not a good sign. She glanced up at the branch she held on to and jumped on her good leg while pulling herself up. Her feet left the ground, and she pulled herself up further. The beast below her lunged, his jaws snatching her boot right off her foot. Falon hoisted herself up and clung to the trunk for dear life. The beasts came at her, nearly biting off her foot. She grabbed the next branch and climbed higher. Not high enough. In their blood rage to get to her, the beasts tore at the bark and, like cats, they climbed after her.

When she could go no higher, Falon pulled herself into a tight ball and prayed to God to save her. As if they heard her prayers, the beasts moved to the side, parting as if they were the sea making way for Moses.

He came in the form of that big-ass wolf she'd left lounging on the bed. Its turquoise eyes locked on hers. Several of the beasts barked, and he growled furiously. Like puppies, the black beasts yelped and went belly up as he approached. Falon watched in silent awe as he moved effortlessly among them.

He turned that big tawny head of his back toward her, and this time his laconic eyes laughed at her. He barked. A command that Falon immediately understood. Get down. *Now.*

It was the last thing she wanted to do, but the pain in her foot was an intense throb now, never mind that half a dozen three hundred-pound brutes were surrounding her with Ginsu knives for teeth. Her only choice was to get down and obey the one who was in control. The top dog, she thought derisively, vaguely cheered by her ability to maintain her humor under such grave conditions. She slowly began her descent and wondered why the wolf and not his master had come after her. Where was he anyway? And how did he control the gold wolf who, in turn, seemed to control these snarling black beasts?

Falon didn't give the absurdity of her questioning thoughts much mind. Her life was one continuous movie reel of surreal. Granted, it had been cranked up several notches recently, but given her history, that was almost to be expected.

She focused her full attention on getting down the damn tree without injuring her leg more. It wasn't easy, especially since her body was shaking. She worked very hard not to feel anything, and in less than twenty-four hours, she had experienced the gamut of raw emotions and excruciating physical pain. She was at a loss as to how to deal with it. So she didn't.

It took time and effort to maneuver down the tree while keeping pressure off her foot, which had swollen up to the size of a grapefruit and hurt like hell. She wrestled back tears and swallowed her fear as she carefully dropped to the earth.

Her fingers slipped, and her bad leg hit the ground before her good one. Falon cried out and crumpled to the loamy forest floor. The gold wolf snarled, his fangs displaying his petrifying fury, and leapt toward her. She had nowhere to go but against the tree trunk. He kept coming until his nose touched her face in something resembling a nuzzle.

A bubble of hysteria lodged in her throat. This close, she could see the possessive gleam in his eyes. He lunged at the big black beast that had ripped her boot off.

Stupefied, Falon watched the big black wolf-thing lie supine, accepting the fury of the gold one. When he had been sufficiently punished, the gold wolf turned to her and slowly approached. She backed up as far as she could, but the tree stopped her progress. The wolf growled low, not threatening but reassuring.

How was it she knew exactly what it was communicating? Thinking? Falon stilled, holding her breath as he sniffed, then pressed his nose to the nape of her neck. He licked her.

The heat of his rough tongue sent a shiver of fear and, *Jesus*, desire through her body. "No," she stuttered, not liking where her deviant thoughts took her. But he ignored her as surely as his master must have last night. His nose traveled lower to her shoulders, then her breasts. He nuzzled her cleavage. His nose traveled lower until he came to the juncture between her thighs. Falon squeezed her legs shut just as she visualized his master nuzzling the same place. He had done wicked things to her with his tongue. He had— The wolf pressed his nose more firmly against her. Falon bit her bottom lip and caught her breath at the warmth that followed his close inspection.

He growled again, then looked up at her as if to say, "We'll get to that later," before continuing to nuzzle his way down her legs until he came to the injured foot. His big warm tongue flicked out.

Despite her fear and the pain, she nearly swooned as he used his tongue to caress her instep, around her toes, and over the—Oh God—the sharp edge of the broken bone that protruded just above her ankle. When she looked down and saw the compound fracture, she fainted.

* * *

THIS TIME, WHEN Falon woke in the strange bed, there was no sign of the wolf. Instead, its owner, the blond Neanderthal, stood at the foot of the bed, leaning against a post with his arms crossed over his chest, glowering at her.

Raising her chin and trying not to appear intimidated, she sat up. Flames of pain radiated through her, and she fell back again.

Her leg.

She looked down to see her left leg, pant fabric torn away, replaced by a plaster cast. The last twenty-four hours flashed in her head, alternating between fast-forward and rewind.

Death. Destruction. Mass confusion. Pain. Fear. And . . .

She looked up at the great beast in front of her, then away.

. . . awe.

Last night he had terrified her with his magnificent anger and prowess with a sword. Today, still terrified, she looked at him through more contemplative eyes. His arrogant air hung just as heavily around him as it did before. More so in his calm state. He was a man who did not ask to be followed; it was a given. A good foot taller than her, his thick blond hair was cut stylishy short, framing a strong, handsome face. He was dressed casually in a fitted black shirt and black jeans.

Falon's cheeks warmed as her gaze swept the length of him. Though his clothes nicely defined his wide shoulders, deep chest, narrow hips, and long, muscled legs, she knew his true magnificence could only be appreciated in his most natural state.

She swallowed hard and refocused her attention to the matter at hand: What was going on here? First that man Conan, then the man before her, Vulkasin, then the big bad wolf, and now Vulkasin again. And all of them somehow connected to her—did her newfound powers feed off them? Were they the conduit?

She rewound to Conan—or *Jager* as he'd called himself—who'd called her Slayer and told her he was going to take her to her people and that they were destined to be one. Her and Conan? She shivered at the thought. And just who were the people he'd spoken of? What was a Slayer?

She had no people. She was an orphan, a drifter, a loner. Yet he'd known her real name, something she'd guarded for the past ten years. That wasn't enough to give the rest of his statements credence though. Was it?

And what of this man? Vulkasin. Did he know *Jager*? What had they been talking about? Did he have anything to do with Mr. D's murder? Or did he think *they* were connected in some way, just like *Jager* had? Because now that she'd woken up in the room for the second time, she couldn't deny it—there was a part of *her* that felt a connection. To the room. To the wolf. And, Lord help her, to the wolf's master.

He continued to glower at her; she felt his gaze on her body, but she refused to acknowledge him. Ostrich, she thought, and stared at her broken leg as if the cast would somehow explain what the hell was going on. When it didn't and it became apparent the man was going to wait her out, she raised her gaze.

Those mocking turquoise eyes stared back as if daring her to speak. His angry aura held a tinge of red—of passion—but stronger than that was the spark of an old, weary soul.

Yeah, well get in line, buddy.

The spirited thought gave her the courage to speak.

"Who are you? Where am I? What did you do to me?"

He put two fingers to his full lips and shook his head. "No answers until I have mine."

Falon's jaw dropped. She didn't know if she wanted to kick that arrogant controlling smirk off his lips or just tell him what he wanted to know so he would tell her what she wanted to know. Both, she decided.

"What do you want to know?" she gritted.

"What value are you to Salene?'

"Conan? Value?" she sputtered. "Hell if I know. I went to Del's for a sandwich; next thing I know that guy is ranting and spewing crap and tells me he killed Mr. D. That pissed me off, and well, you saw the end of that fiasco."

"Where do you come from?"

"Like where was I born?"

He nodded.

"I'm an orphan, and have been on my own since I was fourteen."

"You possess powers."

Falon looked down at her hands and smiled. She raised them and pointed them like pistols at Vulkasin. She pulled the triggers. "Yeah, apparently I do. If you don't let me go, I'll use them on you."

His eyes sparkled. "Don't let me stop you."

His confidence took some of the wind out of her sails. She might be able to slow him down, but she saw what he was capable of. Falon was many things, but she wasn't a fool. But that didn't mean she was a doormat either.

"Who are you? Where am I? What did you do to me?"

For long moments he contemplated her, deciding just how much information he was going to give her. Finally, he shrugged and uncrossed his arms. "I'm Rafael. You're in my house. And I saved your life. Twice."

Falon shook her head. "Before that. Last night, after—after you killed Conan. You—you—"

He smiled, the gesture nothing short of arrogant, and moved to the opposite side of the bed to sit down on the edge. "Your body called to mine. I answered."

"I made no such call. You raped me!"

His smile widened, softening the harsh edges of his face. Slowly, he shook his head. "I wouldn't call it that."

Her jaw dropped at his audacity. "What, exactly, did you take for consent? My dead weight or my complete silence?"

Rafael leaned across the big bed toward her, so close she could see the quick flare of his nostrils and feel his warm breath on her cheek. "I am guilty of many crimes, but rape is not one of them. I asked your permission, and you gave it."

Falon closed her eyes, but she couldn't block the image of him taking her from behind or the way their bodies had undulated wildly as he repeatedly thrust into her. She had wanted him all right. But damn if she'd admit it. Her eyes flashed open, and she shook her head, denying culpability. She'd said yes, but not in reality! "I thought it was a dream. I never would have—"

He pressed his lips to her cheek and kissed her. His warm lips trailed along the curve of her face to her jaw. He dug his long fingers into her hair. Damn if her body didn't spark. "It was no dream," he said against her throat, then dragged his teeth along her jugular. "I wanted you; you wanted me." Fingertips brushed across her tight nipples. Falon gasped and felt a flood of warm moisture between her thighs. Rafael groaned and grabbed her head in the palm of his other hand. "Just like you want me now," he said, his voice raspy with desire.

Falon struggled, very uncomfortable with how her body reacted to his. It lit up like a roman candle that would flare until he chose to extinguish it. It was wrong. *She* was wrong for wanting him.

"Do you want me to demonstrate more thoroughly?" he asked.

"Yes," she said before she realized the words had escaped her mouth.

He grinned above her. "Now who is in denial?"

Falon blinked. "I didn't mean that. I'm hurt. Scared. Just like I was when you brought me here. First, Conan—and then those beasts outside almost killed me—"

Abruptly, he released her and moved to the edge of the bed and stood. "I took care of that."

Her ardor cooled as abruptly as he had moved away from her. She seemed to have more control of herself when he didn't actually touch her. She filed that realization in her memory banks.

He'd taken care of it? How? And what was he referring to? The fact that she'd been hurt? Had *he* healed her? Had he somehow given her the strength to jump that high wall and run like a deer?

"If that's true, then take care of my leg!"

He stalked toward the door and put his hand on the knob. "Until I know you won't pull a dumb stunt like you did this morning, you'll have to deal with being immobile."

He opened the door, and as he walked through the threshold, Falon screamed, "You can't keep me prisoner here!"

He stopped and said over his shoulder, "Any time you want to venture outside those gates and deal with Angor and his pack mates, feel free. But know there will not be a another rescue."

He left her then.

RAFAEL CURSED AS he strode into the great room. The girl was full of contradictions—scared shitless one moment and showing alarming degrees of courage the next. When she'd awoken, she'd acted just how he'd expected: nervous and disoriented, afraid of his wolf even as she'd mustered the courage to mouth off to him. Her answers to his questions were useless—*if* he believed she was telling him the truth, which he didn't.

He'd underestimated her. The bathroom escape was clever. And ballsy. He'd heard the shouts from outside of an intruder and known she had taken off. How she'd gotten over that wall, he had no clue, but if some of his men had been guarding the interior perimeters the way they should have, they would have seen her and gotten to her before she could even try.

He'd had no choice but to go after her himself. And when he'd found her, he'd smelled his mark on her fifty feet away, as strong as it had been when he'd taken her. That the Berserkers hadn't respected it pissed him off, but his anger wasn't directed at the animals, only at his men and himself.

Fools! He should never have underestimated her determination. He'd watched her take on Salene, so how the hell could he have forgotten—she was no beta female, but an alpha, and that was likely what had called to him in the first place, despite the fact she was a human. Or was she? Her powers intrigued him. Though unusual for a human, he knew it was possible. The keepers of the wolves were living proof. Regardless of what she was, arousal buzzed through him at the memory of her body's acceptance of his.

He wrestled with his raging hard-on, pissed off that he wanted her again. He didn't *want* to want her. He had done what he had to do. He'd marked her, but only for the sake of the pack and the Blood Law. That was all he was going to do. No further involvement. Not on any level, and that included sport fucking. He would not do that to himself. She would be dead soon enough, and so he forced himself to think of her as dead to him now.

It didn't temper his rage. All it did was make him imagine her dead, her body broken and bleeding after Lucien was done with her. No longer warm but cold. No longer spirited but faded. No longer . . . anything. No, it didn't temper his rage; instead, it made him uncomfortable. Guilty. Reluctant. And he could be none of those things.

The girl had to die so that his pack could survive.

He stopped in the middle of the great room. Dozens of pairs of eyes stared at him. Minus the elders who kept to themselves in the back of the compound, this was his pack. His only family now. Forty-eight men and thirty-two women, all between his age of thirty-four down to twenty-four. They'd been loyal to him, staying despite the fact they couldn't mark their mates until he did or reproduce until he did. At least he'd finally given them the comfort of the mark.

Like a thick pheromone haze, the smell of sex permeated the hall just as it had his bedchamber. Since he had marked the girl last night, his pack had been wildly fucking. Not mating, that would not come until he and his chosen one became one in mind, body, and spirit. She would have to mark him of her own volition for their bond to be complete. He would not give the woman upstairs the chance.

Rafael shook his head. That was not going to happen. Not with this woman. His pack had become restless and impatient. Lycans were born to procreate. That his pack had not produced one single child in fourteen years was placed squarely on his shoulders. All these years, and still he could not stomach what was asked—no demanded—of him. He had prolonged the inevitable. Now he'd made his mark, and once he was free to mark another, he would pick a Lycan like himself, exchange marks, and watch his pack thrive.

He was as weary of the tension as his pack. He glanced around at their exhausted, lust-glazed faces. It was a wonder they could stand, and the infusion of sex must have addled their senses as much as it was addling his.

Because although he'd ordered the Berserkers let loose to protect the compound against anything that even remotely posed a threat, they should've maintained enough of their senses to ensure the interior security of the compound and the girl Rafe had ordered them to guard with their lives. Yet when she'd escaped, not even Anton had loaded the high-powered tranq guns that could down Angor, the largest of the Berserkers, and gone after the girl. Because of their inaction, she had been hurt. It infuriated him. Yet he could not explain his protectiveness over the girl. While he knew he had to do what he had to do, something snapped inside of him when he saw her in Angor's jaws. Rage and worry infused him. Had the beast's fangs broken her skin, he could not have saved her. He shook his head. When had it become so complicated?

He hadn't made himself clear before, so he would now. "I'll kill any one of you who allow her out of this compound again," he growled menacingly.

"Rafael," Anton said as he approached, his head bowed submissively. "At first we thought she was an intruder. It wasn't until she jumped the fence that I recognized her."

Rafael snarled. "And you then did what?" He grabbed a half-dressed Lana, one of the unattached females. One who had, on several occasions, eased his own sexual tension. Anton's scent was all over her. "Went back to fucking?"

"No. I—"

"Rafael—" Lana said, pressing her full naked breasts against his chest.

Rafael looked down at Lana's big brown eyes that gazed up at him with longing. Many of the pack females had deserted them due to their yearning to take a mate and reproduce. He was grateful to those who'd remained, even the pack whores like Lana. But as her musky scent toyed with his raging libido, he thought of the girl upstairs.

His mouth firmed when he remembered the instant he'd seen her outside, surrounded by the vicious beasts. For a split second, he'd wondered if he should leave her to them to finish. That way, Lucien could do him no harm . . . But her expression, while fearful, had been overridden with bravery, and as soon as he'd seen her bare foot, bloodied, and broken, he'd known he would never let that happen. Possessiveness had swarmed over him, just as it had last night when he'd taken her. She was his. His mate. Even the Blood Law could not deny him that.

Lana slid her hand down his belly to his groin. "Rafael," she softly said, "your need to mate is strong."

He set his jaw. Yeah it was, but not with her. He looked over her shoulder to the slowly sinking sun. He'd heard Lucien's howl last night . . . he would come. Soon. For it was only during two hours each day that they were both in human form—the hour before dusk and then the hour before dawn. And the Blood Law could only be avenged when both brothers were in human form.

Sure enough, as soon as Rafe had the thought, a loud snarling preceded the low, throaty roar of a Harley. The scent, so much like his own, was unmistakable. Lucien was already here.

Six

AS RAFE MENTALLY and physically braced himself, Lucien strode into the great room as if it were his. It had been, a long time ago. At least, it had been *theirs*. Now Lucien was the outsider, and an unwelcome one at that. The only reason he'd made it inside alive was because he came alone, could glamour the Berserkers, and shared Rafael's blood. It was a respect thing with the packs, but if any one of those three factors had been absent, he'd have been eviscerated by the Berserkers. If somehow he had miraculously made it past them, Rafe's pack would have descended on him like vultures on road kill and finished the job. Many of them wouldn't have wanted to. In fact, many would have grieved over Lucien's body. But they'd have done it, because while they'd once been loyal to both him and Lucien, their greatest loyalty now was to Rafael only.

Fortified by that knowledge, Rafael met Lucien toe to toe, flexing his muscles and baring his teeth like the true alpha he was. "My dear brother, to what do I owe your most unwelcome presence?"

Lucien snorted, his message clear: Rafael knew damn well why Lucien was here.

True. Every Lycan in the room knew why he was here. He was here for the girl, exactly as Rafe had known he would be. He just hadn't expected him to come quite so soon.

As Rafe watched, his pack gathered in close, their bodies at the ready. Though he and Lucien were twins and remarkably similar, their looks were also glaringly different. Lucien's features were harsher, a dark counterpoint to Rafe's light. Thick black hair. Tawny eyes with dominant black striations. They shared the same prominent cheekbones, aquiline nose, square jaw, and sadly, the same grim, unsmiling mouth.

Lucien walked around pissed off at the world. Rafe couldn't begrudge him that. He walked around with his share, too. Having most of your family eradicated by Slayers, not to mention having your mother skinned alive in front of you, and your father eviscerated while you were forced to watch, tended to do that to a Lycan. But in Lucien's mind, he had suffered more, and at the hands of his own brother no less.

And if Lucien had his way, Rafe was about to find out exactly how pissed off a Lycan could get when his mate was slaughtered before his eyes. The question was whether Rafael was going to let that happen, right here and right now.

Something touched his arm, and Rafe looked down. He'd completely forgotten about Lana. She'd sidled up to him again, pressing against his body, ignoring Lucien completely. Rafe knew it was a deliberate insult to Lucien, and so did his brother. He was about to push her away when, growling, Lucien yanked her hard to his chest. His nostrils flared as Lana hung hypnotized in Lucien's arms. "My brother doesn't want to fuck you; if he did, he would have marked you years ago. He has found and marked his mate." He raised his nose toward the back staircase and sniffed. "I can smell their sex even through the stench of all your own."

The pack bristled at that, any softness for Lucien immediately leaving them. That Lucien would mock the sacrifices the pack had made over the years—because of Lucien's and Rafe's blood feud—was akin to sacrilege.

"Who I fuck is none of Lana's concern. Or yours, Brother," Rafael snarled.

Lucien laughed and shook his head, shoving Lana away from him. "Come now, Rafe. It's not about the fucking. It's much *much* more important than that. Did you seriously believe I'd forgo personally congratulating you on such a momentous occasion? Your marking a mate is cause for great celebration." Lucien looked hard at Rafe and smiled, showing a perfect set of straight white teeth. "On my part, at least." He threw his head back and laughed deeply, thoroughly amused at the power he held at the moment.

Rafael simmered and swore Lucien wouldn't hold the power very long. In that moment, Rafael's decision about whether to give the girl to Lucien tonight or not shifted in favor of the latter. Obeying the Blood Law was one thing. Allowing his brother to make a mockery of him in front of his pack was something else altogether.

Lucien must have seen the defiance in Rafael's eyes.

"You know what's coming, Rafael. I've come to claim my rights under the Blood Law of the Lycans. A mate for a mate. You're bound by the law to hand over your chosen one to me." He smiled so demonically that if Rafe didn't know better, he'd swear Lucien was possessed by a Slayer. Were that true, Rafe would be as duty-bound to kill Lucien as he was to give him his mate.

Under no circumstances could the blood of Lycan and Slayer mingle. It was the only reason he had destroyed Lucien's mate. Duty to the pack above all else. Even if he hated himself for it.

Lucien ran a finger along the high curve of Lana's breast then looked at Rafe. His eyes widened in mock surprise. "Still here, Brother? Maybe I didn't make myself clear. You're bound by the Blood Law to hand over your mate, and I want her. Now."

Rafael grinned. "Fuck you and your *little* dog, too."

Lucien's eyes widened slightly before he nodded. "Then you've sealed the pack's fate. For a female, Brother." Lucien glanced at the pack that stood behind him, uncertainty and almost fear in their eyes. "You see how your alpha hesitates? He'd sacrifice you all, even though he marked the girl knowing what was to come."

As one, every pair of eyes in the room looked at Rafael for reassurance that Lucien spoke lies.

Rafael shook his head, and their eyes filled with relief.

Lucien was right. The woman's death was Lucien's to command. If Rafe refused, he'd be removed as alpha. He'd lose face with his pack and would be banished. And then the pack would die out, because Rafe knew in his gut there was no other male who could effectively lead the Vulkasin pack as its alpha. Not even Lucien.

Rafael swiped his hand across his chin. Damn it all to hell! What was he waiting for? What did it matter if it was tonight or a week from now? He should just get it over with. It didn't matter that he'd mated her or that he felt a natural possessiveness after having taken her body with his. He had no emotional bond to her. And it would remain so. For everyone's sake, he would hand the woman over to Lucien, then claim a Lycan mate and breed.

He looked at Anton. It was on the tip of his tongue to command him to bring the woman to them.

"Do you defy the Blood Law, Brother?" Lucien snarled.

Lucien's attitude stilled Rafe's tongue. His instinct was to meet aggression with aggression. If he was going to hand the woman over to Lucien, he'd prefer to keep Lucien suffering for as long as possible.

Without answering his brother, Rafe strode away from his pack and started up the stairs.

Lucien followed him.

As each step brought him closer to the woman, even though he'd committed himself no less than seconds earlier, Rafe was not without reservation. The girl was an innocent. She had no hand in what fate had dealt her. Was it right that she would die today, just so his pack could survive?

He should not have to pay. He was just in destroying Lucien's Slayer. Only without indisputable proof that she was, the council sided with Lucien.

Rafe shook his head, angry that he even contemplated the wrongness of what he was about to do. It *had* to be done, damn it! If it wasn't her, it would be another. This wasn't about an eye for an eye, but rather an eye for an entire race. He had made the choice when he destroyed Lucien's mate, Slayer that she was. He'd do it again.

Fuck!

For the first time in fourteen years, Rafael considered how his brother must have felt. Could he blame Lucien for his Blood Law revenge? Rafael was having difficulty as it was, and he had no emotional bond with the woman in his bed.

How had Lucien felt when he was in love and that love had been ripped away from him by the person he trusted the most? Rafael swallowed hard. He didn't want to know. Not knowing was easier, and he swore he'd keep it that way.

He'd never succumb to emotional chains again. He had died a thousand times as he watched Corbet skin his mother alive, then endured the agony in his father's screams for him to stop. Rafael never wanted to experience anything remotely close to it again.

His resolve galvanized. This was right for him and his pack.

Upon reaching his room, Rafael flung open the door.

It was empty.

Shock held him silent until he sensed Lucien's presence just behind him. "Son of a bitch!"

He ran into the bathroom to find the window open and that fool of a woman hanging by her fingernails from the edge of the roof. He shot through the window and grabbed her hand just as it slipped off the roof tile. She screamed as he hurled her back onto the roof, then tossed her over his shoulder and proceeded to shove her through the open window she had escaped from twice!

When he'd wrestled her back into the bathroom, he tossed her over his shoulder again and took her kicking and screaming into the bedroom. Lucien's eyes darkened. Rafael tossed the woman onto the bed. She bounced several times before coming to rest near the edge. She turned a blue-eyed glare up at him. Rafael glared back. He didn't want to feel compassion for her. He didn't want to feel anything except relieved.

He didn't want to feel the wave of possessiveness that rolled over him when Lucien moved toward her, but he did.

Stopping several inches from her, Lucien's nostrils flared. His eyes simmered with the luster of pure gold before he shot a smug smile at Rafael. "It looks like you're the one who's marked a human now, Brother."

Rafael clenched his teeth and rubbed the back of his neck even as he glared at the woman and the mark he'd put on her. "The difference, Brother, is she is not a Slayer of our people."

"So you repeatedly say."

"You still refuse after all these years to see the truth. She had to die or she would have killed us all!"

Lucien sneered. "Admit it, Rafael, you wanted control of the pack. To get it you destroyed me. Your brother. Your *only* brother!"

Lucien's hatred for Rafe and what he had done spewed like toxins into the air. Regret clawed at Rafe. Not for what he had done but for what he had lost. "We will forever be at an impasse. You will see the Blood Law avenged. So do what you must."

Rafael forced himself to turn away from her then. Tried to brush her off as inconsequential. But there was a primal part of him that was willing—no itching—to fight his brother for her.

He had claimed her. Marked her as his. As an alpha, it was unconscionable that another take what was his without a fight to the death. But he could not defy the Blood Law.

Immediately after giving his brother the go-ahead to take her, Rafe turned back and, without thought, moved to stand between the woman and Lucien.

The girl sat openmouthed, staring at Lucien then Rafael then back to Lucien. Then she bolted. Straight out the door and down the stairs, her feet practically flying, despite her injured leg and cast.

Rafe bounded after her, Lucien's disdainful laughter following him.

"Maybe I was wrong," Lucien called after Rafael. "Your chosen one doesn't appear to want anything to do with you let alone to be your mate."

Rafe was right behind her, but by the time he got to her, she was surrounded by the pack, spinning in circles and hissing at them as they pressed in on her.

Rafael grabbed her arm, wrenching her up to her toes. "You're not going anywhere," he said, even as his eyes leveled with his brother's amused face.

"No, she's not. But I'm suddenly feeling . . . amused. Do you have a name?" Lucien asked the girl.

At the question, Rafael jerked around to face her. As he did, he let go of her arm. He'd marked her, been inside her body, and not once bothered to ask for her name. He hadn't cared enough to ask. Hadn't wanted to know. But now, he did.

"Screw you," she threw at Lucien. She turned to face the entire pack. "When I get out of here, you'll all be screwed!"

"You won't be leaving here," Lucien said as he moved closer. "In fact . . ." He yanked her up to him, lowered his head, and ran his nose down her neck and inhaled. "You won't be leaving this house at all. The only question is, how long will I allow you to live?"

The girl looked helplessly to Rafael for aid. His instinct to protect what was his raged. He snarled a warning to his brother.

Lucien paid no attention. All his attention was on the girl, and it wasn't because he was planning where best to inflict a mortal wound. Rafael knew his bother well. As a race, Lycans were highly sexual creatures, but the alphas were hardwired to spread their seed far and frequently. Rafael was no exception, nor were the others.

The surrounding pack moved restlessly around them now. Their need to mate again was reaching a fevered pitch.

Rafe didn't care. Not about Lucien's sexual needs, that of his pack's, or any other person in the world. At that moment, he didn't care about the Blood Law, or that he'd splintered his relationship with his brother for the very thing that was now overwhelming him—an inexplicable need for a human female. Something foreign and hot coursed in his blood, flaring hotter the longer he saw the woman in Lucien's arms. "She is not yours to take, Lucien."

Lucien looked up from the terrified woman, his eyes dark because of his heightened sexual awareness and his impending night shift. In less than fifteen minutes, he would be on all fours. If he could just stall him . . .

"She is mine to kill, though."

"There's a difference," Rafe said, neither agreeing nor disagreeing with him.

The girl gasped and tried to twist out of Lucien's grasp. When his grip increased, Rafael watched in astonishment as she turned to face his brother and glared at him. She thrust her hands and then . . . Lucien howled and let go of her, grabbing his head with both hands.

Stunned excitement thrummed through Rafe. Is this why Salene wanted her? What power was this? Where did it come from? Only a few Slayers he knew possessed it. Yet he sensed no dark magic in her—was he fooled as Lucien had been?

The girl paled and moaned as if she were in pain. Then her body went limp, dropping as if she'd lost consciousness. Wolf-quick, Rafael caught her just before she hit the floor. He set her down and looked up at Lucien, who was slowly lowering his hands from his head. He didn't know what the hell had happened, but whatever it was, he was glad.

Fury twisted Lucien's features. "What trickery do you employ, Rafe?" Lucien moved toward the girl, but Rafe pulled her protectively closer. "Give her to me. Now."

Instead of answering, Rafael stood, cradling her in his arms. She was light, little more than a child. A feeling of admiration swelled within him, and with it, his own urge to mate again.

Lucien's rage exploded when Rafael refused to hand her over. He lunged toward them, but Anton and several others intercepted him, grabbing him by his arms and pulling him back. Lucien howled and tried to shake them off, but more of Rafe's pack jumped in. In total, it took ten of his men to keep Lucien at bay. Silently, Rafael's gaze moved from Lycan to Lycan. His gaze was steady. Theirs not so. They weren't sure they liked what he was doing, but he'd seen the amazement in their eyes when the girl dropped Lucien to his knees.

His pack had recognized the strength in their alpha female and were now willing to give Rafe what he needed: space and time.

Breaths heaving out of him, Lucien roared again and managed to drag the men holding him forward. His eyes flashed red, betraying his rage. As was to be expected, the instant Lucien's fury bypassed a certain threshold, his body went to all fours, then from smooth skinned to furry black beast. Both he and his brother had learned long ago how to shift quickly and easily, nothing like the horror movies the kids loved to agonize over.

His men backed away, all satisfied. Lucien would not avenge his lost love as a wolf.

Rafael clutched the girl tighter to his chest. Lucien's great glossy black wolf rivaled Rafael's tawny version in every way but did not eclipse it. In human or wolf form, they were different but equal in every way in terms of strength. Rafael's only edge was his patience over Lucien's hair-trigger temper. It was the reason they were still alive, because if they truly fought to the death, it would mean both of theirs.

Looking down at his brother, Rafe said, "We'll resume this man to man at dawn."

Lucien snarled at Rafael's back as he strode back up to the bedroom.

His mind swirled in a million different directions. What had she done to Lucien? How had she injured him as no other could? *Did* she possess the same dark magic as the Slayers? And damn it, why had he prolonged the inevitable? An urge to go to the ancient Amorak, his mother's people, for answers pulled at him.

He rarely visited them. It had been years, maybe a decade? When they refused to believe Rafe's claim that Lucien's mate was a Slayer, he'd stormed away in anger, never to return.

In many ways he had cut off his nose to spite his face. The Amorak were wise people, the caretakers of the Lycan since that day three hundred years ago when they were created. Perhaps with them, he could find answers about the woman who was driving an even deeper wedge between the brothers who were sworn blood enemies.

Entering his bedroom, Rafael gently set the girl down on the bed. As he studied her, an amazing thing happened. The anger, rage, and doubt whirling inside him calmed. Thoughts of his brother, his pack, and the Blood Law left him. He worried naught about the pack's fate or even his own. His entire being focused on this girl and how she had the power to call to him.

His hands moved to undress her, but then hesitated. He fought his greatest fear, the one that still managed to linger within him. His fear of love. Of being so bound to anyone, let alone someone destined to die, that he would scream and fall to his knees, and *beg* like his father had, only to be kicked away.

He did not want to see her milky smooth skin or her full breasts or the soft tangle of curls at the junction of her thighs. If he did, he would touch her. Then take her. His cock thickened at the thought of having her again. She'd been so tight and sweet, he could have made love to her all night long. But given how she'd reacted to him this morning, she would have had a heart attack if she'd awoken to find herself linked in a very physical way to his wolf.

He smiled despite himself.

If only she knew what he could do to that sweet pussy of hers with his wolf tongue. His dick twinged and lengthened. Yeah, he could make her howl so loud every Lycan for three hundred miles would know what he was doing to her.

As he stared at her, admiration threatened to turn into something more. Something softer. No, he thought. This was purely physical. It was about fucking, nothing else, and he'd prove it right now. Deliberately, he pushed her hair away and ripped open her top. His hands itched to touch her smooth skin. His lips to taste her.

The ring on his finger warmed. In agreement, his dick swelled thicker. The correlation cooled his desire immediately.

Rafael closed her shirt and stepped back, digging his fingers through his hair.

The ring. The damn ring. He was no one's servant. He was an

alpha who chose when to act, when to fuck. As his mind refused to accept what his body and the ring demanded, he set his jaw. "No. Not again." He was done. He would not use her for simple sexual gratification when he knew he'd be turning her over to his brother in the morning. She deserved at least that small respect from him. He closed his eyes and slowly exhaled.

The girl moaned softly, and his eyes popped open. Her small hand reached out for his. As if he were a voyeur watching someone else through a window, he watched his big hand take hers and their fingers entwine. Her body arched. Through the thin fabric of her shirt, he watched her nipples tighten. Her soft, full lips parted, and her breath accelerated. Rafael pulled away, but her grip was tight. Her eyes softly batted open. The deep blue of them called to him. "Take me again," she softly pleaded.

He shook his head and took a step away. "No," he whispered.

The ring flamed his skin. He hissed in a breath. She raised herself, and with her free hand, she smoothed her fingers into his hair. Imperceptibly, she rose higher, and her soft lips took his. His dick flared, yet he did not give in to her. He could not. *Would* not.

Suspicion clouded his desire. What end did she hope to achieve by seducing him? Did she think he would change his mind? Did she know he could not? That he had no say in the Blood Law?

He refused to go there. He didn't want to feel anything more for her than he did.

But the little bitch was not taking no for an answer. As if guided by some other force, she pulled him to her chest, then pressed him to the sheets and covered him with her body. As she rolled over with him, she tore at her shirt. Rafe swallowed when her smooth, milky breasts popped free and brushed boldly against his chest. Though her pants were hampered by her cast, she managed to get herself naked. When her essence filtered to his nose, Rafael steeled himself.

"One more night, Rafael," she said softly.

He pushed away from her and rolled off the bed.

"You can't run from what you must do, Rafael. At least be man enough to give me a farewell fuck."

He snarled and turned back toward her. "Your crudeness is unbecoming."

She threw her head back and laughed. The laugh of a woman in complete control. "And turning me over to your brother *is* becoming?"

"I cannot change the Blood Law."

She moved back against the pillows. She shook her head and pushed back her thick hair. His mark was plain to see on her neck. She smiled seductively. Her blue eyes burned cobalt in their intensity. She slowly shook her head again. Her dark hair swirled down her shoulders to her waist. Her tits peeked out from between the thick strands.

She was stunning. He could not help the direction of his gaze as it followed the firm dip of her belly to her slightly flared hips. Slowly she spread her thighs. "You can change your mind and take me." Coyly, she opened her thighs wider. He looked down at her soft, dewy pussy and imagined being buried deep. He stepped closer to the edge of the bed.

Blood pounded to his dick. She rose on all fours and crawled to him. With her teeth, she pulled down the zipper of his jeans. He didn't stop her. She kissed him deeply, pushing his jeans down with the palms of her hands.

His cock sprang free, hot, thick, and wanting. Warm air swirled around his hips. She slipped her hands around to his ass and squeezed him. He moaned and pressed against her softness. She felt so damn good. Baby-soft skin. And she smelled good, too. Like the forest just after it rained.

Her lips traced down his neck, and her fingers tore open his shirt, sending buttons flying across the bed, hitting the wood floor in a series of pings. She suckled his nipples. She nipped at his belly and licked a wet trail through the downy hair that led her directly to what made him so different from her. He was rock-hard, his desire so heightened he could not see clearly.

He dug his fingers into her hair and arched toward her. He felt the hot blasts of her breath against the head of his cock. *Jesus.*

"What is your name?" he hoarsely demanded. His sudden need to know it was almost as strong as his need for her body.

"Falon," she breathed as her luscious lips clamped down on him and she sucked his come right out of his balls.

"Ah, Falon," he cried out as he bucked against her, his fingers digging into her hair pressing her harder against his groin. *Falon.* She took all of him, completely down her throat. Her fingers caressed his balls. She mouth fucked his cock until there wasn't a drop of come left inside of him.

He collapsed next to her, his body wrung dry. His sexual satiation was short-lived. The image of his brother slowly strangling Falon as she fought for each breath stirred a violent reaction.

Before he let that happen, he would kill her himself, swiftly taking her life to save her from the slow, torturous death Lucien surely had planned. Then he'd kill his brother.

He opened his eyes and turned his head toward her. She lay beside him fully clothed, as was he. Moreover, her eyes were closed, her breaths even, as if she'd never regained consciousness.

He leapt to the floor. *What the hell?* The ring scorched his finger, mocking him.

He had a raging hard-on. He looked closer at the girl. She was still unconscious. What just happened? The ring flared again. Had he hallucinated the entire episode? His dick throbbed, unquenched. He shook his head and moved away from her.

Had the vision been his subconscious's way of warning him to stay way? To hand her over to Lucien without further hesitation? Because she held a sexual power over him that would be his and his pack's downfall?

It had to be that.

She wanted nothing to do with him, much less sex. And that blow job? That was art. Art born of years of experience. She'd been a virgin twenty-four hours ago. He knew she was not experienced in the art of fellatio and that conjuring it in his mind was probably as unlikely as her being able to do the real thing. So what the hell had happened?

It had to be a warning. Because he would not believe that he, Rafael Vulkasin, alpha of pack Vulkasin, who was renowned for his slow-burn temperament and unshakable will, was at the sexual beck and call of a girl who would die at dawn and a damn ring that had a mind of its own.

Or could it be that Lucien had a hand in the vision?

"Impossible!" he roared. He strode into the bathroom, yanked the wooden towel rack off the wall, and violently slammed it into the window jamb and locked the window by impaling it shut. It would take a jackhammer to open it now.

He strode back into the bedroom and looked down at the slumbering beauty. It didn't matter really.

He was now resolved. She'd be dead in less than twelve hours.

Seven

RAFAEL PICKED HIS way through the gauntlet of naked, undulating bodies in the great room. It looked like a Roman orgy, but that was hardly a surprise. By dawn the next morning they would be paired. But unable to procreate.

Fury forced him to the front doors. There would be plenty of fucking for his pack, but no child would be born anytime soon. The girl would soon be dead, and with her, any hope of his pack's ability to breed until he found and marked a suitable mate again.

The urge to flee, to get away and clear his head, gripped Rafael. He shoved open the two heavy metal-studded oak doors and inhaled the clean night air. As he did, he saw his brother's black custom chopper.

He stopped at the edge of the rough plank porch. A long, deep howl echoed through the forest, coming from the direction where he had found Falon earlier that day. Had Lucien followed her scent?

The ring flared on his hand. He grabbed the damn thing and

tried to wrestle it off his finger. It only mocked him by flaring hotter. Feeling the need to run himself, Rafael hopped on his brother's chopper and headed out. He opened the throttle when he cleared the compound gates and gave the horses their heads. Cool air tore through his hair, but even so, the ride through the mountains didn't clear his mind.

Not tonight. Tonight his head was full of emotions—rage mostly—and he was damn horny. He could not remember ever feeling so out of sorts, so on edge. So off balance. His world was unfurling, and he didn't like it.

His pack normally worked as a well-greased unit. Now they were screwing like dogs in his living room with no thoughts about protecting the compound. He could no more command their libidos to turn off than he could keep the sun from rising each morning. It had been too long for them. They'd had sex, yes—they were Lycan, after all, and would howl at the moon twenty-four/seven if they couldn't—but not as they were now.

Now they were having sex not just for release but for the future of the pack. To decide who would be paired and who would not.

It was the kind of sex he'd had with Falon last night. Profound because it had a reason. Ceremonial almost. Under normal circumstances, he would have hit and run. But there was nothing, he was realizing, normal about the girl who occupied his bed. Salene sensed it as well. Why else would he want a woman who was not of his kind? But what was it about her?

Rafael took a turn wide and opened the throttle. Fury tore through him, then compassion. Because Falon had to know what he intended. Did it scare her? Even now, was she wondering when he would return and lead her to her death?

Gravel took hold of the rear tire. He put his booted foot down on the asphalt, riding out of the slide. He grinned despite the near-fatal accident.

He lived for this shit.

As he gunned the engine, he came around a hairpin turn. Instead of easing up on the gas, he opened it up and took it crossed-up like a short track racer. As he came around the corner, he slammed on the brakes. The headlights of a dozen bikes blinded him.

"Fuck."

He sniffed the air. The stench was unmistakable. Vipers, a local biker gang of human thugs. While the human Slayers were his nemesis, the Vipers were an abscess that kept getting bigger, pussier, and more difficult to treat. They'd been trying to muscle in on Rafael's mountain for the last few years. Rafe smiled in the harsh light. But the Vulkasins pushed them back each full moon. He threw his head back and laughed. It was great sport watching them flee in abject terror. Those big badass mofos. Rafael sobered. But like a cancer, they came back, infecting deeper and deeper into Rafael's territory. He knew the Slayers powered them. And because of that he had been able to hike up his own damage. On the cusp of the Blood Moon rising, Rafael took every opportunity he could to eliminate one more Slayer. It was why he had been prowling the streets of Sacramento.

"Sons of bitches," he cursed, then accelerated and charged them in a dangerous game of chicken. Normally he'd stand and fight them off the old-fashioned way, but right now he wanted speed. And the only person he would stop to fight was his brother. And then he'd tear him apart.

Normally, the Vipers backed down, but as Rafe sped toward them, he realized that wasn't going to happen tonight. They formed a tight gauntlet.

He could drop the bike, shift, and get his speed fix on all fours, but he wasn't in the mood for running or messing up a perfectly good Harley.

He grinned in the harsh light. So it was a fight they wanted? Then a fight he'd give them.

Rafe hit the rear brake and came to a skidding stop inches from Gordo, the heavyweight leader of the Vipers, who were second only in ferocity to the Vulkasin pack. The two groups had a long and bloody history. Pack Vulkasin stayed in the black the good old-fashioned way—real estate and Wall Street—but the Vipers made their living cooking and selling meth. Rafael had a big problem with that. He'd had an even bigger problem when several of his pack got hooked on the shit. And then his problem had become the Vipers' problem.

Rafe had single-handedly destroyed the lab.

And that's when the shit really hit the fan. The Vipers had doubled their efforts to get drugs into Rafe's pack, forming new labs faster than Rafe could find them. Then the economy collapsed. That, coupled with the pack's longing to procreate, had weakened many. The pack had been forced to take on more blue-collar type work. Protection runs and supply runs, so long as it wasn't contraband, he was good with it. They did what they had to, to keep the compound running and the pack fed.

The Slayers had tapped into the Viper gang, as well. Methed-out Slayers were twice as deadly and unpredictable than those that were sober.

Rafael certainly had his hands full.

He needed to give the pack back their reason for being. And he had to defeat the Slayers once and for all. To do that, all of the North American packs would have to unite. But too many of them had allied themselves with Lucien, who refused to look at the bigger picture: their survival as a race. United they could have a chance; divided they were doomed.

In seconds, he was surrounded by twelve bikers, each of whom he'd taken more than a pound of flesh from over the years. He wasn't worried about their numbers. Tonight, he was more powerful. He not only had the ring, but his will to survive was at its zenith.

Rafael was easily a head taller than any of the Vipers, and that was saying a lot. They were some big dudes. Even so, he stood his ground.

"Lupo," Gordo called, his face split in half with a grin. Although the Vipers didn't know for sure the power of the Vulkasins, they correctly suspected they were Lycan.

Rafael looked up at the waxing moon, then back to Gordo. "You picked a good night to die."

The dirtbags surrounding him laughed. One shoved him from behind. Rafe didn't budge. His anger simmered. Not enough to force a shift, but if he wanted to, he could hike it up a notch.

He felt those behind him move together. He jumped and kicked back with his right leg, knocking two down. As he turned, he cut Gordo off in mid-word with a karate chop to the larynx. Gordo screamed and grabbed his throat. As he came down, Rafe smashed his boot into the leathered biker's face.

Eight hundred years of persecution was unleashed. Rafael was so angry, so damn pissed off at the last twenty-four years of his life that, one by one, he disabled the Vipers. But he didn't escape without injury.

Someone stabbed him in the kidney from behind. The shock of the hit stopped him in mid-punch. He grunted in pain and quickly recovered, his adrenaline kicking into higher gear. He whipped around, grabbed the hand wielding the knife, and bent it backward. As bones snapped, the Viper howled.

The knife fell to the ground. Rafe grabbed it. The surrounding Vipers backed away.

Slowly, Rafe tossed the large skinning knife in his hand. Then, grabbing it by the point, he chucked it at the downed man, impaling his broken hand to the dirt shoulder.

A gun cocked behind him. He turned to a loud snarl erupting from the forest edge behind him. Bloodcurdling screams rent the air just as Lucien, in all his wolf glory, leapt out and proceeded to rip apart three of the Vipers. Stunned, Rafael watched the last person he ever thought would have his back tear apart his enemy.

Gordo leveled his nickel-plated .357 at Lucien's back. Rafael hesitated in his mind. If Lucien died tonight, Falon would live. He did not hesitate in body. Lucien was his bother. He leapt high into the air and kicked the gun from Gordo's hand, then punched his bloody face, this time smashing it to pieces. The Viper leader hit the ground with the velocity of a three-hundred-pound brick and didn't move.

By the time it was over, twelve Vipers were either moaning and groaning on the mountain road or dead. Rafe looked over to his brother. Lucien was breathing as hard as he was. He ignored the pain in his side and the seepage of blood down his waist.

"I didn't ask for your help, and I didn't need it," Rafe said, angry at himself for his weakness. He'd saved his brother's life. Why?

Lucien growled and looked at his bike as if to say, "Fuck you, it was my bike I was protecting."

It occurred to Rafael that, even though he hadn't needed Lucien's help, his brother had still given it. Even odder, while he doubted Lucien had saved his life, he had saved Lucien's. He looked up at the waxing moon then down to the ring on his finger that softly glowed. What was the world coming to? The blood feud raged but brothers united against a common enemy. That was it, Rafe thought. Lucien finally got it. Blood was thicker than revenge. His heroic act was nothing more than his need to protect his pack from the virulent biker gang. Rafe wasn't fooling himself though. Lucien would not stop until he personally destroyed his only brother. And he would be prepared.

Rafael looked at the bodies strewn across the road. There would be hell to pay. There were lots more where those came from.

He strode past Lucien and hopped on the bike, started it up, and without looking back, continued his flight down the mountain.

The cool air shredded his hair and stung his eyes. He didn't care. The attack by the Vipers was nothing, but his and Lucien's actions bothered him on every level. There was no way he could have known whether Gordo had a silver round in the Magnum; if he had, Lucien would have certainly died. Otherwise, he'd have been wounded, but he'd have survived. It took more than a regular round to kill a Lycan. Rafe's actions indicated not only was he willing to save his brother's life, but he was even willing to insure he wasn't injured.

He was a fool! He may have prevented the girl's end had he just let nature take its course.

It was the Blood Law—survival of the fittest.

There was no room in their world for weakness. Not weakness of character, weakness of spirit or, he thought contemptuously, weakness of the heart. But Lucien was his brother, his only blood family . . . his nemesis and the only person standing in the way of the packs' unity. How could he convince him to set his vengeance aside for the greater good of the Lycan nation?

Rafe set his jaw and made a quick U-turn. He headed back up the mountain to the hidden road just down the way from the compound. To the Amorak. His mother's people. It was long past time that he got over his temper tantrum. It was time to make peace and get answers.

Five minutes later, the Amorak's permanent campsite came into view. It was an eclectic combination of small structures, large trailers, and rambling tents. Quiet faces stared at him in surprise as he rode down the dirt road to the last cabin at the very end. The Amorak camp was once a place of savory scents, cheery laughter, and industrious energy. Now, sadness and apathy hung over the encampment like a dark, moldy cloud.

He was shocked at the condition of the people and the place. It reminded him of a refugee camp. The death of his mother followed by the clash of her sons had taken its toll. The fallout had been the systematic destruction of the Lycans by the Slayers and the insidious drugs supplied by the Vipers. The Amorak, the human spirit keepers of the wolves, had apparently suffered, too.

Guilt washed over Rafe. He'd wrongly neglected these proud, giving people. He had ignored their attempts to placate. Both his and Lucien's pride had done this. Reduced them to the shadows of their former selves. A prideful people who respected the wolf above all other creatures, including themselves. With them, the secrets of the Lycans were buried deep. With them, the Blood Law was enforced.

With the realization of what his pride had cost these people, Rafael felt as if he had the weight of the entire Lycan race on his shoulders alone. And in many ways he did.

From that moment forward, Rafe would set his anger aside. He would do everything in his power to mend the broken fences, and then together with the Amorak, he would prepare for the rising.

He stopped just outside of the dilapidated cabin. The remaining glass in the windows was in shards; threadbare curtains fluttering in the late night breeze caught against the sharp edges of the glass. Rafael lifted his nose and sniffed. The familiar scent of mint and beeswax mingled with the surrounding pine in the night air.

Sharia lived.

As he raised his hand to knock on the weather-beaten door, it opened. A small, ancient woman wrapped in an old tattered shawl looked up at him. His heart stopped. The cheery brown eyes he remembered from his youth were gone. In their stead were hollowed dull brown spots, sunken into an emaciated skull. Hope was gone. Her life force barely flickered.

"Sharia?" he asked, his heart twisting inside his chest. She'd been his mother's nurse, as well as his and Lucien's. She'd been the one person he'd been able to talk to when he couldn't go to his parents. After their death up to the split of the packs, Sharia had been his and Lucien's lifeline.

Guilt washed over him in a second set of waves. He had abandoned her and her people when they needed him most. He hadn't realized it then, but he did now.

"Come in, Rafael," she softly said, her voice barely a rasp.

He ducked under the threshold too small to accommodate his great height. The interior was small but neat. An old bentwood rocker that she'd once used to soothe him as a babe sat across from a battered straight-backed chair. A cot took up the north wall and a small camp-style stove sat on top of a wooden cupboard with a water hand pump. Behind a tattered screen, he saw the claw-foot of an old porcelain tub.

"Sharia, what's happened?" But he knew.

"The blood feud between blood brothers." It wasn't an accusation but a statement of fact.

Rafael inhaled sharply. To think it was one thing, to have it thrown in your face was another.

"I was young and angry when the council refused to believe me. It was a reason to abandon you." He took her old gnarled hands into his. "Can you forgive me?"

For one so old she squeezed his hands with considerable strength before she let them go. "There is nothing to forgive, Rafa. We must all travel our own path. Yours has brought you back to me."

"Come to the compound with me. I will take care of you. All of you," Rafe softly said, knowing she would refuse.

"This is my home," she said with a shake of her head. She turned and sat back in the rocker and indicated he should sit in the only other chair in the cabin. He did so, gingerly, not sure if his weight would destroy it.

"It looks weak, but it can handle the weight of you and your brother," she cackled.

At her words, Rafael immediately envisioned Falon. At first glance, she had seemed weak, but she had a spine. She had handled Lucien, and she had something inside of her that would not be manhandled. Something, he realized at that moment, not of the human world.

He straightened in his chair, reining in his fear in favor of information.

"You have come about the girl?" Sharia asked.

"You know?" Her question shocked Rafael. It shouldn't have. The reason for the Amorak's being was to protect the Lycans. If the girl posed a threat, they would know. How, was a mystery that would not be solved in his lifetime.

"Her coming has been foretold."

Anxiety gripped hold of Rafael; he slowly released it and told her what he knew. "Salene wanted her. I slew him. She possesses great power, though I sense she is new to it. Who is she? Why is she here? What are the powers she possesses?"

Ignoring his questions, Sharia pointed to his right hand. "How did you come by the ring?"

Knowing it was the topic of conversation, the damn thing warmed on his finger. Absently Rafe rubbed it. "Salene. I took it from his ashes."

"Did you know he possessed it?"

Rafe shook his head. "Having not heard otherwise, I assumed, as we all did, that it was still buried safely in the frozen North."

"Do not remove the ring," she warned.

Rafe nodded again. His instincts told him, despite his frustration with it, to keep it on him at all times.

"Has the girl been sent by the Slayers?" Had she used black magic to ensnare him? Was he as blind as his brother had been? He wanted to know.

"No, but she is dangerous nonetheless."

"Dangerous how?"

Dark brown eyes looked steadfastly up at Rafe. "She has the power to destroy you. She has the power to destroy Lucien, and if she destroys the brothers, she will destroy the Lycans." Sharia leaned toward him. "Gain her trust, keep her close."

"How does she have the power to destroy me?"

"The Blood Law."

Rafe swiped his hand across his chin. Trying to get a straight answer out of Sharia was like chasing his tail.

He held up his right hand. "Does she want the ring? What power does it hold?"

Sharia smiled. "The Eye of Fenrir. What is there not to covet? There is power beyond measure within. So long as you do not release the demon wolf inside, you have a chance, Rafael. Do not remove the ring and do not under any circumstances release the hell within it."

"How do I release it?"

She eyed him cryptically, deciding if he was worthy of such information. "By giving it permission."

Rafe sat back, contemplative. The answer was so simple, it was terrifying.

"What power does it have over me?"

"So long as you wear it, the only power the ring has over you is the power of suggestion. It cannot, however, make the person wearing it do anything he doesn't already want to do."

"But when I resist its call, it heats up. I cannot remove it."

She smiled a crooked, toothless smile. "My boy, it cannot force you to do what you do not want to do. But Fenrir is vengeful. He sees all and hears all. Guard the ring with your life. So long as he is not released, his power is yours."

"What power?"

"Since you slipped it onto your finger, do you not feel more empowered? Stronger? Faster, focused? More determined?"

He felt all of that, and more. "Yes."

"The real power lies within you, Rafa. The ring releases it. On the hand of the wrong person, the Eye of Fenrir is lethal."

"The Slayers will see how lethal it will be against them." They already had. He had almost single-handedly destroyed a gang of Vipers.

Rafael lowered his hand and looked at the ring. It remained cool, the eye unflaring. He felt as if Fenrir was quietly listening. "I am weary of this blood feud, Sharia. My pack is falling apart around me, Lucien has come for his revenge, and while I know I must abide by the Blood Law, I have been wronged by it." He looked directly at her. "And I cannot find a way to hand over the girl."

Sharia shook her head, and her dull brown eyes glittered with tears. "You are no wearier than I. The girl can never completely belong to you or Lucien. Only when you each discover and accept your true mate and the sacrifices you must make to possess her, will there be peace. Only then will the packs thrive. Only then, Rafael, can the Slayers be defeated."

"But what of the girl?" he demanded, moving to the edge of his chair. "Am I to hand her over to my brother? Am I to watch as he destroys her before my eyes as I forced him?"

Sharia's eyes softened. "There must always be sacrifice. Sometimes it is the heart, sometimes, Rafael, the soul. Your parents loved each other with every fiber of their being. Your sire would not have given up one day with Tamaska, even knowing the anguish that would follow. He was brave. A valiant warrior. You are his eldest son. You are an alpha. The pack depends on you and you on them. While your feelings are irrelevant to the survival of the pack, follow your heart, my son. Let it lead you, for it will be your only salvation in the end."

Rafael stood up and cocked his right arm to punch the wall over the small stove, but not wanting to have the meager dwelling come down around their heads, he punched his open palm. "Stop speaking in circles! Do I hand her over to Lucien?"

"The Blood Law must be avenged."

"It's a double-edged sword! Lucien should pay for lying with a Slayer—not me for destroying her!"

"The Blood Law must be avenged."

"My heart tells me to defy it."

"Then it will destroy you."

"How can that be? If I follow my heart as you say, you turn it around and say it will destroy me. Which is it, Sharia?"

"Listen to your questions, Rafael, and also to my answers."

Frustration took hold of him. He could get a straighter answer from a snake oil salesman. He should not have come. New bouts of anger and frustration sparred with his promise to himself not to turn his back on the Amorak again.

"Come with me to the compound, Sharia. I can protect you there—here, I cannot."

"I don't need protection, Rafa. I'm safe here among my people." She slowly stood, her old bones creaking as she did. Reaching out, she took his hands into hers, clasping them tightly. "Go, Rafael, fulfill your destiny."

Eight

RAFAEL'S FRUSTRATION AND confusion reached critical mass. Sharia spoke in circles.

Follow your heart. His heart, his *gut* told him handing over the girl so that Lucien could murder her in cold blood was wrong.

The Blood Law must be avenged. So what choice did he have but to hand her over?

He gunned the Harley and headed back to the compound. Dawn was but two hours away. The pain from the knife wound had intensified, but he could handle it. Pain in one form or another was his constant companion.

His guilt over the divide with his brother and the Amorak's current lifestyle ate at him. His inability to save his parents and his pack's degeneration ate at him. Hell, it all ate at him.

But right now, most of all, he wondered if he would be handing an innocent girl over to her death in just a few hours. And if so, what kind of monster would that make him?

When he returned home, he strode into his room, slamming the door shut behind him. The girl woke with a start. In the gray halo of dawn, he saw her sleepy, hooded eyes. Her hair hung in a wild mass around her slender body. She was wearing one of his T-shirts, forcing a scowl.

Her nipples poked at the thin fabric, and the high curve of her breasts left nothing to the imagination.

He snapped back a snarl and walked past her, flung the bathroom door open, and turned on the faucet of the large, sunken sink. Water flowed in a wide, waterfall sheet as he stripped down to his jeans.

Rafe smiled sardonically at himself in the mirror. Thick, stylishly cut blond hair framed his face. The barest hint of a gold beard shadowed his chin. His turquoise eyes blazed like they were on fire. Blood and dirt smeared from his chin down his neck and across his wide chest. He extended his arms and grabbed the edges of the sink with his raw-knuckled hands while flexing his muscles.

Despite his lousy mood, kicking the shit out of those Vipers had been a huge stress releaser. Gordo had had it coming for a long time. Even so, Rafe scowled.

Unfortunately, Gordo's captain, Sledge, would pick up the reins now. He was smarter than Gordo. More patient and more cunning. He wished it had been Sledge he'd taken out. Gordo had been manageable. Sledge would prove to be more difficult. Because the Slayers had made deep inroads with the Vipers, it was inevitable that pack Vulkasin would clash with the outlaw bikers and their silent backers again.

Rafe shook his head. It never ended, but he'd always known that.

For ten years, he'd watched his father manage the pack when it had been thirty times what it was now. Strong. Powerful. Influential. More importantly, it had been prosperous and, despite the ongoing

Slayer wars, happy, strong, and proud. Rafael had known one day he'd be alpha. He'd craved it, wanted it more than anything.

And now the position was his. He'd earned the right, as well as all the sacrifices and troubles that came with it. He had no regrets. When he was honest with himself, however, he could admit that fear, he had in spades. He wanted the same tight-knit family his parents had created. He wanted a strong mate to stand beside him as they watched their grandchildren play. If he wanted to insure the well-being and future of his people, and his dreams of creating a super-pack, there was still much to do before the Blood Moon rising.

And hanging over his head like his double-edged swords was the Blood Law. Until it was avenged, they could not move on!

He shoved his hand under the cold water and then across his face, washing the night's battle stench from him. Straightening, he threw his head back and shook it, sending water flying, then ran his fingers through his damp hair. Rivulets of water ran down his chest, mingling with the blood then down his belly, stopping at the top button of his jeans. He grabbed a washcloth off the sideboard, wet it, then squeezed the water out. Dawn's gray fingers peeked through the ponderosa pine. As he dragged the towel across his chest, his jawline tightened, and he wondered where Lucien was.

What was he waiting for?

He flexed his right arm. The Mondragon tribal band of his mother's line, the noble head of a black wolf with a series of blades crisscrossed surrounding it, was tattooed around his right biceps. Below it hung two eagle feathers.

In contrast, on his left arm, from his shoulder down to his elbow, was the mark of the Vulkasin. A detailed image of a ferocious Siberian wolf, his fangs drawn, his nose pointed north and interwoven through the wolf's thick pelt, the mighty Vulkasin double swords.

He ran a hand down his right pectoral to his side, swiping a significant amount of blood away. He hissed in a sharp breath when his fingers touched the knife wound.

There was more damage than he had thought. The three-inch gash oozed crimson. He hissed and, even as he did, the sound mingled with another's gasp. His head jerked up and locked eyes in the mirror with the girl.

FALON STOOD IN silent awe at the bathroom door. Even if those black beasts outside were hot on her tail, she could not have dragged her eyes from Rafael's body. He was magnificent in his half-dressed state. His back muscles rippled with his every movement. In an ancient font, the word *Vulkasin* was tattooed across his broad shoulders.

Blood ran from a gash in his back. "Rafael? You're bleeding." She rushed to him. Slowly, he turned to face her. When she reached out to touch him, he grabbed her hand, pushing it away. His touch was hot, feverish. She caught her breath at the heat of it.

Anger took a swift hold of her concern. "Did your brother do this?"

Rafael grinned, then laughed. "Like Lucien could ever get that close."

Falon mentally snorted. Like that was such an impossibility. Lord, the man was arrogant. "It's a knife wound." She moved closer for a better look. Rafael flinched when she touched it. "If it wasn't your brother, who did this?"

"Several someones who won't be able to talk about it."

Falon's jaw dropped. "You killed them?"

Rafe reached past her and grabbed a dry towel and blotted his chest. "What was I supposed to do, ask for a Band-Aid?"

Falon took a step back and crossed her arms over her chest. She was very aware she wore only his T-shirt and a cast. She'd thought about snagging a pair of his underwear, too, but had decided that was going a bit far. The ribbed tee was bad enough. "Why is your brother going to kill me, and why are you going to allow it? And what the hell is the Blood Law?"

Rafael tossed the towel aside and moved past her. Falon grabbed his arm and yanked him back with surprising strength. Her eyes widened simultaneously with Rafael's. "Tell me."

He glowered down at her. "Does it matter?"

She released his arm and pressed her hand to his chest. Looking up at him, she saw the anger and the despair in his eyes. Despite her own anger, something inside of her shifted.

He didn't want her to die, but he would not save her either. "Of course it does. It's my life."

"What will be, will be. I cannot change it even if I wanted to." He tried to move past her again, but she would not allow him. She pressed her other hand against his chest. He was warm, and she could feel the harsh throb of his heart beneath her fingertips.

He must care on some level if he was reluctant to see her dead. If she could just pull him a little more into her camp, then maybe she had a chance.

"Rafael," she softly said. "We're connected somehow. Don't you feel it?"

Yeah, he felt. But he couldn't embrace it. Rafael didn't want to, but he forced himself to look down into her deep lake-colored eyes. He owed her that: to look her in the eye when he told her that not only was she going to die, but he was going to make sure of it.

He swallowed hard as the rage began to build again. If he took Sharia at her word and listened to his heart, he would wrap this brave woman he barely knew in his arms and hold her tightly, protectively, then refuse his brother the right to her death. Instead, he let out a long breath, and as he did, it suddenly occurred to him that he had only minutes before his shift. He looked past her to the window. Pink fingers of the new day infiltrated the thick copse of trees east of the wall.

Where was Lucien?

Rafael lifted his nose and sniffed. Ah . . . there. Lucien was close. So why didn't he show himself? This was the time when they were both human. One hour at dawn and another at dusk. What was he waiting for? He would not dare destroy the girl while Rafael was in wolf form. It was not their way.

"I don't want to die, Rafael," she whispered.

Looking down at her, his gut twisted painfully. In that moment, he envisioned the final glance that had passed between his mother and father before she'd died. They'd been mates in the best way possible. Heart, body, and soul. And now, in spirit.

He set his jaw. Smiling sadly, he reached out to touch Falon's cheek. The words were on the tip of his tongue—how sorry he was to have dragged her into the mess that was his life. But his moment of weakness was over as soon as it began.

He was alpha. Alphas did not hesitate.

He jerked away from her, strode angrily towad the door, and yanked it open. "Don't leave this room," he growled. Then slammed it behind him. Rafe shifted and went on the hunt for his brother.

ANGER, FEAR, FRUSTRATION, and, damn it, longing swirled with the force of a category-five tornado in Falon's heart. Rafael Vulkasin was a stubborn, blind man! There was a reason she was here. A reason he had chosen *her*, marked *her*, and resisted his brother's right to destroy *her*. He had saved her life twice, maybe three times. *She meant something to him, damn it.* Maybe not enough to defy his law, but enough for him to hesitate.

And what did he mean to her? In the time she had been aware of Rafael, she'd witnessed him kill a man who was hell-bent on kidnapping her. Had been as intimate with him as a man and woman could be. Had been thrust in the middle of a crazy primitive blood feud. Her belly roiled nervously. If she were honest with herself, she could admit he meant something. There was more than just their physical reaction to each other. As strong as that was, Falon knew Rafael held answers to who she was. She was as certain of it as she was the sun would rise each morning. In Rafael's presence, her powers came alive. New powers emerged, powers she had not known she possessed. With him she wasn't afraid of them. Inexplicably, with him she felt part of a whole, like she had some purpose. Why, what, or how, she didn't know. It didn't matter. It just was. She didn't contemplate the details. She was going with her instinct. Too many times she had ignored it and gotten into trouble. It was time to trust herself. But first, if she didn't eat, she'd be easy pickings for Lucien.

She strode to the door and yanked on the knob, expecting it to be locked. It opened easily. Food scents hit her broadside. Falon's mouth watered. She could not remember the last time she had eaten.

She could not go downstairs dressed like she was, though. Quickly she ransacked Rafael's dresser and closet. She pulled on a pair of black flannel pajama pants that fit over her cast, and a blue fitted button-up shirt. She slipped out of the room, ever alert for that big gold wolf and Lucien.

A myriad of scents infiltrated her nose. Rafael's familiar one, and Lucien's dark angry one, mixed with the food scents and other people scents from below. Hunger drove her down the long stairway and into the great room. About half a dozen people milled about; some she recognized from her encounter with Lucien last night. All conversation stopped. She stood unsure of what, if anything, to say to them. They met her stare evenly, then turned away. Fine, she wasn't looking for friends either. She was hungry, and once she ate her fill, she'd disappear. Her nostrils twitched, and she followed the food scent.

Just off the great room she entered a large, warm, natural stone kitchen with state-of-the-art stainless steel appliances. She didn't stop to admire all of the amenities; she went for the stove where a large pot simmered. She glanced around. Not a soul stirred. Hunger drove her forward. She lifted the lid of the pot and sniffed. Whatever it was, it smelled heavenly.

Falon rustled through the carved oak cupboards for a bowl and the drawers for a spoon. With each in hand, she dipped the bowl into the brew and was about to take a spoonful when she sensed a presence.

Guiltily she turned around to find two women staring at her. "I was hungry."

"That soup is for the elders," a small pretty brunette with brown eyes said.

Falon's belly rumbled, demanding sustenance. She poured the soup back into the pot. "Sorry." She looked longingly at the pot. "I haven't eaten in days."

The brunette stepped past Falon. She pulled out a large bowl from the cupboard and ladled out enough soup to feed three people. She set it on the counter next to Falon and motioned to the other woman, a petite redhead, to come help her. Together they lifted the heavy pot from the stove and walked past her and out of the kitchen.

Falon grabbed the bowl, and just as she scooped up a mouthful, she heard screams, then a thud, then cries. She set her bowl down and ran toward the commotion. The two women stood frantically swiping the hot liquid from their arms and chest. Falon hurried to the brunette, who was covered in the scalding liquid. With no reservation, she ripped the woman's steaming shirt from her, then her pants. The other woman, who was not nearly as afflicted as her friend, ran past Falon and returned with damp towels. Together they set the brunette down on the floor and cleaned the steaming liquid from her lobster red skin. Falon swallowed back the bile that rose in her throat. The burn areas were already blistering.

"You need to get into a tub of cold water," Falon said. "To cool your skin, then get to a hospital. These burns will get infected." She pulled her shirt off and gently wrapped it around the naked woman, who mutely nodded.

Several people hurried to the scene. Incriminating eyes zeroed in on her. A large blond man took the woman into his arms and strode away with her. Falon looked at the redhead. "Is he taking her to the hospital?"

She only shrugged then proceeded to clean the mess up. Falon wandered back to the kitchen and spied her bowl of soup on the counter. She picked it up and walked back to the redhead. "Take this to the elders."

The woman stood and wiped her hands on her damp jeans. Slowly she took the bowl from Falon. "Thank you."

The acids in Falon's belly burned, and she suddenly felt weak. She needed to eat. Surely there was more food in the kitchen. She looked down at her ribbed T-shirt and groaned. Her nipples were clearly outlined beneath the sheer fabric. The flannel pants were soaked. She needed to change. Her stomach would have to wait.

She closed the bedroom door behind her and kicked off the damp pants, then went into the bathroom. She washed her face and arms and found an unopened toothbrush and brushed her teeth. She shrugged and used Rafael's brush to brush the tangles out of her long hair. Wearing only the ribbed tee, she walked back into the bedroom and stopped dead in her tracks.

Looking like the wolf that had just devoured Bambi, Lucien stood casually against the tall bedpost.

"Leave this room," Falon commanded the unwelcome intruder. She tried to keep her voice strong. Although she was afraid of Rafael in a dark, primal way, Lucien terrified her. Her fear spiked when Lucien unraveled his long, muscular limbs, like a cobra uncoiling to strike its prey.

Her.

His smile deepened. Falon's heart pounded like a sledgehammer in her chest.

"I used to live here, you know." He said it casually, glancing around the room. She couldn't miss the regret in his voice.

"It's a . . . nice room," she conceded, "but you don't live here now. Rafael does."

Falon backed up as Lucien slowly stalked her. She narrowed her eyes. "I'll zap you again," she threatened.

Lucien froze, then threw his head back and laughed. "Be my guest. I recovered immediately. You, however, did not. And Lord only knows what I could do to that body of yours while you lay unconscious in my arms."

Falon gasped at his audacity. "You would not dare!"

"Try me." He cornered her. His heat was palpable, his scent wild and of the loamy earth and pine. Her nostrils twitched, not finding the scent unpleasant. "You wear my brother's clothes well."

He raised his hand to her cheek, and in the process brushed his knuckles across her nipple. Falon gasped, and Lucien just pressed closer.

"Do you have feelings for Rafael?"

She took a swift breath. “That is none of your business!”

“Does he have feelings for you?”

“I’m not a mind reader.” Did he? He’d seemed to, when he’d stood at the sink, staring at her. The way his touch lingered . . .

Lucien shook his head, but his lips quirked. “So brave. So hostile. Don’t you know your death is mine to command at any time?”

“My life is mine to live, not yours to destroy.”

Lucien tsk-tsked as he shook his head. “I can”—he snapped his fingers beneath her nose—“snuff you out in the blink of an eye.”

She clenched her jaw and put her hands on her hips. “Try it.”

He cocked his head and stared at her, eyes blazing and nostrils flaring. But then all that heat was banked, almost deliberately. He took a hand from her hip and brought it to his lips. “How about we make a deal instead, Falon. I spare your life, for now, and you promise to keep my brother company.”

“Okay.”

He shook his head. “A little too eager. You’re not even going to pretend to do what I ask?”

“The first chance I have to blow this joint, I’m gone.”

He gave a long, mocking sigh. “That is unfortunate.”

He clenched his fingers around her hand and pushed her into the corner with his big body. She struggled against him, but even with her newfound strength, he was stronger.

Much stronger.

He pulled her hand up and turned it over, palm up. He looked into her eyes, and the black striations in his pulsed. His lust for her swirled in thick, pungent waves around them. Not just a lust for revenge, but that of a primal animal rutting.

To her horror, when he lowered his lips to her palm, her body warmed. Falon closed her eyes and held her breath, not wanting to be affected on any level by this man.

His teeth sank into the meaty part of her palm.

Her eyes flashed open, she screamed and struggled, but he held her fast. Immediately the copper scent of her blood rose to her nostrils.

"Shhhh," Lucien crooned even as he licked her hand. The tender sound contrasted with his violence so much that she was momentarily immobilized. Eyes blazing gold, he grabbed her by a hank of hair and forced her head back. Her blood mingled with his saliva on his lips. He laughed at the way her gaze lingered on his mouth and lowered his lips to hers. Just like that, she snapped to life.

She snarled and bit his lip.

He snarled in return, yanking her closer to him.

When his lips took hers, Falon stiffened in his arms. Wild waves of emotion crashed through her the moment her blood mingled with his.

Pain, heartache, desire, vengeance, and sheer, unadulterated terror. Some of it hers, most of it his.

Falon twisted and pushed away, but his strength was superior. She closed her eyes instead and focused her energy on him. She could force him from her with her own power and pray Rafael returned in time to save her body from certain ravishment. But she had no reason to believe Rafe would return anytime soon.

Lucien laughed and retreated, though he still grasped her hand. He lifted it to his lips again. Falon tried yanking it away. "No pain, my love," he roughly said, then licked the place where he bit her. Magically the wound smoothed over as if it had never been there. He dropped her hand.

"Rafael will kill you if he knows you traded blood with me. For your own protection, let's keep it between us, shall we?"

Confusion stormed her sensibilities. "What do you care if I live or die?"

He smiled a small but genuine smile. It changed everything about him. "Oh, I care."

Falon had no response. Stupefied by his words, she stared at his laconic eyes.

A snarl from the doorway broke Lucien's mesmerizing hold on her. Gasping, Falon saw the great golden wolf at the doorway. Instinctively, she ran toward him, knowing he would fight to his death to protect her. She sank to her knees on the carpet behind the beast, using him as her shield and weapon at the same time.

Lucien stared at them, but his focus was on the wolf. "I see your babysitter has arrived." His gaze met Falon's. "Remember what I asked of you, and know this: if you 'blow this joint,' I'll find you, and you won't like my punishment."

He moved past her and the great angry beast into the hallway. They both listened to Lucien's happy whistle and heavy footsteps as he made his way to the great room. Moments later, the sound of his Harley revving was followed by the creak of the gates opening. Then the sound of the engine faded completely.

Nine

FALON HADN'T REALIZED she'd dug her fingers into the wolf's thick, silky fur until he took her hand in his mouth and pulled it out of his pelt. She blinked as she attempted to process what had just happened.

Rafael returning injured—stabbed.

Lucien throwing down a bargain to prolong her life.

The bastard *biting* her. She clenched her fist, knowing if she told Rafael, he'd do something stupid, like get her killed quicker. She'd wash her hand with acid if she had to.

And then . . .

She looked down at the wolf. He was so big, his head almost even with her chest. And those eyes. She stared at them. They were so much like his master's.

Falon closed her eyes for a moment and slowly inhaled, then exhaled.

Just like his master's! If she didn't know better, she'd swear . . .

But no. She laughed, recognizing she sounded more hysterical than amused.

In that instant, she knew how Alice in Wonderland had felt when she fell down the rabbit hole. Except this wasn't some twisted fairy tale—this was her life. And Lucien wanted to end it. Soon. And Rafael seemed perfectly willing to allow it.

But she wasn't going to make it easy for either of them.

She exhaled and flexed her fingers. Her life might suck, but she was far from ready to hand it over to some dude who thought he was God. His brother could go to hell, too.

Falon opened her eyes to find the damn wolf watching her again. It even looked like it was grinning, as if it knew exactly what she was thinking. To make matters worse, it turned to look at the bed as if to say, "Let's hit it."

She shivered and her nipples hardened. She was emotionally exhausted and starving to death. "I'm not sleeping with you, if that's what you think."

He growled and nudged her with his big snout toward the bed. When she resisted, he herded her as if she were a spring lamb toward the huge four-poster. He leapt up ahead of her. Although it was so faint she wondered if she was imagining it, she heard a slight whimper escape the great beast. He immediately growled as if to cover it up.

Intrigued, Falon moved to the edge of the bed. She reached out a tentative hand and touched the top of his head. If a wolf could groan, this one did, and damned if it didn't seem like he rolled his eyes as well. She couldn't tell if her touch pleased or frightened him. As if he had anything to fear from her. "It's not like I can hurt you, you brute." Using both hands, she pressed them into the fur just below his neck until she felt the powerful muscles bunch beneath her hands. Slowly, she moved her palms to his great shoulders, feeling for a wound. As her hands traveled down his sides, then to his belly, he growled low in his throat.

She froze. His big head was only inches from her. His eyes piercing. Her heart thumped in her chest. Once again, the expression on his face was so dynamic, it made him seem human. "You're losing it, Falon," she muttered just as he licked her cheek with his big tongue. "Argh!" She swiped her hand across her face. "That was disgusting!"

He barked at her and then gingerly rolled over to his side. Immediately, she saw the bloody fur. "Oh, you're bleeding!"

Gently she climbed onto the bed. As she did, she looked at him, afraid he'd bite her hand off. He laid his big head down on the pillow and closed his eyes, his big tongue lolling out of the side of his mouth.

Warm sticky blood met her fingertips when she probed the wound. It was deep, but as she looked at the wolf, he remained dead still. If his wound was not tended, infection would set in. And even if he let her take him to a vet—she snorted at the thought, earning her a withering glare from the wolf—he seemed beyond that right now.

He turned and licked the hand that pressed against his wound. A warm fuzzy feeling washed though her. She pressed her hand more firmly to the cut. Not knowing why, Falon closed her eyes and concentrated all of her energy on her hand and the damaged flesh and organs beneath it. The wolf continued to lick her hand in long, wet stokes. Her body warmed. Her skin tingled. Energy shot from the center of her being to her arm, then to her hand, heating it to painful.

The wolf's head jerked up and he shifted, preparing to stand. "No," she breathed, "Stay." Something was happening here, Falon thought. Even now, she could feel the wound beneath her fingers closing up.

He didn't lie back down again, but he stilled. Her hand heated hotter. She could feel the heavy whoosh of blood in her veins. In one abrupt jolt, it ended. Falon slowly opened her eyes and looked at the wolf. His hooded eyes gave nothing away. As if he deliberately tried to keep his emotions in check. Jesus! He was a dog. He couldn't think or feel like a human. Falon looked down at the dried blood. She poked the area with her fingertips. It was body temperature warm. No fresh blood, no gaping hole. Just smooth furred skin atop thick, corded muscles. She looked at him in wonder.

"Did I do that?" she asked in disbelief.

He nuzzled his side where the wound had been then looked up at her as if ascertaining for himself that she had the power to heal. She didn't believe it herself, but this wasn't actually the first time . . . She thought back to a kitten her last foster dad had thrown out of the car widow as they drove down the street. She'd pissed him off because she had defended her foster sister when he had wrongly accused her of breaking his fishing pole. Hours later when they returned home, Falon snuck out and found the battered little thing in the gutter. He was alive. Barely. She'd cupped the small fur ball in her hands and prayed that it would miraculously heal. She was answered. It had scared the hell out of her, but she was grateful. She was young when it happened and had truly believed it had been divine intervention. But now . . . She looked at the wolf and where the wound had been. He looked the epitome of health. She had healed him.

The wolf growled low and looked at her, cocking his head as if to say, "I don't get it."

"I don't either," she murmured to herself, feeling out of sorts and confused. What was next? Turning dirt into gold?

He responded with a big sloppy lick across her face.

"Argh," she said wiping her face on a nearby pillow. "I told you not to do that!" He licked her again.

Wanting some time to herself to process everything that was happening to her, Falon moved off the bed and gimped to the bathroom. She shut the door behind her and locked it. She sat down on the toilet, dropped her head into her hands, and rubbed her eyes. Her life had done a complete flip since she first laid eyes on Rafael Vulkasin. Her emerging powers excited and scared her. But just as mysterious and amazing was Rafael's pull. She couldn't deny it, wasn't even sure she wanted to. He was the most exciting thing that had happened in her life. Because of him, extraordinary things were happening around her and to her. Rafael had sparked whatever it was in her that had been pressing for release for so long. Intuitively she knew that without him, her powers would be useless. She looked down at the wolf's blood on her hands.

She'd healed him! She looked down at the cast on her leg and then at the closed door, thinking of the wolf beyond. His master healed her terrible wounds. But he was some—something not of this world. She knew it the moment she saw him. The way he fought Conan all doubled-sworded and walking on the ceiling. Who did that?

Was the brother the same? She rubbed her hand where he had bitten her. If she could, she'd cut off her hand! What did his bite mean? Was it his way of marking her? If he was going to kill her, why did he bother? The answer was simple: Rafael. He did it to taunt his brother. She'd be damned if she'd be used to bait the man who saved her life. Falon turned the water on as hot as she could stand it and scrubbed her hand until it bled.

Then she turned her attention to her ankle. If she could heal the kitten and the wolf, why not herself? Falon plopped back down on the toilet and pressed her hands to the cast above her broken ankle. She closed her eyes and concentrated just as she had on the wolf. Nothing. She concentrated harder. No heat emanated from her belly to her hands. She opened her eyes and scowled. Maybe because of the cast? Or she simply did not have the power to heal herself. Her scowl deepened when she opened the bathroom door to find the wolf staring at her, wearing that irritating wolf smile.

She gimped past him, the day's events and her lack of food taking its toll. Her knees wobbled, and she was beginning to see black spots. She grabbed the edge of the oak dresser, closed her eyes, and slowly gauged her breathing until the dizziness passed. Once composed, Falon turned to the beast and said, "I'm getting dressed and going downstairs to eat." She dug through Rafael's drawers again and pulled out another pair of flannel jammy bottoms and instead of a button-down shirt, she grabbed a black sweatshirt that came down to her knees.

The wolf stood at the open door waiting for her. She was beyond hunger pains. Her body was numb. Carefully, she hobbled behind him down the stairway and into the great room.

Her nose twitched at the latest assault of scents. Sex, hot and heavy, hung like a blanket over the area. How had she missed it earlier? Because Rafael was not with her? New savory scents of something wonderful cooking wafted from the kitchen. Fleetingly she wondered how the little brunette was. She would ask after she gorged herself.

Falon stopped in mid-step when she realized dozens of fresh eyes stared at her. Not the same folks who were present earlier, but some of them she recognized from the night before. A harsh shiver tattooed down each vertebra of her spine ending at the small of her back, where it dug painfully in. She was not welcome here, not by them and maybe not even Rafael. The collection of men and women looked normal, like everyday working folk. They looked like she felt. Tired, wary, hungry. And desperate. Of what was their desperation born? Hers was survival. Could it be that they shared more than the roof over their heads? Were they forced to be here, too?

Feeling self-conscious under their cool, guarded stares and even a few glares, Falon reached for the wolf beside her, digging her fingers into the thick fur of his neck. He growled low and menacingly at the group. Their trance shattered. Immediate chatter and movement ensued.

A very pretty blonde woman sauntered toward her. Her curvy hips swayed, as did her full breasts beneath a thin white T-shirt. Her narrowed eyes gave Falon the once-over, twice. Her upper lip curled. "Leave here while you can, or stay and die," she sneered.

A big, dark-haired man emerged from the group. He grabbed the blonde from behind and slapped her hard across the cheek. The woman screamed, and so did Falon.

"How dare you show disrespect? She is the chosen one," he ground out. With a boot to her back, he forced the woman to her knees before Falon. "On your back. Now!" he snarled. Falon stepped back and shook her head.

"It's okay, really, she doesn't need to do that."

The woman glared at the man then looked longingly up at the wolf that ignored her. She cried out when the man stepped on her neck, forcing her to grovel.

"Please, stop!" Falon moved toward the woman. As she reached down to pull her up, the woman jerked away from her touch. The rest of the occupants in the room gathered around, their faces anxious. Falon didn't know what was expected of her, but she had the distinct impression if she did the wrong thing, these people would turn on her. "Where is Rafael?" Falon asked, knowing he would do something.

The woman on the floor laughed hysterically, glaring at the group. "She doesn't know? She doesn't know!" Her laughter turned maniacal.

The big man reached down to slap her again, but Falon had had enough. An odd tightening in her body seized her. She pushed through it and grabbed his fist, twisting him around. No one was more surprised by her strength than Falon, but she didn't back off. "Never raise your hand to a woman in anger again. Not in my presence, at least." She squeezed his hand. Bone cracked. "Or you will be the one on your back on the floor." She pushed him away.

He dipped his head in a submissive gesture and backed away. "As you wish." The hushed and humbled crowd backed away with him.

Falon looked down at the woman who had gotten up on all fours and who looked at her in awe. Instinctively, she knew if she offered her hand, it would be refused. "Get up."

Slowly, the woman did. The big wolf beside her snarled and moved in on the blonde. Blondie got the message. *Get out of here or get hurt by me this time.*

She hustled off toward the front door, never once looking back. The wolf then nudged Falon toward the savory aromas wafting from the back of the structure. Her need for sustenance overrode her uneasiness. Mouth watering, Falon followed his lead into the kitchen, where the long carved oak table sagged beneath an orgy of food.

She swallowed her drool. The wolf nudged her to the closest seat. Falon plopped down and devoured the display with her eyes.

A cheery-eyed, middle-aged woman bustled in from what Falon guessed was a walk-in pantry. She smiled and said over the counter, "I am Galiya. Anything you want, I will cook for you." She poured Falon a huge steaming bowl of meat stew. Before she could set it down, Falon grabbed a spoon and started to eat. She closed her eyes and moaned. It was the most delicious thing she had ever eaten; she was famished. Falon tossed her manners out the window and ate bite after bite. She could not get the food in her mouth fast enough. The wolf sat down beside her and seemed mesmerized by the sight of her eating. After a few moments, it shook its head as if to clear it, then lay down.

"Galiya," Falon said with a mouthful of stew and bread. "This is so good."

She gobbled down two deep bowls of the wonderful concoction and nearly half a loaf of the most delicious soft honey bread she had ever eaten. She sat back and burped. "Oh, my God, I don't think I can move."

The cherubic woman eyed the big wolf now snoozing on the floor beside her. "No reason to," she said with a small smile.

Falon burped again. If she could, she'd eat more. But there wasn't a molecule of space left in her belly.

She started when a large hand tapped her shoulder. Turning, Falon stared wide-eyed at the big blond guy who had taken the woman who burned herself to the hospital. His clear blue eyes lowered. "Thank you for aiding my sister, Marta. She is better because of it."

Falon warmed and smiled at the man who shuffled his big feet as if embarrassed. Falon gently touched his forearm and said, "I was glad to help."

He looked at the big wolf, who watched him intently. He nodded to the animal then to her before he turned and nearly ran from the room. It wasn't like she was going to bite him or something.

"Yuri is not accustomed to thanking females," Galiya, said, a hint of amusement in her tone.

Falon looked up into the woman's cheerful eyes. "It was nothing, really; if I hadn't helped, someone else would have."

"Perhaps," Galiya commented as she cleared the empty dishes from the table.

Her response challenged Falon. "Why do you say that? I get the feeling this is some sort of big extended family. Wouldn't they each help one in need?"

With her back to Falon, Galiya answered, "Some more than others."

Realizing she would not get more specific on the matter, Falon changed subjects. "Where is Rafael?" she asked, moving from the table to a more comfortable spot on a big-cushioned chair near the warm hearth. She stretched her feet out, and sudden fatigue grasped her. Her hands dropped over the armrests. Her left hand touched the thick, soft fur of the wolf. Absently, she stroked him and knew as long as he was near, she was safe.

"Most days he spends away on business," Galiya answered as she washed Falon's bowl and utensils.

Falon yawned. "What does he do?"

"Mostly real estate."

"Real estate?" Falon scoffed even as a yawn took over her words. "He hardly looks the type." Her lids suddenly became heavy. But she looked around at the beautiful stone and oak kitchen. "Where am I? Why does Lucien want to kill me?" Falon fought through the fatigue that had settled in like a hunk of lead. Hot tears stung her eyes. "I won't stand by like a stupid lamb waiting for the wolf to come. I'm a survivor."

Galiya smiled as she bustled around the kitchen. "Rafael is fair and just in his dealings."

"That doesn't answer my questions," Falon countered. She opened her eyes then narrowed them. Was the room moving in and out? Or—

"Rafael is fair and just," Galiya repeated.

Falon's lids became heavier, as if a hundred-pound sack sat on them. Warmth washed through her. Absently, she wondered if she had been drugged. She didn't care. She felt so warm and cozy . . . "That's nice," she said as she yawned again. "Very nice."

I DON'T CARE if it's the president of the United States; tell him I'm not interested in any deals!"

Abruptly, Falon woke to Rafael's angry words. She rubbed her grainy eyes and looked around. Slowly the fog in her head cleared. She was still in the kitchen. The evening shadows had descended on the compound. Geez! She'd slept the entire day! She pushed herself up to a sitting position to see Rafael standing with his back to her at the doorway. His aura flared red. Anger and passion were but shades of crimson from the other.

"Rafe, it's his daughter, for Christ's sake," a familiar voice implored.

It was the man who'd slapped the blonde. Her body snapped to attention when she remembered her immediate rage at the man and the way she'd challenged him and more importantly, how easy it had been to physically restrain him. What was happening here?

"I've got more important things to do at the moment, or hadn't you noticed? Christ, Anton, in two and a half months—" Rafael looked over his shoulder to find Falon staring at him.

"What happens in two and a half months?" she asked, slowly standing. The room tilted a little to the left then righted itself.

"Nothing that concerns you," Rafael bit off as he strode toward her. His eyes traveled up and down her body twice as if to make sure she was whole.

Falon shrugged, feeling rather smug. Power did that to a person. "I suppose if your brother has anything to do with it, you'd be absolutely correct."

Rafael growled. "My brother can go to hell."

"Rafe?" Anton called. "May I have a word with your—woman?"

Rafael and Falon both turned to face him. When Rafe nodded, he came slowly into the room with his head slightly bowed and his shoulders rounded. "My apologies for this morning," he said to Falon.

Her mouth dropped open. She'd expected the man to be hostile, not so deferential. Noting that Rafael was watching, she raised her chin. "I'm not the one you should be apologizing to, sir."

He looked from her to Rafe. "Lana was disrespectful, she was about to—" Getting no help from Rafe, Anton once more looked at Falon. "Her kind only understands corporal punishment."

"I only understand that it's wrong for a man to strike a woman in anger."

Once again, Anton looked to Rafael for help, but he stood silent. Falon glanced up at him and did a double take. He was grinning! "Surely you heard what happened. Do you think it's funny that he slapped her around and shoved her to the ground?"

Rafael looked down at her, his eyes twinkling. "No, I am amused that my sergeant at arms was brought low by a girl, and he's the one apologizing."

"What would you have me do, Rafe?" Anton implored. "Show the same disrespect as Lana?"

Rafael put his big hand on Anton's shoulder and squeezed. "You know you did the right thing, but that doesn't dispel the absurdity of it."

Falon scowled at both men before she turned her full attention on Rafael. "Why won't you help the man with his daughter?"

Rafael groaned. "I am not the village savior. I pick and choose who and when I help, not the other way around." He looked toward the great room. "Besides, there is nothing any of us can do for his daughter now."

Falon looked at Anton. "What's wrong with the man's daughter?"

"She was murdered. He wants Rafael to hunt down the killer and exact justice."

"Shut up!" Rafael hissed. He looked at Falon. "*None* of this concerns you."

"What kind of man are you?" Falon demanded, shaking her head. Then she remembered. "How could I so easily forget? You're the kind to murder an innocent woman. How could you even think to help your fellow man in his time of need?"

Shaking her head in disgust, she looked down at her oversized, disheveled clothing and realized she didn't have a decent outfit to wear to her own funeral. She also realized that Rafael Vulkasin was as far from being a real estate agent as she was from being Mary Poppins, and it was time for her to get the hell out of here. And she was going to use the man who came to Rafael for help to that end.

"There're fresh clothes upstairs for you." Rafael quietly said.

Perfect. She'd go change, but first a detour. Raising her nose, she walked imperiously past them both. Instead of going straight upstairs, Falon picked up speed and strode into the great room where a crowd of people had gathered. Auras flashed like fireworks around her; the blasts pulsed with energy.

In the center of the crowd, she could just make out a steady bright red and gray aura. She stopped in mid-stride when the pulsing black aura of another flared. Falon's heart rate increased uncomfortably. She'd seen it before. Not frequently, but throughout her life the black auras had come and gone. Instinctively she shied away from them. The last such men, Conan and his friend, were dead. She didn't need an instruction manual to know that they were all connected in a malevolent way. And now, one was twenty feet away. Had he come for her?

Fear skittered around the lining of her belly. Automatically she looked toward the kitchen. Rafael was already coming after her, anger etched along the planes of his face. Despite her fear and Rafael's anger, she felt the pull of the other man. The grieving father. Keeping a cautious eye on the threatening black aura, Falon moved quickly into the crowd, pushing bodies aside until she stood by the man with the red and gray aura. He was dressed in casual yet elegant threads. Bracing herself, she looked at the man next to him, hoping she'd imagined his darkness.

She hadn't. His aura pulsed with a deadly force all its own. The man turned dark, soulless eyes on her. The same dark, soulless eyes of Conan.

Falon shivered but did not retreat, despite the waves of malevolence that washed off him. There was no denying the vibe. It was the same as Conan. They were cut from the same cloth. *Slayers*, Rafael had called them. She looked expectantly at Rafael, his entire focus on her. Couldn't he feel the darkness in the man?

Rafe grabbed her by the arm, pulling her away. She jerked free. He growled low, so that only she could hear. She ignored his warning. She really didn't give a crap. He had his plans, she had hers, and right now, she wanted to know why these two very different men were here.

"Mr. Vulkasin," the man with the red aura said while extending his hand. He would be a handsome man, Falon thought, if not for the deep stress lines etched in his face. She knew they were recent. How could he not be distraught? His daughter had been murdered. In an uncanny way, she felt a connection to this man.

Rafael moved from behind Falon and, with a subtle wave of his hand, cleared the room until only Rafael, Falon, Anton, and the two men remained.

Rafe extended his hand. "Mr. Taylor, I'm afraid there—"

"My daughter was murdered in cold blood," he said, his voice shaky with emotion. "I want the bastards who did it. The cops have their thumbs up their asses. Name your price, and I'll pay you up front. I want them found, and I want them brought to me. Alive."

Rafael turned dark eyes to Falon. "If you will excuse us?"

No way was she leaving. Falon was beyond intrigued. Not that the man's daughter was dead—she was very sad for him—but that he believed Rafael could hunt down the killers. That didn't sound like real estate deals to her.

Unfortunately, her body chose that moment to betray her. She needed to pee, really bad, and though she could really care less about dishonoring Rafael in front of anyone, she knew she would embarrass him if she resisted his request. And despite everything—call her crazy—she didn't want to do that. It struck her, in all of its absurdity, that she had feelings for the man. How and why, she had no clue. But God help her, she did. But she still had to pee. Without a word, Falon turned and gimped away.

As she moved past them, her cast hit a raised plank on the hardwood floor, and she went sprawling forward. Strong arms caught her. At contact, pain burst in sharp explosions in her head. She cried out and covered her ringing ears. As she did, her hand brushed against the man who'd broken her fall.

Bursts of black and white spattered with crimson combined with the screams of a tortured child, flashed like a horror movie in her head.

Dear God, her breakfast roiled in her belly. Falon fought the urge to vomit. She opened her eyes and locked stares with the hard black one above her. Evil lurked behind his eyes. They sparked, and his hands tightened punishingly on her body. She knew he'd guessed what she'd seen.

She shoved away from him and rushed to Rafe. Only when she was safely by his side did she address Mr. Taylor. "Your daughter is alive."

Ten

WHAT KIND OF cruel trick is this?" Taylor shouted as he shoved past Anton and the man who'd stopped Falon from falling. He made the mistake to push past Rafael to get to Falon. Rafael reacted lightning quick and brutal. With one arm around Falon, he maneuvered her behind him and at the same time kept her pressed against his back. With his other hand, he grabbed Taylor by the front of his shirt and flung him across the room. The shocked man landed with a hard thud on the hardwood floor.

"Holy, hell," Anton cursed, hurrying to him at the same time Taylor's companion did. Together they lifted him to standing.

Taylor's face faded to ash, the stress lines on his face deepening to gouges.

"You come into my home asking for a favor and think this is the way to get it? By threatening my woman?" Rafael roared.

"I'm so—sorry. I wasn't going to harm her. But she—she—" He

raised a shaky finger to point at Falon. "She taunts me with her cruelty—"

Falon remained steadfast. "She's alive. I don't know how I know, but I do."

"Sir," Taylor's companion said as he brushed his rumpled clothing, "she's lying." He turned his cold eyes on Falon and Rafael. "We have pictures, we heard the CD. If she isn't dead, after what we saw and heard . . . If God is merciful, she is."

Falon squeezed Rafael's hand then released it. When she stepped past him, Rafael growled low, but instead of pushing her back, he kept stride with her as she approached the two men.

"She's okay," Falon said, looking at Taylor. "But she won't be for long. There are others who want her."

Rafael glanced down at Falon. "Be sure, Falon. What you're saying—"

"I'm sure," she said fervently. She took Taylor's hands into hers. While she did not see the flash of pictures she had with his companion, she felt his desperation and his desire to believe her. "I swear it. She's alive." She felt a spark of hope flare in him.

"Who has her? How do you know?" Taylor implored, squeezing her hands. Gently, she withdrew them.

Falon turned to look at his companion. She lifted an accusing finger at him. "Ask him."

Taylor's eyes widened. "Smythe—" he whispered.

Smythe bared his teeth, glaring at Falon. For the first time she felt afraid. "Lying bitch!"

Rafael unleashed on the man. He backhanded him so hard he went airborne. As he came down, his head hit the edge of a low wooden table with a sickening thud. Even knowing what would happen, Falon hurried over to him. He didn't move. She knelt down and pressed her fingers to his neck. Rage. Pure black, unadulterated rage roiled through him. Falon didn't recoil. Instead, she focused, pushing the rage back, allowing none of it to contaminate her. She touched the rising lump at his right temple.

"What have you done?" Taylor shrieked coming toward his man but hesitating as he remembered what Rafael had done when he moved too fast toward Falon.

"Let him die," Rafael said, striding to Falon, ignoring Taylor, who was completely overwrought. Rafael extended his hand to Falon.

Falon looked pointedly up at him. "If he dies, we'll never find the girl. He's the key."

Rafael swore. "I never said I would look for her in the first place."

The man beneath her fingers moaned. He was coming to. Falon removed her hands, sat back on her heels, and looked up at Rafe. "You'll allow an innocent girl to die when you can prevent it?"

Rafael leaned down and drew Falon up. "I am not the keeper of the world's woes. I have my own problems at the moment. There's no time to waste chasing ghosts." He turned to Taylor. "I'm sorry, but I cannot help you."

"Cannot or will not?" Falon challenged, resisting his pull.

He stopped and looked angrily down at her. Rafael Vulkasin was not accustomed to defiance. He'd just have to get over it. Falon glanced at Taylor. His face had caved. He'd aged ten years in the last ten minutes. She looked angrily up at Rafael. How could he *not* help this man?

"You have no idea what you are asking of me. There is more at stake than you know," Rafael hissed. "Accept my answer. It is law here."

She got that. He walked around here like the Lord Almighty.

And maybe he was, but laws were meant to be broken. "A word with you, Rafael, in private," Falon softly said.

"There is nothing to discuss."

"After everything you have subjected me to, it's the least you can do." Beseeching, she looked at him. "Please." She hated sounding like the damsel in distress, but she needed to be heard. Her focus was on saving the girl, yes, but in doing so, she would save herself. She needed to get out of the compound if she were going to have any chance of escaping this madhouse.

"Jesus." He shook his head and strode angrily into what appeared to be his office, closing the door soundly behind them. She didn't spend time admiring it. She whirled on him and said, "That man with Taylor, Smythe, he's like Conan. Don't you see it?"

"Conan?"

"The *jaeger* dude from the other night."

She watched him bristle. "Salene, the Slayer?"

Falon waved her hands anxiously. "I don't know what the hell that is, but that guy out there has the same dark energy. Same black eyes when he's pissed. He gives me the creeps the same way Conan did. When he helped me up and I touched his hands, I heard the girl's screams, felt her terror. He's responsible for the girl's disappearance. He can lead us to her."

Rafael looked out the window of his office to the others. "I can always sense a Slayer. I do not sense that in him." He looked pointedly at Falon. "His eyes are blue, not black."

"I know what I saw," she insisted. She was not imagining any of this. "Can he hide it from you?"

Rafael's face hardened. Lucien had been fooled; the entire pack in his absence had been fooled. "Sometimes with black magic, if they are powerful enough. But when they are boastful, arrogant, or angry, I can see it in their eyes."

"I saw it!" Falon took a deep breath and slowly exhaled. "What—what do these Slayers slay?"

Rafael looked down at her and smirked. "Vulkasins and anyone associated with them."

Falon gasped, stepping back. That explained the desperation surrounding her. "Why Vulkasins? Conan called *me* a Slayer."

Rafael threw his head back and laughed despite the grim situation. "*You*? A Slayer?" His laugh deepened.

Falon flushed, angry that he was laughing at her.

He sensed her hurt. "You misunderstand my amusement, Falon. You're a brave girl, but to be Slayer, you must possess knowledge of the black arts, and the bloodlust to kill me and mine would have to be as much a part of your DNA as your beautiful blue eyes." He cocked his head and looked at her. "You are not evil. Do you wish to kill me?" He grinned. "Don't answer that." His tone lowered to serious when he asked, "Do you practice black magic?

Falon swallowed hard. No, but it intrigued her beyond normal curiosity, and she had once tried to conjure a spell. It hadn't gone well . . . "No," she croaked. Panic grasped her by the throat, cutting off her breath. What if she *was* a Slayer? Falon pushed the ridiculous thought out of her head. She was nothing like Conan or Smythe. All of that said, at the moment, right now, she had a real Slayer to deal with. "I'm telling you, he's a so-called Slayer, and if that's true, here he is in the Vulkasins' lair. Maybe that's why he kidnapped the girl, because he knew Taylor would come to you for help?"

Rafael's nostrils twitched. He looked out the window again then down to Falon. "You may be on to something there, girl." He nodded and said, "Let's play this out."

ONCE AGAIN, FALON'S intuition impressed him. In his gut, Rafael knew she had tapped into something. For a human, she had extraordinary insight and power. Salene had sensed it, too; perhaps that was all there was to his wanting her. He recognized the power and wanted her so that he could control it. That she could identify a Slayer when he could not bothered him on the highest level. Not that *she* could, but that Smythe's magic was so powerful he was able to hide his identity from a true alpha. With the rising impending, Slayers were positioning themselves any which way they could. The closer the better. And each Lycan they took out, especially an alpha, before the rising, was one less Lycan they had to fight for supremacy. Taylor had come to the right man after all. Rafe would look for the girl, and at the same time go hunting. The last thing Smythe would see in this world was Rafe's sword right before he cut his Slayer head off.

Rafe looked down at Falon, standing so righteously beside him. She was a worthy partner. His belly did a slow, weird roll. He felt a pull from her he had never experienced with a woman before. It should have excited him. Instead, it did the opposite. A deep sense of dread filled the void in him. He needed to focus on saving his race, not think whimsical thoughts of a woman who could be dead by the next sunrise. For now, he would indulge her but keep his hand close to his vest. If Smythe were a Slayer, he would lead Rafael straight to his clan, and then—he smiled inwardly—heads would roll.

Rafe took Falon's hand and led her back into the great room. Nervous energy snapped around them. Rafe looked pointedly at Taylor's companion, "What is your full name, sir?"

He bowed his head submissively. "Harold. Harold Smythe." He stepped toward Rafael and offered his hand. Rafael slowly shook it. He waited for a sign that he was shaking hands with a Slayer but felt nothing but cool, clammy skin. He looked directly into the man's blue eyes, wanting indisputable confirmation that he was what Falon said he was. Nothing. If it were anyone else than Falon who made the claim, Rafe would tell Taylor to take a hike. His own instincts were sharp and they told him to trust Falon's. And so he did, but his cautious nature also told him to be on guard.

"What do you do for Mr. Taylor?"

"Harry is my COO," Taylor said, stepping toward them. "What he does is irrelevant, Rafael. I trust him implicitly with my life and the life of my daughter. His integrity is beyond reproach." He grasped Rafael's arm. "I—I fell for your woman's foolishness, but in my heart I know—" His expression twisted painfully as he looked at Falon then back to Rafe. "At least give me the satisfaction of seeing my daughter avenged. I will give you everything I own."

Rafael's instincts had kicked in, and he now accepted that Falon sensed something he had not. It bothered him that she had an awareness he didn't, but at the same time, he felt proud to be her mate. She was brave. Strong. Special. "I'll look for your daughter's abductors," Rafael said, uncomfortable with the degree of relief that swept over Taylor's face. "But *when* I bring your daughter to you, alive, I will name my price. Do you agree to honor it?"

Taylor nodded vigorously. "Anything you want is yours."

Rafael regarded Falon then Smythe. "My woman says the girl is alive. I want to see your proof that she's dead."

Smythe stammered for a moment then withdrew a manila envelope from his jacket pocket. He handed it to Rafael. "The pictures and a CD arrived in the mail this morning. She's been missing for two days. If it was staged, the producer should get an Academy Award."

Rafael pulled out one gory picture after another from the envelope. It showed the girl strung up, then—he swallowed hard—dismembered. "Jesus," he said.

Falon moved as if she wanted to see the pictures. He shoved them back into the envelope. "You don't want to see them."

"If I'm going to help you find her, I need to see them."

"No one said you would be involved."

"*I* said." She grabbed the envelope from his hand and pulled them out.

Anton made a funny sound. When Rafael shot him a harsh glare, Anton stared at something interesting on the ceiling.

Rafael watched Falon's smooth, honey-colored skin blanch white. Her hand shook, but she maintained her composure. Quietly, she slipped them back into the envelope. She looked at Taylor. "I'm so sorry, Mr. Taylor."

"Are they real?" he demanded.

"They look real, but my gut is telling me she is alive." She handed the envelope back to Rafael.

He withdrew the CD from the envelope. Without a word, he walked over to the elaborate sound system and put it in a player, then pressed the Play button. Terrifying high-pitched screams echoed in the room. Falon put her hands over her ears, the heart-wrenching sounds too much to bear. Rafael stood rigid next to her. Anton remained stoic beside Taylor, who looked like he was going to collapse. Smythe tried to console him. After several minutes of the same heart-wrenching sounds, Rafael hit the Stop button. "Is there more than that? Any dialogue?"

"No," Smythe answered. "Just the buzz of the chainsaw and Ally's screams."

Rafe took the CD from the player and slipped it back into the envelope. "Has there been any demand?"

"No," Smythe answered, since Taylor was too traumatized to stand, much less talk. He had collapsed into a chair. "Nothing."

"Go home, Mr. Taylor. Give me forty-eight hours, and I'll either find your daughter alive or the person responsible for her death."

Smythe helped Taylor up. Taylor moved slowly toward Rafael and took his hands into his. Had he allowed him to, Taylor would have kissed them. But Rafe shook his head and withdrew them. "Go home. I'll take care of it."

As the men exited the building, Falon turned on him. "How could you make such a promise?"

Rafael smiled. "You don't know me very well, my dear."

"But how can you be *sure*?"

Rafael's smile widened, and he did something that completely shocked him even as it felt completely right. With the envelope in one hand, he extended his other to Falon. "Let me help you upstairs so that you can clean up. Then I will show you."

As Falon showered, Rafael stared out the window into the dark. He lifted the envelope to his nose and deeply inhaled. A myriad of scents swirled around him. He pulled out the pictures. Now, fewer scents. But more distinguishable. He sniffed the CD and smiled. Fewer still.

He felt the rush in his blood. Not simply because he'd soon be hunting but because Falon would accompany him. Her powers were formidable, and her Slayer detector honed. Would that each pack had a woman of Falon's talents among them, many lives would be saved. Smythe wasn't the first Slayer to fool an alpha. Lucien's woman had done so with little effort. Rafe would give his right arm to know where Falon came from, who her people were. He believed her when she said she was an orphan. Did she have Amorak blood flowing through her veins? There were few Amorak, and those of blended Lycan and Inuit blood that had the skill to heal. He himself possessed great healing power given to him by his mother, who was a direct descendant of the great mother Singarti. How did a human come by the gift? And that thing she did when she was pissed, shooting off mental lightning bolts? If she did not practice black magic, then how?

He smiled when he recalled what she had done to Lucien. She

may just give his brother a run for his money. His smile tightened. She was too special for the likes of Lucien. Destroying Falon would benefit no one but his brother's bloodlust for revenge.

Rafael looked toward the bathroom door as it opened. His heart caught high in his throat, and blood slammed straight down to his dick. She looked all sexy and dewy wrapped in a big, fluffy towel. She scowled at him. "I don't have any clothes that will fit over this cursed cast."

He set the envelope down and sauntered toward her. He smiled. Couldn't help himself. He wanted to touch her. Run his hands down the soft, sultry skin of her back to her ass. Feel her breasts push against his chest—

"I'll make a deal with you," he said, his voice husky, making no mistake of his desire.

She cocked a suspicious brow.

"I heal your ankle, and you promise not to run away."

"I'll make a deal with you. I help you find the girl, and you let me go."

He respected that she didn't beg for her life. Instead, she challenged him at every turn, making it more difficult to deny her. Most women would be mewling and frightened right now. But not Falon.

"Then you stay here, while I find the girl," he softly said, praying she would not accept his command. He wanted her as his hunting partner tonight.

She smiled then, a big, bright, sexy smile. She stepped into his space. Rising on her toes, she pressed her lips to his but did not actually kiss him. His body tightened as the furnace in his loins flared. "I don't think so." She backed away and dropped the towel. She looked over her shoulder and threw him a slow come-hither smile. His body jerked as if he dangled from the end of a rope. And damned if she didn't bat those long black lashes at him, and ask, "Since when did I become your woman?"

His entire body swelled with desire. He didn't fight it. He was alpha; she was his, damn it. Rafe growled and stepped to her. He touched her shoulders, his fingers instantly reacting to the smooth heat of her skin. He traced his fingertips across the concave of her shoulder and turned her around. His body tightened, more blood slammed to his dick, and his lips dropped to the mark on her neck. He nipped her. She gasped but did not pull away. He nipped her again, wanting to throw her onto the bed and sink into her. *Jesus.* He felt her body loosen, smelled her musky release. What had they been discussing? He closed his eyes and inhaled her scent. It was potent. Hot. Irresistible. He forced his mind to clear. "Since I marked you," he growled in answer to her question. His hands slid down her bare back to her ass just as he had imagined moments before. He rose hard against her belly. She pressed against him. He hissed in a sharp breath. "So long as you live, Falon, you belong to me. You can run, but you can't hide." With every ounce of self-restraint he possessed, and very reluctantly, he set her from him. "Do not forget it."

She stiffened against him. Anger reverberated between them. "What is the Blood Law? What part do I play in it?"

Her questions caught him off guard. They shouldn't have. Of course she wanted answers. "For any organization or civilization to thrive and coexist, there must be a code of conduct and rules by which they are governed. My group is governed by the Blood Law."

"Why does your brother have the right to take my life?"

Guilt stabbed at him. "He doesn't." It was true. "However, the council of elders, our governing body, doesn't agree."

"Then why do you act as if he does?"

Rafe raked his fingers through his hair, not wanting to have this conversation now. Not ever. He could not sway the council, though he had tried. His frustration with them reached a new high. It was not just what they demanded of him.

"It's complicated."

"Complicated?" she shrilled. "You hold my life in your hands, and all you can tell me is, it's complicated?" He stood quiet, unable to defend himself.

"I don't want to die. I *will not* die because of your Blood Law. If that messes with your day, too damn bad."

She grabbed the towel from the floor, her ass brushing against his cock. Rafe swallowed hard. And was grateful when she huffed back into the bathroom, slamming the door behind her.

He let out a long breath and jammed his fingers through his hair again. What was he supposed to say to her? How could he justify her death when he knew with a certainty it was Lucien who should have paid the penalty, not he! Perhaps he should let her escape. Aid her. Cover her scent and hope Lucien did not find her. He was torn in half. There was so much more at stake than one life. He shook his head, forcing that part of his future from his thoughts. The here and now was what was important. Tonight he would hunt. "The clock is ticking. We need to go!" he called after her.

Several minutes later, Falon emerged, dressed in the fresh clothes he had instructed one of the beta females to purchase that day. She looked hot in the tight black jeans, even with one pant leg rolled up above her cast. The form-fitting blue jersey shirt matched her eyes perfectly. She could only wear one of the black leather boots. He imagined her in thigh-high stiletto boots. And nothing else. His dick lengthened again. Damn. He wanted her in the worst way. Right there, right then. Whether she wanted it or not.

He grabbed the envelope before he did something she'd never forgive him for and extended his hand. "Come."

* * *

FALON CHOSE TO put their conversation aside for the moment. Not because she needed Rafael to save her. Thank you very much, she would save herself. Her newfound powers gave her a confidence she had never experienced. She should have embraced her differences years ago. It would have saved her so much misery. But here, with Rafael, she wasn't shunned. Instead, he embraced her differences; he was the catalyst to their fruition. Maybe she and he were more alike than different. For those reasons alone she didn't pursue their conversation. It wasn't like he would indulge her with answers anyway. More importantly, she had a life to save.

She looked at his strong outstretched hand, well aware of the power held within. Separated from him she was not her most powerful. She slid her hand into his. Warm energy thrummed from his body into hers. United, they would be a formidable force. She looked up at him and saw that he, too, understood the potency of their union. When his fingers possessively entwined with hers, Falon followed him out the door.

As if a lightning storm followed overhead, energy snapped and crackled around them. Falon was beyond excited, beyond curious at what the night would hold, and more than anything, beyond fascinated.

Rafael fascinated her. The way he walked as if he owned the world. The way everyone respected him. The compound and its inhabitants fascinated her, and her primal reaction to him each time he touched her fascinated her.

It terrified her, too. While she would escape this place, part of her understood that what was driving Rafael was his honor—an honor that demanded he follow some ridiculous law, even if he didn't want to.

What also fascinated Falon was her emerging personality and

strength. Who knew? She had always hidden. Done everything in her power to stay below the radar. She had taught herself how to blend in so seamlessly she didn't appear to be anything but an innocuous blip. Around Rafael, she felt alive for the first time in her life. Parts of her she hadn't even known existed had emerged. With a vengeance. Least of all her primal sexual awareness. She didn't need to read the headlines to tell her Rafe felt her pull as much as she felt his.

When he had called her "my woman" in front of Anton, she'd been shocked, but in a cavewoman way, she'd also been pleased. Her body trilled when she thought of his big powerful body claiming hers. Her nipples tightened, her breathing became labored, she was wet—

Abruptly Rafael stopped and pushed her up against the wall in the foyer. His eyes flashed, and his nostrils flared. "I swear to God, Falon, if you don't turn that off, I'm going to fuck you right here."

"I—"

Rafael grabbed her to his chest; his lips crushed down on hers. Her body jerked as if she'd been shocked. Every part of her responded. The chemistry between them was as shocking as it was terrifying. As quickly as the kiss began, it ended. Falon could barely breathe, much less form a coherent thought. He pressed his forehead against hers as he struggled for composure. His eyes had darkened to the color of a moonless night, their intensity unwavering. Falon lifted her lips to his, wanting more from him. His jaw clenched. "Don't. Just don't." He grabbed her hand again and pulled her through the large doorway. Dazed and confused, wondering what it was she had done to provoke such a reaction from him, Falon stumbled behind him.

"Saddle up, boys," he called over his shoulder to the crowd they had just passed through in the great room. "We're going hunting tonight!"

Eleven

A FEW SHORT moments later, out in the large circular yard, choppers roared to life. "Release hell!" Rafael shouted to Anton over the revving V-twins.

Hell indeed! Falon stiffened as the pack of those black beasts, the same ones that had chased her up a tree, came galloping toward them. Automatically, she backed away, her gaze riveted to their basketball-sized heads and gaping jaws. Ignoring her discomfort, Rafael strode fearlessly toward the animal that had nearly chomped her foot off. It jumped up, placing its huge paws on Rafael's chest. As if they were long-lost friends, Rafael scratched the beast behind the ears as he spoke to him. Rafael's words were low and commanding, yet respectful and even affectionate. His easy rapport with the beast should have surprised her, but as she was learning, there was far more to Rafael Vulkasin than his good looks and temper.

The animal howled and then bolted toward the closed gates.

Falon watched in stunned awe as he leapt high into the air and over the two-story wall, nary a paw touching.

Rafael straddled his chopper and looked over his shoulder at her. He nodded, indicating she should hop on. And what? Ride off into the night in search of the girl? It's what they were going to do. Why now did she hesitate? A big crazy part of her wanted to throw caution to the wind and ride behind Rafael as if she had some right. But the smart part of her knew to even think about trusting him would be a fatal mistake. Wanting to find the girl aside, this is why she pushed so hard to go in search of her, get out of the compound, and make her getaway. And to that end she nodded, more than willing to ride bitch.

It was not easy. As she tried to mount the bike in a graceful manner, she failed miserably. Her balance was compromised by the weight of her cast. Reaching out, Rafael grabbed her arm, steadying her as she threw her leg over the back fender and precariously settled on what little piece of seat was available.

Unlike some others in his gang, who had bikes with two distinct seats, Raphael rode stag. She glanced at the women who had followed the men out into the yard and found several of them gazing narrowed-eyed at her. Falon raised her chin. The woman in her felt a spike of possessive pride that Rafael wanted her to ride with him. Besides, what did she care what they thought of her? She was not coming back here.

"What about a helmet?" she asked over the low rumble of the engine.

Rafael flashed her a disarming smile and patted her on the right thigh. She caught herself from throwing herself into his arms. His smile, holy moly, it changed everything about him. He was happy once. A long time ago. She knew it as surely as she was sitting behind him. What changed it? "You're safe with me."

"Right. Until you hand me over to your brother . . ." His grin faded. And for that she was sorry. She knew he didn't smile much. That he had for her, warmed her. There she went again; all he had to do was smile at her, and she turned to putty. Jesus, she was losing it. Focus, Falon. Focus on getting away. Far, *far* away.

As the chopper lurched forward, Falon grabbed hold of Rafael's waist. When the gates opened and they swarmed out into the night, she held on for dear life. At the same time, she stayed alert, familiarizing herself with her surroundings. The bright moon was waxing, and oddly, her vision was so sharp she could decipher the trees from the brush and even, if she squinted, see the roosting birds perched on their branches. She shook her head, confused by her continued transformation. In less than a week she had become superwoman. In less than a week she had lost her virginity to a mysterious, powerful man who, though he fought it, was honor bound to hand her over to his brother.

She didn't want to die. Not now. Not here. Not this way. Despite her dreary existence, the night she met Rafael, a tiny flame had sparked in her. Since then, it had ignited into an inferno she could scarcely control. Most of the time didn't want to control it. A flame named Rafael. He'd started something in her she wanted on the most basic level to finish. She wanted to live. She wanted to thrive. She would fight for that right. She refused to be the sacrificial lamb in some blood feud between anyone. But she had work to do first. After having felt the malevolence in Smythe, she could not in good conscience let an innocent little girl be victimized. She would help in any way she could to see that the girl was returned safely to her family. After that? She was gone.

How ironic. Despite their temporary truce to search for the little girl, Raphael, the man who had breathed life into her, could be her demise. But he was also the man who believed her about Smythe. He made it difficult to resist him. In another place and another time, she might . . .

She looked around at the saddled bikers hell-bent on saving a little girl. To all appearances, they seemed like your average everyday people. Even for bikers, there was an air of respectability and intelligence about them. Not the rough trade stereotype. Even more paradoxical was Rafael Vulkasin, who was for all appearances a biker. But he was so much more than that. He looked like he had just stepped out of a *GQ* shoot. His hair was stylishly cut, his clothes designer. He was intelligent, well-spoken, a gentlemen at his core. But he was also lethal. And protective. *Over*protective.

When someone or something threatened her, be it his beloved beasts or that man Smythe, he was on it like white on rice. Was it because he cared for her or because he didn't want her to die by any other hand than his brother's?

Falon's spine stiffened. She'd fight Rafael, his brother, or anyone else who thought they had the right to take her life. She looked longingly into the darkness that sped past her.

Her confidence was building. All she needed was a small head start. She might not be able to wield a sword, but those mental lightning bolts—when they came—worked pretty good. Next time Rafael tried to force her to stay put, she would see how it worked on him.

Rafael.

The tension in her back eased. He did something to her. Something she had no control over. And in a weird twist of fate, she knew she had the same effect on him.

Her arms tightened around his waist. She laid her cheek against his back and closed her eyes. Heat swept though her. Blood pumped through her veins, stimulating nerves and pheromones. As her body awoke, so did his. His scent intensified. Hers responded. This was crazy! He was as aroused as she.

Rafael, why must I die?

The Blood Law demands it.

Falon's eyes flew open and she jerked back, nearly toppling off the bike. What had just happened? Had Rafael heard her? Could he read her thoughts?

Deep, laconic, dangerous laughter reverberated in her head. So similar to Rafael's but so different. Lucien! He was dark, angry, impulsive. He wore his hatred for his brother like a neon sign. Whereas Rafael was the bright light of sanity, and a man who she suspected would move mountains to close the chasm between him and his brother, Lucien was the complete opposite. He would not be happy until he destroyed his brother. Why? What had Rafael done to Lucien to elicit such hatred? She shivered. And for the love of God, how was she part of this feud between them? Laws were meant to broken. Who enforced this Blood Law? And how the hell could Lucien read her thoughts?

My brother may have marked you, lovely, but my blood flows in your veins now, as yours does in mine. I can take you whenever and wherever I like . . .

Falon closed her eyes and mentally shoved him from her thoughts, much like she did when she first met him. His laughter faded away. How dare he invade her thoughts? How was she, a stranger, responsible for settling a feud? She tightened her arms around Rafael. She believed him when he said she was safe tonight. But what about tomorrow? She would die before she allowed Lucien to touch her. And so her determination to run tonight grew stronger.

As the bikes ate up the miles, the night grew darker. Falon kept her cheek pressed to Rafael's back and found peace in his quiet strength. When she looked down at the rushing asphalt, Falon's stomach rolled with nausea.

Up to now, she'd missed them, but running on either side of her and keeping up with the motorcycle were two of those humungous black beasts. The biggest one, the one that had torn her boot off, ran to her right. His long tongue lolled out of the side of his mouth, the only sign that he exerted any energy at all. She looked over her shoulder to see the rest of the pack loping easily behind them. Their powerful legs ate up the road with their long, ground-eating strides.

Where was the big golden wolf? Wasn't he their leader?

She shook her head, allowing the cool night air to tear through her long strands and fought to keep her waning balance. She was living in the twilight zone. In just the few days since Rafael brought her to his place, it seemed as if a lifetime had passed. Each day was more bizarre and confusing than the day before. But really, should that surprise her?

She *was* different. She knew that while she was human, she had otherworldly traits. She could see into certain people's hearts and souls. And now, when she was terrified or angry, she could shoot mental lightning bolts.

And . . . there was something else. Something that terrified her more than the brothers. Her rages were flaring with more regularity. No kidding, she thought. Look at the situation you're in. Anyone would be pissed off. But what happened inside her when her anger flared, barely controllable, bothered her more than her newfound ability to zap people when she felt threatened. Her whole body hurt, down to her bones. She felt as if she were being torn apart, and since her arrival at the Vulkasin compound it had progressed rapidly. She'd seen red when Anton struck Lana. She wanted to tear him apart. The first time she'd felt a hint of this pain was when she was twelve, just before she'd killed for the first time.

Falon squeezed her eyes shut and shook her head, not wanting to think of that night. But images rushed her consciousness.

It had been a bleak night. The kind horror movies opened with. She'd run from her fifth foster home after a particularly severe beating. Her rage had risen with a ferocity that terrified her. Not wanting to hurt anyone, she took off. It was cold and dark, the air still yet full of energy. The only light showing her the way down the dark and dangerous alley was the muted glow of the full moon through the thick clouds. She'd felt out of sorts. The pain she was becoming familiar with had begun. Ironically, it was also the same day she got her period for the first time. Talk about PMS! A man followed her—and tried to force himself upon her. Her survival instinct flared. What came next appalled her, but she had no choice. No control. She'd—she'd torn him apart. Literally. With his blood on her hands, she ran. She was still running.

Her arms tightened around Rafael's waist. Not for comfort but because she was afraid she would work herself up into such a tizzy, she'd fall off the chopper and kill herself or worse be torn to shreds by those black beasts surrounding her.

She wasn't prepared for what Rafael did. He dropped his left hand to her tightly gripped ones over his waist and covered them. His big, fingerless leather-gloved hand squeezed hers reassuringly. When he didn't remove his hand but kept it protectively clasped around hers, she felt herself relax. When he began to absently stroke her skin, she stiffened. So did he. Abruptly, Rafael released her hands and returned his to the handle grip.

His action and her reaction distressed her. What was happening between them? There was a pull toward Rafe she could not shake. At times, she didn't want to. In another place and in another time, social outcast though she was, if she were brave enough, she might have the courage to pursue him until he belonged to her.

A primal possessiveness took hold of her. It dug deep into her fiber. She wanted him, she realized, physically as well as emotionally. Did it make her insane, weak, and just plain brain dead that, despite the fact that he would not lift a finger to save her life, she still wanted him?

Was she psychotic? What had happened to her that she would feel so deeply for a man she barely knew and who did not value her life? She shook her head and sat back on the small piece of seat she was allowed, and released her hands to grasp the sides of the seat. As she did, the bike hit a pothole. In a dizzying tumble, she went flying backward.

Falon screamed, instinctivly tucking into a fetal position to avoid injury. As she did, her fall turned into a slow motion movie reel. Out of body, she heard her screams, high and tinged with genuine fear. She closed her eyes, not wanting to see herself go splat and die. She knew no matter how tight she tucked, her entire body would turn into a bloody pulp as soon as she hit the road. Instead, as she flew toward the rushing asphalt, two strong arms caught her in midair, then pulled her close to his hard body, tucked and rolled at a maddening pace along the asphalt, taking the brunt of the impact.

When they stopped rolling and came to a stop on the gravelly shoulder, Falon kept her eyes closed and her body tucked. Her heart beat so hard, her rib cage hurt. The sounds of the bikes as they idled met her ears. Wet slobbery tongues lapped at her limbs, accompanied by whines of inquiry.

Long, possessive fingers brushed over every inch of her body, touching, pausing, then moving on. Hot spots on her knees, elbows, and her hip flared. Flat on her back, she opened her eyes and looked up to find Rafael's deep turquoise-colored eyes above staring intently at her. He brushed a strand of hair from her cheek. Falon shivered. It was a loving touch. Reverent. She opened her mouth to answer, but words got stuck in her throat. He wanted something from her. Something far more profound than her body. She could see it in his eyes. A deep yearning for something she could not give him: peace.

"Are you hurt?" he asked, his voice low and gravelly.

Taking mental inventory, she shook her head as sensations

registered. Just scrapes, nothing broken, and a shimmering warmth along her skin that had nothing to do with injuries. She could have been bleeding out and she would not have noticed because of the way he was looking at her. The way he made her feel knocked her so far off balance she constantly felt as if she were in a free fall.

"I'm okay. Are you hurt?" she asked, carefully sitting up. Her gaze raked him from his head to his boots. Not a scratch that she could see, and barely a tear on his leathers.

"I'm fine." He stood and instead of helping her up, he lifted her up into his arms and turned with her. "Anton!" he called.

The man dismounted his bike and hurried toward them. Falon realized every eye of the pack of bikers was riveted on her. The men appeared restless. Had they worried about her, too? And how the hell had Rafael managed to save her and remain unscathed?

A red glow pulsed behind his turquoise eyes when he looked down at her. His concern was gone. "What the hell were you thinking? We were going eighty-five miles an hour for hell's sake! You could have killed yourself!" he raged at her.

She twisted out of his grip, knowing that had he wanted to keep her in his arms, he would have. She was gaining strength every day, but it didn't come close to his. Falon stepped back, almost tripping over her cast, but she held her ground. She pointed a finger at his chest and jabbed him. "What the hell do you care if I die right here, right now?"

She looked at the four dozen men surrounding her. At the hunger etched deeply into their faces. A hunger and a weariness that held on to each one of them like a festering plague. It was palpable. Who were they, and what did they want from her?

Rafael reached out a hand to her. "I care."

She slapped his hand away. "You care about yourself."

He opened his mouth to defend himself but thought better of it and closed it. He whistled two short whistles, and the big black beast that had almost taken her foot off trotted over to Rafael. He said something in a foreign language to the animal. It growled. As the growl ended, Falon's blood froze in her veins.

Though she had no idea what they meant, she had heard similar words before. From her mother. A ghost of a woman. The last recollection she had of her was when she was around five years old. There had been a deep sadness in her mother that transcended centuries of pain and suffering.

"What did you say to him?" Falon demanded.

Rafael glared down at her. "It's none of your business." She bristled. He was so bipolar! One minute all caring, now pissed and indifferent. And rude.

Rafael looked over at Anton. "I'm taking your ride, see what Jor-Don can do with mine. You take his bike."

Anton nodded and dismounted his chopper. Rafael mounted it and looked to Falon. "Come. The girl is alive and within ten miles."

Falon's eyes widened. "How do you know that?"

He moved up and stood, giving her ample room to mount. "I just do. Now get on."

Falon did as she was told. Her heart fluttered anxiously. The girl was alive! Sweet Jesus, she had been right! And if she were right about the girl, then she was right about Smythe. She looked up at Rafael before she swung her left leg over the studded seat. "What about Smythe?"

"We'll take care of him after we secure the girl."

TEN MINUTES LATER, Rafael raised his hand in a stop position and pulled over just inside a large, dilapidated industrial park. Nary a light shone from the large, sagging buildings surrounding them. Shattered windows gaped like fanged ghosts at them. Stacks of broken pallets were strewn, some stacked lining sagging cyclone fences. Empty rusted drums lay in disarray as if they were dropped from the air and left where they landed. Large tumbleweeds hugged the fence twenty feet deep, their escape ending there. Old chemical scents lingered faintly in the air. The park looked much like what Rafael imagined the world would look like after Armageddon. Dark, desolate, lifeless. Not even a rat hid among the debris.

Yet, despite the lifeless stillness of the area, Rafael could smell the stench of a Slayer and the pungent scent of a terrified child. Three hundred yards ahead.

Rafe cut his engine and hopped off. "Stay here," he commanded Falon. He watched her stiffen. If the situation wasn't so dire, he'd smile. She was growing quite a backbone. Gone was the confused girl he rescued.

He gave the kill sign to the rest of the pack. The engines hushed, and he had his men's rapt attention. "Slayers ahead. Three hundred yards. I'm going to go get the lay of the land, I'll be back shortly." Rafe whistled for Angor, turned, and jogged north, deeper into the park.

Twelve

AS RAFE QUIETLY approached the warehouse, he motioned for the Berserker to watch his back. He did a quick scan for mounted cameras. None that were detectable. First mistake. Quickly he shifted into wolf form, then jumped nimbly to the roof and trotted over to a large round fan cover. He grasped the edge with his teeth and pulled it toward him, then looked down.

The warehouse was small as warehouses went. Maybe thirty-five thousand square feet of footage, empty space except for a large shrouded platform in the middle. He salivated as the scents wafted up to him. It was surrounded by armed Slayers. His keen sense of smell picked up the scent of a child. He poked his head farther in. Where was she? Hidden beneath the shroud? Had to be. There was no other place in the warehouse she could be. He turned his attention back to the Slayers.

Rafael's pulse picked up speed.

These were not your average run-of-the-mill Slayers; these were clan Corbet Slayers. Direct descendants of the first wolf Slayer, Peter. They were motivated by something more powerful than the black magic they had mastered. Clan Corbet was powered by their untold hatred of wolves and anything or anyone remotely related to them, including the Amorak. And who should be pacing anxiously atop the platform awaiting him? Edward. Second only in command to his brother, Balor, master of all Slayers. He had more than a Lycan versus Slayer score to settle with the bastard. It was personal. Edward had held his mother down while his oldest brother, Thomas, skinned her alive.

Rafe's blood quickened, his thirst for vengeance so strong he could taste it. What a coup. Through his complex network, Rafael learned only recently that Balor was back East, drumming up mercenaries for the rising, which left Edward in charge. If Rafe took out Edward tonight, it would send the entire Slayer community into a panic. They were very much like Lycans in that if their leaders were eliminated, the clans floundered. They needed strong leaders to survive.

Clad in chain mail, the ancient war garb of his founding father, including two nasty looking broadswords, Edward strode back and forth along the platform as if he were king of the world.

He wouldn't be for long. Rafe smelled his anticipation. All of the Slayers were hyped and ready to kill. The chemical stench of meth oozed from their pores. Compliments of the Vipers. Their excitement and eagerness for battle was palpable. But so was his packs'. Rafe resisted the urge to tip his head back and howl. Oh, how sweet his victory would be tonight. He would not have another chance like this. Not before the rising.

He smiled in the dark and backed away, dropped to the ground, and stealthily inspected the perimeter. His nose twitched as he approached the main entrance. He stepped to the door and sniffed.

The fur on the back of his neck stood on end. C-4. He sniffed the entire perimeter of the building, locating the same scent at the smaller back doors. The higher windows, though, were clean. Quickly he shifted and dressed. He whistled softly for Angor, who had shadowed him. Together they trotted back to the pack.

"It's a trap," Rafael softly said as he approached his men.

Falon's head snapped up. "What do you mean?"

"Slayers. At least a dozen, methed out and waiting for us to storm the gates and rescue the girl."

"What are you going to do?" she asked.

Rafael smiled. "Storm the gates and rescue the girl."

"But—"

"Knowing what we're up against will give us the edge."

"But what if they just open fire on you? How can you protect yourself against that?" Falon asked as a cloud of doom darkened her thoughts.

Rafael threw his head back and laughed. "Are you worried about me?"

Of course, she was worried about him! He had—the sex thing alone made her care. There were other more poignant reasons, reasons she ignored. Reasons that if she escaped, wouldn't matter. Not if she were to survive. Falon snorted. "Hardly. If you die, I have a better chance of surviving."

Rafael turned serious. That was true. Truer than she knew.

His gaze locked for a long, silent moment with Falon's. He knew she was special, so special Salene wanted her. So special, Rafael, an alpha, had marked her, a human, before he knew her. So special she could jump high fences, read people's minds, and sniff out a Slayer among a pack of Lycans. So special she could disarm an alpha as powerful as his brother with a glare. Sacrificing her for the sake of the Blood Law was not going to be easy. And it would be a sacrifice.

Despite his hard heart, in just a few days, she had wormed her way under his skin.

If he were the impetuous type, Rafe might sacrifice his life for hers. But his life was invaluable to the Lycan nation. Rafael knew if he died before the rising, so, too, would his people. His chest tightened painfully with the longing that would come when she was gone and the resentment of the law that failed them both as well as regret for what he could not stop, though he would sacrifice anything, save his people, to prevent her death. He forced the debilitating feelings aside. There was no room for weakness in his life.

He raised his nose into the air and deeply inhaled the dark and dangerous scents swirling around him. Tonight would be a good beginning to the end. Twelve Slayers in one fell swoop? It would be like hitting a million dollar jackpot at Harrah's. Salene and his flunky had been nice notches on his belt. The Eye of Fenrir was more than icing on the cake. The Eye of Fenrir had been like hitting a progressive lottery. He was set. The ring flared on his hand in agreement.

Tonight it would aid him in getting his hands on that pissant, Edward. With Thomas's disappearance more than two decades ago, and his presumed death, next on Rafe's list was Balor. With Balor eliminated, the Slayers would run like cockroaches when you lifted the rock they hid under. Each one of them going in a different direction, making it easy for his pack to pick them off one by one, until finally they would be extinct.

If he could do it all before the Blood Moon rising, all the better. Even if he couldn't eliminate Balor or Edward before that fateful night, he would eliminate as many Slayers as he could get his sword into, thus weakening them from the flank and working his way in.

Rafael snarled, anger at his brother's continued solitude infuriating him more than usual. Over the years Lucien's arrogance had mushroomed. He had no grasp of the reality of what they faced. Yes, Lucien did his fair share of hunting, but neither Rafe nor Sharia could get it through his arrogant brother's head that united, they would have had a chance. Divided, they were doomed unless the gods chose to bestow a miracle on them.

Now to complicate matters was Falon. How could he rail against Lucien for his refusal to unite the packs, if he, Rafael Vulkasin, ignored the laws written in his ancestors' blood?

And so it had come to pass. Pack Vulkasin regularly hunted, reducing the Slayer population one soul at a time, and never did his pack go to ground without a kill. The Slayers didn't make it easy. They trained hard and regularly. They also had an advantage in battle. While Lycans were stronger, faster, and more agile, a Slayer could only be destroyed by decapitation, and only by a Lycan sword, whereas Lycans could be destroyed with a single silver bullet to the heart. The Slayers had turned cowardly over the years. Taking long-distance sniper shots or using AKs loaded with silver rounds. Lycans lived on high alert twenty-four/seven. The faintest scent of a Slayer put them on the offensive, and instead of being the hunted, they became the hunter. Tonight would be no different.

"Rafael," Falon said, tugging at his shirtsleeve, jarring him back to the present. He blinked, unable to remember what they were discussing. He looked down into her pleading eyes, and he remembered. He wanted to sink his fingers into her thick, silky hair and kiss her, to reassure her he would survive this night and, gods willing, the rising. But he didn't, because while he may survive, she most likely would not. It ate at him. She held value to the Lycan nation, and she was innocent of his and Lucien's battles. Why should she pay? Was there no way to convince the council to spare her life?

Rafael swiped his hand across his chin. To even challenge the Blood Law was punishable by death. He had no say. He was bound to uphold it. And so he would. Rafe looked past Falon to his men, who moved restlessly about.

"Prepare for battle!"

Moments later, donned in bulletproof vests with triple-ply trauma plates over their hearts, they pushed their bikes to within one hundred yards of the warehouse.

"Do you smell that?" Rafael asked Yuri, his third in command and Anton's first cousin.

The tall blond Vulkasin nodded. "C-4," Yuri growled.

Rafael nodded. "And a lot of it."

Yuri's grim expression reflected exactly how Rafe was feeling. But it didn't matter. Just like the explosives didn't matter. They were here to get the girl, and get the girl they would. But first, they were going to make hash out of every Slayer in there.

They'd show Edward and his men as much mercy as they showed Rafe's mother. Rage swelled as his beast clawed for release.

Memories washed over Rafe. Every year, on the anniversary of Rafe's parents' deaths, Balor managed to get his hands on either a Vulkasin or Mondragon. What he did to them was not fit for hell. Rafael's rage and hatred festered in his belly like an abscess. His yearning for vengeance had mushroomed since the last full moon.

Rafael fought the urge to throw his head back and howl. That night had been a bloody but fruitful raid. More than two dozen Slayers, among them Edward's youngest son, Robert, had fallen beneath their swords. Rafael had taken great pleasure in cutting down Edward's arrogant progeny. Robert had taunted Rafe for years about how his father held Rafe's mother down while his uncle skinned her alive. But what cost the little bastard his life was when during the last raid, Robert wagged a shammy under Rafe's nose. His mother's scent still clung to it. His mother's skin, Robert used it to shine his slick hot rod. Right before Edward's horrified eyes, Rafe skinned his only son alive. Upon returning to the compound, Rafe ordered Stanza, the pack tanner, to retool his chopper seat with the Slayer's skin. Now Robert's skin felt his ass each time he mounted his bike.

An eye for an eye.

Blood Law.

A growl rumbled in Yuri's throat, almost as if he could read Rafe's mind.

Rafe studied his friend. Yuri reminded Rafe of a Viking. Tall, thick, and blond, he was quiet, respectful, highly intelligent. At his core, however, he was a bloodthirsty warrior. His need for vengeance against the Slayers was as strong as Rafael's and Lucien's. Yuri's mother had been mutilated by Balor.

Thinking of his friend's grief, Rafe's rage built. His body tightened. The color of blood clouded his vision. He clenched his fists, setting his jaw. His bones began to shift.

No, damn it! Rafe fought to tamp down the beast within. He didn't want to shift in front of Falon. One, because he didn't want to scare her any more than she was. Two, he didn't want to see the contempt in her eyes when he retook his human form.

It bothered him that he even cared, but he could not deny he felt protective of her—and himself.

He turned back to Yuri. "If it were me inside, waiting for the cavalry to come busting through the front doors, I'd have rigged the C-4 to blow when the doors opened. Anyone within thirty yards would catch the blast as they got bottlenecked trying to come through."

Yuri nodded. "Yet we can't ride through the windows."

Rafael's gaze rose to the high windows and ways to access them. They were only two stories tall. No problem for his Berserkers. "Send the Berserkers to the rear of the building. Instruct them to split in half.

Between the windows. Tell them to make entry only after they hear the blasts we're going to make from the front and rear entry points," Rafe ordered.

Yuri's eyes widened to huge. "Tell them—? Are you mad? They won't listen to me!"

Rafael scoffed. "Angor will take your instruction." As only Rafael could, he alerted Angor to follow Yuri's directions to the letter. "Now go. And, Yuri? Tell them to make a lot of noise when they come in. I want every Slayer in the building to shit themselves."

"Gotcha." Yuri bounded away, stealthy as the wolf he was. Quickly Rafe turned his attention back to the warehouse.

He called his men to his side as he studied the front of the building. "Both sets of doors are rigged to blow. The trip will be when they open." Rafe grinned and looked at Anton. "And we *are* going through them. Line your bikes up, stack column in front of the doors from fifty yards out. When I give the signal, rev 'em big, get that back wheel spinning. Both point riders proceed through the door alone."

Anton's jaw dropped, but he did not say a word. Nor the men behind him who looked at each other with concern.

"Not kamakaze," he assured them. "Jump off the damn things before impact. But be exact in your steering. Guide the bike into the center of the door as fast as it'll go."

Relief flooded their features. Of course they didn't want to die, not without a fair fight, at least. Still, Rafael had no doubt each and every one of them would ride into hell for him. Just like he'd do for them.

"They're ready at the windows, Rafe," Yuri said as he rejoined the group.

Motioning the rest of the crew around him, Rafe moved fifty yards farther from the warehouse and quickly laid out his plan. "The warehouse is roughly thirty-five thousand square. The only thing in it is a shrouded raised platform approximately thirty by fifteen with ramps on either side. It's directly in the middle of the space. I don't want a fatal funnel at the doors. After impact, split right and left into the warehouse as you enter. If the man in front of you goes left, you go right, and so on. Focus on the interior of the building; that will be where the action is. Yuri, Anton, and I will ride in directly behind the front column, so your asses had better be out of the way because we're not stopping. As we enter through the front, the second column needs to be in position to hit right after you hear the explosions from the front column. The Berserkers will be entering through the windows. We'll have these pieces of shit in a vise grip. As always, use your firepower to compromise them so that you can get close enough to take off their heads."

Pounce and start tearing off heads. Yes, it was primal, but then so was the eight-hundred-year war between Slayers and Lycans.

Rafe looked over at Yuri. "We need to get a lock on the girl immediately after entry. I don't exactly know what to expect, but I don't think she's going to be sitting pretty, bags packed and waiting to go." Turning back to the group, Rafe asked, "Any questions?" No one called out. He nodded and stepped back. "Then let's do it."

As they broke, Falon, who had listened but kept her distance, stepped toward him and stated, "I want to go in with you." She had come this far. Why could she not finish it? And she had proven she could hold her own.

The hair on the back of Rafael's neck stood on end. He turned to look at her, feeling as determined as she looked. More so. "It's too dangerous in there, Falon. I want you to stay here." He knew he had been foolish to bring her. But his desire to have her by his side overrode his caution.

"I can help! I can hold my own, Rafael. You know it."

It was not going to happen. Not under these conditions. He didn't need her help. It would be too risky, and for what? Her indulgence? No. He watched her about to erupt again. He moved into her space in an attempt to make a rational case on both of their behalves. He pressed his fingers to her lips, shushing her. He didn't mean to shake his head; it must have been his brain thinking out loud. Her dark brows dipped ominously low over her flashing eyes, then she nipped his fingertip, and to his surprise drew blood. He yanked his hand back in surprise. What a vicious little—

"I bite, too, mister, and if you're not careful"—she swiped at his blood on her bottom lip—"I'll eat you up and spit you out."

She pushed past, then turned to face him. "You gave your word to Mr. Taylor that you would return his daughter to him in forty-eight hours or less. She's in there terrified. How do you think she's going to react when you and your boys come charging in like demon bikers wielding your swords and chopping off heads? I can go to her, let her know not to run. We're here to save her, not hurt her."

"Do you think for a minute those bastards in there don't know we're out here? They've been waiting all night for us; she's the bait. If she isn't dead now, she will be the minute we enter."

Falon raised her nose to the night breeze and sniffed the air. Her eyes widened before they narrowed and turned on him. "She's still alive." She turned then and strode as quickly as her casted foot would allow toward the warehouse.

Rafael stood in shocked silence. Had she just caught the girl's scent in the air? They were almost a football field away and downwind! He looked at Yuri, who cracked a smile. "Too bad the Blood Law prevails. She is more than a worthy mate, Rafael."

"Tell me something I don't already know," Rafe grumbled as he strode after her.

When he caught up, Falon abruptly stopped and held out her hand, palm up. "I want a sword."

He nearly choked. "For what?"

"To defend myself." She snapped her fingers. "Now, please, and while you're at it, heal my damn foot so I can walk!"

Rafael ignored her demeaning command of him and shook his head. "You'll get yourself killed. Stay here and wait for JorDon. He's riding in with backup. I'll entrust you with bringing them up to speed on the situation."

"Backup?"

"Angel Ruiz, southern family. He has some personal business of his own with the Slayers."

Falon shook her head. "I will not stand out here and wait when I can be of use inside! I have a right to go in there. We're here because of me!"

Rafael leaned down into her space. Alphas were never challenged, not even by their mates. Not unless they wanted to learn a harsh lesson. "You have no rights unless I give you rights." The minute Rafe said the words, he knew he was going to pay.

She slapped him hard across the cheek. "How dare you!"

Rafe grabbed her hand before she could strike again. He pulled her so close to him their breaths mingled. "Do not *ever* strike me."

"You are not the boss of me! You're nothing but a brute! Kidnapping is against the law! You have no right to hold me against my will."

Frustrated by her defiance in front of his pack, he shook her. "You accepted my mark. That makes you mine. As such, I am your master, and you will obey me!" he growled as his men began to gather around them.

"You seduced me!"

Not wanting to hurt her any more than he had, Rafael leashed his temper and pulled her away from the gathering group. "I will not have this discussion with you here, Falon. I own you. Accept it."

She yanked her arm from his grip. "If I am truly nothing but a possession of yours, am I so unworthy that you'll allow your brother to kill me if he gets the opportunity?"

Rafael rammed his fingers through his hair. This was not the time or place to discuss any of this. "I cannot turn back time and undo what I have done. The Blood Law trumps emotions and desire. Even mine."

"What did you do to your brother that was so horrible your laws mandate you serve me up to him?"

Rafael inhaled then slowly exhaled. He looked down into her righteous blue eyes and knew he had no right sacrificing her. But didn't know how not to. At the very least, he owed her an explanation. "I took his chosen one from him."

Falon blinked. Confused. "So? I pay with my life for sibling rivalry?"

"I took her *life*. While he was still inside of her!" he roared, years of anger, frustration, and yes, guilt poured out from him.

Falon blanched white before his eyes.

"I *killed* her, Falon. I ripped her heart out of her chest. I watched as she bled out in my brother's arms. I am responsible for all of our woes." He pointed a shaking finger at the warehouse. "In there are a dozen Slayers, one of them directly responsible for my mother's death. I'm going to kill them all. While I'm in there, you will stay out here, because"—he yanked her up to him so that her feet dangled in the air—"because—" He wanted to say because he did not want any harm to come to her. That he cared for her and could not bear to see her destroyed by a Slayer. That if he could challenge the Blood Law for her life, he would. But he didn't say any of those things. Instead, he took the cowardly way out. He let go of her and strode away.

"Rafael!" Falon called. Rafe stopped in his tracks and slowly turned to face her, suddenly willing to take the brunt of her anger. Guilt did that.

"Why did you kill her?" she asked softly.

"My brother was too blinded by lust to see that she was a Slayer." As he said the words, Rafael knew he'd do it again. And again. Lucien had given him no choice then, and Lucien would give Rafael no choice now.

Falon made her way to him and stopped just shy of an arm's length away. She leaned toward him and put her hand on his chest over his heart. She could feel the wild thump of it against her palm. "Conan said I was a Slayer. What if he was right?"

He felt gut punched when he thought of what the law decreed. No Lycan shall lie with a Slayer; to do so was punishable by death. By rights Lucien should be dead, and if Falon were Slayer, Rafael as well. But before his death sentence, could he destroy her? Would he? His heart tightened at the thought of harming her. The ring flared on his finger. He took Falon's hand into his and squeezed. "Then I would take my sword and cut out your heart."

He flung her hand from him and strode toward the warehouse. His men stood in silence as he strode past them.

"Yuri!" Rafael shouted over his shoulder, "Handcuff her to something. I don't want her to play hero or to escape."

He saw her eyes widen and knew she'd really hate him for giving that command. He kept walking, even when he heard Falon's screams of protest and Yuri's grunts of pain. Rafe shut down his emotions and focused solely on getting to the Slayers, not losing any of his men, and, as a possible bonus, getting the girl. Afterward, Falon might refuse to speak to him, but—he cursed—it was better that way. He was beginning to go soft. This way, he'd let her go, telling himself there'd been no future for them anyway.

By the time they had taken their positions, the night had stilled to a dead calm, as if it were going to sit back and watch the action play out. And for the most part, the action would be perfunctory. They had been killing each other for eight hundred years.

Telepathically, Rafe called to Angor, who informed him the Berserkers were in place. He nodded to Yuri, who looked no worse because of Falon, who he could see was handcuffed to a stop sign. He gave the signal to crank the bikes. The engines rumbled to life with a deep, guttural roar, their distinct sound a warning to Edward. They were here, and they were going to fight to the death.

As the engines warmed, the rpm's rose higher and higher. They opened full throttle. Rafe sat back easily, giving his bike gas. He looked over at the two men who were riding point and who would send their bikes through the doors. Staying mounted until the last moment was crucial and difficult, but if anyone could handle it with precision, it would be a Vulkasin.

The back column was set. Rafe gave his bike some gas and moved up to the front and side of the column. Holding in the clutch with his left hand, he gave the signal to go with his right. The two point riders, Jackson and Mateo, their bikes now at a fever pitch, popped their clutches and roared forward. Both the bikes popped wheelies, dropped, and then hurtled like missiles toward the doors. Somewhere between twenty and ten yards out, Jackson jumped clear of the bike, guiding it dead center into the door. An enormous explosion racked the night, the velocity so great, the ground shook beneath their feet and the back draft flared with the heat of an oven across their faces. As the bike slammed the door from its hinges and plunged deep inside the building, flames and debris poured out through the jagged opening.

It was more than Rafe had expected. Was that why the Slayers seemed so complacent inside? Did Edward really think the C-4 would do all the work for them?

Mateo, the second biker, struggled to keep his bike upright after the initial burnout and wheelie. When he neared twenty-five yards from impact, Rafe cursed, knowing Mateo wouldn't have the time or the distance to guide it to target and jump to safety. Even as he watched, Mateo eased his body down over the tank and throttled back as far as possible. The bike lurched and slammed into what was left of the second door with Herculean force. Another fireball exploded, mushrooming through the opening and swallowing both rider and bike. Rafael heard Mateo's screams and imagined his body hurling through space and slamming into the concrete floor with a sickening thud. He didn't have to imagine the bloodcurdling scream that followed as Mateo was killed by a Slayer's sword.

Rage exploded inside Rafael. An eye for an eye. He would avenge Mateo's death this night and the deaths of so many before him.

Rafael kept his focus on getting inside to do it. An explosion at the back of the building announced the entrance of the second column. The sound of shattering glass followed by bloodcurdling snarls filled the air as the Berserkers smashed through the windows and poured into the place. Giving the enemy no time to gather their wits, Rafe howled a throaty battle cry, signaling his men to open throttle and charge through the jagged, smoldering openings of the decimated front doors.

Gunshots reverberated through the building; the clash of metal on metal fused with the grunts and screams of men as they fell.

FROM WHERE SHE stood handcuffed to a damn stop sign, more than one hundred yards from the warehouse, Falon blanched at each explosion, then watched as flames shot high into the night. Her anxiety rose as she paced in a circle around the sign. She didn't like to be separated like this from Rafe. Her place was beside him. She yanked and pulled at the handcuffs. The metal cut into her skin; blood dripped to the asphalt. She jumped when another explosion set the dark to light and a harsh sense of urgency shook her. Nervously she trembled, not understanding her sudden and uncharacteristic agitation. She was supposed to be at Rafael's side. She was his chosen one. Falon squeezed her eyes shut. What was she thinking? She should be running the other way!

She was torn in half. She wanted to run to Rafael. See for herself he was alive. Then fight beside him. The other part of her, the survive-at-all-costs part, screamed at her to escape. To run far and run fast.

No one stood guard over her. She looked down at her bloody, swollen hand. She could gnaw it off. Or, she gulped, she could break the bones in her wrist and pull her collapsed hand through that way.

Anguished screams drifted from the warehouse. Falon's heart beat faster. The terrified cries of a little girl called out to her. Rafael's anger, his bloodlust, his passion transcended the space between them. Her body jerked as if she were spasming. Pain speared her belly, as if she had been stabbed. She heard Rafael's enraged war cry. He was wounded. He needed her. And unable to stop herself, she answered his call.

"I'm coming!" she cried. She did not hesitate. She grabbed her arm just above her wrist and the metal cuff, then threw her weight into it. She twisted then pulled. She screamed in pain as bones crunched. Her world went black just before she saw stars. Her knees shook. She took a deep breath and did it a second time. She screamed louder and dropped to her knees. But she knew it was enough. Before her hand swelled more, she carefully maneuvered it out of the metal cuff. When she was free, she held it gingerly with her right hand. Nausea rolled through her. She sat down and put her head between her knees. She was going to faint from the pain.

Long minutes later, when her vision cleared, Falon ripped part of her shirtsleeve off and, as best as she could, wrapped it snugly around her wrist to give it a modicum of support. Slowly, she stood, inhaled, then exhaled.

This was it.

She had a choice. She turned toward the city lights in the distance and freedom. Then back at the flaming warehouse and Rafael. Freedom? Or death?

She turned toward the beckoning city lights but wavered in her step. What life did she have? Knowing she was different, always running, not knowing who she was, where she came from. With Rafael, she felt alive. Accepted. She had meaning. Had she not had the vision of the girl, she would not have a chance at survival. She turned back to the warehouse. She may not know much about herself, but she knew she possessed power. Power that if paid attention to and honed could be her ticket to freedom. She took a step toward the warehouse.

A lone howl echoed from the building. The hair on the back of her neck rose.

"Rafael."

She took another step and then another. Then she was running. To Rafael, the man who made her come alive, and the man she was determined would not see to her death!

Thirteen

RAFE PULLED THE Slayer's blade from his gut with his left hand before deftly turning it back on the bastard, relieving him of his head. Rafe howled his battle cry as he skidded to a sideways stop directly below the gallows. The top shroud had been lifted. Standing like a hunk of bait on a hook, directly on top of the trapdoor, was a young girl, knees shaking, hands tied behind her back, her head in a black cloth bag, a hangman's noose around her neck.

What a sick fuck Edward was. Using a child to lure them in.

Rafael looked for Yuri across the vast space. He had seen the girl as well and was already riding toward her. Anticipating their approach, a tight ring of Slayers swelled from beneath the gallows as Rafael's men pressed upon them.

Yuri dropped his bike into a sideways slide and let it crash into two of the Slayers, knocking them down like bowling pins. Springing to his feet, he hacked off heads on his way to the steps of the platform.

Ignoring the pain in his side from the Slayer's sword, Rafe gunned his bike forward, surging into the melee. When he was half the distance to the gallows, a Slayer rushed him and took a swing at Rafe with his sword. Ducking, Rafe narrowly missed the separation of his head from his shoulders. Simultaneously, Rafe drew his right-hand sword. In one fell swoop, he ended the Slayer's life but not before the Slayer grabbed the right handlebar of Rafe's bike, causing it to suddenly lurch right and then slam onto the floor and out from under him. Rafe hit the floor, slid to a quick stop, then immediately stood. The hooded girl screamed, twisting and turning against the noose and ropes binding her hands behind her neck. If she kept at it, she would hang herself. Fully focused and running on adrenaline and vengeance, Rafe drew his second sword and hoped Yuri could get to her before Edward pulled the trapdoor lever.

Yuri was closer. He'd made it to the base of the ramp but was stopped by Edward and two other Slayers. Yuri was an admirable swordsman. His sword flew like a nest of angry hornets, slashing against the blades of his opponents. Sparks flew as he pressed his point, forcing them back onto the steps. While this gave the Slayers a height advantage, it also exposed their legs. Yuri took full advantage, cutting through the knee joint of the lowest man. The bone-shattering cut sent a bloody arch into the air and dropped the enemy forward, face-first onto the floor. In another tactical slice, Yuri took off his head. Edward ran for the girl just as Rafe looked up to witness the partitions around the base of the platform fly open, revealing a dozen more armed-to-the-teeth Slayers. They tossed the beaver pelts they'd used to disguise their scents from their shoulders.

Son of bitch! He was a fool to have fallen for that trick. And the fool always paid the piper. Rafe snarled. Not tonight.

"You are an arrogant fool, Vulkasin!" Edward taunted from the platform. He raised his sword. "Come now and taste my vengeance!"

Rafael raised both of his swords over his head. "Vengeance is all mine tonight, Slayer!" Despite the added Slayers and the loss of a handful of his men, Rafael's confidence soared. He was at his pinnacle tonight. Nothing could hurt him! With the help of his magnificent Berserkers, who were making hash out of anything that got in their way, and the power of the ring, he would lead his pack to victory.

Slayers were smart, but he was smarter. Slayers killed because of an eight-hundred-year-old command by a long-dead king. Lycans killed to survive and to avenge the deaths of their loved ones. Tonight, he would avenge hundreds of slain Lycans, including his own mother and father.

He looked up at the ceiling two stories high to several heavy looped metal chains hanging from a swing arm mounted from a thick steel beam. He leapt straight up, grabbing onto a thick, blunt hook looped over the swing arm. He shoved the hook up, freeing it. Securing his right foot in the bend of the hook and wrapping the chain around his calf for leverage, Rafael did a free fall. In a wide, forceful swath, he swung down with both swords drawn, hacking at the rush of Slayers. Bullets zinged past him as the Slayers opened fire, several hitting his vest but not penetrating. As he came in for his first hard hit, he took several Slayers out. As the swing reached its full rotation, he unwound his leg from the chains and leapt onto the bottom of the east ramp that led to the platform, then bounded onto the platform where the girl stood screaming bloody murder.

He swung his blade to cut the rope attached to the noose, but heat seared his hand, forcing him to release his sword instead. He swung his left-hand sword around, and it, too, was shot from his hand. Rafael roared in fury and turned. His gaze clashed with Edward's. The Slayer held a .44 nickel-plated Magnum aimed directly at Rafael's heart.

"Take your best shot, Slayer. It's the only one you'll get," Rafael snarled.

The loud rev of chopper engines rose above the din of battle. Familiar but not friendlies. Vipers.

And right on the heels of the Vipers' revving engines came the sweet sound of sure death—the death of Edward and his Slayers! Rafael grinned. Pack Ruiz. The cavalry had arrived. It was going to be a banner day.

In a high backward somersault, he leapt over the backside of the platform and retrieved his swords. He jumped back onto the platform. Raising them above his head in an intricate pattern, he maneuvered them until they flew in perfect circular symmetry like the propeller of an airplane, producing a whirlwind. Keeping the deadly rotation going, he walked to the edge of the platform then hopped to the floor and walked toward the Slayers and their bullets, the force of the air disturbance from his swords so great he pushed all of them backward into the far wall. The Berserkers who flanked him went in for the kill. It was not pretty, what they did, but the Slayers deserved no less. Several of them leapt high into the air to escape but crashed backward into the wall from the velocity of the whirlwind.

Thick smoke began to infiltrate the building. An evasive tactic by the Slayers. But Rafael could see through smoke. The Vipers swung left and right, swarming in behind him. They were led by a broadsword-wielding Edward, who rode a Vulkasin chopper.

Rafe leapt into the air after him. Edward jumped off the bike and onto the platform, going straight for the girl. Angel's men descended on the Vipers, while Rafe's continued to systematically eliminate Slayers. Rafe went after Corbet.

Edward dropped down in front of the girl. He grabbed the rope that held the noose around her neck and placed the edge of his sword to her throat. "Come a step closer, Lycan, and she dies," Edward taunted.

Rafael sneered. "You overestimated my affection for the girl. I came for you. She just led me here."

Edward laughed, ignoring the havoc going on around them both. Flames eating up the walls, gunfire and swordplay. The sounds of men dying.

"I heard different. I heard you have a telepath in your midst. I heard she possesses the power to bring your brother to heel." Edward jerked the noose, causing the girl to scream. "A trade. My girl for yours."

Rafael's fury soared. How did Corbet know of Falon? Smythe knew about the telepath part, but who in his pack had betrayed him and told him about Falon's disabling of Lucien? Who would dare? "Telepath she may be, but then so is Talia and several others. But with the power to disable Lucien? Someone has been spoon-feeding you bullshit." Rafael stepped closer. "Even if it were true, she bears the mark of the alpha. She is not a commodity to be bartered."

Edward pulled the trembling girl back against his chest. His blade dug into her tender skin. Blood dripped in slow rivulets onto the steel. "So be it, Lycan."

"You looking for me, douche bag?"

Rafael turned, stunned at Falon's voice. He moved to grab her, protect her. Vehemently, she waved him off. He looked back to Corbet, who looked as stunned as Rafael, but for different reasons. Corbet blanched white, as if he saw a ghost.

Falon sidled alongside Rafael and hoarsely whispered, "My left hand is broken; can you do your voodoo and fix me up so I can help you out here?"

Without breaking his stare at Corbet, who continued to gape at Falon, Rafe handed her one of his swords and gently wrapped his fingers around her broken hand. The fighting abruptly stopped.

The only sound, the harsh intake of breaths and the rush of exhales. Blood mingled with death, clogging the air.

HEALING WARMTH INFUSED Falon's broken bones. She and the man threatening the girl couldn't stop staring at one another. There was something disturbingly familiar about him. Instinctively she knew he was bad news.

When Rafael's healing warmth subsided, she flexed her fingers and rotated her wrist. Good as new. She kept his sword. She pointed it at the man on the platform. "Have we met?"

His eyes narrowed. He shifted his feet. She felt more than heard movement behind her. She turned just as Rafael did. A swarm of bodies rushed them, and the fight was on again.

Instead of turning to fight, Falon rushed the platform. Her intent had been to aid Rafael, but he was a big boy and could take care of himself. The girl needed her.

The Slayer with his sword to the girl's neck had bigger fish to fry: Angor. The beast attacked the Slayer.

And to Falon's astonishment, the Slayer held his own. How he did and still lived was a miracle. The man was good. An expert swordsman. As good as Rafael. Maybe better. As she reached the top step, the Slayer rammed his blade clear through Angor's mighty chest. The beast howled in pain, writhing against the steel. The Slayer shoved it deeper into the beast. It fell to its knees then dropped to the planks.

The Slayer yanked his sword from the matted bloody fur and pointed it at Falon. "Seize her," he commanded. Several other men stopped their attacks on Rafael's men and hurried toward her.

Falon leapt over them as they came at her. Above her, Rafael swooped down from the ceiling chain and neatly cut down two of them. Falon choked back a cry as warm blood sprayed across her face. The girl screamed behind her. Falon turned to see the Slayer who had her yank hard on the drop floor lever.

The girl's body plummeted downward, her strangled screams cut off from the yank of the noose. Falon hurled her sword, but Rafael was faster. His sword flew hilt over point toward the girl and just as the velocity of her body would have pulled the noose completely closed and snapped her neck, the blade severed the rope she hung from. She dropped to the floor, hitting it with a dull thud. Falon ran to her while Rafael went after the prick who had tried to kill her.

Falon knelt beside the motionless body so close to Angor's. His blood pooled slowly around them. She pulled the hood off the girl and pressed her hand to her chest. Though faint, her heart beat a steady thud. Compelled by something she could not explain, Falon turned to Rafael's prized Berserker. The same one that had tried to kill her. The same one who nearly did. She crawled to him on her hands and knees, slipping in the sticky blood. Without hesitation, she placed her fingers into the deep wound, and pressed her other hand over it.

"C'mon on, you brute," she whispered. "Find the will to survive."

She felt the slice to his artery with her fingertip. She pressed more firmly into his chest and called upon a greater power than her own to repair the damage. Her body thrummed with warmth—entering through her head then tracking down to her neck and shoulders and into her arms and fingertips. Into Angor. His heart shuddered then beat once. Then a second time and a third. He stirred. His big red eyes opened. His heartbeat picked up a steady rhythm. Thump-thump, thump-thump, thump-thump.

Falon smiled. The beast snarled, his fangs bared. Falon sat back on her heels. So much for being grateful. Big sweaty hands grabbed her.

Falon twisted around and found herself seized by three of the dirty bikers that had come in and fought beside the Slayers. She screamed and kicked at them, wondering where Rafael was. She looked across to the platform to see him chained to the gallows post.

What happened? How?

He'd been captured and chained?

How could that be?

He was stronger. Smarter. His eyes flashed red as she caught his gaze. "Rafael!" she screamed as she was dragged toward the front of the burning building. The thugs jerked her hard, turning her around. Violently, she twisted until she could see Rafael again. "Rafael!" she screamed. "Rafael!" Several Slayers at very close range pointed their guns at his heart. They were going to kill him! "No!" she screamed.

Crazed fury possessed her. Her body tightened. Blood pounded in her ears.

Standing beneath the great weight of the chains, Rafael roared furiously. Red eyes flashed. As she strained to get to him, his body jerked and contorted. His human roar morphed into something primal. Animal. Falon screamed in shock and horror as he dropped to all fours and in less than a heartbeat turned into the big golden wolf that had been protecting her when Rafael was gone. The chains fell from his body. He snarled and lunged toward her.

A staccato of shots rang out. His furry body twitched as bullets ripped into him. "Rafael!" she screamed, reaching out for him. Shock waves slammed into Falon. Rage infused her. Fear of losing Rafe tore her in half. Her vision clouded red. Her bones cracked, her skin tightened. Her body felt as if it were tearing apart at the seams. She shoved at the hands that held her captive, but it was not enough.

She screamed again, her voice raw, sounding like Rafael's primal roar.

His big body slammed into them. Falon went spinning on her

back across the concrete floor and into Anton's arms while the bikers scrambled to get out of the wolf's way. Head down, the great beast stalked his prey.

"Destroy him!" Edward yelled as he mounted a chopper. The bastard was going to take off like the coward he was.

Falon flung Anton's big arms from her as Rafael annihilated the three bikers. Despite her cast, she ran after the Slayer as he throttled his bike toward the back of the burning building. Smoke clogged her lungs, but she continued forward, ignoring the calls for her to stop. All she could see was a red target on the Slayer's back. The smoke thickened, and her lungs ached as she tried to draw in clean breaths. Her pace slowed. She stumbled. Her eyes burned. Her heart thudded like a freight train in her chest. She fell to her knees and was caught by strong arms.

"Falon," Rafael breathed, pulling her close to his bare chest. "You're going to get yourself killed."

Falon looked up into his blazing turquoise eyes and said, "Like you care."

His fierce face froze; his eyes searched hers then softened. "I care, damn it," he growled.

So did she. She opened her mouth to tell him, but the velocity of an explosion shoved her harder into his arms, the percussion of it deafening. Fiery shards of the building rained down upon them as Rafael shielded her and called to his men to get out. It was the last thing she heard before her world went dark.

FALON WOKE TO wild laughter, lurid female screams, and the hard cadence of rock and roll.

Slowly she sat up. It was still dark, but the gray fingers of dawn were just tinting the night's dark a shade lighter. She was in Rafe's room. How? They had been hours from here. She realized she was naked and that her cast was gone. She wiggled her toes and rotated her ankle. No pain.

In a wild, mad rush, the evening's events slammed into her. The blood, the gore, the girl, but predominant was the vision of Rafael when he turned into a wolf!

The big blond wolf!

Since the night she'd met Conan, her life had become a Halloween classic. None of it made sense. Yet all of it fell into place. She was different. Rafael was different, and in their differences, they were somehow connected. She'd known it but ignored it, because all of it terrified her.

Falon hurried to the bathroom, took a quick shower, and put on the fresh pair of black jeans and skimpy black half top left for her. She strode to the door, intending to get to the bottom of all of this. This—whatever *this* was. She'd get her answers, and then she'd get the hell out of Dodge!

She pushed open the door and was hit with a cacophony of sound and sex smells. A hard shot of desire zapped her right between the legs. Her nipples hardened. She shook her head, fighting off the overpowering urge for sex. Not just sex, *mating* sex.

Primal rutting, and not just for the sake of letting off some steam with an available dick. No, her body craved one man. She swallowed. In this case, she supposed she craved one wolf.

Falon shook her head again and took a step back into the room. Rafael had turned into a damn wolf! Right in front of her. How was she supposed to deal with that? "Oh, hey, love your fur coat."

It was fantastic and crazy and . . .

When she had seen him chained and about to die, something deep and viciously primal in her had reared its head. She had felt it. An uncontrollable rage. The desperate need to protect Rafe. It fired her up, nearly consuming her. Had the same thing happened to him when he'd seen her being dragged away? Had that brought about his change?

Falon squared her shoulders. In some unexplainable way, she was connected to Rafael. It had nothing to do with sex, his brother, his people, or the Slayers. It was more organic than that. It was as simple and as complicated as destiny.

She cursed. Destiny be damned. She was a sitting duck here.

As she descended the staircase, her nose twitched. Sex, hot, heavy, pungent, permeated the sultry air. Wild laughter both male and female filled the structure. She stopped in her tracks at the edge of the great room. Her jaw dropped; her body flamed red with shocked embarrassment. Dozens of naked writhing bodies tangled into a wild mass of heaving, grunting debauchery. Unable to move and just as unable to tear her gaze from the grotesquely erotic sight, Falon gaped.

She'd heard of orgies. Had read about them in some tattered magazines left behind in some of her flophouse rooms. And while she wasn't naive, she'd never really thought that people, women especially, had sex with more than one man at a time. Apparently she was wrong. *Very* wrong.

Her body warmed, partly because of the hedonism playing out before her but mostly because she knew she was being watched. Slowly her gaze rose and caught the molten stare of Rafael's. He was the only person clothed! He grinned, a wild, mysterious grin. Falon held her breath, fighting her natural urge to go to him. He watched amused as she mentally fought with her desire for him and her resistance to what they both knew was their destiny. He held out his hand to her, giving her the choice both of them knew was already made.

Falon's limbs loosened. She felt like melting wax. She put one foot in front of the other, careful not to step on a writhing body part on the floor. A large hand grasped her bare foot. She gasped. Rafael growled a warning. The hand slid back into the naked fray, and she took another step, then another, until she had crossed the room without further assault.

Rafael took the final step to her.

"Welcome to the celebration," he said hoarsely, taking her hand into his big warm one. His long fingers wrapped possessively around hers.

She shivered, wondering if he would try to entice her to indulge here, with his pack. His deep laughter rumbled from his chest into her. She looked up into his hot gaze. "I don't share, Falon. *Ever.*" His eyes reddened.

She nodded, not wanting to think of what the consequences would be to any man who touched her as intimately as the men on the floor touched those women. Possessive rage swelled in her chest, making it difficult to draw a breath. She cocked her head and shot him a possessive glare. "Nor do I." Her words surprised her, but more than saying them was the realization that she meant them.

He threw his head back and laughed, the full baritone of it reverberating along the beamed ceiling.

She shoved him and looked down at the wildly undulating bodies. "It's an orgy, Rafe!" Mostly two men to one woman, but some women had three men penetrating every orifice. Falon's skin continued to flush as her body tightened.

Rafael ran his fingertips down her bare arm; an army of goose bumps followed, standing at attention. "We won the night, Falon. There is much to celebrate." He pulled her into his arms and twirled around with her. "Let's go upstairs, and I'll show you how to really celebrate."

She shook her head, wanting him but more afraid of lying on the big bed with him and knowing what that would mean. Another hook.

Deeper. Harder to remove. "No, no. Wait. I want to know where the girl is. And . . ." Her eyes widened. "What you did back there, the wolf—and that man, Edward. Who is he? Why did he want me?"

His eyes glittered with excitement. A low growl rumbled from his chest. "The girl is in a safe place until her father can claim her later tonight." He strode with her in his arms toward the stairway to his room. "You don't need to concern yourself with Edward Corbet. He and his nest of Slayers will be handled."

Falon stiffened. "Corbet?" *She* was a Corbet. Amid all the chaos in the warehouse he had looked at her as if he knew her. She had felt a jolt of recognition as well. She shivered in Rafe's arms. Dear Lord, were they related somehow? If they were, what would Rafael do?

"In less than three months' time, every Corbet on this earth will be wiped from it. Permanently." His voice had deepened with righteous fury. And so she had her answer. His voice lowered as he pressed her more intimately to him and said, "About the wolf thing?" He laughed. "What can I say? I turn into a beast when I get pissed."

Tightening his hold, he ran up the stairs with her as if she didn't weigh more than an ounce.

"I'm hungry!" she protested grabbing at straws to slow him down. She needed to know more about Edward Corbet.

"I'm famished, too," he said, squeezing her.

Falon struggled to get out of his ironclad embrace. "Not that kind of hungry, Rafe." She pushed away in earnest. He kept a solid grip on her. "I'm tired. I'm confused." *I need to know what you will do if you learn I'm the enemy.* How could that be? She didn't have a mean bone in her body. She was not full of hate or a killer. She relaxed some. Maybe it was just a coincidence. Corbet was a common enough name . . . besides, if she were remotely related to a Slayer, wouldn't Rafael know? At least sense it? She didn't use black magic to hide her identity like Smythe had.

When they entered the room, Rafael locked the door behind them and tossed her onto the bed. "Get undressed," he commanded as he unbuttoned his shirt.

Falon stiffened. "I will not!"

He flung his shirt to the floor and started to unbutton his jeans. "Yeah, you will, or I'll undress you myself."

Falon rolled over to the opposite side of the bed, then to the floor, putting the large bed between them. "No." Did he think she had no pride? At some point, he was going to hand her over to his brother, for God's sake!

He shucked his jeans and boots. And despite her anger, confusion, and fear of the unknown, Falon could not help but look down. Dear Lord. Damned if her body didn't warm. His thick arousal jutted arrogantly toward her. Parts of her melted. Other parts heated. All of her remembered the glorious feel of his thick heat inside of her. Her gaze swept the length of him. He was magnificent. Every inch of him was hard and lean with an underlying power that defied reality.

"You can't force me," she said with little conviction. He could, and they both knew it.

"I have no intention of forcing you to do anything you don't want to do, Falon," he softly said.

"Then leave me alone."

He crawled on top of the bed. On all fours, he came toward her. His eyes burned bright, penetrating to the truth she denied both of them. Corded tendons strained beneath the thick, sculpted muscles of his neck, shoulders, and arms. She tried to swallow, but her throat was too dry. His large penis and balls hung heavy between his thighs, swaying with his graceful movement. He reminded her of a great wild beast coming to claim his mate. Her body loosened. A primal urge, so powerful Falon could barely breathe, overcame her. His eyes hypnotized her.

"You can't fight it, Falon. We are mated. You bear my mark. You are mine. Mark me before the sun rises, and I am yours."

"Wha-what does that mean?"

"It means I am alpha. As my mate, I will protect you against anyone or anything that threatens your life. I choose you to stand beside me as my equal. Your enemies are my enemies. It is your blood I have chosen to blend with mine so that my legacy lives on."

What if she were his enemy? "What about the wolf thing?"

"I am Lycan, Falon. As are my people. I cannot change it, nor would I if I could."

"What exactly is a Lycan?" She was afraid she already knew the answer.

"My ancestors were wolves. But I am human, a human who possesses the skills and instinct of the wolf, and who shifts with the sunrise and sunset."

"Is—are the people downstairs like you, too?"

"Yes."

Oh shit. Falon closed her eyes and inhaled deeply. This was crazy weird. But then so was her life. Was she really all that shocked? She opened her eyes. "What if *I* were the enemy? Would you protect you from me?"

He scoffed, shaking his golden head. "I would never hurt you, Falon. Have I not proved that?"

He had, but—"Would you protect me from your brother?" If he would not, there was nothing more to be said or done between them.

Rafael's eyes flared red before returning to the deep turquoise that was unique to him. "I will kill him if he touches you."

Finally! He put her before the ridiculous Blood Law! Falon caught herself from turning into an emotional pile in front of him. Yet emotion welled up so thickly in her chest she didn't think she could speak without her voice revealing her relief and happiness.

She blinked back the hot sting of tears. "What changed your mind?" she croaked.

He smiled that mysterious smile of his. Every part of her thawed. "Let me show you," he said.

Falon swallowed hard and coughed. Her throat was so dry. Her chest was near to bursting. She wanted to throw herself into his arms and never leave his side, but there was more she needed from him. "Am I free to leave here?"

Rafael's gaze flared with angry possession. Yes, he had marked her and vowed to protect her, but she knew by his hesitation that the answer was yes and that it would kill him if she walked out that door. And she might die, too. But right now?

Her trembling hand reached up to the top button of her little half shirt. She slipped it through the eye. Then the next one. Her chest rose and fell in stuttered breaths. Her nipples were so tight they ached.

"That's it. Now slide it off your shoulders," he urged.

She did. Her breasts plumped under his hot gaze.

"You are extraordinary, Falon." He reached out a fingertip and touched a turgid nipple. When it puckered more beneath his touch, he groaned. He slipped his other arm around her waist and pulled her hard against him. His lips devoured her. Falon's body turned liquid in his embrace.

"You are so warm. So soft," he murmured against her breast. He raised his head and looked hotly into her eyes. "And so fierce." He pulled her harder against his bare chest. "You were something else tonight, Falon. Amazing." He kissed her hard. His lips commanded hers to accept; his tongue took her breath away.

He yanked her jeans off in one fluid movement and pushed her onto the bed. He crawled on top of her, his cock thick and swollen, the dewy head weeping for entry. Her legs opened, and he entered her in one thick, deep stroke. Falon cried out in shocked pleasure. She was so slick, so tight, she could feel the contours of his cock inside of her. She raised her knees up so that he could fill her completely. He was big and warm and felt excruciatingly divine.

He thrust into her in long, slow strokes. The tension built. Falon stretched out beneath him, pulling him deeper inside her. She felt as if she had done this a thousand times but that it was also their first time. He was so right. He nipped at her neck, his teeth drawing blood. He licked her skin, slowly, savoring the taste of her. Her lust intensified.

The overwhelming urge to do the same thing to him nearly overtook her. He growled as if he could read her thoughts. His thrusts became more urgent. She looked up into his eyes and caught her breath. His gaze was red and blazing. The cords in his neck strained against his skin. His momentum increased, his thrusts so deep and powerful she wasn't sure if she could hold on.

His body tightened. For a long moment, he held himself suspended above her, his muscles straining and taut. His skin was slick with sweat as he fought something. She realized the sun had broken the horizon and in clarity understood.

He was only human at night. Was he going to shift? Now? Inside of her? Dear Lord, no!

He squeezed his eyes shut and in a quick movement turned her over. "I have time, Falon. A few moments," he hoarsely said.

"Before I leave you, though . . ." He dipped his head between her ass cheeks. She heard him inhale. Her womb constricted, releasing more of her slick essence. His tongue flicked out and against her swollen lips. "Oh, Rafa," she moaned. He growled against her slickness at her term of endearment for him. She didn't know where it came from, but she liked it. And would say it again, for his ears only.

His tongue slid across her lips again, the tip penetrating into her.

She nearly came off the bed. Gently, he licked her hardened clit and suckled it against his lips as his tongue flicked teasingly back and forth. The tension in her body threatened to snap.

To relieve the incredible pressure inside her, Falon screamed. But it wasn't enough. Her orgasm built, one monster wave atop another as he slid his tongue back and forth across her dripping wetness, lapping and sucking at her like he was eating a melting sundae.

She snapped, climaxing with such ferocity her nails dug into the mattress. Her hips undulated, her bottom pumped high in the air, and still that long, luscious tongue of his lapped and sucked and lapped and sucked her. Another hard climax hit her before the first one faded. This time she threw her head back and howled.

In a hard, slick thrust, he growled low and penetrated her, his cock so thick and swollen she wasn't sure if she could take all of him. He filled her to his balls. And she knew there was no other more sublime experience than this. As if one thousand lights burned from within, her body lit up, every nerve ending dancing, electrified. Wild, wanton visions flashed in her brain. Of them making fervent love. Of them in the woods, naked and running free. Of Rafe taking her on soft green moss. His big, powerful hands all over her body. Claiming her and letting it be known to man and beast that she was his.

He grazed his teeth along her jugular. She could feel his incisors, sharp and dangerous, press into her skin. She could feel the hard throb of her pulse against his lips. The urge to mark him as he had marked her struggled with fear of what that would mean. If she took that final step, she knew he would never allow her to leave. And she needed to. It was imperative she know if she were connected to Edward Corbet. Until then, she could not completely give herself to Rafael. Because he would not want her.

He came in a wild, furious frenzy.

His teeth sank deeper into her skin. The pain of his bite, mingled with the hard, frantic thrusts of his orgasm, pushed her over the edge once more. Her thighs widened, her hips dipped lower, she threw her head back and cried out as white-hot desire crashed into unimaginable pleasure. The shock of the hit left her breathless and shaken to the point of collapse. Rafael slid an arm around her belly, steadying her, his breaths harsh and ragged behind her.

Neither one of them moved, save for their great gulps of air as their slick, heaving bodies struggled for composure. They remained as one. Her on all fours, him buried deep inside her from behind.

After long minutes, she felt his erection subside. When she moved forward and he slipped from her, she turned to look at him. To see if he was as affected by their wild, lustful mating as she was.

She caught her breath and moved away from him.

He looked wild. Primal. Violent.

In that terrifying second, he shifted into his mighty golden wolf.

Fourteen

IT WAS NEVER good to fear the truth, but she did. Falon moved back against the carved headboard as the wolf in front of her bared his great white fangs. Images flashed through her mind. Images of the same wolf tearing men apart.

Consciously she knew this wolf was Rafael, that he would not hurt her. In theory anyway. But her instinct also told her he was unpredictable. That the wolf part of him would override the human part.

She didn't move one single muscle and barely breathed as the wolf sniffed her hair, her cheek, then her shoulder. She held her breath when his warm wet nose nudged her breasts. When his long tongue lapped a nipple, Falon hissed in a breath. Her nipples tightened, which caused her embarrassment enough. But when he licked her again, slower this time, sending shock waves shooting straight to her pussy, Falon whimpered. She opened her mouth to demand he stop, but he licked her again; this time his teeth grazed a sensitive tip.

"No," she breathed, stilling the restlessness in her body. He growled, and with his big head, he pushed her back into the rumpled sheets. Unsure of what he would do if she did not comply, Falon lay as flat as her spine would allow and as still as a corpse.

He pressed a huge paw on her thigh, stilling her. Pinning her down. As if she'd be dumb enough to try to escape. He sniffed her breasts, his nose warm and damp as he nudged them. Then he sniffed again. Falon squeezed her eyes shut. He continued to sniff her body. Lower now to her belly. He stuck his nose in her belly button. It tickled. Falon clenched her hands closed. He licked her belly. She gasped because the sensation was far from unappealing. Hedonistic cravings tempted her to offer no resistance . . . at all.

He licked her again, this time a long, slow swath from one hip to another. She flinched and squeezed her eyes tighter. Her skin pebbled and her body tingled. It warmed in parts it should not have warmed. She felt his head move lower, just above her mons. She was still hot and wet. Falon swallowed hard again and dared to open her eyes. She caught her breath. He stared right at her, his jaws only inches from where he had been as a man. Her chest rose and fell in shallow waves. He made a funny noise and then opened his jaws just enough to look as if he were smiling.

Slowly she shook her head. "Don't you dare, Rafael."

He growled and licked the inside of her thigh instead. She hissed at him. So close to where he should not go. When she made to move away from him, he plopped a big paw on her arm, staying her. He growled low and gave her a look that said, *I won't go* there, *but I'm not done with you. Yet.*

"Behave yourself," she warned but lay rigidly back against the sheets. He settled down beside her and licked her fisted hand. She pulled it up, but he pulled it back to her side. Fine, she thought. He can lick her hand. And he took his time, too, his big, warm tongue slowly, gently licking it open and then her fingers until she began to relax.

Her tight muscles loosened. She closed her eyes. Her breathing deepened then steadied. His touch felt good, comforting, sensual and, oddly, safe. She trusted not only his calm licking but the possessive paw on her arm and thigh. The faint brush of his soft fur and warm body beside her. Yet each time he lulled her back into a warm, comfortable place, his big tongue would overlap her hand to catch the outside of her thigh. Each time it did, she held back a cry of surprise; and damn her, pleasure.

Falon forced herself to go to a calmer place. A place where she could leave the turmoil and rest in peace. She had mastered mediation years ago. It had been her salvation when the craziness that was her life became too much. In time to the wolf's slow, steady licks, she slowed her breathing and allowed her body to loosen. Her mind cleared. She was floating. She exhaled, and her body fully relaxed. Ah, here was where she felt most at peace.

Soft and warm, as if she were being carried away by a protective cloud.

She pushed away the bloody visions of the night before. Of the horrific battle. Of Rafael shifting into a wolf. Of the little girl's screams of terror. Of the frantic orgy. Of that man, the Slayer Edward Corbet, and what, if any, connection she had to him. Her thoughts turned to the good visions. Of Rafe's promise to protect her and of her giving herself completely to him. She smiled. She could feel him as a man again in her deep meditation.

Her body tingled, and suddenly the wolf and man merged in her mind.

His fingertips traced along her spine. Falon melted into the touch. Her nipples hardened, her body trembled. Warm lips pressed against the tender skin behind her ear.

Bold hands slipped around her waist to her belly then possessively pressed against her still-slick mons. Falon arched and moaned. She felt herself liquefy. "Rafa," she breathed.

"*Corazón*," his deep voice whispered. Huskier than usual. His term of endearment warmed her insides. Emotion filled her chest to heavy. His touch created such evocative sensations.

Fingers stroked her swollen lips, slipping effortlessly along their slick folds. Falon's hips rose, wanting more. She spread her thighs and was rewarded when a thick finger slid into her waiting warmth. With slow in-and-out thrusts, he swirled his finger deep inside of her, tapping that sweet place that drove her mad. Tension swept across her body. Her pussy wept for more. Falon bit her lip, holding back a feral cry of pleasure. She was wanton. What would Rafael think of her?

"I think you are beautiful," he whispered.

Her skin flared with heat. His voice. The timbre deep but different. His scent the same, but different.

She pressed her hips up to meet his palm. She opened her mouth to scream as her orgasm hit her out of nowhere. His lips captured hers, silencing her cries of pleasure, and his tongue violently fucked her mouth as his finger pressed the secret place inside her, forcing her orgasm to deepen.

She opened her eyes, expecting to see blond hair and turquoise eyes.

She did not.

She didn't see Rafe's wolf either.

The jet-black hair swirled around the angry face of the tortured brother. His deep, tawny eyes molten in lust or fury she could not tell. His power, his energy, his sensuality smashed into her, stifling her to stunned silence.

Lucien.

He smiled against her lips, then nipped at her bottom lip. Her body thrummed with sensation. She stiffened, tore her lips free, and screamed in terror at the exact same time the orgasm exploded inside of her, tearing her apart.

Terror mixed with raw ecstasy created a leviathan of sensation overload. Darkened eyes watched in supreme satisfaction as her body gripped and writhed around his finger, the vestiges of the orgasm racking her body like harsh waves pounding against pilings during a storm.

Lucien! She shook her head and pushed away from him, wanting separation, yet her body cried out for more of him. He cupped her hot mons and pressed his finger more deeply into her. Wide-eyed, she arched, as her eyes rolled back, her lids closed. Gasping for breath, she strained against him.

"I am in your blood, Falon." He pushed her back into the downy comforter. "You can never be rid of me." His lips descended onto a hard nipple.

Falon swallowed hard, licked her dry lips, and with every bit of will she possessed, she arched, trying to push him from her. He only clasped her tighter to his naked body. His lips hot as fire, scorching her skin.

"No!" she cried. Rafael! Where was he? He promised to protect her. With his life. She screamed. He would never forgive her if his brother took her! She could not bear his rejection. She could not bear his disgust. Her heart ached for him. She would never put him through that.

"Say yes to me," he commanded.

Falon twisted out of his grasp, wondering how she had managed it. He was stronger. She backed up against the headboard. "I will *never* say yes to you, Lucien. Never!"

He was on all fours. His black hair a wild mane around his head. His golden eyes sparked in passion. He reached out a big hand and traced his fingertips across her knee. Shivers, not completely unpleasant, ran across her body. Guilt washed over her. She would never betray Rafael. Falon pushed back harder, kicking him. He grabbed her foot and kissed her instep. In fascinated horror, she watched him lick a slow, deliberate trail up to her knee. Her body shook.

Hypnotic gold eyes glittered, never once wavering from her. He put a hand on each of her knees, then slowly pushed them apart, exposing her pink glistening opening. Falon bit her lip, mustering the power she knew she was capable of.

Her musk scented the air. Lucien closed his eyes and inhaled. "My brother's scent mingles with yours." He inhaled again, this time deeper. "I see he hasn't lost his touch."

Falon held her breath. If he trespassed further, she'd rip his heart out. He opened his eyes and stared directly at her.

"My scent will override his."

Falon stiffened to tempered steel. "I will kill you if you trespass again."

He threw his head back and laughed so loud she thought the ceiling would come tumbling down around them. "Your body cries out for mine. Why do you deny what nature intended?"

Falon shook her head. "I thought you were Rafael."

"You came in my hand, your eyes wide open."

Falon shivered. "You tricked me. It was too late."

He laughed low. Sensuality and danger oozed from him. "You cannot deny you are attracted to me. Part of you knew it was me. Reveled in *me*."

"I didn't! I will deny you. Always. I have no interest in you other than I demand you release Rafael from your ridiculous Blood Law."

Lucien smiled a thoughtful half smile. "So he told you."

Falon dragged a pillow across her chest, leaving her bottom region in plain sight. When Lucien's gaze dropped to her thighs, she tucked the pillow safely between her legs. His gaze dragged up, and he smiled a most disarming smile. "I envy my brother. You are a mate worth keeping." He looked over his shoulder to the sleeping wolf beside them. Falon gasped, just noticing Rafael still in wolf form for the first time. How could he sleep when she was practically being raped?

"He cannot hear us, Falon. You and I, we share blood. It is just the two of us in our own little world. I can come to you at my leisure, and Rafael will know nothing of it. Unless you choose to tell him. Then"—Lucien shook his head—"what do you think my brother will do when he discovers his chosen one came to me in every sense of the word?"

Falon kicked at him. If she told Rafael what happened, he would shun her, and in the process might get himself killed taking his revenge. "Tell him, and I'll give you a headache you won't ever forget."

Lucien threw his head back and laughed again. "You cannot harm me, Falon. But mark my words; I intend to destroy my brother just as he destroyed me."

"Your woman was a Slayer! She would have destroyed all of you!"

Lucien's head snapped back; he eyed her suspiciously. "So says my brother."

"How did he know?" she asked, her voice suddenly shaky. If she were related to Edward, that meant she was a Slayer by blood. Could Lucien see it in her?

"He says she showed herself to him. Slayers' eyes go black when they reach the height of passion. Whether it be anger, lust, or blood-lust to kill."

"He-he saw her eyes turn black."

Lucien looked down at the wolf and sneered. "My *brother* could not handle the fact that I had taken a mate and would become solo alpha. He concocted a lie and killed her."

Falon did not believe it. Rafael was noble. High above lies. "You're a fool, Lucien. A jealous, selfish fool. You will sacrifice all for your petty revenge!"

He pounced on her, shoving her back into the covers. His body was blistering hard. His scent earthy with a hint of ocean, like the Monterey pines meeting the turbulent Pacific. He was as primal in his anger as Rafael was in his passion for her. Lucien's fury rose thick and hot against her thigh. He forced her legs apart. "I would have given my life for my brother, but instead he took mine when he took my chosen one from me." Lucien dropped his head down to hers. "Did he tell you how he did it?" he hoarsely demanded against her neck. His teeth skimmed along her jugular.

"Yes," she breathed.

"Everything?"

"Yes."

"Did he tell you that he ripped her heart out of her chest as I made love to her? That she died in my arms?"

"Yes," she said, barely able to say it, unable to imagine Rafael doing such a heinous thing to his brother. His twin. A spark of compassion for Lucien ignited in her heart. Rafael may have been right, she was a Slayer, but she was still the woman Lucien loved.

"I'm sorry, Lucien," she whispered.

He snarled, ignoring her words. His ragged gaze pierced her. His lips drew back from his teeth in a nasty smile. "What poetic justice it would be if I took you right now. If I fucked you and ripped your heart out of your chest and left it here, on the bed for my brother."

"No," she whispered. She didn't want to be someone's vengeance.

"No. That would be too easy. He needs to suffer longer. Harder." Lucien bit her. His fangs pierced her tender skin where Rafael had earlier, then sank deep into her flesh, muscle, and artery. Falon screamed and arched into him. Straining in a macabre sexual dance. She wished death over his taking of her, but she could not stop her body's lustful response to him any more than she could stop the moon from rising.

Lucien's body responded in kind. He lifted his hips, forcing himself upon her. Panic seized her. She tried to calm enough to gather her powers, to force him from her with her mental lightning bolts, but she was too afraid if she took even the slightest part of her attention from his taking of her, he would seize the moment.

The head of his cock tapped her nether lips, then slowly rocked back and forth between them. A shock wave of sensation hit her body. Falon bit her lip so hard she drew blood. The copper scent added fuel to his raging flame. His fingers dug into her skin, and his body tensed as he prepared to take her. "Stop, Lucien!" she commanded. "I will despise the sight of you forever if you do this."

"I don't care what you think of me," he snarled. His body tightened, his hips moved against her.

Falon opened her eyes and caught her breath. His eyes burned red-hot. His wild black hair fell down into her face, shrouding them.

"Yes, you do," she breathlessly said. "You're an alpha, Lucien. A leader." His muscles clenched as a sheen of sweat broke out across his dark skin. His jaw clenched, his lips drawn tight, revealing straight white teeth, his breathing labored. "Please," she softly said, "Act as a true alpha would, and release me."

He rolled from her with a curse but yanked her up by a hank of her hair, so close to his lips she thought he was going to kiss her. "I'm not done with you." He shoved her back onto the bed. He looked down at the stirring wolf on the bed beside her. "Or my brother."

Falon closed her eyes, knowing she was safe. For the moment. When she opened them again, Lucien was gone, but the big golden wolf stood over her with a questioning look on his face.

Confusion reigned supreme. What the hell had just happened? She sat up and looked toward the closed door, then around the room. Where had Lucien gone, and why hadn't Rafael gone after him? The wolf licked her hand. She looked at him. Her body trembled. Her head ached. Had she dreamed Lucien? She touched her neck where both brothers had marked her. Fresh blood stuck to her fingertips.

More for comfort than anything else, Falon reached out to pull the great gold beast to her. She was cold, afraid, and confused. He licked her neck where she had just touched. She flinched. He pressed his nose to her skin and sniffed. He snarled viciously, snapping at her. She screamed, pushing away from him. He snarled again and jumped from the bed.

Dear God, Rafael knew.

Her body iced. She looked at Rafael, who continued to snarl viciously at her. His words so recently spoken came back to haunt her. *I don't share. Ever.*

She slipped from the bed, wanting to explain but not daring to. Though it had been a dream to her, it was real to him. Lucien's scent mingled with her musky scent and hung damningly between them. "Rafael—I'm sorry," she whispered. And knew as she said the words, whatever they had shared was gone.

Rafael turned and bolted against the thick door, sending it flying off the hinges. Falon stood naked and terrified in the middle of the room.

Her instinct screamed at her to go after Rafael, demand he listen to her, force him to understand that she had no hand in what happened. Lucien tricked her, using her love for Rafael against her.

Falon gasped, slapping her hands over her mouth. Love! When had love happened?

"Rafael!" She desperately called. "Come back!"

But he would not. She knew it as sure as she knew she loved him. Crazy as it sounded, she did. That love took hold of her determination to get her man back.

Quickly, she dressed.

Fifteen

ALL HER LIFE Falon had run. Run from who she was, what she was. Run because she was different and feared those differences.

She was done running.

The only running she was going to do now was toward answers.

She'd already started. She had discovered and embraced her powers here in the compound. Not only that, but she had been emotionally and sexually awakened, not by one man but by two. One man she loved; the other she despised. The first was lost to her because of the second. Or was he?

As unconventional and different as Rafael was, she loved him. She belonged to him. He had marked her. He had trusted her! Promised to protect her from Lucien. Her place was by Rafael's side. But how? He was a stubborn, testosterone-driven man *and* beast, and both were convinced she was guilty of a crime far worse than death. Adultery, with his nemesis of all people, akin to treason in his mind.

Grief clogged her throat, making it difficult to exhale. As did the feeling of hopelessness seeping into her soul. She had lost something so precious, so profound, something that had breathed life into her hollow soul. She realized when she saw him chained by the Slayers and about to be destroyed that she loved him, would die for him. She had found him only to lose him. No amount of begging, borrowing, or stealing could get him back.

It was as if their connection had died. Once a life was taken, there was no rebirth.

Argh! She threw the pillows across the room. Even if she could convince him she did not have sex with his brother, she had to leave. What, dear God, what if she *were* a Slayer? Rafael would destroy her on principle alone. There was no staying here. Not now.

She must go, and she could not come back to him until she knew who she was. Falon prayed to every god imaginable that she was not remotely related to any Slayer. But, if by some terrible twist of fate she were, she would move the entire Sierra range if that's what it took to convince Rafael she was a worthy mate, that she loved him above all others and would stand beside him and battle each and every Slayer that walked the earth. *If* she were Slayer, and she could love him, a Slayer with no hate in her heart toward Lycans, only love, then surely there could be peace between their people.

Though her heart ached, a sliver of hope shone through the bleakness that had become her despair. She would discover the truth about herself and, regardless of what that truth was, she would force Rafael to face it and accept it. Then he would accept the truth about Lucien. The truth about her.

There was only one person who could give her answers now: Corbet. She would find him and demand he tell her who she was. Why she had been abandoned. Whatever information she learned, she'd use it to leverage an end to this craziness between Slayers and Lycans.

New resolve filled her with a confidence she had never experienced. The bloodlust between Lycans and Slayers made no sense to her. Did they kill each other just because their ancestors had? How meaningless was that? She'd show them the stupidity of their eight-hundred-year war and why it held no relevance in today's world. She'd help them heal. Could she make them BFFs?

No, that could never be, but there could be peace.

Falon dressed, then kicked out the glass of the bathroom window Rafael had staked shut, and this time when she jumped, she cleared the compound fence by several feet. She was stronger now. Faster. She hit the ground running. To the warehouse, from there she would track Corbet. Her feet flew over the soft, loamy grass. She hurdled downed logs and exposed boulders. Everything smelled crisper, cleaner, sharper. Her vision was that of a cat's. Each forest sound was distinct rather than a resonant mixture.

Behind her, she sensed the warm breaths of several Berserkers. She didn't fear them. She had saved Angor. Instinctively, she knew he would not harm her. Unless . . . Falon stumbled. Unless Rafe gave the kill order, something he might do, given his belief she'd betrayed him. Betrayed him with . . .

She picked up the scent she had come to fear. Fear on so many levels, and yet the fear of losing Rafael was greater than the fear of his brother.

Lucien was close. He would know where Corbet was. But she didn't dare go to him. She would do that later, after she discovered the truth. And asking him questions or favors wouldn't be her purpose.

In the back of her mind, Falon had the ridiculous notion that she could reunite the brothers. That she could mend the hatred that clogged both their hearts. Only then, she realized, could there truly be peace.

So many vague memories muddled her brain as she ran, her

thoughts focusing on that night in the warehouse. On the ring that had brought her here to Rafe. On the niggling thought in her subconscious that she'd seen the ring long before she'd encountered Conan at Del's market.

She stumbled again as memories solidified. She had seen it! As a child, not just on Conan's hand. God help her, but had it been her father?

Dear Lord, was he a Slayer?

Was she?

A new scent drifted in the air. Female and distinctly Lycan. Familiar. Not from Rafael's pack but strangely from long ago. Falon slowed her frantic pace, coming to a dead stop. She lifted her nose and quieted her thoughts.

The scent escaped her as another one overpowered it. Lucien. He was closer now. She could hear his deep breaths, feel the pounding of his heart.

You can run from me, but you can never hide.

Falon took off, ignoring Lucien's words. She could run and she could hide, and when she had her answers, she would use all her power to force him to confront Rafael and tell him what hadn't happened. Rafael would accept she'd been a victim of Lucien's manipulation. That she hadn't been a willing partner in his sex games. And then, maybe, Rafael would soften.

Lucien's scent intensified around her.

Angor, she silently called. *Help me.*

The great black beast growled behind her. Had he heard her, or was he going to attack her? Falon turned to plead her case and to beg him for his help. As she turned, he leapt toward her. She ducked and stumbled backward, preparing to ward him off. But he jumped over her into the darkness. His pack followed him.

Vicious snarls reverberated through the trees. Falon changed direction and headed for what she knew was the main road that led to the compound and down the mountain. From there she would head toward civilization. And Corbet.

She ran for what seemed like hours. Each time a car approached or passed, she ducked back into the woods. The female scent she had picked up earlier returned. She felt drawn to it. A safe haven. In another place and another time, she would pursue it. Not tonight. Tonight she would learn her true identify and with that knowledge fight for the man she loved.

Finally, she came upon a small encampment. The scents were strong and, again, oddly familiar. Much like the female Lycan scent shadowing her. Like a wolf rather than the cat she'd thought of earlier, every sense in her was heightened. Had the mark of the Lycan brothers given her wolfen power? It didn't matter. She was glad for it, felt comfortable with it, and would use it to her advantage.

She stopped at the forest's edge then stealthily crept toward the village. She heard a small whimper. She hunched lower, looking for the source. The hair on the back of her neck rose when she realized it had come from her. A tightness in her gut mingled with a longing in her heart. For what? Why here, why now? She moved in closer. The air swirled with old-world human scents. Distinct and not of this time. The mood of the people who milled about was sad, forlorn. Despondent. Her vision honed.

Were these the Amorak Rafael spoke of? But if she was a Slayer, why this sense of familiarity? They could not be her kin.

Confusion washed through her in chaotic waves. The more she discovered, the more confusing it all became. Could a Lycan pair with a human and produce a hybrid of sorts? She was all human, albeit one with some wacky shit going on, and Rafe had said he chose her to carry on his legacy. Was that allowed? Was it possible she was both Lycan *and* Slayer?

Impossible, according to Rafael. She shook off the questions. She had to focus.

The small houses were in bad need of repair. Several cars that had seen better decades clogged the narrow dirt road that ran down the center of the place. If she could just get to one . . .

THE SUN BEGAN its final descent as Rafael reached the northern tip of his mountain. He shifted in mid-stride, never faltering. He coughed up the ring he swallowed each time he shifted, slid it on his hand, and continued to run naked through the pines. As man and beast, rage filled every cell, every pore. His entire being.

Betrayed by his chosen one! With his brother! He snarled and continued to run. How could she allow Lucien to mark her? Didn't she know or care about the significance of her treachery? Even if he could forgive her, the pack never would. What she had done, fucking his brother while she bore Rafael's mark, was paramount to treason.

She would be ripped apart.

He threw his head back and howled in pain, frustration, and longing. He loved her! His chest ached, not from the exertion of his endless running, but in heartbreak.

He had defied the Blood Law for her! And in return, she'd allowed Lucien to come to her, take her, then mark her.

They must have traded blood for Lucien to so easily come to her while he slept. How had he *not* known? Had he been so caught up in his own plans for vengeance he had overlooked it?

He stumbled, dropping to one knee. The details didn't matter. They had united and in doing so had forged an insurmountable abyss between himself and Falon.

He pounded the rocky earth with his fists. He welcomed the pain. The ring flared. From the moment he'd taken it from Salene and put it on his finger, his life had shattered into a million pieces. He had no control, and just as Sharia had told him, Falon would be his destruction. His honor and his destiny forsaken for a traitorous bitch! He grabbed the ring and tried to wrestle it from his finger. It flared hotter, burning into his flesh. He knew what it wanted: *Falon*. If he could not have her, neither would Fenrir. And neither would his brother!

"Never!" he roared. Birds took flight from the trees, and deer sprang from their hiding places in the brush, dashing past him to safer ground. He would *not*, could *not* take her back. Even, gods help him, if he wanted to. He had only one option, and it was something he should have done long ago.

Destroy Lucien.

With no leader, pack Mondragon would have no choice but to reunite with pack Vulkasin, and together they would destroy clan Corbet. What happened after that, Rafael did not want to think of. Without Falon, his life would be . . . what? As empty and despondent as it felt now. Would he ever recover? Did he want to? Anger was so much easier to endure than heartbreak.

He stood and stared up at the darkening sky. The orange moon rose full. He would be his most powerful tonight. He would hunt Lucien down and strike a fatal, final blow. And if Lucien had not avenged the Blood Law, then Rafael would. Unspeakable pain tore him apart. His jealousy ripped his heart to shreds. He wanted nothing more to than to snap Falon's neck. But to do so would kill him. He knew it. But his pride, how could his damn pride allow her to live when she had betrayed him so heinously?

Were it not true, if he had one shred of doubt, he would cling to that. But he saw the mark and smelled their sex.

Rafe howled at the moon, then said to the ring, "Fenrir, *my* will shall be done!" Then he shifted, swallowed up the flaring ring, and ran as if the hounds of hell were on his heels back to the compound.

He smelled the Amorak miles before he reached his home. He also caught other scents, familiar and unfamiliar. He knew why Taylor was there, but why the Amorak? They had not come to the compound in years. Had they caught wind of Falon's treachery? Would they hold Lucien accountable as well? Would they demand Rafael hunt her down and slay her? Blood rage clouded his vision. He was a step ahead of them.

Not wanting to engage with his pack, Rafe avoided the secured front gates and instead cleared the high fence that surrounded the compound, then leapt onto the roof and into the shattered window of his bathroom. Though her scent lingered, he knew Falon was gone. She had run. He'd watched her and let her go, even though doing so had been almost as painful as watching Corbet skin his mother alive.

He forced the fury and heartache from his soul. He was alpha. There was no room in his heart for sentimentality. Falon had seen to that. He quickly shifted, coughed up the damn ring, slipped it on, and took a shower then dressed.

Several of his pack paced the vestibule to the great room. In his anger, he had run off at dawn, leaving them without instructions, with no leader in his absence. Their tension was palpable. They immediately settled when they sensed his presence, relaxing even more when they physically saw him. They knew something significant had occurred. They looked expectantly at him, then past him for their alpha female. Rafe leashed his emotions. "Good evening," he said, ignoring their questioning eyes.

"The Amorak are here. They're edgy and angry, Rafael. What happened?" Anton asked, his head down, showing his respect despite his demand.

"I suppose I'll have to ask them," Rafael said, his voice steel, leaving no room for more questions. "But first, I want to conclude my business with Taylor. Escort him to my office." Rafael strode past Anton and said over his shoulder, "Alone."

Rafael paced his office when Anton failed to bring Taylor in quickly enough. He wanted the human gone. Their business was concluded. He had other much more important business to attend to.

"Come in," Rafael roughly called at the knock on the door. He turned and faced Taylor. In forty-eight hours, the man had aged a lifetime. Still, his smile and the tears in his eyes belied the deep stress lines in his face. He rushed to Rafael, extending his hands. He grabbed Rafe's hands and vigorously shook them.

"Thank you, thank you!" his voice cracked, and tears ran down his cheeks.

Rafael stiffened and extracted his hands. He looked past him to Anton, who stood quietly at the threshold. "That will be all for now." His sergeant at arms retreated from the room, closing the door behind him. Rafael moved around to his desk and sat down, wanting distance between himself and Taylor. He was in no mood for human touch. His gut roiled when he thought of Falon and the smoothness of her skin, of her sweet scent. He growled. Of her treachery!

"Mr. Vulkasin?" Taylor said, a tremor of fear shaking his voice.

Rafael looked up and forced a smile. "Sit," he said, nodding toward the empty chair in front of his desk.

The man sat and leaned forward. "I don't know how you did it, and I don't give a damn. All I care about is that my daughter is home safe and sound." He wiped a tear from his eye. Rafael sneered at the man's weakness. He would never go there again. *Ever.*

"I'm a man of my word. Name your price, and it's yours."

Rafe sat back, contemplative, in his big leather chair. If Falon were here, she'd want to know how the girl was. He did, too, but not because he was overly concerned for her health. He wanted to know what she saw. What she knew.

"I trust your daughter is no worse for wear?"

Taylor nodded his head vigorously. "Barely a scratch on her. How she's going to do emotionally, only time will tell."

"Does she recall anything of her rescue?"

Taylor furrowed his brows and pursed his lips. "No. None at all. She has no recollection of the entire ordeal."

Rafael nodded. With time, her memories would return. Slowly at first, then in a rush. He'd blocked his parents' death for almost a year before he could face it again in his mind's eye. Now, there was not an hour that passed when he did not relive the horror of that day.

Taylor's head snapped back. "She was rambling when we drove her home, none of it making sense, but she did ask about a pretty dark-haired lady who saved the dog. Would that be your, uh, girlfriend?"

Rafael's organs twisted. "No."

Taylor nodded in understanding but pressed on. "I'd like to thank her. I owe her as well. If it hadn't been for her, my daughter would still be missing and Smythe would still be in my employ." Taylor sneered. "He won't be surfacing anytime soon." Their gazes locked in understanding.

"Falon also will not be surfacing anytime soon."

Taylor sat back in surprise. "Did she—"

"She is gone, Mr. Taylor, that is all you need to know." Rafael stood. "I'm afraid I have urgent business of my own to attend to."

Taylor stood. "You haven't named your price, Mr. Vulkasin."

Rafael had every intension of being compensated, when the time was right.

"Give me some time to think about it."

"Your call. You have my number."

"Keep your phone with you at all times. You never know when I'll be in touch."

Taylor nodded and held out his hand. "I will. And thank you for giving me back my daughter."

Rafael clasped the man's hand, glad for the first time that he had allowed Falon to interfere. At least one man would sleep easy tonight.

Rafael stood for a long moment after the door closed. Emotions chipped away at his tightly held defenses. He pushed them back, hardening his resolve, refusing to allow his emotions to play any further role in his future. The chaos in his heart and soul began to subside as his brain wrestled the last stronghold of his heart. No anger, no heartache, no regrets, no vengeance. Just steely resolution.

He was alpha and, as alpha, his sole reason for being was to protect, provide, and procreate for the greater good of his pack. He had failed them once out of fear and nearly destroyed them because of love. He would see the Blood Law avenged, then choose another mate and wildly procreate. He needed to do what he should have done all along—sacrifice Falon and then move on.

The scent of the Amorak intensified. Slowly, the door opened. Through the threshold, Sharia wobbled on her old, unsteady legs, accompanied by Talia's adopted brother, Daniel. The man glared at him.

Talia.

Lucien's captive. Her loss had been devastating to the pack in many ways. Not only was she their healer, their calm voice in the storms of chaos, she was their direct link to the Spirit Mother. She was also Rafe's spirit guide. Mostly, she was his friend. He missed her.

When he demanded the council step in and force Lucien to return her, they once again refused him. He took matters into his own hands then but failed to free her.

Mentally Rafe hung his head in shame. Another failure as alpha. He shook off the guilt. By sunrise, he swore to himself, Talia would be home.

"Rafael," Sharia softly said. "Your chosen one seeks the Slayers. You must stop her at all costs."

Sixteen

RAFAEL'S HEART STOPPED for one inexplicable moment before it kicked his chest with the velocity of a mule team. Unbridled fury that she would dare betray him yet again raged white-hot in his chest. But to Sharia and her shaman, he remained outwardly composed.

"She is dead to me," Rafael said evenly. "The Slayers will do what Lucien has failed to do. If they do not, then I will slay her myself."

Sharia's feeble body wobbled toward him. "Tonight is *the* night. The moon is full and you are at your strongest, Rafael. The Slayers will not destroy her. They will protect her and use her powers on all Lycans. You must go after her. Tonight."

Rafael swiped his hand across his chin and began to pace his office. Sharia moved into his path and grabbed his shirt in her gnarled fists, shaking it. "You have allowed your guilt and emotions to rule for too long, Rafael. Your refusal to take a mate has prevented the pack from reproducing. Your failure to mate has inadvertently prevented Lucien from taking another mate, as well. The packs are dying. Reclaim your chosen one. Only then can destiny play out."

Rafael snarled. "She betrayed me with my brother! Even now, she runs to the enemy. I will never reclaim her!"

"Set your emotions aside!" she hissed. "If you do not reclaim her, the Slayers will triumph, and every Lycan will perish before the coming of the Blood Moon. Is your pride worth the lives of an entire nation?"

Despite his fury, Rafael gently disengaged the old woman's hands from his shirt. He looked over to Daniel, who had said nothing. He didn't have to. The recrimination in his eyes spoke volumes. Rafael inhaled sharply then slowly exhaled. He was alpha. As alpha, he was the one who had to make the hard decisions. He was the one, not Lucien, who bore the weight of the Lycan nation on his shoulders. He had let them down too many times over the last fourteen years. He promised himself he would not do it again. He would take charge in whatever capacity was required and do what had to be done to preserve his people and their future existence. But asking him to rescue his chosen one, the same chosen one who betrayed him with his brother then ran to their mortal enemy, was too much. He did not know if he possessed the self-control not to harm her the next time he laid eyes on her. "What am I to do with her once she is reclaimed?"

"Allow the Blood Law to be avenged," Sharia softly but firmly said.

Rafael shook his head in disbelief. It made no sense. "Reclaim her, and wait for Lucien to come for her?"

Daniel nodded as Sharia said, "Yes."

The reality of what they asked of him struck him speechless.

"It is the only way to move past it, Rafael," Daniel said, speaking for the first time. "Avenge the Blood Law, and wipe the slate clean. You will be free to take another mate, and Lucien will follow. The packs must unite if they are to rise with the sun the day after the Blood Moon rising."

"Once the Blood Law is avenged, life will spring from the loins of all Lycans. It will be a great time to rejoice. The rebirth of the Lycan nation will come with the rising, but only if the packs are united. See it through, Rafe, then be done with it! The wounds have festered too long." Sharia's voice held strong with conviction.

Rafael jammed his fist into his open palm. How could he take Falon back? Did Sharia expect he take her back into his bed as well? He would not. Never.

He would not breed with her. Now he was relieved she had not marked him. Until she did, she would not conceive. He would reclaim her, but in appearances only. Let Lucien come for her. Let him avenge the Blood Law; only then could Rafael walk away from the chains of guilt that held him captive all these years and walk to freedom.

Though his heart had closed, he nodded. "I will see it done."

Sharia nodded and smiled a crooked, knowing smile. She patted Rafael's hand, then brought it to her lips and kissed it. The sweet gesture in the midst of such harsh words took him by surprise. "Your parents would be proud of you, Rafael. You have finally, after all this time, taken control of your destiny." She lowered his hand and let go of it. "I promise you, in the end you will be glad you did. With your sacrifice, the glory of the Lycan nation will shine brighter than a thousand full moons. You will see."

She turned from him and, with Daniel's assistance, made her wobbly way out of his office. Daniel quietly closed the door behind them.

He replayed Sharia's words in his head. The ones about his parents being proud of him. He hadn't been doing right by them, but today that would end.

The debilitating yoke that he had dragged around since the day he slew Lucien's chosen one, lightened. With it gone, he would be invincible. He growled and yanked the office door open.

"Anton, Yuri, tell the boys to saddle up! We're going hunting!"

NESTLED HIGH IN the Oakland hills, Falon stood outside a large building that resembled an old medieval fortress. Though it had taken all day, it had been easy to track them. She'd returned to the burned-out warehouse and, like a wolf to its prey, she lifted her nose to the air, caught their lingering scents, then followed them to this place. Oddly, there didn't seem to be an elaborate security system like at the Lycan compound. She guessed when you were the hunters, you didn't need one.

Dozens of old cars and vintage motorcycles lined the perimeter of the rustic stone structure. Not a soul stirred. The sun had set a half hour before. She'd watched since then, hoping to catch a glimpse of Edward. He was here, his scent dominant.

She had no more of a plan now than she had when she'd run from the compound. How could she get answers then walk away a free woman? Promise Edward something? He would want nothing less than Rafael.

The wide iron-strapped wooden door to the building swung open. She ducked behind the dilapidated car she had driven down in. When a man stepped out and abruptly stopped and turned her way, she ducked deeper. Holding her breath, Falon peered at him through the windows. Edward. And he was not alone. Lana! Collared and on a leash, she cowered beside him. So that was how Edward knew what she had done to Lucien. She was partially clad and looked more than a little roughed up. Her head lifted in the slight breeze, and she, too, turned toward where Falon hid. Damn it, the wind had shifted, and she was now upwind of them. She backed up, hunching down until her knees creaked.

"Do not be afraid," Edward called, his deep voice reverberating off the cars. As he moved toward her, Falon moved stealthily around the cars, putting distance between them. "I will not harm you." The hair on the back of her neck stood on end. His soothing baritone lulled deceptively. "Come out, tell me why you are here. Who are you?" he cajoled.

Falon felt the pull of his voice. She nearly stood. While she didn't trust him, she felt on a gut level that he was as intrigued by her as she was by him. But he had her at a disadvantage. She was at his lair with everything to lose, and he had everything to gain. She smiled wryly. If Edward thought he could use her to draw Rafael out, the joke would be on him. The last thing Rafael would do was put himself or his pack in danger for her safety. Her stock had dropped suddenly and dramatically, thanks to Lucien.

So, what *did* she have to lose at the moment? Maybe a day or two of a forced stay until Edward figured out Rafael would rather hand her over to the Slayers than lift a finger to save her? She'd take her chances.

Slowly, like the phoenix rising, Falon stood. She startled in surprise to find Edward standing on the other side of the hood of the car she hid behind. He was as tall as Rafael was, but blond, blue-eyed, and pale-skinned. She'd consider him a handsome man if she didn't know the truth about him. He smiled a wide, disarming smile. Yet his eyes glittered malevolently. Falon's nostrils flared as she inhaled his scent. The blood of the Lycan nation screamed out for vengeance. She stiffened.

"She is Rafael's bitch!" Lana accused, scrambling up behind Edward. Without looking behind him, he threw out his left arm and hit her in the chest with his fist. Lana landed with a sickening thud on the asphalt. Instinctively, Falon moved toward her. Edward stuck his hand out, palm open, like a stop sign.

"She is not worth your attention."

Falon slapped his hand away and gloated inwardly at his shocked expression. She bet most people, women especially, didn't defy him. Falon dropped down beside Lana. Blood pooled behind her head; her dazed brown eyes looked up at Falon.

"I'm sorry," she mumbled.

Falon shushed her, gently rolled her head into her open hand, and pressed her fingertips to the gaping hole in the back of her skull. Energy warmed her chest, reverberating into her shoulder, down her arm, into her hand and fingertips. Lana closed her eyes. "You'll be okay," Falon whispered, before carefully setting her head down on the concrete. "Do not move," Falon instructed, then stood, wiping her bloody hand on her jeans. Lana would heal shortly.

She turned to Edward and demanded, "How are we associated?"

His lips thinned as his gaze scalded her from head to toe. "You are a healer?"

She shrugged. "I know how to use a Band-Aid."

He reached down and yanked Lana up to him, grabbed a hank of her hair, then twisted her neck around so that the back of her head was exposed. Lana squeezed her eyes shut, biting her bottom lip. Instinctually Falon understood: Edward was a sadist. He thrived on pain. Lycan pain. Lana didn't give him the satisfaction of showing hers.

"Do you always pick on women?" Falon demanded, wondering how long they were going to stand out in the parking lot challenging each other.

Edward shoved Lana from him, then yanked back on the leash, jerking her backward. She splayed out on all fours and began to cry.

He sneered, then looked directly at Falon. "She is Lycan. As such, she does not deserve my respect."

"Then why bother at all?"

He threw is head back and laughed. "You are not an ignorant woman. You know the power I wield, and yet you challenge me?"

"I challenge any man who treats another being with such contempt."

He shook his head. "Come inside, my dear champion of the world, come see what Lycans have done to my people; then tell me how you feel."

When Falon crossed the threshold into the fortress, she felt like she had walked into the thirteenth century. The interior of the building was what she imagined an English castle to be. Flaming sconces adorned thick block walls. Between the sconces hung rich tapestries, each one depicting battles scenes. Slayers versus Lycans. And piled along the walls were towering heaps of . . . ? Wolf pelts. At that moment she was grateful she had not eaten. Her stomach did several somersaults, yet she managed to maintain her composure and continue to observe her surroundings.

Long trestle tables and rushes covered the floor. A huge walk-in hearth blazed with fire; several spits rotated large hunks of roasting meat. At the far end of the hall, a dais with two large carved thrones was prominently displayed. On either side of the thrones was a large, square iron cage, both of them empty. Falon didn't need anyone to tell her what the cages were for. Edward handed the leash over to a burly man, who dragged Lana kicking and screaming to the cage on the left. He shoved her in, kicking her in the behind for good measure. The door clanked shut, and the brute turned a skeleton key in the lock.

Contempt sprang into Falon's next words, "I assumed since you were human you would be civilized. I was wrong."

"There is no civility between my people and Lycans." He looked down at her and menacingly said, "On any other day, you would be in the cage next to her. You have cavorted with Lycans!" His voice lowered, and he stepped closer. "The *only* reason you are not is because you are a human who, for the moment, intrigues me."

"What of those of mixed blood?" she asked.

He threw his head back and laughed an ugly, demonic laugh. "Do you mean Lycan and Slayer?" he asked incredulously.

"Yes."

"Preposterous! A Slayer would never stoop so low as to bed a dog. It is forbidden, not even discussed!"

"So you're saying there has never been a coupling between a Slayer and Lycan."

"Blasphemy! Speak of it again and lose your tongue!" he raged.

Falon blanched at his outrage, yet her mind whirled with thoughts. Did Edward not know that Lucien's chosen one had been a Slayer? Was he in denial? Or had Rafael been wrong? Had he killed an innocent woman? Dear God, what if he had?

"My apologies, Edward." She forced herself to touch him by placing her hand on his arm. She blanched at the malevolence that swirled within him. He flung her hand from him as if he knew she could see into his soul. She had made a colossal mistake coming here. But she persevered; she would have her answers. "I am new to your world, thus misunderstanding the dichotomy between Slayers and Lycans."

He stared hard at her, sensing she was being honest. In truth, she was. Rafael had been less than forthcoming with information. Falon took several deep, cleansing breaths to calm her rattled nerves. They continued toward the far end of the hall.

A multitude of cloying scents wafted around her, clogging her nostrils.

The people, dear Lord, the people were dressed like Conan. Was she at a medieval reenactment? She glanced at Edward and saw that while he wore more modern garb, several pieces, like his leather boots, were lined with what she was sure was wolf fur. His wide leather belt and tunic-style shirt were reminiscent of the Old World. The hair on the back of her neck rose when she looked closer at the people in the hall. Many of them were not whole. Limbs were missing. Some just missing hands or maybe a foot. Some with severely ravaged faces. Good God, what happened to them?

Edward smiled bitterly at her astonished face. "The work of pack Vulkasin." He strode toward the end of the hall. Every person in the place stopped whatever chore they were about and stared uneasily at her. Every part of Falon screamed for her to run. But she knew if she were to understand herself, she must stay, because here she knew she would find the answers she sought.

"What are you?" Falon asked as she stepped deeper into the bowels of the building.

"You know who we are. We are Slayers."

"Why?"

"Our king decreed it eight hundred years ago. Until no wolf walks this earth, we will hunt them and destroy them."

"But, Lycans are human."

"They are wolves first."

Falon didn't belabor the point. So they were wolves some of the time. Apparently that was enough to get you killed by a Slayer. She stopped and looked up at the tapestries. The ones farther back depicted witches and sorcerers casting spells. The black magic Rafe spoke about. The last and most elaborate tapestry illustrated a large blond man richly garbed in Old World threads with his hands raised to the heavens and a huge black wolf that hovered among the ominous clouds. Falon stepped closer and gasped. The ring on the man's finger. It was Rafael's ring! And Conan's before him. And perhaps, her father's before that. Falon cleared her throat. "Did he encourage your use of the black arts?"

"Necessity dictated we embrace magic. When the wolves were given human life, we had no choice. We do not abuse the power."

"When were the wolves given human form?"

"Three hundred years ago. During the great war of the North, my ancestors were on the verge of eliminating the last packs from the earth. The northern gods took pity on them, knowing they could no longer survive as they were. So they were given human life."

"So you went against the gods to obey a dead king?"

"You insult my clan. We do not worship the gods of the Lycans. We are Christian men and women as was our king!" He stepped back and extended his hand toward the hall and the people within it. "I'm sure Vulkasin has spoon-fed you lies about us. We are not animals like the Lycans, but civilized, and honor bound to our ancestors. Until the last wolf is no more, we live as my ancestors lived. We are steeped in our traditions and will not rest until the king's work is completed."

Falon nodded. So much for love thy neighbor. She pointed to the tapestry. "What of the ring in the tapestry?"

"The Eye of Fenrir, a gift to my ancestor from his king for his loyalty and good work." He turned narrowed eyes on her. "It belongs to me. You know Vulkasin wears it."

"I do, but I was not aware it was yours."

"Did Vulkasin send you here to spy?"

"No." She looked directly at him and continued, "I have been cast out."

"Do you take me for a complete fool? I saw how it is between you and that cur." He cocked his head and looked sideways at her. "I also know if you leave here, you will die by the hand of his brother. Vulkasin will not stop him."

She knew that but asked, "Why not?"

Edward took her elbow and steered her to an upholstered chair near a smaller hearth and indicated she should sit. He pulled another chair over and sat facing her. "Do you know why I have not separated your head from your neck?"

Falon swallowed hard and shook her head. "No, why?"

"Because you are not Lycan. Because I am the only one who can save you now. Because you can deliver me Vulkasin, but truth be known, more than all of those things combined, there is something compelling about you. I felt it the moment our eyes met. I know you felt it, too."

Falon nodded, unable to deny it. It was why she was there. "Tell me why Rafael will not stop his brother from killing me."

Edward snapped his fingers; immediately, two women dressed in ye olde garb set a tray of food and wine on the small table next to Edward. They disappeared as noiselessly as they had appeared. Yet when Falon looked around, she felt like a speck under a microscope. The people had slowly stopped what they were doing and quietly watched her. She couldn't say they were unhappy. Their auras, though black, were tinged with green and yellow. Content colors.

She dragged her attention back to her host. He poured a goblet of wine and handed it to her then poured one for himself. She watched him warily. He smiled and sipped the wine. "It is safe to drink."

Falon took a sip and found it surprisingly sweet and tasty. "Tell me."

"The Lycans are ruled by two things, both of equal importance to them. The Blood Law, their covenant, and their thirst for Slayer blood. The Blood Law dictates an eye for an eye. Vulkasin slew his brother's chosen one. The law decrees Mondragon has the right to exact the same as payment for the injustice done to him. He despises his brother and will see it done. Only then can Vulkasin take another mate and add his devil's spawn to the mix."

"Some say Lucien's chosen one was Slayer," Falon ventured, bracing herself for an explosion.

Edward's face reddened, but he did not break his stare. Slowly, he said, "A lie. Never has a Slayer lain with a Lycan."

"Why would Rafael lie about that?"

"At the time, the brothers were co-alphas. Vulkasin felt threatened by his brother's taking of a mate, so he destroyed the threat and made up lies that she was a Slayer to justify his actions." He laughed contemptuously. "Vulkasin didn't plan on the fallout or how it would weaken the packs."

Edward poured another cup of brew and drank deeply from it. "Vulkasin's continued reluctance for more than a decade to take a mate has worked in our favor as well. Until the alpha breeds, the pack cannot. Vulkasin's refusal to take a mate has kept the packs small, and we have been making them smaller."

"Why are you telling me all of this? You know Rafael has marked me?"

Edward looked at her as if she were a dunce. "Because I know that his brother will destroy you. Because you are human and value your life. You will fight for it. You are safer here with me than anywhere else in the world. And even if I believed Vulkasin cast you out, which I don't, the Lycan has no choice but to come for you if he will ever be able to take another mate. For me, for my clan, you are a means to two ends: Vulkasin's life"—he sneered—"and the return of my ring."

So it really had been a mistake to come here. He had no intention of allowing her to freely go. The cold fingers of fear scurried down her spine. She fought the shivers. "Other than being Lycan, what has Rafael ever done to you?"

Edward stood so quickly, the chair he had sat upon flew back against the wall, hitting it with a thud.

"He took my son!" he roared. "He skinned him alive not more than three months ago! Right before my eyes!" He slammed his fists against the block wall. "I will do the same to him!"

Falon sat stunned. She had seen Rafael kill. Understood it even. If she believed Edward's statement—and she did—she understood his hatred. But his son was a Slayer, and were not all Slayers fair game to Lycans, as Lycans were to Slayers? "How old was he?"

Edward turned bright onyx eyes on her. Falon caught her breath and sat back. They turned, just as Lucien had explained they did when a Slayer became enraged. "A day shy of eighteen."

Dear God, just a child. "Why would he do such a terrible thing?"

"Because it is what Lycans do. It is why eight hundred years ago a great king charged my ancestors to destroy the wolves. They were rabid thieves, preying on humans, stealing our children and feeding them to their young. They are evil. They procreate evil. They must be eliminated!"

Falon sat for long moments, digesting what she had just been told. In that moment, she realized that the hate between Lycans and Slayers was so deep, so profound, and such a part of their DNA fabric that there was nothing anyone could do to broker peace between them. There would only be peace for one side or the other when the enemy was extinct. She was foolish to have come here and even more foolish to think she could be the catalyst to peace between the warring people. Yet, in some big or small way, somehow, somewhere, she had a place in this all. But where?

She drew in a deep breath and looked squarely at Edward, a man her lover—the Lycan she loved—had vowed to destroy. "My name is Falon Corbet. What does that mean to you?"

Seventeen

EDWARD'S STUNNED EXPRESSION caught her off guard and filled her with instant dread. Just as quickly, however, his face smoothed back into a normal mien. "It means nothing. Corbet is a common enough name."

She'd seen his shock. Why? She stood and took a step toward him. Toward the truth.

"Then how do I know you? You said yourself we have a connection. You felt it. *Who am I?*"

He averted his gaze for a second before staring straight at her. "Tell me about your parents. Perhaps there is a distant blood tie."

"I don't remember my parents. I was a foster kid. My only tie to my past is my name."

"Perhaps your foster parents gave you the name?"

Falon shook her head. "No, I'm sure Corbet is my family name." She thought for a moment then asked, "Are there any of your clan who have broken off to go on their own?"

"The clan never separates. Our strength is in our numbers."

"Is there some way you can tell if I'm a Slayer? A test or something?"

"You have failed the only true test of a Slayer."

"I have?"

"You do not posses the one thing all Slayers are born with: hatred for Lycans. You have shown the opposite, having lain with one, an animal."

Falon bit her tongue. She took exception to that last remark. "But what if I wasn't taught to hate? Could I still be a Slayer?" She had to know!

"Our hatred is woven into our genes."

Why was he not questioning her more in depth? His demeanor had noticeably shifted from highly curious to indifferent. As if he had lost all interest in her. This was not going anywhere close to how she had imagined. What *had* she imagined? That he would ask her questions then reveal who she was based on them? Well, yes, sort of. At least she had one answer, the important one. All indicators pointed to a non-Slayer status. For that she was eternally grateful. One less bullet Rafe could use against her, and just as important, she thought Slayers sucked. Hugely.

Part of Falon's anxiety relaxed. She was not a Slayer, but—she eyed Corbet cryptically—while she may have read more into her initial meeting with him, there was more to all of this. "Why did you try to capture me at the warehouse? And how did you know Rafael would show up?"

He shook his head at her like she was a child. "The answer is not plain to see?"

"I'm not good at cat-and-mouse word games, Edward."

"Why capture you? Bait. If I could not destroy Rafael then, he would come for you, and I'd destroy him now. In my own environment, I am unbeatable. How did I know Vulkasin would show up?

Smythe, may he rest in peace, maneuvered his employer seamlessly. It was Harold who kidnapped the daughter, then suggested he go to Vulkasin for help. Harold's magic is—er, was—strong. He hid his Slayer status, but then you, my dear, saw through it."

"How do I see through it?"

Corbet shrugged again. "That is the question of the day now, isn't it?"

"Why did you kill Smythe? He's one of you."

"I would never kill a Slayer. His employer discovered his duplicity and"—he shrugged nonchalantly—"he was eliminated."

"So let me get this straight: your guy gets whacked, and you could care less. You used an innocent child as bait, who you would have allowed to die had Rafael not cut the rope. Your war with the Lycans spreads into the innocent human world. What honor is there in that?"

He shrugged, nonplussed. "Collateral damage is a sad fact of our quest. It does not happen often."

He was so blasé about it. Not one shred of remorse. No wonder Rafe couldn't wait to chop off this guy's head. She might beat him to it.

Edward looked past her shoulder and motioned for someone to approach. Falon turned to see several large broadsword-armed men walk toward them. Her heart almost jumped out of her chest.

"You have nothing to fear from me, Falon, or anyone here," Edward said. "I can protect you from both brothers. If you will allow me to."

Because she was human, he'd said, and that was it. Right. Falon coolly regarded him. He was not offering anything for free. "My ability to pick a Slayer out of the crowd when a Lycan alpha can't doesn't have anything to do with your invitation, does it?"

His eyes glittered with excitement. He nodded. "Among other things."

"I'll take a rain check. I'm not going to be your worm on a hook.

Besides, I have unfinished business with *both* brothers. You'll have to find someone else to use as bait."

His face drew tight, his lips thinned, his eyes darkened. "Whatever that business is," he snapped, "let it go. If you step outside of this building while either brother is alive, you are as good as dead."

"Thanks for caring," Falon flippantly said. Nervously she smoothed her hands down the front of her jeans. "I'll take my chances."

"I'm afraid, Falon Corbet, that I cannot allow you to leave at the moment," Edward said, standing.

"I had a feeling you were going to say that. But I really do insist on leaving." Imperceptibly, he nodded to the men who had gathered close behind her, forming a semicircle. Trapped like a rabbit in a snare. She had only one way to go, into the stone wall. Or . . . Immediately she shut down the fear that flashed like a sputtering neon sign and focused on extracting herself from her stupidity.

She leapt straight up into the air, stomping on Edward's head and using it to propel herself higher. She did a high backflip and landed behind the goons and Edward. He turned slowly, smugly, his confidence unflappable. "Very impressive. If I did not know better, I would say you were a highly trained Slayer."

In a blur he jumped high in the air. As he came down to land in front of her, Falon focused every brain cell in her head on shoving him back into the thugs who closed menacingly in on her. Just as Edward's feet touched the floor, his body slammed backward into the wall, unhinging a corner of the tapestry of the Slayer with the ring. Falon didn't waste any time to gloat. She leapt toward the thick wood door and hit it feetfirst. It splintered into a dozen pieces as she tumbled out of the building. As she mentally slowed the velocity of her fall, she pushed off the steps, continuing her high leaps. A large hand grabbed her right ankle and yanked hard. She went hurtling backward onto the stone steps that led to the fortress. She hit with such velocity, the sound of cracking bones overrode her painful cries.

"You will never best me, Falon Corbet," Edward said as he yanked her up and threw her damaged body over his shoulder. He pushed what was left of the door out of the way with a flick of his hand. Incredibly, as if they were whole, they slammed shut behind them, the thick steel bars slamming into place.

She was a prisoner.

PACK VULKASIN MADE good time to Oakland. It was a ride Rafe had made one hundred times, and each time he'd added a kill notch to his belt. Tonight he would add more.

The night air was cool in his hair, and Falon's scent messed with him the entire ride down the mountain, onto the Sacramento flats and along the salty breeze of the bay. Each time his heart ached for her, he forced the emotion aside. He refused to think of her as anything less than an enemy of the state. Even if he gave her the benefit of the doubt—perhaps Lucien had tricked her?—her flight into the enemy's arms destroyed it.

But his love could not save her.

He shook the emotions from his heart and soul. Like the exhaust fumes from the chopper, they evaporated into the night air. He was not destined to live with his true love. He was destined now to choose a second mate that would be best for his pack, not his heart. Never again his heart. He and Lucien lived by the same curse. Neither brother would have their true chosen one beside them.

As many alphas before him had done, Rafael would sacrifice his own desires to do what was required to keep the pack safe and thriving. That he had put his own selfishness before the pack's well-being gnawed at him. Could he help that he was not a cold-blooded murderer? Could he really condemn himself for failing to take a mate, when doing so would be handing her a death sentence? On the other hand, hadn't he acted quickly and without remorse, killing Lucien's mate when it was the best thing for the clan?

He should have immediately chosen a mate, made the sacrifice, and moved on. But the injustice of it all prevented it. He had obeyed the Blood Law, damn it! Rafe clenched his jaw so hard his teeth ground. What was done was done, and now he must see the rest through.

It would eat him alive if he dwelled on the right and wrong of it. He must focus on the task in front of him. Capture Falon. Destroy Edward.

With Balor back East drumming up soldiers for the rising, Edward would not have reinforcements. But Rafe did.

He glanced behind himself and nodded. Pack Ruiz joined them in Vallejo, pack Casares pulled up behind them as they screamed through Richmond. Clan Corbet was strong, well-armed, and had a very defendable fortress, but Rafe had the element of surprise, the benefit of numbers, and the full moon on his side.

He glanced up at the rising moon. By midnight it would be at its highest for this cycle. Rafael, too, would be at his peak strength. The timing was in the Lycans' favor tonight. It was a rare full moon when a Lycan fell beneath a Slayer's sword.

As the packs approached the off-ramp to the road that would wind high up into the hills, Rafael slowed, allowing the bikes to condense. They swarmed off the highway onto a wide boulevard, blowing through one red light after another. Not a cop in sight. They would be noticeably scarce for the rest of the evening—Rafe's call to Taylor had insured it. The man was connected. Calling off the cops in advance would make what Rafe had to do go that much smoother.

Falon's scent intensified. Overriding her fresh natural scent was the pungent smell of fear. He growled, wrangling with his instinct to protect her. In his mind, he heard her calling to him for help. To come for her. Begging for forgiveness, for something she had no control over. But more urgent was her warning that Corbet was waiting and to stay away. He clamped his jaw so tight it threatened to snap.

Once again his gut told him he had overreacted when he woke that morning, that she was an innocent in a deadly game to which she didn't know the rules. That he was too quick to a temper when it involved Lucien, and he'd let his emotions overrule his reason. The very least he should have done was to hear what she had to say. Instead, he assumed the worst.

He closed his mind and his heart to her pleas and warnings. He would not soften.

Rafael turned off the main road to a less traveled one and began his ascent into the foothills. After a few miles, he slowed then came to a complete stop. The packs swarmed around him. He cut his engine and motioned for them to do the same. When nothing but the distant traffic could be heard, he said, "In an eighth of a mile we're going to turn off onto a dirt road. We'll dismount, shift, and surround the fortress." He looked over to Amon, his armorer, who pulled up behind them in a blacked-out van. "I was not going to use them until the rising, but we'll need them tonight if we're to survive until then." He looked over at the van. "Amon has flack jackets and thick, leather studded collars made especially for Lycans. Half of us will shift and we'll outfit them. Once that's done, the rest of you will shift and Amon will outfit you."

Amon slid open the panel door to reveal stacks of flack jackets.

"The collars will help prevent beheading, and the jackets will stop most caliber silver bullets. Do not shift back to your human form unless I give the command. We'll form a wide noose around the fortress and slowly draw it tight. Under no circumstances can any harm come to"—a rise of emotion caught in Rafael's throat—"my chosen one. Tomorrow night I will deliver her to Lucien, and the Blood Law will be avenged."

Collective sounds of surprise rippled through the packs, followed by knowing yet sympathetic nods. They knew, as he did, it must be done.

"When we have the fortress in sight, I will shift and find a way to breach the structure. Once I locate the woman, if there is a way for me to extract her without a full-out assault, I will choose that route.

"Once she is extracted, we'll go in and do what is necessary." He looked across the sea of determined faces. Their days of being the hunted were coming to an end. Tonight Edward, tomorrow Balor. Rafe's only regret was that the man who slew his parents, Thomas Corbet, was nowhere to be found. For that Slayer he would be extra specially vicious.

Rafael lifted his nose to the air and inhaled. The scent of Slayers was strong. His blood quickened.

At heart, he was a predator. They all were. It was how they'd survived, but their humanity had tempered much of it. Wolves in the wild did not kill for the sake of killing; they killed to survive. That it thrilled was a by-product. Rafael and his people were no different. Yes, there were those like his brother who lived to kill. His pack was bloodthirsty and untrustworthy. Pack Vulkasin was more civilized. And it had cost him, Rafe realized. If their positions were reversed, Lucien would not have hesitated to take a mate so that Rafael would avenge the Blood Law. Once done, Lucien would have chosen another and begun to build his dynasty. Rafael had stumbled by not wanting to have a hand in killing an innocent. Everyone he cared for had suffered for it. It was what separated him from his brother. Rafael valued life and was compassionate. And maybe, too, there was a part of him that wanted Lucien to suffer more. He failed to admit his woman was a Slayer. And so Lucien lived while Rafael would have to sacrifice an innocent.

"Do not spare one Slayer life tonight," Rafe said. "Each one you take is one less we will battle in the coming months, and one less threat to the Lycan nation." He looked over at Amon, who nodded. "Pack Vulkasin and pack Ruiz, shift."

Less than thirty minutes later, Rafael sat upon the slanted roof of the northern wing of Corbet Keep. Falon's scent cried out to him for rescue. His anger flared at her stupidity. What did she think Corbet would do when she approached him? Welcome her with open arms? She was marked by the most powerful alpha in North America. Corbet would never allow her to leave. The only reason she lived now was because Corbet had known even before Rafael had that he would come for her.

He had no choice, just as Sharia had said.

He slid a heavy smoke vent aside and peered down into the bowels of the hall. Immediately his gaze trained on the two metal cages. His nose twitched. Lana! He realized she'd betrayed them all by giving Corbet the heads-up on Falon. Now she paid the price. As much as he despised her treachery, he would not leave her here for the Slayers to rip apart. He would bring her home where her pack would exact their justice.

His eyes traveled across the ridiculous thrones to the other cage. A small pelt-covered lump lay balled up in the corner. His heart thudded in his chest.

Falon.

Her head snapped back. She looked up. Their gazes locked. The longing in her eyes tore him in half.

Rafa, you came!

I came for my pack. You belong to my brother now.

She sat up. Grabbing the metal bars, she winced in pain as she tilted her head all of the way back so that she could fully see him. *No, Rafa! I am* your *chosen one. I would never willingly go to your brother.*

You already have.

She stifled a cry. *Lucien tricked me. He came to me in my dreams. I thought it was you, but he never, we never—there was no consummation, Rafael, I swear it!*

Did Corbet trick you, too?

"No." She stared up at him, grasping the metal bars as if she could pull them apart. *I came here for answers. I realize now it was foolish!*

Silence!

But it was too late. Corbet materialized beside Falon. He grabbed her hair and yanked her head hard against the metal bars. Falon snarled and grabbed him, digging her nails into his skin, shredding him. Corbet shoved her away and looked at his bloody hand. "If I didn't know better, I'd say you were a bloodthirsty Lycan bitch." He looked up at Rafael, who leashed his primal urge to drop on Corbet and tear him apart.

"You came as expected, Vulkasin, the full moon and all," Corbet sneered. Armed Slayers stacked up behind him.

When I drop to the floor, use your powers to blow the front door off its hinges, Rafael instructed Falon.

She nodded and turned toward the front of the hall. Corbet continued to stare up at Rafael.

"Come down, Vulkasin. And let us discuss a reasonable exchange."

"The lives of my entire pack for what? You killing my chosen one for the hell of it?"

"Give me the Eye of Fenrir, and I give you my word I will release her and allow all of you to leave in peace."

Rafael laughed. "Your timing stinks, Corbet. I left the ring behind." A lie. As he'd always done before, he had swallowed it. If Corbet knew he had, he'd gut him.

"That is unfortunate for your whore. But fortunate for me," Corbet said, grabbing Falon's leg and yanking her hard against the metal bars. He shoved back her pant leg and ran his hand along her smooth calf. "Such supple skin. You do remember, Vulkasin, how skilled I am at skinning."

Rafael snarled as the beast in him fought for release.

"Robert paid for your despicable acts, Corbet. Do you want your daughter to pay for another?"

Corbet shrieked with such fury the sound reverberated against his ears. The Slayer drew his short blade, sliced Falon's ankle, and ripped a slice of skin from her. Falon screamed in pain, yanking her leg back through the metal bars. Stunned by the vicious act, Rafe looked down at the bloody pulp of her skin. His vision clouded crimson. Corbet would regret he was ever born. An eye for an eye. He would exact more than a pound of skin from him.

He may have to take Falon's life to settle the Blood Law, but no one hurt his chosen one. No one. Rafael howled, his rage so complete the beast in him took over. He dropped to the floor in full wolf.

Eighteen

FALON FOCUSED ALL of her energy on blowing out the front door, but she couldn't get the visual of Rafael in all his wolfen fury out of her head. And something else was happening to her . . . she was having trouble focusing. Her vision honed then blurred. Her bones ached. Her organs were tight. Primal fury clawed at her from her insides out, demanding release. Only she didn't know how to release it.

Each time Rafael lunged at Corbet, taking a bite out of him, the Slayer got in his own licks. Her mate's blood splattered in a high arc into the air. Warm drops spattered across her face. Falon snarled and lunged at the cage. Her teeth gnashed at the metal bars while her hands and feet dug and tore at the corner. Her vision clouded. Her heart beat furiously. When she couldn't break free, she sat back on her haunches and looked around the room, seeing it so clearly it was like 3-D magnified.

More Slayers circled Rafael, each taking a hack or a stab at him.

Some paid for it with the loss of a hand, but the combined efforts began to take their toll. Blood smeared his beautiful coat. His lunges were shorter, his bites less accurate. Falon turned toward the door and the howling from beyond. *Hurry,* she urged the pack before turning back to Rafael. The Slayers closed in a tight circle around him. He snarled and lunged, tearing into them. But for each bite he took, two Slayers wounded him. Blood dripped from his fur to the stone floor. His front legs buckled beneath him. She felt his weakening.

She strengthened. He needed her.

Falon grabbed the bars to her cage and pulled, never taking her gaze off Rafael. The howls outside of the building intensified. The Slayers within rallied, their weapons drawn as they prepared to battle. She knew she had to find a way to let the pack in, but she knew if she focused on the door, Rafe would fall beneath Edward's sword.

"Fight me as a man!" Edward screamed, jabbing Rafe's right flank. "Or die like the cur you are!"

"No!" Falon shouted. If Rafe shifted back to his human form, he would have no weapon, no protection. It was best for him to remain in his wolf form.

Rafe snarled, snapping at Edward's hand. His fangs sank deep into the Slayer's flesh and bone. Corbet kicked Rafael from him into another Slayer, who impaled Rafael from behind through the shoulder blades, pinning him to the floor. He howled in agony.

Another just as excruciating howl followed. With jarring reality, Falon realized the sound came from her.

Edward turned to look at her, shock registering on his face. At that moment, all movement stopped. Eerie silence followed. The Slayers stared at her as her skin rippled. Realization, shock, and horror slammed into her but was quickly followed by relief.

She was Lycan.

Her gaze swept to Rafael. He'd dropped to the floor, the sword buried to the hilt between his shoulders. Its bloody blade protruded just below his neck into the floor.

Agony twisted and tugged every fiber of her body. He could not die! She would not allow it!

His deep turquoise eyes darkened, and through them she saw into his soul. The turmoil of his life played out in front of her. His pain, his heartache, his life as an alpha that refused to mark an innocent for the sake of his brother's revenge. And there, in the middle of it all, she saw his love for her. Despite what he thought she had done, it burned bright and hot. Only death could extinguish it.

Falon threw her head back and howled another ungodly howl. Her hands pulled at the bars, then slipped off, no longer able to grip. Her bones crunched and stretched, her heart rate spiked, her skin tightened. She lost her balance and fell in agony to the floor of her cage. She closed her eyes, wanting to fight off what she was sure was the most torturous death imaginable but instead welcoming it. Because even if it meant her death, she would save the man she loved.

RAFAEL SHIFTED AND lay in stunned silence. He could not believe what he witnessed. Falon shifting into a sleek black she-wolf. When it was done, she opened her wolfen eyes, and he was mesmerized by their deep blue depths. She snarled, lunging through the opening she'd made in the cage, and dove into Edward. The Slayer was as stunned as Rafe, enabling his hesitation to give her the opening she needed. A clear shot to his throat. Corbet screamed and raised his sword to defend himself, but she was too quick. Like a pit bull—no, like a wolf protecting its young—she latched on to Rafe's enemy and hung on, her head viciously shaking back and forth, until Corbet's screams became only gurgling whimpers. He dropped to his hands and knees, tearing at her fur, and still she hung on. Rafael lay impaled, having lost too much blood to offer his assistance. Seeing their leader downed by a crazed wolf, the Slayers who had attacked Rafe fled toward the back entrance.

Falon finally released Edward's limp body and turned her attention to Rafael. She hesitated slightly before approaching him. She licked his face, making small whimpering noises.

Automatically, his hands reached out for her, burying themselves in her coat. He closed his eyes, relishing her touch even as he choked out, "The door, Falon, open the front door."

In three bounding strides, she was at the door. She pounced on the thick metal bar with her jaws and pulled it up. The door swung open as she bounded back to him. Rafe was able to raise himself on an elbow but could not remove the sword. Falon frantically licked his wounds, her tongue warm and healing. His pack bounded after the retreating Slayers. Yet Falon acted as if she was not aware of anything but him.

Overcome with emotion, awe, and recrimination, Rafe lay quietly against the floor. How had he not known she was Lycan? He understood in that instant that Falon had not known it either. She'd shifted hard, like he had on his sixteenth birthday. But at least he knew what would come, how it would feel and what he should do. While he'd had the support of his pack to help him through it, she'd had no one. He swallowed hard. He was not there for her, his own chosen one. The Blood Law aside, he should have known. Should have prepared her.

His pack was in for a monumental surprise. Sacrificing a human was one thing, but a powerful Lycan, and one who had saved their alpha's life, was entirely different.

He dug his fingers into her thick, luxurious coat and hugged her close to him. Moist heat stung his eyes as he was once again overcome with emotion. Even with how he'd treated her, even after he'd sworn to kill her, she had risked her own life to save his and, in so doing, had destroyed his mortal enemy.

"Falon," he said against her fur, "I'm sorry."

She licked him fervently, her emotion as high as his. He even felt her tail thumping against his leg. And wolves did not wag their tails. He couldn't help laughing as her tongue licked his belly, tickling him. She soothed away the deep wounds, just as he had done for her the night he killed Salene.

"Rafaél!" Anton called as he came running naked toward them. "The Slayers have fled into the woods. We caught a few, but I sense more are on their way. We need to get you out of here." He looked at Falon, blinked his eyes as he processed the scene before him. As realization surfaced, his jaw dropped in shock.

"Get this damn sword out of me," Rafe cursed, trying to sit up. Save that wound, Falon had smoothed away the others. He wasn't losing as much blood, but he was still losing some.

"Jesus, Rafe," Anton said squatting down behind him. "The bastard nearly decapitated you." He firmly gripped the handle and slowly pulled. Falon growled low when Rafe hissed in a sharp breath. As the blade cleared his back, blood leaked down his chest.

"Now finish off Corbet," Rafe gritted as the pain of his wound burned.

Falon immediately licked the wound between his shoulder blades. Rafe closed his eyes and lay back, enjoying, despite the dire situation, the warmth of her touch while Anton deftly separated the Slayer's head from his body.

He tossed the sword onto the floor and bent down to help Rafe up. As he did, Yuri approached in human form and tossed clothing at them. He stopped short when he saw Falon. He glanced at Rafe, then at Anton, and back to the black she-wolf. A smile tugged his lips.

"Is that who I think it is?" he asked Rafe.

"Damn straight it is," Anton, answered. "I knew she was special, shoulda known she was Lycan." He looked up at Yuri as he helped dress Rafe. "Ripped Corbet's throat out as he was about to send Rafe to the Great White Spirit in the sky."

Yuri's smile widened. "Thank you, Falon," he said. She barked and nudged Rafe to get a move on.

Anton helped Rafe dress then dressed himself. With Yuri's help, they each looped one of Rafe's arms around their shoulders and proceeded to help him out.

"What about me?" a female voice screamed. "You can't leave me here! They'll come back and kill me!"

At Rafe's side, Falon snarled. Rafael, however, would not leave one of his own, traitor or not, behind. He looked down at Falon, "She is one of us. Do you know where the key is?"

She growled in assent.

"Take it to Lana. She can let herself out. Make sure she comes with us."

All of the Lycans save Falon had shifted back to human form. They were dressed and mounted. Though still wobbly on his feet, Rafael didn't mount his bike. "Amon, take my bike. Lana, you ride bitch. Anton, load yours up, I want you to drive the van."

"Rafe," Angel, pack Ruiz's alpha, said, stepping toward him. He extended his arm, and each man grasped the other's at the elbow. "Edward's death will not only weaken the clan but empower the packs. Many thought him undefeatable. With his death, the Lycan nation will rise to do the same to his brother and all who call themselves Corbet."

Damon, pack Casares's leader, offered his arm, as well. "Well done, my friend."

Rafael appreciated all of the praise, but they were thanking the wrong person. He shook his head and looked down at Falon, who lay quietly at his feet. “Don’t give me the props. I didn’t touch him. Falon shifted and ripped that poor bastard’s throat out. Thank her.”

A wave of confused mumbles and questions echoed through the packs. In one collective step, they all moved closer to get a better look at the sleek black she-wolf who had single-handedly saved the day. “She killed Corbet and saved my life.”

“But she is human?” Angel said.

“Apparently not,” Rafe said, smiling like a proud parent. If he could have conjured up the perfect mate, Rafael could not have topped Falon. She was one of a kind. And she was his.

“It will not change the Blood Law,” Lana sneered.

Every eye turned on her. Low snarls erupted around her. She paled and stepped back. Falon rose and walked stiffly toward the woman who had the good sense to hop into the van.

Rafe turned back to the packs. He saw the reluctant agreement with what Lana had said on their faces.

His heart could take no more of this. He turned and fiercely said to the packs, “Falon is my chosen one! She is Lycan as are we! She saved my life, an alpha’s life! She destroyed our mortal enemy, an enemy scores of Lycans have lost their lives to. Does that not count for something? Surely, the Blood Law can be avenged another way!”

The pack leaders shook their heads. “Rafe, you of all people know it cannot be changed,” Damon said. Regret laced his words.

“I slew my brother’s chosen one, it is true, but she was a Slayer! Our laws decree we kill them, no questions asked. I have maintained that fact for almost fifteen years. I refuse to pay the price Lucien demands. We are on the precipice of extinction if we do not unite.” He looked down at Falon, who stood calmly regarding them. “If we destroy our heroes and those who can do nothing but strengthen the Lycan nation for generations to come, we are destroying ourselves.”

"Rafael," Angel said. "Force a council meeting to order. Plead your case to the alphas this time, as well as the Amorak. Only they can change our laws, as they created them. They will reconsider. They must!"

Angel was right. It was Rafe's only chance to keep Falon alive. He looked the two alphas in the eye. "Do I have your support?"

"I never doubted you from the beginning, brother. I have your back," Damon said. Angel echoed his words and added, "I will spread the word. The council has only the power we give them."

"Thank you."

Falon pressed against his leg. He looked down into her cobalt eyes and smiled. They had a chance. For the first time since he brought her home, he believed they had a chance.

"I'll demand the council. Now I need to get back to the compound before I turn into a pumpkin."

As pack Vulkasin roared north to the Sierras, Rafael reclined in the captain's chair of the van and tried to sleep. But his mind raced with wild, wondrous images of himself and Falon carefree and smiling, knowing the Blood Law no longer mattered as they made love in an emerald green meadow, on the sunny slope of a pond not far from the compound.

She laid her head in his lap. He looked down into her big, soulful eyes, and something so deep and so profound moved within him he could not put a name to it. Emotion he was not aware he possessed rushed up into his chest, filling him to whole, making it nearly impossible to take a breath. She was his. No man, Lycan, or law could say otherwise. He would protect her with his life, freely giving it if it would save hers. He knew she would do the same for him. She had proved that tonight.

"Anton," Rafael softly said, "is the American River cabin stocked?"

"To the hilt."

"Take me there."

Anton nodded and slowed to the shoulder of the highway. When Yuri pulled up with questioning eyes, Anton said, "We're going to take a little detour. Go on ahead."

AN HOUR LATER, Rafael stood in the large shower stall of the cabin his parents had built before he was born. It was a bittersweet reminder of them, but a place he had always flown to when he was troubled or just wanted solitude. Tonight he wanted time alone with Falon. He didn't know when she would shift again—in the beginning it was hard to control—but he wanted to be with her when she did. She would have a million questions. He grinned as he lathered his belly and his thickening cock. There was that, too. He wanted her. Was on fire for her. He couldn't wait for her to shift so that he could lose himself in her.

Just as the gray fingers of dawn peeked through the tall, whispering pines, Rafael shifted into his wolf form and lay down on the big bed beside his she-wolf. She snuggled up to him, and in moments, they were both sound asleep.

Nineteen

PAIN FLARED IN every inch of Falon's body. Her bones cracked, her muscles ripped, her organs stretched. Falon moaned and writhed on the bed as her body contorted to take back its human form. She tried to calm herself, to keep her breathing even, just as she had when she'd shifted into a wolf. Then, like now, she'd been surprised by the pain, but she hadn't panicked. She hadn't been afraid.

Rafael lay beside her, watching, waiting, comforting. She closed her eyes as she had when she shifted into the wolf and just allowed her body to do what it needed to do. She didn't fight it; she allowed it to happen. When her body finally stilled and her aches and pains subsided, she took a deep breath and slowly exhaled. She wiggled her toes and her fingers.

Warm lips pressed a kiss to her nipple. Her body immediately responded. She moaned and opened her eyes to look into two deep aquamarine-colored ones.

"How do you feel?" he softly asked.

She drew his lips to hers and kissed him deeply. His warm, naked body slid against hers, drawing heat in its wake. "Better now," she said against his mouth.

He dug his fingers into her silky hair, gently combing out the tangles. "Do you want to tell me when you turned Lycan?" he teased but a serious tone underwrote his casualness.

She closed her eyes and tried to think. *Really* think. "I've always known something was different about me. I never fit in and had unusual tendencies and later, rages that I—I had difficulty controlling. There were the heightened senses, the odd aches and pains." She looked at him. "The urge to kill was the craziest part. It terrified me that I could feel so—so vicious. It only happened a few times in my teens, but when I was overcome with the feeling it was when I was being threatened or witnessed someone being victimized." She traced the line of his full bottom lip. "But the night I met you, things really started to kick in. New emotions, feelings, stronger urges. Latent powers." She shook her head. "Okay, not really new; it was just more of what I had been ignoring, because it's always been there; I just didn't know what *it* was."

"Tell me what it," he whispered as he stroked her neck with his fingertips, "is."

Her body ripened. It wanted him. Now. But she needed to clear the air first.

"Rafa, about Lucien—"

Rafael stiffened. She pressed her fingers to his lips. "Shh, let me talk; then we will not discuss him again."

His body eased some. But his gaze remained fixed.

"He bit my hand."

"Where was I?"

"It was the morning I healed you in your wolf form. That morning he was at the compound. He tried to kiss me. I—I was scared, angry, so I bit his lip. I didn't realize what the repercussions of that action was. I tasted his blood, so I guess some of it got into me. He healed his bite mark on my hand saying I would pay the price, not him. Not wanting to upset you, I didn't tell you. Then I scrubbed my skin so hard I bled. I was afraid you would be angry. I had no idea what would happen, but I knew something bad would." She swallowed hard. "That morning, after we made love, and you marked me again, I fell asleep to your licking. I was in such a contented sleep, I dreamed of you awakening me and making love to me. But—Rafe, Lucien got into my *head*, not physically—and I made him stop. He didn't, we didn't—" She took his angry face into her hands and said, "You are still the only man who has completed me that way. There is no other, and there never will be." She kissed him deeply. While he did not engage her, he did not push her away either. She sat back and looked at him.

"When you said Edward's last name was Corbet, I freaked out. *My* last name is Corbet. And even though you said you could detect a Slayer, you missed Smythe, and Lucien didn't know with his chosen one. I-I thought I might be a Slayer. So I went to the person who could tell me where I came from, if indeed I am a Corbet clan Slayer. I was not running to the enemy, Rafa, I was going to find out who I was and then come back to you and demand you hear me out, and Slayer or not, accept me!"

He smiled. "You are Lycan."

"Apparently so. Maybe that's why my parents abandoned me. I would give anything to know who they are."

"There are Lycans who go off on their own and take human mates. Children are born to them and though still Lycan, they are not as powerful as a full Lycan." He traced his fingertip around an impudent nipple. "I suspect by your powers, you are full Lycan." He leaned toward her and licked the turgid tip. "There is much you need to learn about your people—"

"Can we talk"—she dragged his fingers from her neck to her breasts down her belly, then lower to the warmth between her thighs—"later?"

Rafael smiled and lightly swept his fingertips across her mons. She moaned and undulated beneath his hand, opening for him. Ravenous hunger for him overcame her. "You do not know how many times I woke, ready to take you while in my wolf form."

She nipped his chin. "That could be interesting. Why didn't you?"

"I didn't want to scare you." His fingers circled her stiff clit, dipped into her heat, then out, slowly circling her with her own moistness. She moaned and closed her eyes. She lifted her hips to his finger. He cupped her heat with his hand, rocking gently against her.

"More," she breathed. He sucked a nipple into his mouth then teased it with his teeth, gently tugging. Falon moaned, arching her back, reveling in the sweet torture. Wild, wanton desire caught fire in her belly. Low, primal sounds erupted from her chest. Impatient with Rafael's slow seduction, Falon pressed his hand more firmly against her slick, swollen flesh.

"What do you want, Falon?" he breathed, his breath scorching her skin.

"You. All of you," she begged. "Now."

Rafael nipped the underside of her breast and quickly kissed the sting away. In a slow, scorching trail, he kissed his way down her belly to her navel. She strained against his slow hand, wanting penetration. He tortured her with the slick circling of his fingertips on her plump, juicy folds.

His lips hovered above his hand. God, she wanted him to take her. "I love your sweet scent," he said, his breath caressing her flaming skin with each syllable.

He slipped a long, thick finger into her waiting heat. Falon melted around him.

"I love how your body responds to mine."

Her hands fisted around the sheets. As he hit home, his lips pressed against her full, throbbing clit. Falon's hips rose skyward. He took her into his mouth and gently sucked to the languorous cadence of his finger inside of her. It was pure, blissful torture. Her body writhed and bucked beneath his lips and hand. Sensations, so much more than ever before, crashed against each other inside her, igniting a feral fire.

"Rafa," she breathed, squeezing her eyes shut. She wanted to tell him there was no one else for her, that there never would be, that only he would ever touch her as he touched her now. But her body's desperate hunger for his was too strong. His slow, methodical seduction of her body trumped words of love and devotion. His cadence picked up tempo, his lips sucked harder, the tension became unbearable. In a defining cataclysmic moment, the dam broke. Air escaped her lungs, perspiration erupted over every inch of her skin. Her body convulsed as an orgasm swept through her. It liquefied—then it completely surrendered all to him.

Muscles heavier than lead, eyes closed, Falon lay sprawled on the large bed, Rafael still between her thighs. Gently he licked her as the shock waves continued to reverberate in her body, though in time, they slowly receded. His fingers massaged her pussy. And his tongue, God, his tongue . . . it slid and swirled and prodded.

She gulped for air, licking her dry lips. She wanted more of him. Now she would take it.

Regretfully, Falon pulled herself up and away from that wicked mouth of his.

On her knees before him, she raised a brow. He smiled a slow, sated smile, his beautiful eyes jade dark. He reached out and grabbed her hand, pulling her to him. She came but shook her head and rolled him over onto his back. Her gaze raked over his hard, muscled body, from his wide chest to his taut belly and lower to his beautiful straining cock, and swollen balls. There was nothing soft about Rafael Vulkasin. He was the epitome of alpha. And he had chosen her.

Now—she looked down at his passion-strained face—she would choose him. She crawled along his long legs up his thighs, dragging her female against his male. He grabbed her hair, pulling her toward him, rising to take her.

"No," she said. "Your turn to be patient."

In a slow, seductive slide, she rubbed her slick cunt up and down his anxious cock. Rafe strained beneath her, his hands fisted at his sides, fighting the urge to lose himself inside her, knowing if he touched her, he would roll her over and take her. Her musky scent mingled with his, creating an erotic perfume.

On her knees, Falon held herself from him. His cock rocked against the inside of her thigh. Her body quivered, her skin flushed roses. She cupped her breasts, threw her head back, then, reverently, she lowered herself to his waiting shaft. He grabbed her ass, moaning loudly as he filled her. She had no words to describe the sublimity of him filling her. It was pure, unadulterated bliss.

THEIR GAZES MET and held. This was it. The connection she had searched for without ever realizing what it was she sought.

"Falon," he breathed. The muscles in his neck corded as he tried tamping down his need for her, tried not to rush. But it was too much to ask. He moved boldly up into her. "I'm sorry I doubted you."

Tears stung her eyes. She threw her long hair over her shoulder, leaned down, and pressed her lips to his. Her tears sealed their deep kiss. “I am yours as you are mine. I would never betray you or our people.”

His arms wrapped around her. “I would die for you,” he hoarsely said. Their lips met in a wild torrent, as their hips rose and fell in perfect frantic symmetry.

Wild, wicked abandon grabbed hold of Falon. Any lingering inhibitions she’d held on to were tossed away. Her urge to mate, to connect, to make love to this man was more than desire, or need—it was crucial to her survival, like air and water. She came in a hard, violent crash. She threw her head back and cried out a long, pealing cry as each wave of the orgasm rocked through her. Their bodies had slickened. She felt Rafael’s body surge and knew he was about to explode inside her. As he lifted high into her, she sank her teeth into his neck. Her teeth broke skin and sank into muscles, then deeper. His warm blood was an instant aphrodisiac, stoking her appetite for more. It met then mingled with hers, cementing their destiny as one together. Rafael’s hoarse moan and wild undulating body arched beneath her as she scraped her teeth along his jugular, forever marking him as hers.

Rafael wrapped his arms around her waist and rolled her over. He filled her, giving her all of himself in one long, fierce release.

Their forced breaths mingled as their bodies, still one, could not quench the need for the other. Rafael entwined his fingers with Falon’s and raised her arms above her head. He kissed her deeply, his tongue meeting hers in a slow, deep, intimate kiss. Falon strained beneath him, wrapping her legs around his waist, not satisfied to have him once. She wanted more of him, all of him. Now.

She arched her back, inviting him deeper into her. Her hunger had not been slaked, nor had his. His hips moved hotly against her, the sweat of their bodies warmed with the friction, adding more sensation to the erotic movements.

When she tried to rise to him, he kept her pinned to the bed, deepening his kiss. Her body frantically undulated beneath his as primal desire drove her almost to the brink of madness. She tore her lips from his to gasp for breath, arching against him again and again as the wild beast in her demanded the beast in him.

Her unbridled passion for the man above her launched her high into the stratosphere. Her chest burned from the swell of emotion that overcame her.

"Rafa," she cried as their future flashed, bloody, dark, and destitute in her mind. She closed her eyes, shutting out what she knew she could not change. Destiny was written, and while they could fight it, it would win. It always won.

He smoothed her damp hair from her face and looked down at her with such fierce love she couldn't stop the reactive tears that erupted. "Rafa," she cried, hugging him close.

"My love," he shushed, kissing her lips to silence. "I will protect you. I swear to you, I will allow no man or Lycan to hurt you."

But what of you?

He looked deep into her soul.

I will grow into an old, old man with you and our children by my side.

They tumbled into a long, soul-searing orgasm so intense, so profound, so prophetic they did not recover until the wee hours of the morning.

RAFAEL WOKE TO Falon's muffled cries against his chest. Her body quaked softly. Her fingers tightened around him, her breaths short and shallow. He pressed her soft body into the sheets and kissed her lips, quieting her dark thoughts. Their connection complete, he could see into her dreams, feel her pain and her fears. And though he told himself they were for naught, that he would fight to the death to keep her alive, he knew it would be the battle of his life.

He'd never feared raising his sword against a Slayer. He lived for the challenge and the vengeance. But a dark trepidation settled in his soul when it came to challenging the council for the unfettered right to his chosen one. He'd attended only one council meeting in his life, and that was right after the packs split. He was nineteen, angry, arrogant, and inexperienced. His pleas fell on deaf ears then. Would they again?

"Rafa?"

He smiled and looked down into two of the most beautiful blue eyes he had ever seen. As deep and blue as Lake Tahoe, and just as bright. She was striking in a most memorable way. Her beauty wasn't the classic type; hers was deeply sensual. The kind that imprinted on a person's brain, never forgotten.

He smoothed her cheek with his fingertips and smiled. "You were dreaming."

As if a dark cloud passed by the sun, the brightness in her eyes dimmed. "I'm afraid. I can't shake the feeling."

"I told you—"

She pressed her fingers to his lips and shook her head. "I know what you said, but it doesn't change the reality of our situation."

Rafael leaned up on one elbow and tried to convince her as much as himself. "My brother took a Slayer into our pack. He intended to mark her as his. The Blood Law forbids mixing of Slayer and Lycan blood. It's a death sentence not only by Lycan law but Slayer law as well. Had Lucien marked her, he would have been executed for bringing our mortal enemy into the pack. I saved my brother from sure death and prevented the introduction of Slayer blood into the pack. He should have thanked me, rather than insist I pay for my actions with the life of my chosen one."

"Why didn't anyone else see that she was a Slayer?"

"The Slayers have mastered the black arts. As Smythe did, she very skillfully concealed her ancestry."

"Then how did you know she was a Slayer?"

"As he—took her from behind, she was arrogant enough to show herself to me, challenging then mocking what she thought I was powerless to prevent. He could not see how her eyes turned to ebony as Slayers' do when they are on the precipice of destruction. I did. I had no doubt then, and I have no doubt now."

"If you prove she was a Slayer, would the Blood Law be revoked?"

"Only Lucien can revoke it. It is his right to see it carried out, but not mandatory."

"Then the Blood Law is not written in stone?"

"It is, but there is some discretion. Let's say Lucien, as the offended party, decided he wanted something else in lieu of your life, I would have to give it to him."

"Anything?"

"Anything. Taking one's chosen one is the most grievous offense in our world. Therefore anything else is considered less. I agree with the law in principle, but I cannot and will not pay the price of your death for destroying a Slayer. Any other Lycan would have done the same thing. That it was an alpha's chosen one, an alpha who couldn't see through the lust-induced spell she cast on him, is not my problem. I pled my case fourteen years ago, and I'll plead it again. This time, I will be heard, and the law will be amended."

"If there was a way you could prove she was a Slayer, would they heed your challenge?"

"Yes."

"Where is she buried?"

"There is no body; a Slayer returns to dust when they die a true death. Some immediately, some over the course of a day or two.

Lucien and I nearly killed each other after I killed her. When we came to, the curse was cast. The day after the Slayer's death, Lucien's room was torched. The evidence went up in smoke. But Talia remembers seeing only the body when she found Lucien and me dying, nothing more. Perhaps she can meditate to see what she did not see all those years ago."

It was Falon's turn to lean up on an elbow. "What curse?"

Rafael's lips thinned. "Lucien and I are evenly matched. We'd fought to our deaths. As we lay dying, Talia, pack Vulkasin's healer, pleaded to Singarti, the Spirit Mother, to restore our lives. She did. With conditions. Until the Blood Law is avenged, I roam the nights as a man, a wolf by day, and Lucien does the opposite."

"But I've seen you both as men at the same time."

"One hour at dawn and another at dusk we are both men."

"Who is Singarti? Tell me of the rising."

Rafe smiled. "Three hundred years ago in the far North, during a Blood Moon rising, a great battle between Slayers and my ancestors who were wolves ensued. The wolves were being slaughtered at an alarming rate. The Inuit people respected my ancestors and called to their spirit gods to save the wolves. The most powerful of them is Singarti. She gave the wolves human life so that they had a chance to survive the Slayers. Singarti also banished Fenrir, a supernatural wolf who betrayed his own kind, to the ring Edward gifted Peter the original Slayer with." He raised his hand. "I took it from Salene the night we met. It holds great power. The gods foretold an Armageddon of sorts during the next Blood Moon rising. Lycan versus Slayer for the whole enchilada. The rising is in two months."

"All or nothing?" she asked.

He kissed the tip of her nose. "All or nothing. But do not fear, my love. The Lycan nation will rise and destroy every Slayer on this earth."

She believed him. But first things first.

"So clarify for me the curse details. The only way you and Lucien can both be men and shift when you want is when the Blood Law is avenged?"

He kissed her forehead. "Yes."

"Is there another time when we automatically shift?"

"When we are incredibly pissed, it's almost impossible to prevent, and upon every full moon there is no force on earth that can prevent our shifting. During the full moon, we are at our most powerful."

"Last night was a full moon."

"Yes, and I'm betting, since you had no idea what you were, and had no pack to nurture you, your inner spirit knew you would not survive until you were with your own kind. But more than that, you were marked by an alpha, and you saw your mate being threatened, which triggered the beast within. And all during a full moon." He kissed a nipple. She hissed in a breath. Her scent thickened with desire. "You didn't stand a chance." He kissed the other nipple, and Falon moaned, rubbing her mons against his thigh. "You are a shameless hussy, Falon Vulkasin."

She giggled and rolled over on top of him and licked the raw mark on his neck. "I like marking you. I'm going to keep marking you so every female—human, Lycan, Slayer, or goat—knows you're mine."

"You know, there are other places you can put those naughty lips of yours . . ."

Her eyes blazed neon blue. "Oh, really?" She kissed his nipple. His body tightened.

"There?" she asked smiling mischievously up at him.

"For starters."

She kissed his other nipple. "Then you must mean here." She sucked it, flicking it with her tongue.

"Maybe," he moaned.

She dragged her warm, wet tongue down his belly just below his navel. His cock warmed, thickening. She licked the soft golden hairs that formed an arrow to his groin. "How about here?"

"Yes," he groaned.

Her hair brushed across his burgeoning erection, teasing him, testing him. Pushing him to his limit. If she didn't take care of him soon, he'd have to take matters into his own hands.

She licked just above his rod then down the inside of his thigh. "Here?"

"No," he hoarsely said.

"Oh, then you must mean here," she teased, licking the inside of his other thigh.

His hand slid down his belly to his raging hard-on. He wrapped his fingers around himself and slowly began to pump. "You go ahead and play your silly games."

She pouted prettily but watched him as he slowly stroked himself. She put her hands on each of his thighs, dipped her lips down to the head, and inhaled. "Our scents blend well." She laved her warm, wet tongue across the head of his cock. He squeezed his eyes closed and fought back his eruption.

"Did you mean there?" she asked against his skin, her lips barely touching him, yet creating more havoc than before.

He clenched his jaw. "Yes," he groaned.

She dipped her head and licked one of his balls then the other and up the base of his cock. "Or did you mean there?" she coyly asked.

"Falon," he groaned. His cock was thick, hard, and throbbing in his hand. He wanted her lips around him, her tongue teasing the head, her fingers cupping his balls . . . She dipped her head, and in a slow, deep swath she licked around the tip of his dick. He held it up toward her in offering while he continued to stroke himself. Her lips opened wider to take just the head into her mouth. Then slowly and deeply, she sucked, as she would savor a Tootsie Pop. "Jesus," he hissed. "That feels so damned good, Falon."

Her mouth widened as her tongue lapped and licked the sensitive skin just below the inside of the head. Her saliva dripped down his shaft, lubricating his hands. His hips rose and fell as his hand continued to stroke and she suckled him. When her fingers slid down, pushing his away, taking more of him into her mouth, Rafael squeezed his eyes shut and held his breath, fighting back the rush of semen that threatened to erupt.

Twenty

BEING TAKEN BY Rafael was mind-meltingly incredible in itself, but the way he reacted to Falon when she touched him, his body firing up, stringing taut to the limit because of what she did, instilled a deep sense of pride, possessiveness, and power in her.

His long fingers tangled in her hair. His big, powerful body was hers to command at will. She reveled in it. As she took all of him into her mouth, she gently cupped his balls. Rafael hissed in a sharp breath. She tightened her grip on him, swirling her tongue around the head of his cock. No, *her* cock. He. Was. Hers. He belonged to her. And *only* her.

She would destroy anyone who stood between them.

And she realized with vivid clarity that no matter what the council decreed, she would fight Lucien for her life, even if it meant taking his.

She'd have to. Rafael could not challenge the council if they refused to believe that Lucien's chosen one was Slayer. He could not challenge their decision to uphold the Blood Law. Rafael was an important alpha; to remain alpha, he was sworn to uphold the law. As yet, she had made no such declaration. Her loyalty was to her mate first, the pack second. The council last. It would be her, and her alone, who would have to redirect the winds of fate. God help any Lycan who stood in her way.

To even suggest she would go willingly with Lucien to die was ludicrous.

Ferocious thoughts reverberated in her head. She growled.

"Easy, my love," Rafael hoarsely said.

Immediately, she realized she was about to maul her man! Her body loosened, as did her lips and hands. She slowed down, and then, with excruciating care, she slid her hands to the base of his shaft and sucked deeply, moving in perfect cadence to his hips.

She felt his quickening. She swirled her tongue around him, slightly moving her head in a circular motion. She cupped his balls with one hand while she continued to slowly pump him with her other. Perfectly synchronized, she brought him to the surface as he wildly thrashed beneath her. Tensing, Rafael grasped her head, minimizing her movements. In a long, suspended thrust, he released. She held him steady and slowed her sucking, bringing him back to earth.

His body collapsed back into the damp, rumpled sheets. His eyes closed, his chest heaved, and he lay in a sated sprawl. She wiped her mouth on the sheet and slid up his slick body, snuggling against him. They lay quiet, their emotional and physical bonds forged and unbreakable. No matter what their future held, Falon was confident the bond created here would stand the test of time, war, and, God willing, the Blood Law.

He stroked her cheek with his fingertips. "The sun rises, my love. Prepare to shift with me, and I will show you a whole new world."

She looked up at his smiling eyes. "How do I make it happen?"

"Think it, see it, feel it, then be it. Soon it will happen, even before you realize you wanted it to happen." He kissed her quickly on the lips, and an instant later, Rafael, the great golden wolf, stood on the bed beside her. He licked her face.

Falon smiled, digging her fingers in his thick mane. She closed her eyes. She could do this. *Think wolf. See herself as sleek, black, and ferocious. Feel the essence of primal. Run with the wind . . .*

Moments later, Falon was running beside Rafael through the dense forests. No beast dared challenge them. Not the black bear and her two cubs or the humans. Every sense was wide open. The scents of flora and fauna were crisp, clear, and distinct, some distracting but most pleasant. The human scents made her nose twitch. Perfumes, deodorants, and other man-made smells clung to them. They were easy to detect. Their cloying smell would hang like pesticide in the air for days after their passing. With amazing clarity, Falon realized how easy it was to let the human in her go. To be wild and free, at one with nature and her mate, was incredibly satisfying. She could let go of the human world entirely. And never regret it.

The air was brisk, but the sun was high and warm. They splashed through a stream, along fallen logs and protruding boulders. Rafael showed her how to hunt rabbits, deer, and birds. Her reluctance to eat them was momentary. She was famished. He licked the blood and stains from her fur, and she him. They napped along the riverbank, the sun warming them. When the sun finally began its descent over the western mountains, they made their way back to the cabin. As they ran up the steps, they both shifted at the same time.

Rafael grabbed her hand, led her into the large bathroom, and turned the shower on. Warm water sprayed her face, washing her free of all scents.

Her hunger for him had only grown in her wolf form. His thick erection nudged her hip. He was as voracious for her as she for him.

He lathered her up, his big hands sliding along her slick skin. He pressed her against the tile wall and took her from behind. His teeth grazed her neck, obliterating Lucien's mark, replacing it with his own. His ferocity when he did it shook her to her foundation. His possessive nature instilled not fear but understanding; he would allow no man or Lycan to trespass ever again.

As he thrust into her, he slid his fingers into hers, pulling her arms over her head and against the wall. "You are mine, Falon," he roughly said against her ear. "If Lucien dares to come to you again, kill him." His hips thrust hard into her as if he had to make his point by hurting her. But she enjoyed his raw, possessive nature. It was, after all, the nature of the beast. As his female, she understood it and would want it no other way. "I will."

She spread her legs wider. He bent his knees behind her to accommodate her new position. But he did not gentle his touch. She cried out in bittersweet pain as his big body pressed her harder into the tile. His fingers tightened to painful around hers. He stretched her body by pulling her arms higher over her head. His deep thrusts forced her sensitive pussy against the tile with each undulation. Her body flamed.

She leaned back into him, exposing her neck. He growled so ferociously she cried out in real fear. His body swelled behind her, his cock long and thick inside her. He bit her from behind, and as he did, her world exploded into a thousand tiny pieces.

Rafael came in a harsh, violent rush, lifting her off the shower floor. She cried out, reveling in his furious passion.

The water turned cold before they were able to separate. Her legs felt like Jell-O; her skin still burned as if someone had set a match to it. Her heavy breasts tingled, as if Rafael still nipped her. But it was her swollen nether lips and her womb that still called for him.

Falon shook her head. What was wrong with her?

"Rafa," she said, barely able to speak, her energy spent. "My body is possessed by yours."

"Do you still ache for me?" he asked finally, gentling as he nuzzled her neck before carefully helping her from the shower. He sat her down on the stool and knelt beside her and lovingly began to dry her.

She dug her fingers in his damp hair. "I burn for you."

"You always will, but especially until you conceive."

"What?" This news startled her. She was not ready to become a mother!

He rubbed the towel over her head, playfully keeping her in the dark. "Your burn is confirmation our bond took. It doesn't always happen so quickly." He pulled the towel from her head and dropped it to the floor. He pulled her up into his arms and strode with her into the bedroom. He tossed her onto the rumpled sheets and followed her there. She lay back as he crawled over her, opening her thighs. He filled her in one slick dive. She rose to meet him, wanting nothing more than to stay connected to him like this for the rest of her life.

We must return to the compound, Rafael said.

I don't want to go. Not yet.

He gathered her up into his arms and gently rocked into her. His body, just like hers, had only one design. To join. Lycans had a sex drive like no other creature on earth. Even when not bent on procreation, they were highly sexual.

Her orgasm reverberated from her body into his own, shaking him to his foundation. He fought back the beast that clawed for release. It had become increasingly determined to destroy the one thing that stood between his and Falon's happiness: his brother.

* * *

THEY DROVE HOME in the van, Anton having taken Rafe's bike. It was still early when the gates opened. But what awaited them was as much a surprise to Rafael as to Falon. The entire pack was there to greet them, clapping and cheering; the faces that had so recently been drawn tight with fear and angst smiled brightly.

"It seems the pack has accepted you with open arms, Falon," Rafael said. He reached over and took her hand and looked meaningfully at her. "Do you know what that means?"

She was too overcome with emotion to answer, so she shook her head.

"It means they will die for you. My mother was the last female that received such an honor."

Hot tears stung her eyes. "Rafa, I am truly honored, but I don't want anyone to lose their life because of me."

He leaned over and kissed her. "It is *their* honor. It will be mine as well."

"No! Don't say that! We will find a way, Rafael, we *will* find a way!"

"I will call for the council meeting tomorrow night."

She swallowed hard. "So soon? Can't we have another few nights together?"

He shook his head. "There's treachery about, Falon. The entire Slayer nation is preparing a final defining battle with the coming of the Blood Moon. In two months' time, if all Lycans do not come together as one to fight, we will lose all. And I mean *all*. We will fail to exist as a nation."

"What of your brother?" she spit. "Will he insist, regardless of what the council decides, to seek his own vengeance?"

"It doesn't matter what Lucien plans. I will make sure he will not stand in the way of the packs uniting. United we have a chance; divided we fall."

"But that means—"

He kissed her to silence. "My loyalty is to the Lycan nation as a whole. I will do everything and *anything* in my power to preserve it."

The van had come to a stop, and the pack had begun to gently rock it, calling for their alphas to emerge.

Rafael squeezed her hand and smiled. "I think they want us to come out." He looked out at the sea of happy faces then back to Falon. "Shall we, Madame Vulkasin?"

Falon smiled and nodded. "Yes."

To say the pack was happy was an understatement. They were ecstatic. Even Lana, who had been shaved, wore rags, and had been relegated to the lowest rung of the pecking order, smiled when Rafael lifted Falon up. He proclaimed her master Slayer slayer! The house reverberated with loud cheers and hearty hoorays. Music piped in from hidden speakers, mass quantities of food covered tables, beer and wine flowed. The party was on.

Minutes later, Falon found a private moment with Rafael. "I understand everyone being excited about Edward's death. But"—she looked around at the laughing crowd that acted more like mischievous teenagers than mature adults who were at their core warriors and had seen more than a seasoned veteran—"why are they so *happy*?"

"I have much to teach you about your people. But, if I had to hazard a guess, I'd say their joy stems from the fact that we have marked each other, and now, when you conceive, so, too, will the other females."

It suddenly dawned on her that there were no children and didn't appear to be anyone younger than herself.

Rafe read her thoughts. "When the alpha female dies, reproduction stops until the alpha male takes another mate. Or a new alpha comes in and either has a mate or chooses one. When the alpha female conceives, the rest of the pack conceives almost immediately as well. Since my mother's murder, there has been no accepted alpha female." He tipped her chin up with his finger and kissed her. "Until now."

And it explained why she was a walking sex addict—her body wanted her to conceive as soon as possible so the pack could flourish. She pressed against her alpha. She felt his erection against her belly. "Well, I think, for the sake of the pack, we should go upstairs and get on it."

He slid his hand down between her thighs. "I can feel your heat for me, and"—he nipped her ear—"you are so wet, I could fuck you right through your pants."

Falon rubbed against his thigh as he pressed it between her knees. He rode up on her, and she nearly came. "Rafa," she breathed.

He backed her into his office and deftly shut and locked the door behind them. He drew the blinds and had her clothes ripped off her before she could turn around. He lifted her to the edge of his desk and ravenously assaulted her breasts. Falon caught her breath and leaned back on the slate desktop. Her scent was thick and musky; even she could not ignore its call.

Rafael's arms tightened around her waist, pulling her hard against his mouth as he ravaged her nipples. Falon surrendered to him.

Your scent is intoxicating, Falon.

Falon stiffened at the sound of Lucien's voice. He was right behind her! His fingers traced along her spine.

Dear God, did Rafael know?

I have powers of my own, corazón. He cannot smell me or even hear me in your head. Unless you tell him. And I don't think he's going to be very happy with you if you do that.

Falon went rigid.

Shall I tell my brother you covet my touch? It is *why you call to me, is it not?*

She gasped.

"Don't be shy, Falon," Rafael hoarsely whispered. "No one will dare come through that door."

"I-I'm not afraid of that," Falon squeezed her eyes shut, terrified to tell Rafael and spoil everything or not tell her beloved and spoil everything. If she could destroy Lucien while he was in her head, she would. But she had no idea how. "I'm hungry," she lamely said.

"So am I," Rafael breathed as he slid down her belly to her thighs. He dropped to his knees and pulled her into his ravenous mouth. Falon hissed as her body liquefied.

Your musk is powerful, Falon. Lucien said from beside her. *It makes me think of things a man and a woman would be ashamed of.*

She swallowed hard, unsure what to do.

Rafael licked her moist slit. Falon hissed in another breath and rose off the edge of the desk. Dear God. With his hands on her knees, he spread her wider, then pressed his tongue deeper into her opening, lapping her honeyed folds. Falon closed her eyes, her body delirious with desire. She ignored Lucien.

Let him watch. Let him see what Rafael did to her. Things he would never do. Falon dug her fingers into Rafael's thick hair and pressed him against her, and as she did she leaned back and looked his brother straight in the eye.

He laughed, shaking his head. *Oh, little one, you would challenge me?* He leaned over her and nipped at a turgid nipple. Falon gasped and slapped him hard. Her body vibrated from the velocity of it.

"Easy," Rafael whispered against her swollen, weeping folds. He slid a finger into her, and she came off the desktop. Lucien grabbed a hank of her hair and pulled, drawing her body taut. He forced her shoulders to the desk, and from above her, he cupped her breast and again took liberties with her.

Rafael sucked her clit, as his finger slowly slid in and out of her. Lucien licked and sucked her breast. She raised her hand to slap him again, but instead she grabbed a large hank of his hair and before she knew it, pulled him more firmly to her. She squeezed her eyes shut, unable to look at the man who she despised more than any other man in the world. Her desire for him would show, and she could not bear that he knew. Shame and guilt washed over her. It was because his blood, little as it was, ran through her veins. He *made* her want him.

Rafael tightened his lips around her hardened, sensitive nub and sucked hard, launching her to the moon. She cried out, arching her back, riding the orgasm out as her chosen one lapped at her drenched pussy and his brother mauled her nipples then shocked her when his lips took hers. His thick tongue invaded her mouth. She tried to wrench her mouth free, but he grabbed her chin with a powerful hand, forcing her to accept him.

Falon gasped, caught up in an erotic maelstrom. Fear clashed with the shocking reality of what was happening to her. Her body ached for Rafael and she could not help but respond to him, but Lucien's hands and mouth heightened the experience. It did not matter to her body that her mind and heart didn't want him. How was that possible? What did that make her?

Rafael pulled her to a standing position. Lucien's lips painfully tore from her lips. She bit back a cry. Rafael smiled. "Your cheeks are flushed, Falon. Did you like that?"

"Yes," she helplessly said.

"I love when you come in my mouth."

Mutely, she nodded, trying to keep from glaring at Lucien, who now stood behind his brother.

I see there is one thing my brother and I can agree on. I'm sure I will enjoy you coming in my mouth even more. Knowing that my brother will be howling at the moon as I take you will be my greatest pleasure.

I'm going to kill you, Lucien.

I look forward to you trying.

Get out of here.

Oh, no, I'm having too much fun. Do you know what I'm going to do to you when my brother fucks you?

Shut up.

I'm going to fuck you from behind.

You are foul.

"Rafa," Falon said, as he began to undress. "I don't feel very well. Can we, can I go to bed?"

He'll know you're lying. You will never convince him you don't want to fuck.

"Not feeling well?" He touched her cheek. "You're flushed and warm."

A large warm hand stroked her ass, then slipped down between her cheeks. Falon bit her lip and pushed back against the edge of the desk. She heard Lucien's head whack the edge

Damn, woman.

Get away from me, or I'll do more than that.

Falon took Rafael's hand and pressed it to her cheek. "So much has happened in the last two days, hell weeks! I'm feeling a bit overwhelmed."

She looked up at him to see if he was convinced. The sharp glint his eyes told her he wasn't.

"What's really wrong, Falon?"

She took a deep breath. "Lucien, he—" She had to tell Rafe. Or Lucien would plague her the rest of her life.

"Does he intrude?" Rafael raged. His eyes flared red, and she watched him fight the beast. Falon backed away, genuinely afraid at his instant fury. She had hoped he would not flash, but knew when it came to Lucien, Rafael had a zero flash point.

"No! No, I-I was just thinking—what if he tries to, you know, do something underhanded?"

Rafael pulled her into his arms, instantly calming. "He is weak, Falon. His vengeance drives him. It will be his downfall."

My brother fools himself.

You are half the man your brother is.

You will pay for that, corazón.

Falon wrapped her arms around Rafael and stood up on her toes. "I love you, Rafa. I could never love anyone as I love you." And she meant it. "Now take me, before I start howling at the moon."

Twenty-one

WITH DELIBERATION, FALON turned around and set her hands on the edge of Rafael's desk. Lucien stood on the other side facing her. She wagged her naked bottom at Rafael, who stood behind her. "Come to me, lover. Take me, mark me, then take me again." Her glare never wavered from Lucien's except when Rafael entered her and she closed her eyes, savoring the thick heat of him. Her nipples beaded, but her skin pebbled when she opened her eyes to see the fury contorting Lucien's face.

He refused to allow her to look away. Rafael's hands held the cradle of her hips as he thrust into her. She arched her back as sensation mounted on top of sensation. Rafael's taking of her while Lucien watched was oddly thrilling. When Rafael pulled her hair back, arching her back into a C, her breasts jutted out only a foot from Lucien. Her nipples were hard and sensitive, craving a man's touch.

Rafael swirled his hips as he thrust deeper into her. He hit that sacred place, and she felt her body begin to liquefy. The scent of their sex was thick in the room. Her skin slickened with perspiration. Her breaths became harsh and ragged. She threw her head back as the orgasm reared. She closed her eyes.

Open your eyes. I want to watch you come.

Falon opened her eyes. Lucien had moved closer. His face was drawn tight in sexual tension. She could smell his anger and his lust.

Rafael leaned into her as he pulled back her head. "Mine," he said roughly and scraped his teeth along her jugular. Falon screamed. The combination of the orgasm, the pain of Rafael's bite, and Lucien's voyeurism was too much. It pushed her over the edge, and she tumbled headlong into a wild, raucous climax. With a roar, Rafe followed her.

Falon collapsed back against Rafael. When he slipped from her, she deliberately kept her gaze off Lucien, but it was more difficult to do so than she would have expected. Turning in Rafael's arms, she pressed against him, kissing him deeply.

"Let's go to bed," she whispered.

He dressed, wrapped her in an Indian blanket folded on his sofa, and carried her upstairs. Again, she didn't look to see if Lucien lingered. She didn't care, she told herself. If he showed up in her head again, she would find a way to kill him.

Rafael left Falon sleeping soundly in their bed. The festivities were still well underway when he went back downstairs. He motioned to Anton and Yuri to follow him in to his office. He laughed when he opened the door. Falon's musk hung like an "I had sex here" sign. His own scent was as prominent. He stopped short and sniffed. The hair on the back of his neck rose. Another dominant male scent mingled with theirs.

Lucien! Damn him!

"Lucien was here earlier today," Anton said, reading Rafael's reaction to his brother's lingering scent.

Rafael whirled around. "Why am I just being told about this?" His brows drew together in a hard frown. "What did he want?"

"Falon," Yuri said when Anton hesitated.

"We told him to go take a flying fuck," Anton said, closing the door behind them.

Rafe wished the statement filled him with satisfaction, but all it did was make him tense with dread. "I take it he knows of her Lycan status and Edward's death?"

Anton nodded. "He also knows you're insisting on a council meeting. He didn't seem to care."

"He said your Slayer ploy didn't work fourteen years ago, and it wasn't going to work now," Yuri elaborated. "We didn't tell him you had the backing of key alphas."

"We've been busy while you were gone, Rafe," Anton said, coming around to stand beside him. "We've contacted the northern packs. Your father's kin are anxious to come to your aid, as are several unrelated eastern packs."

Rafael shook his head. "How?"

"The Internet is a beautiful thing, and since we created all of their systems, it was a no-brainer to use technology to get the ball rolling. They will be here by sunset tomorrow."

Rafael clasped Anton on the shoulder and squeezed. "Good work, Anton. I will go to Sharia and ask for the council to meet here then. But we have a more immediate dilemma. I'm going to need Talia."

Anton and Yuri looked at each other then back to Rafe. "Why?"

"Talia saw the body, though she doesn't remember what happened to it. I *need* for her to remember! I need her to talk about how crazy Lucien was around his Slayer. Talia can spot black magic ten miles away. She will support my claim that the woman had a supernatural hold on Lucien. You all felt it; the council must believe me!"

Anton shook his head. "By the time we got to you, Talia had called upon the Great Spirit Mother and you were wolf and Lucien human. Other than the blood, I don't remember seeing the Slayer's body."

"Could she have turned to ash so soon?" Yuri asked. "I thought only the old guys went up like that."

"She either turned to ash and we all overlooked it because our emotions were riding so high at the moment, or someone removed her body and buried her ashes."

"Will Lucien allow Talia to testify?" Anton gravely asked.

"I will demand the council call her as a witness on my behalf." Rafael paced the room, thoughts of his brother infuriating him. "He's going to be the downfall of the entire Lycan nation if we allow him to do what he's doing. He needs to be sanctioned, but the council refuses to take action."

"The council has a weak spot for both of you," Anton said. "You and Lucien are the golden sons. I almost feel like they're awaiting a miracle that will magically mend the bad blood between you two."

Rafael flung his hand up into the air. "Each day that goes by, my hatred for my brother deepens. He has pitted pack against pack. Why the council has steadfastly refused to see his hand in our destruction is beyond me."

Both men shook their heads. There was no answer. It was what it was. And for the first time in nearly fifteen years, Rafael had a clear, concise game plan.

"What if Lucien refuses the council's request to produce Talia?" Yuri asked.

"If he refuses to bring her when she can offer key evidence, then they will have to find him in contempt!" Rafael strode to the door, but before he opened it, he said to his two most trusted men, "Keep an eye on Falon. I don't trust Lucien any farther than I can throw the bastard. Have the women prepare for guests. I'm going to see the Amorak."

Rafe was glad for the time to clear his head, but it only confirmed his resolve: Falon would not be sacrificed because he'd killed a Slayer. He'd been well within his rights as alpha to do it. He was the one who'd been wronged, not Lucien. And he would prove it.

The small village was brightly lit when he approached. Energy crackled in the air. What had them so energized? Had they heard about Falon and her slaying of Edward? It had to be.

Rafe rode straight to Sharia's small hut. She was waiting for him on the dilapidated porch. He scowled and killed the engine on his bike.

"You knew I was coming?"

"Of course," her old voice crackled. "Of course." She turned and wobbled her way into the small candlelit space.

Rafael followed and was surprised to see Daniel and Maleek, an elder from the North, seated on two new chairs. That was good for Rafael. Maleek had a strong dislike for Lucien. Both men nodded, acknowledging him. "Sit, Rafa," Sharia said, pointing to a short stool by the window.

Rafael helped the old woman into her worn rocker before he sat. When he did, he sat forward and said, "You have heard of my desire for a council meeting?"

"Word travels fast, Rafael, as you know," Daniel said. "We are preparing."

"Good." He turned to Sharia, "As the elder here, I ask that you instruct Lucien to bring Talia to the meeting to bear testimony on my behalf."

"What testimony?" Daniel asked.

Rafael scowled and thought before he spoke. "With all due respect, Daniel, I choose not to divulge my reasons as it may prejudice my case."

"With all due respect, Rafael, I insist."

Rafael sat back in his chair. "No."

Daniel sat forward, his face tightening. Maleek put his gnarled hand on Daniel's, staying the man's next words. The elder looked to Sharia, who nodded. "You are free to have any person present to bear witness. It is my understanding Talia is being held against her will in the Mondragon compound?"

"Yes," Rafael angrily said, sitting forward. "The council has done nothing to secure her release. Lucien has been allowed to run roughshod over the entire nation to its detriment."

It was Sharia's turn to place a quieting hand on Rafael's arm. "My son, the council does not act or not react without great debate. There are valid reasons for action or not. You must trust us. We act with only the Lycan nation's best interest at heart."

"Then why has Lucien been allowed to divide the nation?"

"Destiny, my son can not be undone, not even by the council."

Rafael stood and swiped his hand across his chin. He wanted to pace, but there was no room to do so. "So you're trying to tell me all of the shit we've had to endure since I don't know the hell when is destiny?"

All three nodded in unison.

"I am in charge of my own destiny! No other entity, including the council or the Blood Law, can dictate to me how I live my life!"

"Destiny works in mysterious ways, Rafael," Maleek softly said. "Do not fight it."

"I will fight for my beloved! Lucien will not destroy her! Under *any* circumstances. Tell that to your destiny!"

He took the two steps necessary to reach the door. He turned to the three who sagely watched him. He felt like the joke was on him, only he didn't know it yet.

"The alphas converge as I speak. They will have arrived by dusk tomorrow. Will destiny permit the council to convene then at my compound?"

Daniel scowled while Sharia and Maleek showed the hint of a smile. "Destiny has already set the time at dusk tomorrow."

Rafael nodded. "Of course she has."

The ride home was quick. His heart, body, and soul yearned for Falon. He needed to feel her in his arms, to know she was real, alive, not a dream. This all *felt* like a dream. He was not the same man he'd been the night he rescued her from Salene. His life before Falon had been a haze, one ruled by guilt and resentment. He hadn't truly been alpha until he'd found her, and even then, not fully until she'd marked him. Her love fortified him in ways he had never imagined. She brought everything down to its most basic level. His mission to unite the nation and defeat the Slayers was possible now because of one thing—he not only believed it could happen, he knew with certainty it would happen, with Falon at his side.

He had always thought he was fighting for his people and, while that was true, he was now fighting for the woman he loved, as well as their unborn children. In just a few weeks, he had discovered what mattered most. He understood his parents' adamancy that he and Lucien not leave their hiding place when the Slayers came that day. To his parents, he and his brother were the most precious things on earth. The things they would die to protect. And they had.

He swallowed hard. Just as his mother and father had died so that he and his brother could live, so, too, would he die so that Falon could live.

His mind was made up. If the council refused to see the truth—if it gave Lucien license to destroy Falon—he would destroy his brother, even if it meant facing his own death sentence. But at least Falon would live.

* * *

FALON WOKE TO Rafael's lips kissing hers. She stretched, smiling.

"I missed you, love," he whispered against her lips.

"Mmm, I missed you, too."

Rafael pulled her against him, stroking her hair as she snuggled into the crook of his neck. Her fingers caressed his chest. "I love you," she murmured before her breaths took on the deep, even cadence of sleep.

He kissed the top of her head. "And I you."

He glanced at the window just as the blush of dawn seeped beneath the curtains. With dusk, their fates would be decided. And God help them all.

Twenty-two

FALON WOKE SLOWLY to bright sunlight and Rafael's furry body stretched out beside her in the big bed. She smiled, digging her fingers into his thick fur. His big body pressed closer to hers. She wanted to wake up like this every morning.

No, she wanted to wake up to Rafael's human body every morning.

Realization of what was to come struck her with the force of a lightning bolt. This could be their last morning together.

She rolled over and buried her face in his fur, trying not to cry, trying to be strong, and trying to believe that Rafael could convince the council to set aside the Blood Law.

In her heart, she knew it would not come to pass. Even so, she was determined to survive Lucien.

Her body stiffened as she remembered his intrusion last night. He was determined to destroy what she and Rafael shared. His methods were underhanded, and if she were less of a woman and not as committed to Rafael, it may have worked.

But she was alpha of a great pack. She stood beside a great man. She had destroyed a great Slayer. If left no choice, she would destroy Lucien as well.

Careful not to disturb Rafael, Falon slid from the bed and into the bathroom.

Twenty minutes later, when she emerged from the shower, she peeked in on him. He still slept. She wanted to go to him, but knew he was exhausted.

Besides, the savory scents wafting up from the kitchen called to her.

She was hungry, and she knew with the coming meeting and the many out of town guests expected, there was work to be done downstairs. She welcomed it. Anything to keep her mind off tonight.

The women of the pack smiled, casting their eyes downward as she walked into the hub of action. They were busy cleaning the remnants of the night's revelry, but there was an underlying, undeniable tension in the air. Not, she realized, because she had walked into the room, but because of what was to come that night.

"Falon?" A petite blonde woman who she had seen on several occasions with Anton humbly approached her. Falon's natural instinct was to tell her not to act so subordinate, but she knew that she could not. There was a definite and defined hierarchy in the pack, and she was at the top. But she would always treat those under her with fairness and love.

She smiled, easing the woman's nervousness.

"I'm Glenna, keeper of the house. If you would permit me, I'd like to show you around, explain how things have been done. In case you want to make changes."

"Thank you, Glenna. I would love to, but first I need to eat. I'm famished."

Glenna nodded. "Galiya has outdone herself this morning. Come,"

Glenna, said, extending her hand and waiting for Falon to precede her toward the back of the house.

As Falon sat down to a feast for dozens, she invited Glenna to join her.

The woman's cheeks flushed. Falon could tell she wanted to refuse, not out of disrespect but from fear. Falon sipped her coffee. "I only bite Slayers."

Glenna's big brown eyes widened. "How did you defeat Edward?" she gushed, dropping into the chair beside Falon and raptly awaiting the tale. Falon smiled inwardly as several other women, who just happened to find themselves near the kitchen, drew closer.

Falon plopped a piece of the most delicious cinnamon roll ever baked into her mouth and slowly chewed. The other women seemed to be waiting for permission to approach. She waved them over. Just as Glenna had, they hurried to take the available seating and turned expectantly toward her.

Shrugging, Falon said, "He threatened my man, so I ripped his throat out."

Glenna's eyes shone bright. "I heard you ripped apart a metal cage first and even took pity on that treacherous bitch Lana."

"My treachery was the act of a woman scorned," Lana said from the doorway. "I realize it was wrong now."

"Do you really, Lana?" Glenna demanded, narrowing her eyes at the lesser female. "Or do you realize it was wrong because you got caught?"

Lana bared her teeth at Glenna but did not come farther into the room.

"Your desire for an alpha has been your undoing, Lana. Rafael and Falon may be forgiving, but the council will not be," the pretty brunette next to Glenna said. "You will not survive the night.

Now be gone with you." She waved Lana away as if she were an annoying gnat.

Falon chose not to interfere. Lana had committed high treason when she went to the Slayers. It was Lana who'd told them of Falon's coming and her handling of Lucien. Because of Lana's treachery, several of the pack had not returned from the warehouse.

Lana curled her lips and snarled. "You act so high and mighty, but with the coming of the Blood Moon we will all die!"

"Do you have so little faith in your alpha, Lana?" Falon asked, rising and walking toward the traitor. "*If* your life is spared, what part will you play in seeing the battle won? Or will you run to the enemy again?"

"What alpha?" Lana spit, not caring about her disrespectful tone. Glenna hissed in a breath and stood. Falon waved her off. Lana continued her tirade. "Lucien's position will be upheld by the council. Rafael will die to save you. Then what will we do? Unite under Lucien, who cares for nothing or no one but himself?"

Her words sent a ripple of apprehension through the gathered women.

"You give Lucien too much power, Lana," Falon softly said, but the edge in her tone was unmistakable. "Rafael will not die trying to protect me. Lucien will die when I rip out his throat."

The women gasped. Falon continued toward the woman, who now hunched and quaked by the doorway. "You saw what I did when I saw Rafael fall. I tore those metal bars apart. I shifted into a powerful wolf, and I ripped Corbet's throat out. Do you think Lucien would receive less from me?"

"You underestimate me, Falon," Lucien said from behind Lana. Stools and chairs scraped across the wood floor as they were hastily vacated. Every woman in the room, save Lana, scrambled behind Falon.

In Falon's head, Lucien was formidable. Here in person, he exuded such a lethal sensuality she could smell the terrified females around her exude come-fuck-me pheromones. Lucien was the ultimate bad boy. And as with all bad boys, they were no good for any woman.

Falon's temperature rose. Not in lust but in anger. How dare he show his face here?

Lucien caught Lana's chin in his hand. As if she were on a cloud, she rose to him, all flushed and fluttery. He kissed her. Sharp breaths hitched behind Falon. "My thanks for your confidence, Lana my love. Despite your low opinion of me, you will be rewarded." He turned his golden eyes to Falon. "Prepare yourself, *corazón*; tonight you will share my bed, and tomorrow?" He smiled menacingly. "Tomorrow you will die."

Falon squarely faced him, focusing every ounce of energy and concentration on him. "Tonight will be your last on earth if you think I'll go with you."

He smiled that wicked smile of his. "You will come," he softly said, the double entendre clear to her.

Falon thrust her hands at him and watched in fascination and triumph as he went flying backward across the threshold, landing on the slick wood floor beyond. She strode toward where he lay stunned and furious. He had the good sense not to attempt to rise. "As I live and breathe, I will never come to you!" She thrust her hands at him again, and his body shot farther along the hardwood. She continued toward him, determined to kick him out of her home.

She raised her hands again and, just as she was about to give him another shot of whatever it was she had, he shifted into the big bad black snarling wolf that nightmares were made of. Falon didn't give it a second thought—she shifted as well. The hair along her back stood straight up. Snarling rage tore through her.

He snarled and hunched, about to leap. She hunched to meet him in midair. Then an amazing thing happened. The females behind her shifted, snarling and growling. They leapt over her, landing solidly between her and Lucien, forming a Lycan wall around her.

Lucien snarled and snapped his jaws, frustrated by the females' audacity to challenge him. Another deadly but familiar snarl erupted from behind Lucien. Rafael leapt across the room, slamming into his brother. Black and gold fur blurred as the wolves fought. Their big bodies rolled into furniture, slammed into walls, shattered glass and mirrors.

They were evenly matched.

When one got the upper hand, the other countered. Falon shifted back into her human form, quickly dressed, and followed the brothers out into the yard. Blood slicked the wood floors. Panic ripped through her. They would kill each other! She ran to the edge of the porch where the wolves viciously tore into each other. As she had moments ago, Falon focused her energy on them. She raised her hands and, just as she had done to Lucien, she propelled both of them backward. They separated at her forceful shove, their bodies tumbling in the dirt. Instantly, both were on all fours, lunging at each other again.

"Stop!" Falon shouted. She rushed forward. "Stop!" she screamed. She jumped toward them, shifting in midair. Sharp fangs sank into her back and her chest. She howled in pain and then . . . It was over.

Still in wolf form, Rafael stood stunned and protective over her. The women gathered around her, as well. Beside them, the men of the pack had arrived, forging a wall to keep Lucien at bay.

Falon lay in the dirt, breathing hard. Bleeding hard. She was sure she'd heard a bone or two snap earlier, but the pain from the bites was bearable, and she would do it again.

At least the fighting had stopped.

Not sure if she would be better off as a wolf or a human, Falon shifted. Rafael snarled and turned to lunge at Lucien, who stood oddly silent except for his heavy breathing behind the gauntlet of men. Falon reached out and grabbed Rafael's leg, "Rafa, I'm okay. Let him go. Please."

Rafael snarled but turned his attention to her. He licked her face and the two deep fang marks that punctured her skin just above her right breast. He snarled as he licked. She understood.

Go, Lucien, go before more Lycans die.

But he was already gone.

The women carefully gathered her up and gently carried her to her and Rafael's room. They tried to minister to her, but Rafael growled them out of the room. When the door closed behind them, a hot wave of emotion rushed Falon. Yes, she was glad Rafael was alive, and glad she was no worse for the wear, but what touched her more than all of that combined was how the females of the pack had come together to protect her, when she should have been the one to protect them! She knew they were terrified of Lucien, yet each one had risked her own life to protect Falon's.

Rafael nudged her back onto the bed. She was naked and bleeding. He licked her chest, his tongue warm and soothing, and in time the pain lessened and the wound healed. But she was still bleeding. She rolled over onto her belly, exposing her back and the bites there.

Rafael snarled and whined, then snarled again. He was furious. Furious because of the wounds, yes, but more furious with himself. When she'd jumped between the brothers, she'd been bitten by both of them. Rafael just realized that.

"It's okay, my love," she soothed, stroking his neck. "You didn't know."

As he had before, he licked her wounds, ever so gentle, ever so loving. Ever so sorry.

In less than an hour, Falon had healed enough to shower, dress, and return downstairs, this time with Rafael by her side. She was greeted as a hero and with much fussing over by the women. Even Lana asked if there was anything she could do for her.

Falon fought back tears and thanked each female and male. They seemed humbled by her heartfelt thanks. Her heart swelled with pride as she looked around at the pack. They had accepted her and would fight for her. She was one of them and was proud to be their alpha.

She stood in the middle of the great room that had been a shambles just an hour before. Now it gleamed with polish and shine. The debris had been removed and, with some of the furniture gone, it opened the room up nicely.

"That was some spring clean," Galiya said as she approached with a tray of food. "Your breakfast got cold, Falon, but here's your lunch. Eat all of it. You will need your strength."

They all would.

Pack leaders arrived as the afternoon sun set. Falon greeted each one of them with Rafael by her side. There were eight in all, but there were others who would travel from all corners of the world with their packs for the Blood Moon rising.

An hour before dusk, the alphas were situated and the compound ready for the historic council meeting. Falon knew Lucien would return, arrogant and defiant and absolute in his belief that he had the right to take her life. Falon shivered, not afraid of death but of not living with the man she loved.

Rafael gently took her hand in his jaws and tugged her toward their room. Falon smiled, knowing what he wanted. She wanted it, too; she had been waiting for him all day.

Twenty-three

RAFAEL SHIFTED AS they hurried up the stairway. Falon gasped at the vicious gouges in his back, arms, and chest. The flesh was torn, the wounds raw. "Rafa, you're wounded!"

"I'm fine," he said pulling her toward the bedroom. He lifted her into his arms and ran the rest of the way, kicking open the door, then slamming it shut with his foot. He leapt onto the bed with her in his arms. His lips captured hers, silencing her protests.

Was he crazy? He was wounded and bleeding, and he thought they . . .

She struggled, determined to heal him. He was just as determined to rid her of her clothes. Impatient, he ripped them from her body. His lips captured hers in a deep, desperate, never-ending kiss.

"Ahhhh." Arching into him, Falon surrendered. His fingers dug into her hair, his long, hard body pressed hotly against hers. Falon wrapped her arms around his neck, pressing her body firmly against his, wanting to touch every inch of him, never wanting to part.

He tore his lips from hers. Holding her head in his hands, he stared deeply into her eyes. Emotion clogged her chest. She saw into his soul. She felt his desperation, his heartache, and even his fear of losing her. "Rafe," she cried, "We will be together, I swear it."

His face softened. "I love you, Falon. You are the other half of my heart, my soul, my life."

She lifted her lips up to his. "As you are mine," she whispered.

He took her then, in a slow, deep slide. She met him, liquefying as emotion overwhelmed her. They clung to each other, their hips moving in slow, agonizing rhythm, desperately holding on, prolonging the inevitable, wanting just one more minute, one more second, one more heartbeat.

One more breath.

The kiss that began their union ended only when the final wild rush of sensation claimed them both. It was a poignant explosion that ebbed right along with their heartbeats and finally their breaths.

For a long time, they lay connected, man to woman, alpha to alpha, heart to heart, soul to soul. Neither wanted to face the gathering below, but they knew they had no choice. It was who they were, what they chose, how they would live.

Lycan.

"Falon," Rafael hoarsely said as he caressed her cheek with his fingertips, "I will protect you; I swear it."

She smiled and kissed his fingertips. "As I will protect you."

He smiled, but it tore her up inside to see the moisture gather in his eyes. "Spoken like a true alpha."

MOMENTS LATER, HAND in hand, they descended the stairway into a time and place that would irrevocably change their lives forever.

The tension was thick; anxious scents clogged the air. The council was seated in a semicircle. Each of them was dressed in the traditional white-fringed leather of the Great Spirit Mother, Singarti. Sharia, Daniel, and Maleek, he knew. The three others he did not recognize but knew they were from the great white North. He recognized their authority by the eagle feathers woven into their gray hair. The one closest to Maleek was an ancient, shrunken man who was hunched so far over he had to sit back to gaze upon the gathered. The one next to him was an old medicine woman. He knew this by the beads and fur pouches filled with herbs that hung from her sealskin belt. The man beside her was younger, as was Daniel; his long black braid hung down the front of his right shoulder.

Eight alphas sat in support of Rafe. Four to each side of the council.

As Rafael and Falon entered the room, bodies parted, allowing them to pass. Rafael sniffed the air.

His anger flared. Lucien.

He looked across the room to see him standing arrogantly to the side with his own supporters. Rebel alphas Lucien had lured to the dark side. Where was Talia? He needed her to support his case. His heart pounded against his chest when he could not locate her or pick up her familiar scent.

Lucien would dare defy the council's demand? How could he have a fair tribunal if she could not verify the violence of that day and hopefully give them a clue to the Slayer's ashes? He tamped down his temper. He refocused on what he had control of, and that was the truth.

As they approached the dais the council sat upon, Anton took up his position to Rafael's right and Glenna, his mate, took her position on Falon's left.

"My thanks to the council for agreeing to this meeting." Rafael's deep voice reverberated across the beams. Sharia, Daniel, and Maleek nodded, but the other three sat stoically staring at him.

"Do you agree to abide by the council's verdict?" the hunched ancient demanded, his voice clear and deep for one so old.

Rafael squeezed Falon's hand. She clutched his. "I do."

The old man turned in his chair and sat back to regard Lucien. "Do you agree to abide by the council's verdict?"

Lucien stepped forward, his eyes locked on Falon. Rafael's beast inside roared furiously at his brother's arrogance. "I do," he clearly said.

"Then let us proceed." The ancient sat back and calmly regarded the floor.

Maleek stood and read from an old leather scroll. "The Blood Law is the ancient law of the Lycans. The founding Lycan fathers swore to uphold its commandments. They are never to be challenged, changed, or ignored. The first Blood Law decrees it high treason, punishable by death, for a Lycan to lie with a Slayer. The second law decrees, when a Lycan steals, slays, damages, or destroys another Lycan's property or person, the victim of such acts has the right to demand an eye for an eye. If the victim is unable to demand justice due to death, his or her next of kin has that right." Maleek lowered the scroll and looked at Rafael. "Rafael Vulkasin, you slew the chosen one of an alpha. As the Blood Law is written, in keeping with the code of an eye for an eye, the offended has the right to the same. Do you dare challenge the Blood Law on this account?"

Rafael let go of Falon's hand and stepped forward. "I do not challenge the Blood Law , but I disavow my brother's claim of my chosen one on the grounds that *his* chosen one was in fact a Slayer. It was only because of my duty to uphold the Blood Law that I slayed her."

Maleek looked stone-faced at Rafael. Did he still believe Lucien had the right to Falon?

"She was a Slayer!" Rafael roared. "Lucien broke the first law of our people. It is *he* who should be punished, not I."

"She was not!" Lucien growled stepping toward the council.

"Silence!" Maleek commanded, staring down Lucien. "You will have your chance to speak."

Lucien cast a sneer at Maleek. It did not go unnoticed by the councilman. His eyes narrowed at the insult.

"Can you prove she was a Slayer?" Maleek asked, turning back to Rafael.

"Talia was the only one who was in the room after I slew her. She can attest to the condition of the room. She can also attest to the woman's behavior before her death. It was Talia who called me from my spirit journey because she was afraid of the unnatural hold the woman had on Lucien. "

"Did you not investigate immediately after?" Maleek asked, surprised.

Rafael shook his head. He was still kicking himself all of these years later. "All hell broke loose after that. I was more concerned about holding my pack together. By the time I gave it thought, it was too late."

"But now that you do not wish to sacrifice your own chosen one, you decided to consider what you should have considered years ago?"

"In truth, Maleek, I had nothing to fight for." He looked back at Falon and smiled. His heart briefly stuttered to a stop. Pride swelled in his chest. She stood proud, the regal epitome of an alpha female. He turned back to the council. "I do now. I come to the council with the truth and ask only for the Blood Law to be upheld."

Maleek looked at Lucien. "Produce Talia."

Lucien turned and pulled the small healer from the group of defiant alphas surrounding him. Rafael's heart soared. Talia! She caught his gaze but did not return his smile. Her petite frame was rail thin and her dark eyes were sunken deep into her skull. Rafael swore but checked his temper. Lucien had so much to pay for. He would gladly give him his due.

Rafael did not miss the angry glances from his pack, as well as several of the alphas who knew and loved Talia as he did. It was apparent she had been neglected. Abused. The council had failed him when he'd demanded they force her release, as well as when Lucien refused to attend the meeting. That he was here today to claim Falon told Rafael he felt confident he would be victorious.

It would not happen.

"Talia Vulkasin, did you witness the death of Lucien's chosen one?" Maleek asked when she stood before them

"No," she softly said.

"Were there any indicators up to the time or after her death that she was Slayer?"

"She—" Talia glanced at Lucien, then said, "No."

Rafael steamed. She was lying!

"When you came upon the brothers at death's door, did you see the body?"

"Yes."

"What was its condition?"

"Bloody, lifeless. I only glimpsed it. I was too focused on Rafael and Lucien."

"After the brothers were revived, did you see the body?"

"No."

"Had it disappeared?"

"I—I don't know. I was tending to Rafe and Lucien, who were ready to kill each other again. There was so much commotion afterwards."

"Were there ashes where the body had lain?"

"I don't know. There was a fire the next morning. The entire suite burned up."

The fire had been deliberately set. Rafael had always thought it was Lucien bent on revenge, but could it have been to hide the evidence of the Slayer's ashes?

"My pardon, Maleek," Rafael said.

The man scowled, not liking the interruption. He nodded.

"A question of my brother if he will give his word to answer truthfully."

The ancient elder leaned back and shot a glare to Lucien. "There will be nothing *but* the truth spoken here this night!" he roughly said.

"What answer do you seek, Rafael?" Lucien laconically asked.

"Did you set the fire that morning?"

Lucien's eyes narrowed. "Would that I could claim responsibility, I would." Of course he would. After that night Lucien had done everything in his power to destroy all that was Vulkasin.

"I take it that's a no?" Rafe asked.

"I did not set the fire."

"Do you have knowledge of who did?"

"Do you mean, did I order it set?"

"There is no room here for semantics. Were you, in any way, shape, or form, responsible for the fire?"

"No."

Oddly, Rafe believed him. So, who had set it, and why? To cover something up.

Rafael looked back to the council. "There has never been any doubt that the fire was deliberately set. We could smell the gasoline used as the accelerant. All other scents were drowned out by the smoke. With the pack separated and fighting at the time, there could be only one reason for the fire. To hide a Slayer's ashes."

"So you claim," Lucien sneered.

Maleek shot him a sharp glare then looked at Rafael. "Do you have any further questions for Talia?"

"I do," Rafael said. He walked up behind her. When she refused to turn, he knew why. Lucien had broken her. He gently touched her shoulder. She flinched. "It's me, Tal. I won't hurt you." He turned her to face him, and his heart broke for her. Her big brown eyes shimmered with unshed tears. Rafe cast his compassion aside.

He glared up at the council. "How can you ask me to accept your verdict when you cannot enforce the release of one taken against her will?" He looked down at Talia. "But you're home now."

"Her home is with pack Mondragon," Lucien said, striding toward them.

Talia stiffened and looked up at Rafael, her face impassive. "I have been free to return here. I chose not to."

He didn't believe her! Rafael's hand fell to his side. "You don't have to lie. Talia, you're safe here."

She shook her head and strode back to where Lucien stood, then turned to face Rafael. "I choose Mondragon."

Rafael's beast clawed and scratched for release. He leashed it. It would do him and Falon no good for him to lose control. One thing at a time.

Rafael strode toward the dais. "It is understood that Talia cannot lead us to a grave so that we can see the dark ashes of the Slayer for ourselves nor bear witness to verify ashes on the sheets. But that does not mean she was not Slayer. It only means I am the sole witness to her identity."

Maleek nodded. "What proof did you have that she was Slayer?"

"When I walked in on them, her scent was laced with black magic. Black magic she used to blind Lucien to what she was. Lucien's lust for her shielded what he refused to see. Her stench was thick and cloying, but when he was about to mark her, she showed her true self to me. She taunted me with the fact that Lucien would be sole alpha, and she would reign by his side. Her eyes turned hard and ebony black as a Slayer's does when impassioned. I did not imagine it. She had intentionally maneuvered Lucien to choose her. Once she conceived, she would populate the pack with Slayers. I could not permit that." He stepped closer to the council and said, "If given the opportunity to go back and change what I have done, I would not. She was Slayer. I destroyed her as is my birthright. My duty. My only regret is that Lucien has had to endure the pain of her loss all these years, but more than that, he has failed to understand that in the end, there was no other way."

"Would you swear this on the lives of your pack?" the ancient medicine woman asked.

Rafael turned to her and nodded. "I would swear it on the souls of my parents; it is true. For fear of his own death sentence, Lucien refuses to acknowledge his folly."

"Not a folly, Brother!" Lucien sneered. "Your jealousy that I was to become sole alpha drove you to the edge. She was no more a Slayer than your chosen one! You killed her for your own gain and no other reason."

Rafael turned on his brother. "And what, Brother, have I gained? My family spilt in half? The hopes and dreams of our parents cast away like trash because of your hatred for me? The lives lost because of your rogue marauding and pillaging? What did I gain that I have not lost one hundred fold?"

Lucien turned to the council. "How dare you swear on our parents' lives!" Lucien stormed. "It's sacrilege. They died so that we could live, and you use them as if they are your personal get out of jail free card."

"I loved them as much as you, Luca. The day they died is burned in my memory for eternity. If either one of them stood here now, we both know what they would do."

Lucien strode toward Rafael. "Yes, we would, what they always did, take your side."

Lucien whirled around and faced the council. "I swear on *my* pack's life that my chosen one was human, not a Slayer. She was not perfect, but she was mine. I demand an eye for an eye. I demand my blood right." He turned and pointed at Falon, who stood silent and proud. "I demand she be given to me so that I can exact my vengeance!"

"Seek your vengeance on my body. I freely give it to you," Rafael pleaded.

A collective gasp rippled through the room. Falon vehemently shook her head.

"Oh, no, Brother, that would be too easy for you. You will bleed like I bled. I want my due. Now." Lucien looked back at the council. "I demand it!"

Rafael strode back to Falon and took her hand into his. Their gazes caught and held. He wanted to tell her to be strong. It was not over yet. But he could not. "Falon slew our mortal enemy, Edward Corbet. She saved my life and the lives of my men. Is that how the council treats a hero? Is there no leniency? The Blood Moon will rise in two months' time. If the council allows Lucien to destroy her, the packs will fall into further disarray." He turned to his brother, pleading not only for Falon but for their people. "Divided, Lucien, we lose all to the Slayers. United, we have a chance."

Pack Vulkasin cheered, demanding justice for Rafael. The alphas who came in support of Rafael and Falon joined the chant. Lucien's mobsters chanted, "Kill, kill, kill."

Red rage clouded Rafael's vision. His beast snarled. His body tightened. He fought it, holding tight to the human part of him. If he succumbed to the beast, he would kill Lucien and his minions.

"Silence!" Sharia shouted over the roar, her old voice surprisingly sharp. "How dare you disrespect this council?" Immediately, the voices lowered to irritated mumbles, and the shoving stopped. Rafael struggled for control. Falon squeezed his hand and pressed against him. She stroked his tight jaw. "Rafa, fight the beast. I need you here."

The beast snarled and backed down but did not leave altogether. Instead, it hunched in Rafael's gut, waiting to pounce, then kill.

Rafael looked around and saw the desperation on his pack's faces. He felt their anxiety. They began to move nervously, anticipating the council's verdict. Desperation was not unique to them only. It tore his guts apart.

Falon's hands tightly gripped both of his. He looked down into her terrified eyes.

I'm afraid.

He forced a reassuring smile he did not feel. *You will not die.*

He cleared his throat and carefully extracted his hands from hers. He approached the council for the last time. "I have proven to be a worthy alpha. I have defended the Blood Law, hunted Slayers, conducted myself in the human world as a model citizen. I have not disrespected my heritage or the Lycan nation. Even when my own blood brother has pillaged and plundered what is mine, I have shown tolerance for him, even though I did not have to be so tolerant. While he has spent the last fourteen years giving no thought or preparation for the future of the Lycan nation, I have prepared for years for the rising. I have earned the trust of my pack and the alphas of many other packs." The alphas seated on either side of the council nodded. His pack behind him nodded. "With all due respect to the council, this tribunal comes down to one answer. Do you believe me when I say I slew a Slayer, or do you believe Lucien that I slew an innocent for my own gain?"

A hush fell over the entire building. Rafael had hit home his point. The scowl on his brother's face proved it. They had a choice; believe the good son or the prodigal son.

A new hope flared in Rafael's chest. How could the council choose to believe Lucien over him? Falon squeezed his biceps. He looked down at her and smiled.

He tried to read the council, but every one of them remained stoic.

"Lucien Mondragon, do you have final words on your behalf?" the ancient one asked without leaning back.

Lucien strode arrogantly before the council. "With all due respect to the council, while my brother paints a lovely picture of himself and casts me as the villain of the world, let me remind all of you who it was that brokered the deal for one thousand silver swords to arm all Lycans for the rising. Let me remind you all who it was that funded that buy. Let me remind you that it was me who made sure that the sacred battleground of our forefathers in the North was overlooked for development." He laughed low, looking at the three elders from the North who could not hide their surprise quick enough. "Yeah, mighty elders from the North, that was me. *All* me. While I may do business differently then my fair-haired brother, what I do, regardless of method, is for the greater good of the Lycan nation." Lucien turned and faced Rafael. "Do not ever question my loyalty to my people."

He strode back to his place, turned with his hands locked behind his back, and faced the council. "I anxiously await your verdict."

Twenty-four

FALON'S BELLY DROPPED at Lucien's impassioned words. Not that she felt anything other than contempt for him, but the council had reacted to them favorably, whereas they had not done so with Rafael.

She had wanted to scream at them to do the right thing. To insist that Rafael would not kill his brother's chosen one as a power play. But she knew if she said anything, she would be revealed for what she was: prejudiced. A woman who did not want to be sentenced to death. A woman in love.

Why couldn't they all see what she saw? Rafael was not perfect, but she knew he'd believed the woman was a Slayer. Was she? If Rafe believed it, so would she. But would the council?

"The council will retreat for the evening. Return at dawn for our verdict," Maleek decreed. As the council left single file to the cabins that had been prepared in the back of the compound, Falon put her hand over Rafael's heart. It thudded powerfully against her palm.

He raised her hand to his lips as the pack swelled around them, oddly quiet.

Falon caught Lucien's gaze across the room. For once, the arrogance was gone. Instead, sadness lingered. It sank in at the moment for Falon that Lucien truly in his heart didn't believe his chosen one was a Slayer. He'd loved her. He had lost his parents, his friends, and all he had was his brother, and in Lucien's heart, his brother betrayed him. He still had not come to terms with the pain after all these years.

Do not pity me, corazón. The verdict will play out as it should. Prepare yourself.

She stiffened. Ah, the arrogance was back. *I'll see you in hell first,* Luca.

Falon turned her back on the prodigal son to gaze upon the good son. Her mood softened. Rafael had done the right thing for the right reasons, and for his efforts, he was being crucified. She slid her hand into his big warm one and smiled up at him. It was a travesty what happened to the brothers' parents. They should be there for each other. But from what Falon had witnessed, Rafael had extended the olive branch, and Lucien had refused it.

For there to be such virulent hatred, there had to be great love first. The line between love and hate was razor thin, and just as sharp. Would the split packs ever stop bleeding? Could they?

A deep sadness settled within Falon's heart. The greatest tragedy of all was the demolition of a great family. A three-hundred-year dynasty had fallen, with no hope of resurrection.

"Rafe," Anton said, his anger apparent. "Lucien has warped the truth to make himself seem like a misunderstood rebel with a cause." He spit on the floor.

"Rafe," Yuri said, "the council sees through Lucien's schemes. It is common knowledge he is a thug among our people."

Rafael shook his head. "Lucien's chosen one was murdered. It's all he can see."

"It's all he wants to see," Falon muttered.

"It is what it is. I have tried to get through to him, Falon. His anger prevents any chance of healing."

Rafael stood for nearly an hour as one person after another congratulated him on his speech, voiced their support, then turned around and disparaged Lucien. Despite what was at stake, Rafe had grown weary of Lucien bashing. Maybe he had chosen to see only what he wanted to see in his brother. There was good before. There could be good again.

Falon never once left Rafael's side. When the pack finally drifted off, he pulled her into his arms and kissed the top of her head.

She lifted her lips to his. "Let's go for a run."

"Excellent idea."

They undressed in their room, shifted, and exited through the open bathroom window to the roof.

Side by side, they ran for hours. For Falon it was cathartic. She knew if the council came back in Lucien's favor, she would have only one day to kill him if she were to live. He intended to use her first. She would kill him before he laid a hand on her. Her gut told her to do the deed here, before the council, the alphas, and her pack, but Lucien had given her a better idea when he'd said he would take her before he killed her. If she killed him here, there would be witnesses, and she would not get a running head start. In his lair, she would.

She stopped suddenly and shifted. Rafael skidded to a halt and did the same. Naked, they stood facing each other, their chests rising and falling heavily from their exertion.

"If the council rules in Lucien's favor, I will fight for my life, Rafa. I will have no choice but to kill your brother," Falon softly said. "Do you believe I can do it?"

Rafael walked toward her. The moon was shrouded behind dark clouds, but there was plenty of light for a wolf. His features reflected his sorrow and his desperation. "He is as strong as me, Falon."

She crooked a smile, though she did not feel carefree. "Are you insinuating I can't take you?"

He shrugged as his gaze raked her body. "Let's find out now," he slyly said.

"Rafa, listen to me," she seriously said. "If the council finds in Lucien's favor, promise me you will not attack him."

He looked taken aback. "I will not promise that. Though it would tear me up to do it, I will kill him before I allow him to harm you."

"He has plans for me before he exacts his vengeance."

Rafael snarled, "I will kill him if he touches a hair on your head."

She pressed her hand to his chest. His heart beat wildly against her palm. "Listen to me. We must plan now for a future together if we are to have one. If you kill Lucien, I live and you die. If *I* kill him, we both live."

"I will not live without you, Falon. I will not let you be his, not even for the time it takes you to kill him."

"*You must.* The entire Lycan nation is at stake. Listen to my plan."

He shook his head, wanting to hear none of it.

"Don't be obtuse, Rafe! If the council finds in his favor, put up a fight, argue, rant and rail, but allow me to go with him. After he drags me off like a conqueror, I, too, will plead for my life, grovel, cry, act submissive. When we are alone, and he is least suspecting, I will strike! I will send word with Talia. She lied, Rafa. I felt her aura. She's miserable. With Lucien gone, she will return. As you prepare for the rising, I will lay low. Upon the rising, I will meet you, fight beside you, and when we triumph, we will write a new covenant."

He shook his head. "No."

Frustrated, she pounded him hard on the chest. "Your pride refuses to see the reason in my plan. It will work!"

"Too risky."

She punched him again, this time harder. He grunted, grabbing her fist. She punched him with her free hand. He grasped that one, too, wrapping her arms behind her back. "Do not assault me, Falon. I am your alpha. You will obey me," he growled low.

She struggled against him. A thin film of perspiration from the run made it hard for him to hold on to her. Her anger mounted. If she had to beat him into submission, she would. She would not allow him to sacrifice his life for hers when he did not have to. That he lacked the confidence in her spurred her on.

"I refuse to allow you to sacrifice your life for mine, when neither of us has to die!" she cried. She twisted out of his grip and darted past him. He grabbed her arm and yanked her back hard against his bare chest. Angry, frustrated, and terrified, she pounded him with her fists, crying, screaming, and begging him not to do it.

He held her tightly in his arms and allowed her to take her fear and frustration out on him.

When she felt his erection against her thigh, she became more infuriated. "Is sex all you want from me? How can you want sex when I'm pleading with you for your life?"

He tried to kiss her, but she bit his lips, drawing blood.

He snarled, real anger. His grip tightened. "You little bitch." He pushed her down to the ground. Thick, loamy moss buffeted the impact. He dropped down on top of her, grasping her fists when they came flying at him, yanking them over her head.

"How can I think of sex at a time like this?" he hoarsely asked. "Ask me how I cannot breathe." He nipped a swollen nipple. "How can I think of sex at a time like this? How can I not when you stand before me, angry and desperate to take a chance with your life for my own?" He nipped the other nipple. "How can I not think of sex when your body glows with sweat beneath the moon? So perfect. So damn fuckable." He pressed his forehead to hers. "How can I not think of sex when I watched you stand proud, regal, and beautiful as my chosen one before my peers and the great council." His cock thickened against her. He dipped his head and kissed her parted lips, melting into her.

She moaned and arched against him. He tore his lips from hers. Her musky fragrance scented the air. "By all that is holy, Falon, how can I not want to make love to you when your body calls to mine? How can I not think of making love to you when I see your love for me shine in your eyes? Tell me, how am I not to think of the most sacred act between a man and a woman when I am with you?"

Hot tears burned her eyes. He kissed them away.

"My love, the day I stop thinking of having sex with you is the day you bury me."

He moved into her then, slowly, reverently, exquisitely. His lips captured hers in a slow, spiraling kiss. Their slick bodies rose and fell in perfect synchronicity. Tears leaked from Falon's eyes. This could be the last time she felt Rafael inside of her.

Warm lips kissed the moisture from her cheeks. Thick fingers smoothed across her face. "Don't cry, my love. Trust in me."

His gentleness was too much. She didn't want gentle. She wanted rough; she wanted him branded into every inch of her body, a reminder of who she belonged to. Falon snarled. Hatred for Lucien exploded inside of her. How dare he destroy what she held so near and dear to her heart!

"Gentle," Rafael softly said.

Falon arched into him "I am yours, Rafa! No one can change that!" she cried.

His body tightened; his fingers dug into her hair. He cupped her head with his big hands as his thrusts turned from slow and languorous to deeply urgent. She felt the beast in him roar. He grabbed her hands and raised them above her head. His body drove into hers. His teeth nipped and laved her nipples raw. His fingers dug into her wrists. His body continued to slam into hers. Tears ran down her cheeks. The bittersweet pain of his lovemaking nearly broke her. How could she live without this man?

Her beast snarled. She would not.

This was how she wanted him: fighting mad, passionate. The tension built; her anger, fear, and frustration increased with every thrust. Her beast lunged and scratched for release.

She heard Rafael's beast snarling for freedom. Her own answered.

A HARD WAVE of down-and-dirty primal desire crashed through Falon. Her body thrummed, her pussy creamed, her breasts swelled.

She wanted Rafael's beast within. He pulled out of her and roughly turned her over onto all fours. When he mounted her, he nipped her neck, holding on to her slick skin. Falon's thighs quivered in anticipation. Just as he fully penetrated her, she felt his body shift. Falon gasped at the sensation and followed his lead.

The animal aspect of their mating was nothing like Falon expected. It was more, it was less, it was basic, primal, and simplistic. There was no courting, no sweet words of encouragement, no soft caresses. But they didn't need any of that. Stripped down, raw, they mated. There was no other word to describe the way Rafael's wolf cleaved to her she-wolf. It was just as profound, and as much a part of them as their human side.

Just as their mating reached a fevered pitch, Rafael shifted. Falon growled, and breathlessly she followed him.

Rafe pulled out from her. "No! Rafael, stay, stay!" she screamed. Her pussy was on fire. Her need for him inside of her was so acute she could not see. Only feel. He grabbed her hips roughly and flipped her over onto the soft loamy ground. She lay splayed on her back, her thighs parted, her body undulating wildly out of control.

She looked up into Rafael's stormy face. His eyes blazed, his chest heaved, his glistening red cock jutted arrogantly toward her. He crawled over her, his cock and balls hanging heavy between his legs. Falon grabbed him, reveling in the power of his sex. She raised her hips and guided him into her. He thrust high inside her, his heavy balls slapping against her ass. "Rafa," she cried.

He thrust harder. Deeper. "Is that what you wanted, Falon? To know what it was like?"

Unable to speak, she could only nod.

"Was it all that you expected?"

"Yes," she gasped.

"Do you want me to shift, to feel my beast inside of your woman?"

The suggestion of such a thing was so taboo, her cheeks flushed. He thrust again. Falon shook her head. "I want you like this." If this was the last time they would be together, she wanted to remember the man she fell in love with. She raised her knees higher, giving him more access to her.

"Let go, Falon. Let go like you have never let go before."

She ached at the realization that he mirrored her own fear that this could be their last time together. Falon obeyed her alpha. "I love you, Rafael. I love you with every breath I take."

He gathered her up into his arms and claimed her lips with a deep, soul-scorching kiss. Falon wrapped her arms around his neck, holding him so close their heartbeats thudded in perfect harmony. As one their passion spiraled up and out of control, then released them both at the same time, for the hard, earth-shattering drop into sexual oblivion.

For nearly an hour, they lay on their backs, their bodies steaming, their breaths unable to stabilize, and their yearning for the other no more quenched than when they ran up the mountain hours ago. It would never be quenched, Falon realized.

Rafael rolled over and kissed her forehead, her eyelids, her nose, and finally her mouth. "It's time to return, my love."

Falon closed her eyes. "I don't want to go back there."

He laughed, though there was not much joy in it. "We must." He stood and hoisted her up.

They began the return home, hand in hand, and despite the great wolf sex and human sex, nothing had changed Falon's mind. If anything, she was more determined. "Rafael, my way will work."

He let out a long breath. "I could not live with myself if you succumb to Lucien's vengeance."

She stopped and faced him. She placed her hands on either side of his face, holding him a captive audience. "Have faith in my abilities and determination, Rafa. I swear it—we will be together on the eve of the rising. It is our destiny."

Finally, she saw him waver. She pushed for victory. "I will not live without you if I don't have to." She nipped his chin. "Believe it and be it. It will happen."

"You are asking me to give my sanction to murder my brother because though I swore to accept the verdict, you won't."

"Not murder, Rafe. I have no part in your blood feud. My only crime is being in the wrong place at the wrong time that night at Del's. Do not underestimate me. I will defend myself. I will kill before I am killed."

He nodded in understanding, though she knew it cost him to

acquiesce. He would never forgive himself if she didn't survive. So she would have to see that she did. She smiled and hugged him. "Now, let's hope this is all for naught."

Dawn came too swiftly. As they had at dusk, everyone converged in the great room.

Rafael watched the council's faces for a "tell" as they filed in. They refused to look at him or any of his pack. Trepidation shivered along his spine and with it, the beast roused. Falon was oddly quiet, reserved. He was anxious. Lucien stood across the room from him, his gaze locked on the council. The council refused to look at him as well.

As the elders sat, Maleek remained standing. The room was tombstone quiet. He looked across the room, his eyes settling first on Rafael then Falon then on Lucien. "Lucien Mondragon, Rafael Vulkasin, and Falon Vulkasin, please approach the dais."

Hand in hand, Rafael and Falon approached as did Lucien to their left. Rafael between his brother and his woman.

Maleek opened a leather scroll. "After careful consideration of all the facts presented here, the council has come to a verdict."

Everyone in the room held their breath. Maleek looked at Falon. "Before I render our decision, understand that while you, Falon Vulkasin, have proven to be an invaluable asset to the Lycan nation, it had no bearing on our verdict. Our verdict was based on the facts presented and what would be fair and righteous considering the impasse we find ourselves in the midst of."

He cleared his throat and read, "It is the decision of this council that Falon Vulkasin's life be spared." Cheers erupted around them. Lucien snarled.

Falon gasped, clasping Rafael's hands. Joy exploded in Rafael's chest. It hit him with the velocity of a fist. He could scarcely breathe, he was so overcome.

"The council could not determine if Lucien's chosen one was in fact a Slayer, but Rafael believed she was. Although he cannot prove it, Rafael Vulkasin is a Lycan reputed for his honesty, and with such a reputation, the council gives him the benefit of the doubt."

Falon's body shook with excitement beside him. Rafael wanted to pick her up in his arms and dance.

"However, Lucien Mondragon's claim cannot be ignored. Therefore, the council grants Lucien full blood rights to Falon Vulkasin with the understanding she is not to be harmed in any way, and if she is, Rafael has the right to avenge her."

Shocked gasps rent the air. Rafael stood stunned, unable to comprehend what he just heard. As the verdict registered, in that one moment in time, his heart shattered, and all hope for his future crashed and burned.

Falon's fingers dug into his hands; her body shook violently.

"Lucien Mondragon, if you choose not to accept Falon Vulkasin as your chosen one, then she is free to remain with Rafael."

Lucien looked as stunned as the rest of them.

"Do, you, Lucien Mondragon, understand that if you choose to take Falon Vulkasin as your own chosen one, in so doing you agree to give her all the rights due an alpha's true mate?"

Lucien turned his bright golden eyes on Falon. His face remained impassive. But when his gaze rested on his brother, his lips quirked. He turned back to the council, then hoarsely said, "I do."

Then all hell broke loose.